PICTURE OF LIES

PICTURE OF LIES

C. C. HARRISON

FIVE STAR
A part of Gale, Cengage Learning

GALE
CENGAGE Learning™

Detroit • New York • San Francisco • New Haven, Conn • Waterville, Maine • London

LIBRARY OF CONGRESS CATALOGING-IN-PUBLICATION DATA

Harrison, C. C.
  Picture of lies / C.C. Harrison — 1st ed.
    p. cm.
  ISBN-13: 978-1-4328-2506-5 (hardcover)
  ISBN-10: 1-4328-2506-2 (hardcover)
  1. Women journalists—Fiction. 2. Missing children—Fiction. 3. Navajo Indians—Fiction. 4. Family secrets—Fiction. 5. Monument Valley (Ariz. and Utah)—Fiction. I. Title.
  PS3608.A7833P53 2011
  813'.6—dc23   2011025021

First Edition. First Printing: October 2011.
Published in 2011 in conjunction with Tekno Books and Ed Gorman.

Printed in the United States of America
1 2 3 4 5 6 7 15 14 13 12 11

In memory of
Fred Martinez,
TWO SPIRITS and a sweet soul
And
John E. Taylor,
archivist extraordinaire

ACKNOWLEDGMENTS

My sincere thanks to Miriam Kleiman, Public Affairs Specialist, U.S. National Archives in Washington, D.C. She graciously took time out of her busy schedule to answer my endless questions about the National Archives. Her wealth of information freely shared allowed me a generous peek behind the curtain at the inner workings of the amazing National Archives. Because of security concerns, I took literary license and fictionalized some aspects of the day-to-day operation as it relates to my story. Any mistakes or misrepresentations are mine, not hers. Thank you, Miriam. You made my story richer.

Thanks to Special Agent Manuel Johnson, Federal Bureau of Investigation, Phoenix Division, and Angela Bell, Public Affairs Specialist, Federal Bureau of Investigation, Washington, D.C., for sharing with me their professional expertise as I wrote this story. I always try to get the FBI stuff right, and they help me with that.

Thanks to Lee Lofland—author, blogger, and veteran police investigator, always available for a quick answer to my law enforcement questions. You're the best. Really.

Thanks, BK. I'll miss you.

And a special shout-out to Billy Bob Thornton. "Hey, Billy Bob!"

CHAPTER ONE

This was supposed to have been a make-up vacation. A week in Cabo San Lucas, just the two of them. Keegan Thomas arrived a day late because of a deadline change on her story for *Offbeat Arizona Magazine.* Jeffrey Wright arrived three days late with no explanation whatsoever.

They'd bickered all afternoon.

Now it was the middle of the night. Keegan, floating in the weightlessness of a half sleep, had been listening to the muffled burble of a telephone without answering it. Because she didn't recognize the ring tone, she thought she was dreaming.

Her personal cell phone ring tone was Billy Bob Thornton's voice. But Keegan's phone was on the charger, turned off. Jeffrey's phone signaled with Johnny Cash's *Ring of Fire,* and she could see it right there on the bedside table beside him. Keegan heard something she didn't recognize, something smooth and sexy that reminded her of champagne and satin sheets.

Quietly, she unfolded herself from the armchair where she'd been dozing and stood in the center of the room, head tilted, listening. The musical ring was coming from Jeffrey's briefcase on the floor next to his partially unpacked travel bag, the unpacking having been interrupted by the squabbling, then later abandoned when the argument really picked up steam.

Jeffrey was a man who preferred those sinfully expensive soft-sided camel-hide briefcases, the kind that could be stuffed with thick files and still double as a weekender. The kind whose supple sides gaped open, revealing its contents when its angry owner neglected to zip it shut. A faint tell-tale glow coming from an interior pocket showed Keegan where the phone was hidden. Guilt nipped at her fingers as she reached for it, but curiosity compelled her to pick it up. The ringing stopped when it was in her hand. A moment before the screen went dark, she saw a phone number with a 206 area code and a name.

Cindy.

A grunt and a snore from Jeffrey snapped Keegan's head around, and she stood there feeling like a child caught in the midst of a deliberate misbehavior. When he rolled over and fell back into a travel weary slumber, she narrowed her eyes at this phone she'd never seen before.

With unabashed nosiness, she flipped it open and pressed the last call button. The last call and all the previous calls were from or to Cindy. Somehow, when Keegan wasn't paying attention, someone named Cindy had slipped into Jeffrey's life in such a way that she required a dedicated phone line.

Keegan stared, dumbly bewildered, trying to sort out her emotions. Wounded indignation, certainly. And betrayal.

Jealousy?

Yes, some.

And it would have been easy to hammer away at him with accusations, but she refused to act like a wounded bitch. Nor was she going to play the part of some pathetic cheated-on victim, quietly acquiescing to now and then liaisons outside the relationship. She looked at the call directory again. The number of calls indicated Cindy wasn't a now and then liaison.

"Wake up, Jeffrey."

At the sound of her voice, his eyelids twitched then lifted, revealing eyes murky with interrupted sleep. It took a few seconds for his eyes to focus on the phone in her hand, but when they did, Jeffrey came fully awake. He sat up and lowered his feet to the floor, gave her a look that said *busted!* and waited for the inevitable confrontation.

"What's this?" she asked, holding out the phone in a manner that suggested she was not offering it to him, but might very well smack him on the head with it.

He averted his gaze, looking instead at the floor, attempting with his silence to make the kind of quick pact they'd made a million times before about other things. But this time, she didn't want to let it drop, so she pressed on.

"Who's Cindy?"

He scrunched up his face, put his hands to his head, and vigorously scruffled up his hair in that familiar male morning head-scratch wake-up routine. Then he leaned forward, rested his elbows on his knees, and let his hands dangle, fingers loosely entwined. She allowed the silence to stretch, hoping it would drag an answer out of him. At last, he released a long, resigned sigh. Or was it a *relieved* sigh, she couldn't help wondering.

"She's someone I met."

Keegan waited for more, the phone burning like a hot coal in the palm of her hand.

"Where? When?"

"In Seattle. A month ago . . . two."

That would have been the commodities trading conference. He'd been gone a week.

"Look," he said, raising his hands then letting them drop again. "I didn't mean for it to happen. I wanted to tell you about her. I didn't want you to find out this way." He was babbling now. "It's just that, I . . . need more," he finished lamely.

"More . . ." she said, drawing the word along toward a question, "sex?"

He sat up quickly and shook his head. "No. Well, yes . . . But, no, not just that," he said with finality. "It's not like that."

"Well, what is it like?"

His eyes traveled over her face. "Keegan, I need someone who's available."

"Available," she repeated, thoughtfully.

"Someone who's . . . present."

"Present?"

"Someone who's not so . . ." He hesitated and twirled two fingers in the air as if trying to stir up the words, ". . . wrapped up in other things."

"Are you talking about my work?" she asked. Suddenly on the defensive, she didn't give him a chance to answer. "You have no idea what it takes to do my job, what it does to someone. In here." She tapped her fingers on her chest. "Writing about mothers whose children have been kidnapped, children who sometimes turn up dead, mutilated."

"No, Keegan, it's more than that. Ever since Daisy . . ."

"Ever since Daisy *what?*" she challenged, her heart picking up pace.

He gazed at her a long moment. She could see a serious debate going on behind his eyes, the words in his mouth seeming to huddle there for safety. Finally, he forced them out.

"Ever since Daisy disappeared, you've been . . ."

"Sad?" she offered, grimly. "Angry? Yes, Jeffrey. I'm damn angry. My daughter was stolen from me. Taken by a stranger. Do you know what that feels like?"

"No, I don't, but I'm sure it must hurt like hell. I know it's killing *you*. I'm sorry."

"Just because the police have given up on her doesn't mean I have! I'll *never* give up on her." Keegan plopped into an armchair and pressed the heels of her hands into her eye sockets, pushing back at the tears burning inside.

When the danger of them spilling over passed, she stared out the sliding glass doors. On the floor of the patio lit by diffused lighting, square tiles were set in an alternately repeating two-three-two pattern of Saltillo and tumbled stone surrounded by a wrought iron railing with five elaborately entwined posts between each stucco pillar.

"And that, too," Jeffrey said, making her jump. He was looking at her, letting loose an enormous sigh of irritation, making a point she didn't get.

"What?"

"That."

"What? I didn't say anything."

"That counting thing you do."

"I wasn't counting," she said, even though she had been.

"Yes, you were," he shot back. "I could see your lips moving. It drives me crazy and people think . . ."

"And people think *I'm* crazy," she finished for him. She pulled in her lips between her teeth and held them. He was right. Her compulsion to count things had begun as an odd quirk in childhood that moderated as she grew, but still manifested in her adult life when she was tired or upset.

"If you weren't so involved with those damn missing kid articles you write, if you just once could think about something else besides your work. You've got to have a life away from the job if you're going to stay sane on the job. If you got more sleep, you wouldn't be so stressed all the time."

"Wait a minute," she said, waggling her hand in the air, bristling at the censorious tone in his voice. "This is *my* fault? You're comparing my work ethic and an annoying habit with your . . . *infidelity?*"

He opened his mouth in what appeared to be a last gasp attempt at defending himself, but apparently thought better of it and said nothing.

She gave him a long *you're-such-a-dick* look, then slowly shook her head. With undeniable clarity, she could see she wasn't as truly connected to this man as she'd imagined she was.

Canceled lunch dates, delayed vacations, and now a secret cell phone made it clear how far she'd stretched his patience, how much she'd taken him for granted. How blind she'd been.

She hated to admit it, but maybe she couldn't blame him for seeking connection outside the relationship. She'd tried to love him. But no man could fill the empty spaces in her life left there by the absence of Daisy.

They'd run out of words, and there was nothing left to argue about, so she gave a vague wave of her hand. "I think you'd better go," she said.

Apparently he thought so, too, because he stood up, pulled on his jeans, then slipped his feet into his deck shoes. Without bothering to put on a shirt, he picked up his clothes from the back of the chair, and shoved them into his bag. He started for the door carrying his suitcase and briefcase, then stopped and came back to stand in front of her, looking chastened. He held out his hand and motioned to hers. "Could I have my phone?"

She gave him a protracted stare and handed him the Cindy-phone.

"There are eighteen calls on there," she said with devilish intent, lifting the corners of her mouth in a satisfied little smile. "And one message. I counted."

She knew he would have slammed the door in annoyance on his way out if his arms hadn't been full. Through the window, she saw him stalk down the stone path toward the resort's main lobby. Briefly, she wondered if he'd call a cab or check into another room. She sat a long time listening to the crashing of the waves on the rocky beach below.

When Daisy disappeared into the mist on that beach in San Diego, Keegan had been carried away by an infinity of despair, its end forever receding. After the police investigation fizzled out at a dead end with no leads, her anguish was infused with anger. That anger, the fuel for her energy, was the only thing that kept her going, making her feel bigger and stronger than she could ever be. It was a strength she felt she would need if she ever wanted to see her daughter again.

Until she learned anger also clouded her judgment and alienated and pissed off people she cared about or needed to help her. After that, she wisely redirected her energy into her writing. The gravitational pull of normality reasserted itself, and she came back to life a little.

Her job at *Offbeat Arizona Magazine* suited her. It provided her with work she loved and a structure to her hours, until eventually the memory of that horrible day Daisy was taken lost its power to send her to her knees.

She wrote about other missing children and their grieving moms and dads, kids the authorities were unable to find despite their best, and sometimes not so great, efforts. The result was an award-winning series of articles that had garnered enough national attention to bring five of those missing children home alive. That alone confirmed her belief that anger sometimes got things done, so she let the fire in her belly burn steady even though its ferocity exhausted her.

Making a decision, she took her phone off the charger and hit speed dial, then sat on the edge of the bed waiting for Diana Delgado to pick up, which she did, grumpily.

"Is the sun up yet?" Diana mumbled.

"It is here. I'm sorry. I wasn't sure of the time change."

"Are you still in Cabo?" Diana asked on the tail end of a yawn.

"I am. But Jeffrey left."

"Left?"

"We broke it off. Well, *he* broke it off."

"*Hummph.* You're better off," replied Keegan's boss, who was also her friend.

"Don't start."

Silence.

"Are you all right?" Diana asked.

"I'm not heartbroken, if that's what you mean." But she had taken a hit, and it *did* hurt. She felt like she'd been discarded for a newer, cheerier model. A more *available* one.

"What are you going to do?"

"I don't know." Silence.

"You push yourself too hard. You should take more time off. You're supposed to be on vacation. Your first one since . . ." Diana stopped.

There was that word again. *Since.* Every event in Keegan's life was marked off by that word, chronicled by that event. Since Daisy disappeared, her life had been divided into a before and after.

Keegan could hear Diana breathing, waiting for her to say something. "Maybe I'll go away for a while."

"Okay," Diana said.

"I'm thinking of taking a road trip."

"Where will you go?"

"Do you remember I told you about that old picture my cousin sent me? He found it in a box in the attic at my grandfather's house after the funeral?"

"Yeah, I think so. Where did you say it was taken?"

"In Monument Valley. My grandfather was a government doctor on the Navajo Reservation when he got out of med school, back before he opened his practice in Phoenix."

"Is *that* where you're going? Are you sure you want to?"

"I'm thinking about it. I was thinking about those people in that picture, wondering who they were and what they're doing now. They knew my grandfather back then. If I can find them, and talk to them, it might be a good article for *Offbeat Arizona.* I know my family would be interested. What do you think?"

There was thoughtful silence on Diana's end. "Well, you

could use a break from the missing children stories." She paused, considering it. "Do you think you'd be able to find anyone now? That picture was taken fifty years ago."

"I don't know. But I thought I'd drive out there and ask around. Even if nothing comes of it, getting away will do me some good. Clear my head. I need some rest," she admitted.

"Then do it," Diana said, warming to the idea. "I can run it as a Where-Are-They-Now? feature next fall," she added, her enthusiasm growing. "And, Keegan, you do need a break. How long do you think you'll be gone?"

"A couple of weeks?"

"Take as long as you need."

CHAPTER TWO

Every morning since Daisy's disappearance, Keegan woke to see pain stretched out ahead of her, its end forever meeting the horizon. She didn't expect to be free of it until she had Daisy back, so she was always surprised at the intermittent interludes of diversion that dislodged thoughts of her daughter and allowed her a reprieve. The six-hour drive to the Navajo Indian Reservation provided just such a measure of peaceful respite.

She drove the back roads, the blue roads on the map, where the views were magnificent. Sheer-walled mesas and colorful buttes and pinnacles formed by eons of erosion created an otherworldly earthscape that stretched as far as she could see. Changing colors and shifting shadows across the rock faces and rippled sand dunes added to the enchantment. It was quiet. Nothing stirred except an occasional hawk on the wing. Little by little, the tension flowed out of her body.

Radio reception became a lost cause in the deepest part of the desert. When it disappeared completely, she slipped in a CD. Billy Bob Thornton kept her company the rest of the way, his deep chainsaw of a voice coming from the 4Runner's speakers lamenting his love for a big shot in the movie biz who Keegan always suspected was Angelina Jolie.

She arrived in Monument Valley in the middle of a red, pink, orange, and purple sunset so dazzling it took her breath away. Exhausted, she got a room at Goulding's Lodge, ordered a hamburger and fries to go, and took her food to her room.

While she ate, she studied the old photograph.

Some of the people in the photo appeared to be her grand-father's age or older. Perhaps, like her grandfather, they'd already passed on. She harbored a hope that some of the younger ones were still around, but the passing years would have changed their looks, adding pounds and maturing their faces beyond recognition. Now that she was here, she could see it wasn't going to be so easy finding anyone in this vast, empty expanse.

There was only one way to begin, the same way she and every other reporter gathered information. Talk to people, show the picture, snoop around, and ask questions.

She slept so late the next morning that by the time she got to the dining room it was already filled with tourists. Luckily a table cleared next to a window and she was seated there, for which she was grateful. The view was even more resplendent in the morning sun.

Within minutes, a menu was in her hands, a pot of coffee was on the table, and a pretty Navajo waitress had come over to take her order.

"Good morning," she greeted with a smile. "I'm Vicki. I'll be your server this morning. What can I get you?"

Keegan ordered her usual breakfast on the road—orange juice, fruit, and a short stack of pancakes—then held up the old photo.

"Excuse me," she said to the waitress, "but do you by chance recognize anyone in this picture?"

The waitress stared at the photo a moment with wide expressive eyes. Looking as if she were struck by a memory, her pleasant expression started to collapse. After a brittle second, her smile reappeared.

"No," she said. "I'm sorry. I don't. Can I get you anything else?"

19

"No. That's all, thanks."

"I'll be right back with your order," Vicki said and hurried off.

Keegan unfolded the *Navajo Times* she'd picked up on her way in, and began reading an article about the first ever casino on the Navajo Reservation, construction scheduled to begin next year.

Vicki Bedonnie couldn't get out of the dining room fast enough. One look at that picture set her heart pounding so hard she could feel it in her ears. Now her chest was tight, making it hard to breathe.

Quickly, she snatched the receiver off the wall phone in the kitchen and dialed with a shaking finger. She closed her eyes, took several audibly shaky breaths, and waited for someone to answer.

"Emerson Bedonnie's office."

"Hello, Bertha. Could I speak to my grandpa? It's important."

"Sure, Vicki, hold on."

From where she stood in the kitchen, Vicki could see through the gap between the door and the door frame into the dining room when the servers went in or out with trays or dishes. The white lady with bright blue eyes and shiny dark hair was sitting in the booth reading the newspaper. The picture lay on the table in front of her.

"To what do I owe the pleasure of a phone call from my granddaughter so early in the day?" Emerson Bedonnie didn't talk on the telephone, he boomed into it.

"Grandpa," Vicki whispered, turning to face the wall. She covered her mouth with her hand so no one could hear. "There's a white lady here showing a picture. She asked me if I knew anyone in it."

"A picture of what?" her grandfather asked.

"Uncle Will's in it. And Lulu."

Vicki heard her grandfather's startled gasp. "What did you tell her?" he asked quietly, as if he, too, didn't want to be overheard.

"I told her I didn't know anyone. But, Grandfather, I don't like to lie."

"No," he replied, quickly. "I don't want you to lie."

"But what should I do?"

"Don't talk to her."

"Okay, Grandpa," Vicki said, and hung up.

One of the cooks, stirring a pot of luncheon special Dried Corn Stew, eyed her suspiciously, but she wouldn't look at him. Instead, she went into the employee break room, untied her apron, hung it on a hook in a locker next to the bulletin board with the OSHA and Department of Labor bulletins, then picked up her purse, and walked out the back door.

Keegan looked up from her newspaper, checked her watch and decided that twenty-seven minutes was long enough to wait for breakfast. Not seeing the server who took her order, she flagged down a passing busboy and inquired.

Thirty seconds later, the manager hurried over, apologized profusely, poured water, more coffee, and took her order again.

"I'm sorry you had to wait so long for your meal," the manager said, apologizing for the second time when she came back with the food. "There was a mix-up in the kitchen. Please accept breakfast at no charge, along with some freshly made Navajo fry bread." The manager placed a plate of delicate, sweet smelling, powdered sugar–dusted, irresistible looking pastries on the table.

Keegan thanked her, but stopped the woman before she walked away. "Excuse me," she said. "Would you mind taking a look at this picture? Do you recognize anyone?"

The young woman took it in her fingers, studied it a moment, then shook her head.

"No, sorry. But I can tell it was taken around here," she said. "Maybe over near Oljato," she said. She smiled and handed it back.

Well, that's a start, Keegan thought, gazing at the picture and wondering where Oljato was.

The photograph was old, cracked at the creases, and a little faded, taken well before Keegan was born. She couldn't identify anyone in it except her grandfather. Lincoln Cole, at the time a dashing young doctor, had been sent to Monument Valley by the Bureau of Indian Affairs to provide medical care to the families living in that most inaccessible part of the Navajo Reservation.

He was standing with a gathering of Navajos in front of a log structure with a peaked roof of crisscrossed logs, looking comfortable and at ease. Those with him looked equally at ease, despite their rigid posture. To her grandfather's right stood two elderly women in traditional dress of the time, long cotton skirts gathered at the waist, tops made of fabrics that looked to be soft velvet or shiny satin. Wrapped around their shoulders or tied close across their middle were deeply fringed shawls that, though the picture was in black and white, Keegan was certain were brilliant with color. An old man sat on a boulder in front and off to the side. A chevron-patterned blanket covered him from waist to ankles.

On her grandfather's immediate left stood a young Navajo woman with a toddler in her arms, both of them cocooned in a shawl. Next to her were two other women, a little older, one holding the hand of a small boy. The faces of the individuals in the back row were blurry and hard to make out, but they looked to be older adults or even middle-aged. Everyone was solemn-faced and unsmiling, except for her grandfather and the two black-hatted men in back. They grinned openly.

It looked like the kind of photo a group of friends might have taken to celebrate or commemorate some event. She narrowed her eyes and moved closer to the light, studying the figures in the photo, bejeweled, straight-faced, stoic, resplendent in magnificent ropes of beads, their fingers, arms, and waists adorned with silver rings, bracelets, and belts.

She tried to imagine what it was like living in this desolate desert fifty-odd years ago, tried to capture a sense of what life had been like then. The lodge hadn't been here, of course, and the roads weren't paved, though she knew visitors had arrived in cars even then over barren, dusty roads. Yet people had lived here, grown up, had families, loved and died here. They had survived.

After breakfast, Keegan visited the gift shop, where she bought a map and a guide book to the Four Corners. The two sales clerks were friendly and helpful, if reserved. They smiled and chatted pleasantly as they rang up Keegan's purchases, but positively stiffened when she showed them the picture. Both women turned away with head shakes and averted eyes before becoming engrossed in paperwork or other behind-the-counter duties.

Keegan left the shop and went next door to peek at the John Wayne movie museum, a tribute to Wayne as well as to all the old western movies filmed in Monument Valley, classics like *Stagecoach* and *The Searchers*. Inside were movie posters, film scripts, call sheets, candid black and white photos of casts and crews. Many movies had been filmed there during the past five or six decades, and no self-respecting automobile manufacturer had neglected to shoot a modern day television commercial there, either. Clearly, John Wayne was well remembered.

She drove down to the main highway and parked at the roadside Indian Market, a straight line of makeshift, plywood stalls where Native American artisans sold their handmade crafts and jewelry. She stopped at each vendor to make a purchase and show the photo. Some of the Indians refused to even look at it. Others studied it with interest, but handed it back with a head shake and a shrug.

Soon, the sun was high, bright, and hot, but Keegan wasn't ready to give up. Feeling like a bit of a nuisance, she stepped into the shade of a low-roofed shed on the end of a run of plywood shacks leaning with the wind.

The old man seated behind the counter had a face as wrinkled as a dried apple, and the same color, too. A Navajo boy in his teens sat at a folding card table in the corner, a high-intensity lamp focused on his workspace as he strung a colorful assortment of beads and stones into a bracelet. The old man greeted her with a nod, and Keegan selected a pair of gloriously beaded earrings. After she paid for them, she took out the picture.

One glance and the old man turned his face away, swept his arm through the air as if batting away something awful, and spoke to her in Navajo. She didn't understand the words, but the tone and his expression made clear the degree of his annoyance with her.

"Grandpa!" the teenager at the table admonished, getting up from his chair and approaching Keegan. He had hair in a ponytail down his back and was wearing a backward baseball cap, khaki shorts, and a long sleeve T-shirt that said *University of Arizona*.

"Let me see." Ignoring the scolding look from the old man, he held out his hand for the picture. "Don't mind my grandfather," he said to her. "Some of the old ones don't like to look at pictures of people who are dead. But I'm a history major," he said. "I'm interested in stuff like this."

He looked at the picture, concentrating hard, taking in the

details. "Where did you get this?"

"We found it after my grandfather died. I was curious and thought I might be able to find these people, if they're still around."

The boy, head down, studied the photo, clearly interested. "Yeah, maybe," he said, nodding. Then, "I don't recognize anyone, but why don't you take it over to the high school? Somebody there might. Maybe one of the teachers. Even if they can't help you, they might know someone who can."

Monument Valley High School was around the corner and up the road a short distance from the Indian Market. She pulled into a space in the Visitor Parking next to a newer model Jeep heavily dusted with red dirt. School was in session, the student parking lot full of vehicles ranging in age from shiny new to nearly ancient, mostly pickups or short, squatty compact cars.

Beyond the parking lot was a long, low, red mesa that extended for miles east to west. Nearly vertical in places, the not quite level summit held piñon trees and juniper in greater abundance than on the surrounding desert floor. At the base of the cliff were boulders that had broken away from the mesa wall, leaving a tumble of large and small sandstone rocks.

Keegan went inside and found the school office. She waited at the counter while a slender Navajo woman with waist-length black hair talked to a man wearing cargo pants, camp shirt, and hiking boots thick with dust the same color as that covering the Jeep outside. When they finished their business, he gave Keegan an appreciative once over on his way out. Behind his back, she returned it.

"Can I help you?" the woman behind the counter asked. She had dark, slightly slanted eyes, an open friendly expression, and Keegan liked her right away.

"Hi," Keegan said and introduced herself. "I was wondering if someone might know anyone in this picture." She laid it on the counter. "It was taken here in Monument Valley. It belonged to my grandfather."

"I'm Jilly Wolf. Nice to meet you," the woman said, picking up the photograph. Her eyes lit immediately when she looked at it. "Oh," she said, smiling, then again, "Oh, Agnes, look at this." She showed the photo to a plump faced older woman seated at a desk behind her, who also grinned and nodded when she saw it.

"They're all wearing the old style clothes," the woman exclaimed.

"Some still dress like that now," Jilly said, speaking to Keegan but looking at the picture.

"My grandfather was Lincoln Cole," Keegan said, pointing him out. "He used to be a BIA doctor here back in the fifties."

"I'd love to show this to my class," Jilly said, eyes sparkling with delight. "I teach Navajo Studies. My students would love to see this."

"Do you know who any of these other people are?" Keegan asked. "I don't want to invade anyone's privacy, but I thought if I could find someone, I might be able to talk to them, give them a copy of this picture. I'd like to write a story for the magazine I work for if they didn't mind, and I was hoping someone might remember my grandfather."

"No," Jilly said, thoughtfully, looking closer. "No, I don't recognize anyone, but my grandmother might," she said, smiling up at Keegan. "Why don't you come for dinner tonight? You can meet her and show her the photo. Would you mind?"

Keegan was surprised at a dinner invitation from someone she'd just met. "Oh, I'd love to, but . . ."

"Oh, please. Please come, it's no bother," Jilly said, meaning it. "My grandmother has to see this. Even if she doesn't know anyone, it will give her pleasure."

"Are you sure she won't mind looking at it?"

Jilly shook her head. "The dead don't scare her. She worries far more about the living."

"Okay," said Keegan. "I'd love to. Thank you."

"Here," Jilly said, "I'll write down the directions to my house. Come at six." She took a pen and paper and began writing, then drew a little map. "When you get to this intersection," she pointed with the tip of her pen, "turn off the highway and go two more miles, and you'll see a fence post just before you get to Alhambra Rock. Stop there, and call me. What cell phone service do you use?"

When Keegan told her, Jilly flapped her hand as if to say forget about it. "Well, that won't work on the reservation." She went to her purse atop a file cabinet, took out a cell phone, and handed it to Keegan. "Here, use mine. Call the house phone when you get there. You can give me my cell back then." She wrote down the number. "I'll drive out to meet you, and you can follow me the rest of the way. You'll never find it on your own."

CHAPTER THREE

Jilly was right.

Two miles off the pavement, the road, such as it was, cut through a slash in a broad mesa then disappeared. Keegan braked to a stop, letting the engine idle. Jagged rock formations with steep plunging sides spiked up from rolling terrain carpeted with red sand and rabbitbrush. The walls of a mesa in the near distance were painted with horizontal streaks of gray shale, pink sandstone, and yellow caliche, making it look like a massive layer cake made of rock.

A few yards ahead, a fence post poked up from the rocky ground, sun-bleached, dried to splinters, and unconnected to anything resembling a fence. A gust of wind blew across the flatland, snicking red sand against the side of the 4Runner, turning the air pink.

She let the 4Runner roll forward, then stopped at the fence post, and looked around once more. The scenery in every direction was huge, beautiful, and a hundred shades of red. No people, no houses broke the never-ending landscape. Long shadows cast by massive stone monoliths stretched across the sand. She took out Jilly's phone and dialed.

Less than two minutes later, Jilly arrived in a moving cloud of dust, handling a dark blue Chevy Tahoe like it needed to be taught a lesson. She grinned and waved, turned a wide circle, and motioned Keegan to follow, which Keegan did, through deep desert sand, and up, down, and out of gullies and wide washes.

Jilly stopped on a hard packed patch of dirt in front of a pale green cinderblock house tucked into a nook that had been scooped out of the side of a shallow mesa by millenniums of wind. Fifty feet away from the house were a couple of small outbuildings, and animal pens minus any animals that Keegan could see. In the back was a new looking pole barn.

Keegan parked next to a pickup truck that had seen better days, with rust and gray primer showing on the fenders and hood. She caught a glimpse of the interior. Green shag carpet scraps and an assortment of yellow and pink artificial flowers filled the ledge next to the windshield.

"That's *shimasani*'s truck," Jilly said, smiling and coming around to greet Keegan. "My grandmother. She lives with me sometimes. Whenever I can get her to. But every few weeks she goes back to her place. She lives in a hogan and tends a small flock of sheep." Jilly went up the steps of a low porch and reached for the screen door. "Come on in. We're having Navajo Tacos."

Aromas coming from the kitchen immediately made Keegan's stomach react. She could see something delicious-smelling was steaming on the stove. At the kitchen counter, a deep-bosomed Navajo woman wearing a blue print ankle length cotton skirt, shocking pink satin top, workout socks, and Keds sandals was tossing a circle of dough back and forth from one flour covered hand to the other. Six-inch long beaded earrings swung from her ears, and ropes of turquoise and cabochon lay on her chest. Two huge silver and turquoise rings rested atop a blue velvet drawstring bag placed on the window ledge over the sink.

Jilly did the introductions, speaking louder than normal for the sake of the old woman.

"*Shimasani,* this is Keegan Thomas. Remember I told you about her? I met her at school today. She has a picture I want you to look at." She turned to Keegan. "This is my grandmother, Earlene Cly."

The grandmother looked up and nodded, greeting Keegan with a smile that was as warm as her words, none of which Keegan understood because they were spoken in Navajo.

"She said welcome to our home," Jilly interpreted, "and she hopes you will enjoy a traditional Navajo meal. She understands a little English, but doesn't speak it much," Jilly explained, her dark eyes stirring with affection, "and doesn't much want to learn." She shrugged. "I don't make an issue of it."

The grandmother spoke again, and still smiling tipped her chin in a shooing motion.

"Okay, *shimasani,*" Jilly said, then took Keegan's arm. "She wants us out of her kitchen while she cooks."

Jilly led Keegan into a living room furnished with old but comfortable looking chairs and sofas, deeply upholstered and covered with Navajo blankets. Stunning Navajo rugs were scattered over the linoleum floor.

"These are so beautiful," Keegan said, admiring them. Though clean, they were faded with use and wear. Keegan couldn't imagine anyone actually walking on them instead of framing them as wall art.

"My grandmother made them," Jilly told her. "That's why she won't stay here all the time. She doesn't like to be away from her hogan too long. She misses her sheep, and enjoys caring for them. She needs help with shearing and during lamb season, but she still cards the wool herself, and weaves. I tell her she can bring her loom here, but she's not ready to do that. Independent, you know, like all us Navajos."

"Does your mother live here, too? I mean nearby in Monument Valley," Keegan asked, thinking how lovely it was that three generations might live close enough to see each other every day.

"No. My mother lives in Albuquerque. She's a professor at the University of New Mexico. I guess I take after her when it comes to teaching. My father's a heart surgeon there, but medicine as a career never interested me."

Keegan settled into one of the soft chairs. Jilly, on the sofa, propped her sneakered feet on a coffee table made of rough wood.

"I lived there for a while, but then my grandmother got older and couldn't stay by herself anymore. I came back here and got a teaching job at the high school so I could look after her." Following a glance into the kitchen, she lowered her voice. "Though she thinks she's looking after me."

Keegan laughed softly, understanding. She thought of her own grandmother, exuding haughty elegance in her younger days, frail now with a heart condition but bearing herself with dignity. She, too, was a tough, independent woman who did things her own way heedless of warnings or advice from family members. And, as often happens in families, genuine bonding skipped a generation. Keegan was closer to her maternal grandmother than she ever was to her own mother.

"But, hey," said Jilly. "Here I am going on about myself and my family. What about you? Where are you from? Tell me about your family? What do you do?"

Keegan gave her the short version. Mother living in Tucson. No brothers. No sisters. Father gone off to chase some greater need. She didn't mention it was with a younger woman, and she didn't mention Daisy.

"I live in a small town in Arizona. Cave Creek, one of the last cowboy towns. I'm single . . . well, divorced," she added quickly. "It was a friendly divorce, though I never see my ex. Brady works for the government and lives out of the country most of the time. Maybe that's why I can say it was friendly. We never see each other."

Jilly raised her eyebrows and nodded, understanding, which made Keegan wonder if she'd had a similar experience with an ex-husband.

She went on. "I write for a magazine. I've been working on stories about the families of abducted children, how it affects them, how they hold up, how they cope. You know, mothers never give up the hope of seeing their child again no matter what."

Jilly was looking at her with sympathy. "Oh, that must be a very hard job," she said.

Keegan nodded. "It is, sometimes. The last story I worked on—" She stopped abruptly.

"What?"

"Well, sometimes the child is never returned, and the families are devastated for life. Nothing is ever the same for them again. The last child I wrote about was found dead. The mother ended up in a hospital with a nervous breakdown. I cried for a week."

Jilly's grandmother came to the doorway and spoke to them in Navajo.

"Come," Jilly said to Keegan. "Dinner is ready."

A Navajo Taco, a scrumptious combination of ground meat, onions, pinto beans, shredded lettuce, and chopped tomatoes on moist rounds of fry bread, filled her plate. The tea was iced and herbal.

Earlene Cly, with Jilly interpreting, entertained Keegan with traditional Navajo stories and legends. She spoke of the Four Sacred Mountains, and the Navajo philosophy of a harmonious life in daily living.

Keegan was fascinated, wishing she could take some notes, but the food was so delicious, she didn't want to stop eating long enough to get paper and pen from her purse. And besides, she was afraid they might think it was ill-mannered of her to do so.

"Spider Woman instructed the Navajo women how to weave on a loom," Jilly said. "The legend tells us she was the first to weave her web of the universe, and taught the Dineh . . . ," Jilly stopped to explain. "That's what the Navajo people call themselves. Dineh. Anyway, Spider Woman taught our people to create beauty in their life, and spread the Beauty Way of living by bringing mind, body, and soul into harmony."

"Oh, what a lovely story," Keegan said. "And a lovely way to live your life." Keegan wondered if she'd ever be able to achieve such a state of being.

"Yes, it is," said Jilly, "but sometimes children are also told that Spider Woman has a special way of finding bad little kids, and when she does, she boils and eats them." Jilly laughed. "I have four brothers and three sisters and lots of cousins. That story kept us all in line, I'll tell you."

After a dessert of peach crisp and ice cream topped with whipped cream and piñon nuts, Jilly got up to clear the table, insisting her grandmother had already done too much and should sit and rest.

"Keegan, show her the picture," Jilly said as she began gathering plates from the table.

Keegan retrieved it from an envelope in her leather bag, and put it on the table in front of the old woman. Earlene Cly's eyes narrowed a fraction, and she stared at the photo for several long moments, not moving, her wrinkled face frozen except for lips that pinched imperceptibly. At last she spoke.

"John Wayne," Earlene Cly said decisively.

Keegan straightened, surprised, and looked at the old woman, puzzled. Jilly moved from the sink where she was squirting detergent and running hot water into a dishpan.

"What? John Wayne? Let me see that," she said, drying her

hands on a dish towel.

The old woman, her face expressionless, handed it over to Jilly, who stared in amazement, then chuckled.

"She's right," she said. "That's John Wayne in the back row. See? Right there. Look close. That other white man next to him might be John Ford. You know, the movie director who made all those John Wayne western movies here back in the forties and fifties."

Earlene Cly got up from the table, and gently taking the dish towel out of Jilly's hands, resumed the dishwashing duties at the sink.

"That might explain the reason the photo was taken," surmised Keegan. "A visit by a Hollywood star and a movie director would certainly warrant a photo op."

Jilly nodded, her eyes still on the photo. "Are you sure you don't recognize anyone else, Gram?"

There was silence and a stiffening of shoulders from the woman at the sink. The conversation about the photo was over, at least, as far as Earlene Cly was concerned.

"Well, I'll ask my mother," Jilly told Keegan, unperturbed. "She teaches anthropology and Navajo history. Maybe she can tell you something about it. Do you have another copy?"

"No," Keegan said, "but if there's a place I can go to have copies made tomorrow, I'll give you one."

"You might have to drive into Kayenta," Jilly replied, handing the photo back, "or Farmington. I'd make copies at school, but the copier in the office quit and the repairman can't come until next month."

Outside, headlights bounced over the roller coaster terrain coming toward the house. A Jeep stopped, the engine was turned off, and a man sat behind the wheel.

"Oh, that's Dante," Jilly said, getting up to go to the door. "He always honors Navajo custom by waiting outside until he's invited in. I forgot he was coming over to bring me an outline of the presentation he's giving to my Russian exchange students."

"You have students here from Russia?"

"Yes," said Jilly. "It's been a huge project. I'll tell you about it." She threw the door wide and waved and called to Dante to come in.

On the porch, he stomped some of the dust off his boots, then crossed the threshold into the living room, looking at Keegan with curiosity.

Rugged, with a handsome suntanned face and sun bleached hair tied back with a piece of rawhide, his male presence filled the small living room. He was well over six feet tall, with powerful shoulders, and good looking enough to hold any woman's glance longer than was considered polite. His erect posture and easy bearing gave off an impression of both physical grace and virility. It was the same man Keegan had seen talking to Jilly in the school office that afternoon.

Jilly introduced them, and Earlene immediately went to the stove, arranged a Navajo Taco on a plate, and set it on the table, motioning him to come and sit. He wasn't shy about doing so, either. After greeting Earlene with a gentle hug and a kiss on the cheek, he sat down at the table and began to eat. He seemed quite comfortable with this family.

"Dante is an archaeologist. He's taking some of our kids on an overnight field trip. We sent fourteen Navajo students to Siberia last semester on a cultural exchange program, so now we have fourteen Siberian students staying with us," Jilly explained, bringing Keegan up to date.

"How interesting," said Keegan. She sat down with the other two, who had joined Dante to keep him company while he ate. "But isn't that a problem? I mean with the languages being so different. How do the kids get on with each other?"

"It's not as different as you'd think," Dante replied.

"Teenagers are the same everywhere," put in Jilly, "and historically, the two cultures are related in the distant past. Some words in their language are the same as in ours. Or close enough to be understood. We also found that culturally, some of our myths and legends are similar, also."

"Like the story you told me about Spider Woman?" Keegan asked.

Jilly laughed lightly. "Well, I don't know about that."

"Thirteen thousand years ago, there was a land bridge connecting Asia and what is now northwest Alaska," Dante explained between bites of Navajo Taco. "Historians believe Native Americans descended from Asian peoples who migrated into North America over that route."

"Navajo people believe that, too," said Jilly. "When we were kids, *shimasani* told us stories about the People from the Cold or the People Left Behind. It was a story passed down to her from her grandparents and their grandparents before that."

"When glaciers melted about ten thousand years ago, the sea level rose and covered up the land connecting the continents. You know, the Bering Strait. There's a national preserve up there now," explained Dante.

"Anyway, Dante is taking the kids on an overnight trip to see ruins and artifacts in Mesa Verde. I need to have his course outline and itinerary approved by the school board."

"Oh, here," he said. He took a folded sheet of paper from his shirt pocket and handed it to Jilly, then looked at Keegan with gorgeous gray-green eyes and continued.

"There are no ruins anywhere in the world like the ones in the American Southwest. Everyone wants to come see them. Archaeologists from other countries salivate at the thought of participating in a dig here. I'm really lucky. I'm freelance, so I get to pick and choose my projects. I usually team up on university digs. Or sometimes the tribe hires me. Right now, I'm doing preliminary work on a possible ceremonial site. There are lots of digs going on around this area, all the way from Farmington, New Mexico, to Blanding, Utah."

"That's true," said Jilly. "There are so many archaeologists working in Navajoland, the joke is that the typical Navajo family consists of a man, a woman, two children, and an archaeologist. Dante's ours," said Jilly. "We claimed him."

Keegan could see why they'd want to. Discreetly she studied him from across the table. There was something compelling about him. He was gentle and polite, thoughtful and modest. He spoke with a quiet earnestness.

Dante finished eating, pushed his plate aside, and casually folded his arms on the table. "What brings you to Monument Valley?" he asked Keegan. He looked at her with genuine interest.

"I have this old picture," she said, taking it out again to show him. "I'm working on a possible story about it for *Offbeat Arizona Magazine*," she said. "I'm a reporter."

The ice in Dante's gaze could have created its own land bridge between them. He regarded her in frigid silence, his face frozen, his mouth clamped shut.

"My grandfather was a BIA doctor back in the fifties," Keegan sputtered, feeling urged on by his fierce expression to explain herself. "He ran the Indian Health Service clinic in Monument Valley."

Earlene Cly, standing at the stove, turned and stared, then her eyes shot to the floor, and right then Keegan knew there were secrets in this house.

CHAPTER FOUR

Well, it looked like she'd offended just about everyone she'd met on the rez so far. And it was only the *first* day.

Keegan sat on the balcony outside her second floor room at Goulding's wearing jeans and a cotton turtleneck shirt, bare feet braced on the railing, drinking her first cup of coffee on the bright blue dazzling morning of the new day.

She'd yet to figure out exactly what had put such a damper on the previous evening. It was as if she'd plopped a steaming mass of road kill in the center of the kitchen table when she'd laid the picture there. Earlene abruptly disappeared into a back bedroom without a goodnight, and Dante Covelli's ebullience deflated like someone had blurted out the punch line to his best joke.

After that, the flow of conversation died, and though it tried to come to life in uncomfortable fits and starts, the evening ended on an undefined sour note. When no one knew what to say next, Keegan had taken out her car keys at the same time Dante stood up to leave. It was Jilly who suggested Keegan follow him out to the highway as a safeguard against getting lost.

Dante didn't object, but neither did he take any pains to make it easy for her. He slammed his SUV into gear and took off in a spin of sand and stones, not seeming to care that Keegan wasn't as familiar with the route as he was. His taillights disappeared a few times, and she'd had to push the 4Runner harder than she liked to keep up.

What the hell had happened? She liked Jilly and hated to think she'd said or done something disrespectful to her or her family. Or her culture.

It had to do with the picture, she was sure of it; she suspected Earlene knew more about it than she'd let on. The elder had stared at it a long time, working hard to keep her expression unreadable, but Keegan could see something going on behind her dark eyes.

The moment had passed, but later on, in front of Dante, Earlene got upset again. What did Dante have to do with it? Maybe nothing. Maybe Earlene had seen something in the photo she hadn't noticed when she'd looked at it the first time.

And Keegan had no idea what had set Dante off. Talk about looks that could kill.

But the day hadn't been a total loss, she thought, as she got ready to go down for breakfast. She'd been able to identify at least two other people in the photo besides her grandfather. John Wayne and John Ford. In the movie museum, she'd learned that John Wayne spent time in Monument Valley even when he wasn't making a film. Finding out during which visit the picture was taken, at least on what occasion, might point to other helpful information.

And, she now had some idea where the picture might have been taken. The manager at the restaurant said it looked like it was near Oljato. She'd already checked the local map she'd bought, and was happy to see that Oljato was only eight miles up the road.

In the dining room, the waitress named Vicki was nowhere to be seen. In her place was another pretty Navajo girl who greeted Keegan pleasantly, took her order, and delivered it promptly with a smile.

After breakfast, Keegan planned her day. A drive to Oljato was first on her list, to look around, ask a few questions. Then a stop at the high school to find Jilly and apologize if she'd somehow upset the evening. She made a mental note to find a place to make copies of the picture.

Two lanes of pavement plowed straight through red desert toward Oljato once she got past the airstrip and the gas station. Sun-baked mesas, low and squat, glorious in the morning light flanked the road. Up ahead, two black crows picked at something on the yellow lane divider. She swerved to miss them, but glossy black wings spread and flapped as the birds rose into the air only to reunite on the road and continue their meal after she passed.

Coming up on her right, an old, weathered plywood shack leaned to the side, pushed that way by many years of desert wind. A peeling white sign with the word *CAFÉ* painted in red was propped next to the door, but the door was hanging on its hinges. In back was an old trailer with arched windows and limp cotton curtains hanging on a sagging rod. At the end of the driveway, a wooden cross with a grapevine wreath of forlorn looking plastic flowers memorialized the death of someone who had been killed there.

Spontaneous roadside shrines such as this one, tangible evidence of extremely personal pain, erected by loved ones at the scene of traffic fatalities, were familiar sights along byways of the Southwest. She'd seen many of them on her way here.

She slowed her speed and read the words *Danny Cloud, three years old* still showing in faded blue paint. Keegan's heart gave a painful little squeeze. She wouldn't have been surprised to find out the parents' grief at the loss of their son precipitated the neglect and decline of the café.

The road ended at the edge of Oljato, though it was hard to tell where the little enclave actually began and where it ended. The pavement turned into a dirt track leading to a cluster of homes and buildings situated at the base of a red sandstone mesa. Beyond that, it continued as a sandy rut disappearing into the distant wilderness.

She drove slowly past the Oljato Chapter House and further on, the Oljato Senior Center. It was quiet, nothing was moving except a hawk circling overhead.

She turned around the way she'd come and pulled up next to a sturdy old adobe building that looked to be a hundred years old. A sign identified it as the Oljato Trading Post. She wasn't sure it was open, but she got out anyway, hoping to get something to drink. The door swung in six inches, then stuck on the stone doorstep, and she had to shove it with her hip to get it open wide enough so she could get inside.

Chest-high counters and display cases ran along three walls in a bullpen design displaying all manner of merchandise from candy bars to hunting knives. A girl, about thirteen, stood behind an old-fashioned cash register. Behind her, an old Navajo woman sat in a rocking chair smoking a cigarette. Both the girl and the woman smiled in greeting.

"*Ya'at'eeh,*" the girl said.

"Hello," Keegan replied. She looked around feeling like she'd stepped into the previous century. "Could I get a cold bottle of water?"

"Sure, right behind you in the cooler," the girl answered.

Keegan turned, surprised to see a modern beverage cooler. She took out a liter bottle and paid for it with cash.

"Can I help you with something else?" the girl asked. "Would you like to go on a Jeep tour?"

Keegan, feeling like she ought to know better, risked showing the picture again.

"No, thanks. I was driving around trying to find where this picture was taken." Maybe that was a better approach than asking about the people. "They told me at Goulding's it was taken somewhere around here."

The girl took the picture. Keegan noticed she avoided show-ing it to the elder. The old woman said something in Navajo, but the girl shook her head and said something back. The old woman let out a nicotine cackle and put her rocking chair in motion.

"This looks like it was taken somewhere between here and Goulding's," the girl replied. "That ridge line there, see? I recognize that. You probably passed it coming here." The girl kept gazing at the picture. "That's John Wayne, isn't it? Are you from Hollywood, too? Are they going to make another movie here? Are you a movie star?"

Keegan laughed, a little amazed someone so young would know who John Wayne was, but apparently he was an icon in Monument Valley.

"No," she answered. "I'm a writer. I was hoping to find some of the people in that picture. But for now I'd be happy to find the spot where it was taken."

The girl tipped her chin in the general direction of Gould-ing's. "I think it's that way," she said. "Maybe you can see it from out front. Come on. I'll show you."

Keegan followed her out the front door.

"There it is, see?"

Keegan turned her gaze to where the girl was looking, comparing the hazy ridgeline in the distance to the one in the picture.

"Go back on that same road and drive slow. Keep looking to your right. You'll probably see it." The girl looked at the picture again, then handed it back. "Good luck."

Keegan thanked her and headed back, driving slowly, scour-ing the irregular ridge line. She held up the picture and compared the uneven chevron-patterned mountains in the distance to the background in the picture.

Her eye caught sight of a double humped angular landform

that resembled the shape of the butte showing over John Wayne's shoulder in the picture, but she couldn't be sure because his head blocked part of it. Touching the brakes lightly, she swerved off to the shoulder and backed up, very slowly, her eyes picking out points of similarity. The long, sandy flat of stones and scrub leading to the spiky landform looked the same. The longer she stared at it, the more convinced she became that it was the right place.

Faint tire tracks crisscrossing the desert floor, overblown a little by the wind, led off the highway toward the rocky rise. The terrain looked similar to what she'd driven over to get to Jilly's. But still she hesitated. This was wilderness. It looked desolate back there.

And she was alone.

And most especially she wasn't dressed for it. Having grown up in Arizona, she knew better than to venture into the desert wearing strappy sandals.

On the other hand, it was daylight. She had a full tank of gas, and a 4 × 4 that could take her anywhere regardless of driving conditions. She didn't plan to get out of the car, and she didn't plan to drive far, just far enough to put the horizon into perspective with the background of the photo. If she was careful to take a slow, straight overland route, keeping the highway always in sight behind her, she couldn't get lost.

Making up her mind for good or for bad, she shifted into four-wheel drive and thumped into and out of the drainage ditch that ran parallel to the roadway, then headed over the rolling land in the direction of the erosion ravaged plateau.

Determination in the face of obstacles and possible failure was a personal characteristic she nurtured. Even as a child, she had a will not easily deflected from its course. Her parents and grandparents called it bullheadedness. She preferred to think of it as tenacity, an indispensable characteristic required of any successful journalist.

It was a bumpy proposition. The ground wasn't as flat as it looked, rising and falling in shuddering dips that jarred her high-riding vehicle, and in turn, her. Guided by some invisible imperative, she continued on, not knowing what she actually expected to find. Maybe the simple thrill of standing in the same spot her grandfather stood fifty years before, listening to murmurs of the past. That was enough to spur her on.

It wasn't long before she discovered that distances over massive expanses of land were deceiving. The farther she drove into the desert, the farther away her landmark seemed to recede. The wind picked up, blowing little dust devils spinning and skipping across the desert floor, but the sky was clear. No clouds threatened rain. A high-flying bird screeched a call as it disappeared over the jagged ridge.

She followed barely visible tire tracks of vehicles that had made passage along this route at some time in the recent past, tracks that diminished as she moved along. She hadn't looked at her watch, hadn't set her odometer, so didn't know how far she'd gone in time or miles. Convinced the faint track she was following led somewhere, she continued on, crawling over boulders and plowing through sandy soil.

And then the trail abruptly ended.

She found herself on an upland plateau with a hard, rocky surface drenched in silence and solitude, overlooking a badlands of intricately stream-dissected canyons. The sun plunged off precipitous ledges into sheer emptiness, and if she went any farther, so would she.

She turned around and was stunned to find the highway was no longer in sight. Somehow she had steered off course. She stared into the distance for one breathless moment, tamping down a tiny bubble of panic. The 4Runner's tread marks were still visible. All she had to do was follow them back to the highway.

As she retraced her route, it became clear she hadn't been driving in a straight line at all. She'd been thrown off by the uneven ground, and by having to swerve around shrubs so large that if carefully tended and trimmed they would have been trees.

After a few hundred yards, other tire impressions, some more recent than others, branched off right and left in a direction that angled off behind her as she'd moved forward. She hadn't noticed them and now found herself staring at a series of forks in the road, unsure which way she'd come.

The Indians probably knew every inch of this desert, guided by the visual memory of the topography, but she hadn't been here long enough to develop that skill. She hadn't realized she'd have to.

Scanning the landscape, she took what looked to be the most heavily traveled trail. A shallow, fairly level dry wash ran parallel to her trajectory, and she edged over into it, making the drive smoother.

The embankments on either side of the arroyo gradually steepened until she found herself entering a deep slot canyon with high sandstone walls rising close on either side. She followed the creek bed a short distance until she remembered hearing about a group of tourists who'd been swept away in a flash flood as they hiked in a slot canyon just like this one. Days later, Navajo guides, who'd warned them it was risky, found their broken bodies miles downstream.

She shoved the gearshift into reverse and backed up to a wide spot where she was able to turn around. Breathing easier when she was out in the open, she scoured her surroundings, searching for anything that looked familiar. She thought she recognized a landform, an exaggerated step-down of craggy ridges, so she headed in that direction along a sandy trail that quickly deteriorated.

Her tires began to lose traction. It felt like she was driving through two feet of snow, and she dared not stop for fear of getting stuck. Her only option was to accelerate and hydroplane through the thick sand until she reached solid ground. She stepped on the gas, gripping the leather-wrapped steering wheel with both hands. The 4Runner moved forward a couple yards, then came to a wallowing halt, its chassis beached in the giant sandbox.

She struggled with it for a while, rocking the big SUV back and forth like she would to extract herself from a snow bank. She made a little progress forward, then heard a clunk, a thunk, and a grinding sound.

"Oh, no," she said, wincing, fearing the worse. When she got out to take a look, her stomach plummeted. Her vehicle was tilted at a crazy angle, one side sunk into the sand up to the frame, the undercarriage snagged on a boulder. She wasn't going anywhere. She reached inside and turned off the ignition, her mind spinning.

Taking deep breaths to calm herself, she focused on her surroundings. A narrow footpath branched off toward a range of warped and buckled low mountains, and she followed it until it ended at an overlook that wound down to viciously hard and unforgiving boulders at the bottom of a steep ravine.

Standing on the brink, she was surprised to see Oljato in the near distance. To the east, Goulding's Lodge was visible tucked into the base of a red butte. Framed in the notch of two conjoined sandstone towers, a strip of paved highway was visible below. A car drove by noiselessly, and she stared after it, instantly realizing that though she could see it from up here, no one could see her from down there.

She went back to the Runner and leaned against the front

fender, thinking. The day was calm, windless and noiseless. Silence pressed in on her ears. A bird circled overhead, drawing a bead on something on the ground behind her. She moved away quickly, thinking about snakes.

She opened the car door and grabbed her bag from the passenger seat, took out her phone, and with faint hope, flipped it open. The screen lit up, but showed no signal. Jilly was right. Her phone was useless on the reservation.

The sun was almost straight overhead. Soon the heat would be oppressive. She couldn't stay there, and she couldn't count on someone coming along to help her out. She'd have to walk.

She took her keys out of the ignition, dropped them in her bag along with her cell, put on her sunglasses, grabbed her water, and started out. Though she could see a bit of the highway, distance had no context. The snowcapped far ranges looked like they could be reached in an hour's walk, although she knew they were in Colorado, at least seventy miles away. Using that as a gauge, she figured Oljato was close to three miles away, Goulding's a little farther, and the highway maybe a mile. All walkable distances if she could get off this rocky mesa to flat ground.

Walking straight downhill wasn't possible. She had to keep veering off around rock piles and deep arroyos. The heat radiating off the rocks was becoming unbearable. She hooked two fingers in the top of her turtleneck, pulling it away from her sweat soaked neck, and considered taking it off. Instead she rolled up her sleeves and plodded along counting her steps.

One hundred and four, one hundred and five, one hundred and six.

Her compulsion to count things had begun in grade school but moderated as she got older. When she was little, she settled into her surroundings by counting everything in sight—the number of wrought iron uprights in a fence, the number of steps to the school bus, the number of times a character in a cartoon said a certain word, the number of windows in a downtown high rise. It had frustrated and annoyed her mother, who endlessly scolded her for doing it, like it was something she could control. She couldn't, and the odd quirk still manifested when she was tired or stressed.

She didn't know herself why she did it, but counting things soothed her. It kept her mind busy on something benign instead of running away with itself during times of stress, confusing and confounding issues that needed to be dealt with or sorted out. It helped her focus, stopped her from panicking, allowing some other part of her mind, the problem solving part, to do its job and come up with answers.

For now, there was nothing she could do about her vehicle. She couldn't move it, and she didn't know what to do about it, so it would have to remain where it was until she found help from someone who did know. The only thing she could do now was take it one step at a time.

Literally.

Four hundred forty. Four hundred forty-one. Four hundred forty-two.

The shade of an overhang invited her to stop, offering the promise of cooling respite. She sat on a rock and took a long drink. She was sure her water would last a while—it was a big bottle—but her head throbbed from the heat, and her face felt like she was standing next to a bonfire. She let her leather bag slide off her shoulder onto the ground, and set her bottle on a flat rock.

She wiped perspiration from her forehead with her sleeve, and rolled up the legs of her jeans to her knees. After a brief rest, she pulled off her shirt and wrapped it around her head as protection from the sun, using the sleeves to tie it in place under her chin. Briefly, she debated the wisdom of continuing on in her bra, bare skin exposed to the sun unprotected by sunscreen, but she decided to risk it in return for temporary relief from the unrelenting sun beating down on her head.

When she reached for her water bottle, something slammed into the back of her hand, driving pain up to her elbow. She let out a yell and jumped as a scorpion scurried away, its little lobster-like body disappearing into a crack between the rocks. Fire jumped along her nerve endings, and swelling began instantly giving rise to genuine alarm.

Truly frightened now, she let out a moan, pitching it up to a panicky squeal. Horrified, she watched burning redness flare over her skin. Supporting her throbbing hand with her other arm, she started off again, taking one unsteady step after another.

Eight hundred sixty-one, eight hundred sixty-two, eight hundred sixty-three.

The swelling was getting worse, and pain of the highest order shot up and down her arm, paralyzing her fingers. She didn't know if a scorpion sting would kill her, but if she didn't get out of this desert, she would die from exposure. Inhaling deeply, trying to keep her breathing regular and her heart rate normal, she kept going, carefully placing one foot in front of the other.

Two thousand sixteen. Two thousand seventeen. Two thousand eighteen.

Suddenly, the smell of burning wood touched her nostrils, and she looked up to see a thin sheen of smoke over the ridge on the opposite side of a wide wash up ahead. Lazily, it drifted at an angle before dissipating on the breeze. On a sandy plateau on the other side of the wash, tire tracks on a rise of land vanished into a notch that cut through a ridge at its lowest point. She could see them only because of the elevation on which she stood and the angle of the sun.

Warily, she started down the slope, digging her heels into the deep sand. It was unsteady going, eventually turning into an expanse of boulders that called for more scrambling than walking. She reached the sandy bottom, but was now in a wide gully and had to follow the dry creek bed downstream to find a low spot in its eight-foot height.

Finally, she was able to scramble up the other side. When her eyes cleared the rim, she saw a tent, and a vehicle half hidden behind an outcropping. Buckets, shovels, hand tools, and other digging equipment were scattered around the campsite. Smoke from burning embers rose in a stone fire ring. A laptop computer was set up at one end of a primitive wooden table. There were three metal-framed folding canvas sling chairs, one by the computer, one by the fire, another next to the table.

She jogged across the flat toward the camp. She'd only gone a few yards when her whole body jerked with alarm as a shadow loomed over her from the top of a rock as big as a house.

"Stop right there," a man yelled. "Don't take another step!"

Chapter Five

When Dante Covelli met Keegan Thomas at Jilly's kitchen table, he felt like he'd been poled in the stomach. He hated reporters. His attorney had tried to explain that they were only doing their jobs, but since when was it anybody's job to destroy a man? Not for one minute did he believe her bullshit story about looking for people in an old photograph. That was nonsense. He knew who she was looking for. Him.

Why couldn't they just leave him the hell alone? Hadn't they done enough damage? No one on the reservation knew what had happened in California. He'd thought, *hoped,* that was all dead and buried, but here it was, coming back at him. People never survived media scrutiny. Some of the mud always stuck, justified or not. And in his case, it was. He was guilty. One stupid mistake had brought his whole world crashing down around him.

He knew, as she also must, the terrible damage that could be inflicted by bringing all that up again. The reputation and credentials he'd worked so hard to rebuild would be destroyed a second time.

But that wasn't the worst of it. If she knew where he was, it wouldn't be long before the others knew, too.

How *had* she found him?

She was a cool one, he had to give her that. He'd never heard of the magazine she said she worked for and wondered who really sent her. Probably one of the tabloids. They'd love to know where he was now. Questions about his involvement had lingered even after the charges against him were dropped.

It was incredible. After all this time, they were still after him. Those vultures never gave up until they'd fed on the last morsel.

Unfortunately, he knew they weren't the only ones who would like to know where he was. There were others just itching to exact payback. He didn't have to wonder who his enemies were. He knew. Certain people from his past, with grudges and ambition. People strong enough and rich enough to finish him off, this time for good.

After he'd chucked it all in California and come here, he'd done his best to remain open and friendly without getting too involved. His work was satisfying and interesting, and it paid him enough to live on, even allowing him to take jobs or turn them down as he wished.

But he rarely turned down a dig project.

The nature of his job suited him. He liked working in blissful solitude down in the cool of an excavated kiva, or far up in hidden canyons searching for solstice markers, or inside canvas tents and ramshackle buildings where the detritus of centuries lay spread out on makeshift tables waiting to be catalogued.

So when he saw Keegan Thomas running toward his campsite in rolled up jeans, skimpy sandals, and a purple lace bra with her shirt wrapped around her head, he was more than surprised. He was damn aggravated.

"Stop!" he yelled. "You're running through my midden pile!"

The sound of his voice nailed her to the spot. Squinting into the sun, Keegan looked up to see Dante Covelli scowling down at her. He stood there, hands on hips, legs apart, looking at her with an expression of unpleasant surprise veneered over suspicion.

Remembering she was practically topless, she snatched the

shirt off her head and clasped it modestly in front of her, grimacing as stinging pain bloomed in her hand.

"I was trying to get down to the highway," she said. "I'm stuck in the sand back there." She tipped her head in the general direction she'd come.

He took his time absorbing that information, looking down at her like he expected her to apologize for it.

She showed him her inflamed hand. "I got stung by a scorpion."

His muscles were wiry, his stomach flat, and his long-legged clamber down the irregular surface of the rock was surefooted and practiced. His hiking boots were well-worn and coated with dust. Clearly he was used to making his way over rocks and broken ground. He executed a final little leap that dropped him to the dirt a few feet from where she stood. Without touching her, he looked at her red, swollen hand.

"Yeah, you did."

Abruptly, he turned and walked away. She followed, stepping carefully, unsure where to put her feet. She didn't want to get yelled at again.

"Sit down over there," he said over his shoulder, nodding toward one of the canvas chairs. "I can put something on it."

She sat where he indicated, and he ducked through the flap in the tent, staying inside long enough for her to put her shirt back on. He returned holding a paper cup and a box of baking soda. He shook some into the cup, added a little water from a jug, and stirred, making a thin paste.

"Here," he said. "Give me your hand."

She held it out, and swallowed a whimper. The back of her hand was now bright red.

Dante dipped his finger in the cup, scooped out some of the white mixture, and gently spread it over the skin of her hand. He didn't change expression or say a word. When she couldn't stand the uncomfortable silence any longer, she spoke up.

"I'm Keegan Thomas," she reminded him. "I met you yesterday at Jilly's."

"I remember," he replied, his voice flat.

Icy silence settled in again. Keegan pondered Dante's unyielding expression, a carryover from the night before. She didn't know what she'd done to offend him, and hoped she'd have a chance to smooth it over. He was a friend of Jilly and Earlene, almost a member of their family. Keegan didn't want to offend her new friend by seeming to be rude to someone close to her.

"Where's your hat?" he asked gruffly, interrupting her thoughts.

"I beg your pardon?"

"Your hat," he said, finally looking at her. "Anybody with any sense knows you don't come into the desert without a hat." He eyed her dirty feet and fancy jeweled sandals, now covered with dust, but didn't comment.

"I'll remember next time," she replied coolly, meeting his unflinching gaze.

His face and arms, and his legs beneath his shorts, were tan, the result of regular outdoor work. Faint creases slanting upward alongside his eyes indicated there were times in the past when he must have smiled.

But he wasn't smiling now.

He finished applying the homemade balm, rinsed his hands, and wiped them on a paper towel. "That might help some, but you should probably be seen at the clinic." He tossed the cup in a trash bag.

She nodded. The baking soda was beginning to soothe the burning pain. "Thank you. I'm sorry if I disturbed your dig. Your . . ." She tried to recall his word. "Your middle pile."

"It's a midden pile. That's a fancy name for a trash dump.

I'm not digging yet. I'm just doing some preliminary fieldwork." He paused and gave her a long, hard look. "What are *you* doing here?"

Accusation swirled in his gray-green gaze, making her feel like she had violated a rule of the reservation or breached some unwritten tribal etiquette.

"I was driving around hoping to find the spot where that picture was taken. The picture of my grandfather I told you about at Jilly's."

His eyes clouded with doubt, and he stared a moment longer, then uttered a grunt of disbelief. "Why don't you leave the Navajos alone? Stop bothering them."

She caught the condemnation in his eyes and instantly her defenses went up. "I'm not bothering them."

"Navajos don't like to talk about the dead," he explained in a tone that told her he thought she was a total idiot.

"Some do," she countered. A stubborn impulse rose up, one that made her dig her heels in. "Some of them are very interested in pictures and stories of the past. Jilly and her grandmother were. And a boy at the Indian Market told me he was a history major and—"

"You're exploiting them," he interrupted.

"No, I'm not—"

"Just like eighty percent of the other white people who show up on the reservation," he went on, not letting her finish. "They all want something from the Navajos."

"No, I don't, I—"

"Where did you say your car was?" he asked, ignoring her attempt to explain. His look was stern, the corners of his lips pulled in tight with harsh impatience.

She blinked and snapped her mouth shut, holding her own in a staredown. "I'm not sure," she replied after a moment, matching his sharp tone. "I turned off the highway just outside Oljato and followed some tire tracks. I got lost. It's hung up on a boulder."

"Great," he mumbled under his breath, then sighed and cursed at the same time. "Okay, come on. I'll drive you down to the clinic."

Oh, how she wanted to say *no-thank-you-I'll-walk!* breaking down the sentence into individual words for emphasis.

But she wasn't that stupid, so she grudgingly accepted his offer, acknowledging it with a deferential tip of her head.

He doused the fire, closed the laptop, zipped up the tent flap, then tramped off toward his truck, boots crunching dry earth. Without a word, he climbed behind the wheel and fired up the engine. She got in the passenger side and sat stiffly, cradling her hand and looking straight ahead.

He followed a winding trail downhill, efficiently avoiding the deepest of the ruts, deftly maneuvering around rocks and holes washed out from a previous rain. The ride passed in silence save for the rumble of the truck and the clang of something metal in the back stowage when they went over bumps. Dante's reluctance to converse expanded the silence inside the truck.

Twenty minutes later, after one last aggravating bump, they were on the blacktop speeding east. Dante pulled up in front of a low-spreading, one-story building at the base of a russet colored butte. A sign above the door said *St. Michael's Medical Clinic.*

"Thanks," she said, getting out.

"I'll wait," he replied.

She could see the red rooftops of her motel a quarter mile down the road.

"No thanks," she said with dour satisfaction, savoring the little triumph of denying him any more good deeds for which she might be beholden. "I'll walk."

"Not in those shoes, you won't."

She snatched a breath to argue, then thought better of it. One of the straps on her sandals had broken and chafed a sore spot on her instep.

"I'll wait," he said again, slouching down in his seat. "If you're allergic to the scorpion venom, you might die and they'll need me to identify your body."

He didn't smirk, but she could see a smirk go through his mind.

She gave him a look that might have melted lesser men, but he didn't even flinch. She couldn't help admiring that, but she'd be damned if she'd let him know it.

A nurse practitioner checked her out, took her vital signs, washed the baking soda off her hand, and applied a topical ointment.

"Here's some ice," the NP said, handing her a plastic bag filled with ice cubes. "This will help a lot. Twenty minutes on, twenty minutes off as needed." Then she glanced at Keegan's foot. "And you might want to soak that and put a Band-Aid on it."

With pain pills in hand, Keegan exited the clinic to find Dante still waiting as promised. He drove down the hill to the motel, and she directed him to her room. When he braked to a stop in front of it, she got out.

"Thank you," she said again, softer this time. "Really."

He gave her a steady look. "Stop bothering the Navajos," he said, his hand on the gearshift. *"Really."*

His brake lights flashed as he rounded the curve and made his way back down to the highway.

The red message light on the room phone was blinking when she unlocked her door. Jilly had left a voice mail saying her mother had agreed to take a look at Keegan's photograph. Keegan was relieved to hear the warmth had not left her new friend's voice.

Before she returned Jilly's call, Keegan telephoned the Navajo Nation Police to report her stranded car and was advised that someone had already reported it, and a tow truck summoned. They gave her the name and phone number where it was being towed and told her she could check on it tomorrow.

Keegan then called Jilly and filled her in on the events of the day.

"So you're without a ride? Well, don't worry about it. You can use my grandmother's truck. She's ready to go back to her hogan, but I'll drive her. She doesn't need transportation out there. I'm sure she won't mind if you borrow it."

Though Keegan tried to politely decline Jilly's generous offer, Jilly wouldn't listen to any of it, and in the end Keegan agreed. "Thank you," she said, truly grateful.

"Can you come with me to Window Rock tomorrow?" Jilly asked. "My mother will be there for a meeting. We can all have dinner, and you can show her the picture before she goes back to Albuquerque."

"I'd love to. Thanks for setting that up."

"Then after," Jilly went on, "some of my students are riding bull at the rodeo grounds there, practicing for the National High School Rodeo next month. I told them I'd come and watch. Do you mind?"

Keegan didn't, and plans were made to leave at an unspecified time the next afternoon.

Exhausted from the day, Keegan hung up, stripped off her filthy clothes, took a long shower, got dressed, then sat on the deck icing her hand. For as far as she could see, walls of red rock glowed brilliant orange, the distant sandstone cliffs set on fire by the setting sun.

She wondered who had called about her car—if it was Dante or one of the Natives—and hoped it wasn't damaged too badly. She was of two minds about borrowing Earlene's truck. On the one hand she was grateful not to be marooned without a way to get around, but on the other she felt a mighty weight of responsibility to be driving an old woman's battered though flowered-bedecked pickup.

And she was grateful to Dante Covelli, too. She might still be up on that mesa if it weren't for his help, despite the reluctance with which it was given.

It was a puzzle to her why he was so dead set against her showing the picture around. As an archaeologist, a historian dealing with antiquity, she would have thought he'd see the value of a gift from the past. It was true some of the older Navajos were unwilling to look at it, but for the younger ones, it was different. The men and women in that picture were someone's grandparents, someone's great-grandparents, and she couldn't believe the younger generation wouldn't be thrilled to see the faces of their direct descendants.

The children in that picture wouldn't be very old now, only in their fifties or sixties. Chances are they were still around.

She sat a moment, and it suddenly occurred to her that Dante was doing more than protecting the Navajos. Something else was going on behind those cool gray-green eyes of his.

CHAPTER SIX

The morning was mad with color. The blood-red sunrise had faded to a wash of dusty rose and amber, painting the farthest cliffs with deeper shades of russet and auburn. Keegan lingered over breakfast, enjoying the show from the big windows in the lodge before returning to her room.

She had the morning to herself and spent it on the phone. First she called the garage where her car had been towed and was dismayed to learn that she'd snapped the drive line. They were trying to locate parts now, but couldn't tell her if it would take three days or three weeks.

"I don't know how long it will be," said the gruff Navajo mechanic. "When we find the parts, we'll fix your car. All I can do."

Next, Keegan called Diana and filled her in on the events of the last few days.

"A scorpion sting! That must hurt."

"It's a little better now. The pain pills help. My arm is still swollen up to my elbow. I've been icing it."

"Have you found anyone in the picture yet?"

"No, but I'm sure there's a story there." She told Diana about Earlene Cly's cryptic reaction, and Dante Covelli's rebuff. "I have a feeling they both know something they don't want me to know. I'll keep digging."

She gave Diana the phone number of the lodge, told her which room she was in, then added, "But I'm going to get another cell phone. Mine doesn't work here. I'll call you when it's activated."

Next she called her mother, half hoping she wouldn't answer. Ellen Cole Flowers, who had many reasons to be happy, often chose to carry on her shoulders the bitter burden of a philandering husband, even though he'd been gone fifteen years. Through the earpiece Keegan listened to the rings, counting them, and reflected on her parents.

They must have loved each other at one time, but Keegan's earliest memories were of chronic, low-grade domestic warfare. Not physical battles, no pushing, no shoving, no hitting, but engagement of a more subtle kind; a constant seeking out of reasons to criticize and fault-find, each parent seizing on small errors to correct about the other, done gleefully.

By the time Keegan entered high school, she had chalked it up to heredity, or perhaps nurture, since she saw the same enmity in the home of her maternal grandparents. However, at some point, her grandparents must have negotiated a sort of truce, because they stayed married. Her parents didn't. Her father left her mother when Keegan was in college.

After many rings, voice mail clicked on and Keegan breathed a tiny sigh. She left a quick message giving her mother the short version of the last two days, then sat on the balcony waiting for Jilly, her swollen hand soothed by a fresh ice pack.

The view was long. Miles of rugged plateau, punctuated by landforms in receding perspective, spread before her, rock formations that had names. She'd seen them on her map. Eagle Rock. Setting Hen. King on His Throne. Bear and Rabbit. The Mittens. The Indians could see things in those rocks, and named them accordingly.

On the reservation, things moved at their own pace. No one seemed in a hurry. Her car would be fixed when it was fixed. Jilly would be here when she got here. Keegan made an effort to slow her own internal time clock, synching it to the beat of this new locus.

From where she sat, she could see the medical clinic Dante had driven her to, the building low and squat under the blazing sun. She wondered briefly if that had been the site of her grandfather's clinic, though the building looked to have been built in more recent times.

At last Jilly arrived, and they spent the next hour going back and forth with the vehicles. They left Earlene's pickup parked outside Keegan's room for her use until the 4Runner was repaired, then set out to meet Jilly's mother.

Just outside Kayenta, Jilly steered off onto the side of the highway next to an elaborate roadside memorial. Plastic flowers draped over a crudely erected wooden cross about three feet high. Ribbons of all colors attached to the crossbar fluttered in the breeze.

"I have to stop here," Jilly said. "I'll just be a minute." She cut the engine, reached into the back seat, picked up a small box, and got out.

Keegan followed.

The memorial didn't look more than a few months old, decorated with many bouquets of plastic flowers, drawings, prayer cards, and a white ceramic angel.

Black lettering spelled out the words *In loving memory—Averill Redhorse*. Hanging by a ribbon attached to the wreath was a silver wrist cuff bracelet with the words *Don't Hate Me Because I'm Beautiful* engraved on it.

"Averill was one of my students," Jilly said. She took a candle from the box, placed it in a glass holder at the base of the cross next to a stuffed animal, and lit the wick, cupping her hand to prevent the wind from extinguishing it. Her movements were slow, almost reverent, her brow pinched with sadness. Glossy eyes held back tears.

"What happened?" Keegan asked.

"He was murdered." Jilly lifted her gaze and let it rest on a spot several yards into the desert. "His body was found over there in that shallow."

Keegan looked into the powder dry dust of the high desert at the place a young boy's life had been deliberately snuffed out.

"He was *nadleehi*," Jilly said. "You know, Two Spirits."

Keegan shook her head, not understanding.

"Transgendered," Jilly explained quietly. "In our culture it's a special gift to possess both masculine and feminine traits. But Averill was killed for having them. By someone from off the rez."

"Oh, how awful," said Keegan.

Jilly nodded sadly. "He was on his way home from a party. A white boy followed him, dragged him out of his car, and beat him to death." Her voice was tight with emotion. "His mother is a friend of mine. She's very traditional, and is now torn between not speaking of the dead and wanting to get her son's story out. She spends most of her time traveling now, trying to raise funds to produce a documentary. I promised I'd watch over the marker and keep it up while she's away."

The two women stood a few moments, Jilly in her own thoughts, Keegan decrying the horrible reality of a young life obliterated before it's time and the manner in which it happened. Jilly said a short prayer in Navajo, and then they left.

They made a quick stop at the Radio Shack in Kayenta to make copies of the photo, then forsaking the interstate, Jilly barreled through the desert over unmarked, sun beaten mostly unpaved back roads she seemed totally familiar with.

Window Rock got its name from the hole in the two-hundred-foot high sandstone formation located there and was the administrative center of the Navajo Nation, housing the Navajo Nation Council Headquarters. But even here in the semibustling capitol of Navajoland, the desert flowed right up to the motels and restaurants lining the main drag through town. Jilly's mother was waiting for them on the patio of a Mexican cantina.

Conservatively dressed in black slacks and a pale yellow, sleeveless, tunnel-neck sweater, her smile was wide and genuine. She wore a choker of tiny seed beads. Turquoise triangles dangled from her ears. Beautiful raven hair twisted into a high bun shined with its own life. She had a pleasant, remarkably unlined face, and skin the color of pale cinnamon. Keegan guessed she had to be in her fifties, though she didn't look it.

As they approached the table, Sandra Wolf stood and greeted her daughter with a hug, then Jilly did the introductions.

"Thank you for finding time to have dinner with us," Keegan said to Sandra. "I know you're busy at the university. Jilly said you were working on an oral history project with your graduate students."

They took their seats and settled at the table. A waitress came right over with menus.

"Yes," Sandra said, picking up the conversation. "I had to come to Window Rock this morning to meet with some of the council members. I'm asking them to participate in the program by doing oral histories with the elders in their families. I dropped off some tape recorders."

The waitress returned to take their orders. After she left, Sandra smiled at Keegan.

"Jilly tells me you have an old picture you want me to look at. A picture of your grandfather? I understand he used to be a doctor on the reservation."

"Yes." Keegan handed the photograph to Sandra. "I'm especially interested in the people with him, and when it was taken and maybe who took it. Can you tell me anything?"

Sandra put on a pair of tortoiseshell frame reading glasses, and looked at it. A smile turned up the corners of her mouth, but it was a poignant one. She nodded sadly.

"You recognize someone?" asked Keegan.

"Yes, I do." Sandra's voice was soft and sad. "This little girl. I remember her from when I was little. She was kidnapped."

The awful words went straight down from Keegan's ears into her heart, where a mother's terror lives.

"What?"

Sandra nodded, her eyes, lustrous now, still on the picture. "Missionaries took her."

Keegan quelled a sudden ache in her heart, the ravaging grief only the mother of a kidnapped child could truly understand.

"They promised to bring her back, but they never did," Sandra said.

"How do you know that, Mom?" asked Jilly.

"Because I was there when it happened," Sandra answered, causing Jilly to stare openmouthed at her mother.

"You never told me that," said Jilly.

"Well, it's not something I like to talk about or remember." Sandra shrugged and handed the photo back. "But things like that happened here back then. Even though the government's policy of forced assimilation had ended, there were still plenty of do-gooders around. Some church activists felt within their rights to take the children and rid them of their culture and heritage, which at that time was perceived as evil."

The waitress came over with their meals, set the plates around, and bustled away.

"What happened to this little girl?" asked Keegan.

"I only have a vague recollection of it now," replied Sandra. "I was only, oh, five or six myself at the time."

She paused, reflecting, eyes narrowed, looking into the past. "I remember I was at my Aunt Mary's house. That's *shimasani*'s sister," she said to Jilly in an aside. "Anyway, the little girl was there with her mother. I remember her mother got sick, and so did Aunt Mary.

"A neighbor came over to help the sick ones, and she brought her two little boys." Sandra's eyes went distant and she paused in thought. "I don't remember their names."

"What happened next?" asked Jilly.

"All us kids were pretty scared, because we didn't know what was going on. We were all crying, the little girl's mother and my aunt were coughing and throwing up. And then I think they got worse, because the neighbor said they needed to see a doctor. But nobody had cars in those days. She had to go ask another neighbor, and he came over in a wagon with his young son.

"They put the little girl's mother and my aunt in the back of the wagon, but the man didn't want to go alone with the sick ones. There was a big argument about it. The women didn't want to leave the children alone, but the man with the wagon didn't want to take the sick people by himself. I guess he was afraid they'd die in his wagon. Finally, the adults left. They told the oldest boy to watch over us kids until they got back."

"How long were they gone?" asked Keegan.

"Until the next day."

"The children were left alone?"

Sandra shrugged. "It couldn't be helped. The women were sick. They needed medical attention. The oldest boy was nine or ten, old enough to watch over us. Little kids were pretty self-sufficient back then. We could get along for a short time." She gave a low laugh. "Not like now. Kids can't do anything for themselves. And you can't let them out of your sight."

"Then what?" urged Keegan. "The missionaries just appeared? How many were there?"

"I do remember that. A little while after the grownups left, two women came down the trail in a wagon and stopped. They said they were from one of the missions. I don't know which one. One of the women picked up the little girl and talked to her, then put her in the wagon. She told us to tell the parents she was taking the girl to school and would bring her back when she was twelve."

A precise sorrow filled in the space around Keegan's heart. "Did they?"

Sandra pressed her lips, and she shook her head. "As far as I know, nobody ever saw her again."

A sad silence descended.

"How old was the little girl?" Keegan asked when she could collect herself.

Sandra slanted her eyes in thought. "I think she was about two or three. She could walk, but didn't talk very well."

"What about her mother? Didn't she report it to the authorities?"

"I never heard what happened." Sandra sighed. "But you know back then, the Indians were very poor. Especially in Monument Valley. It was so isolated, so far away from the populated part of the reservation. And there was so much sickness and death at that time. Lots of people died, and children were left homeless. Navajos always tried to take them in, but sometimes they couldn't. Everyone was hard up. I wouldn't be surprised if the mother thought the little one was better off with someone who could feed and clothe her properly. At least she'd be educated and taken care of."

"Do you know what school they took her to?" Keegan asked.

Sandra shook her head.

Keegan looked at the picture again. "Where is her mother now?"

Sandra touched her lips with her napkin, and pushed her plate away. "Oh, I have no idea."

"What about the father?"

Again Sandra shrugged. "I'm sorry. I wish I could be of more help, but I don't know any more than I've told you."

Keegan sat stunned. She's hardly touched her dinner. The enormity of the story seized her, taking away her appetite. Her thoughts were on Daisy, and a sob was working its way up her throat. She took a sip of water to hold it back.

It occurred to her that the doctor they visited might have been her grandfather. She wondered if there was any way she could get her hands on her grandfather's files from back then, maybe medical records. She'd have to ask her cousin if he'd found anything like that in her grandfather's files.

The rest of the meal was filled with conversation of work and family. Sandra talked about her oral history project and asked after her mother, Earlene. Jilly talked about her exchange students and asked after her father. A summer dance and drum festival was being planned, and they talked about that at length. Afterward, there were goodbyes with warm hugs and promises to get together again soon.

"Let me know if you find anyone in that picture," Jilly's mother said to Keegan in the parking lot. "And if you need anything else, I'll be glad to help if I can."

Sandra sat behind the steering wheel, splayed fingers pressed to her lips, watching through shimmery eyes as the Tahoe pulled out of the parking lot. When it disappeared from sight, she took out her cell phone, and with dread forming in her gut, dialed the personal cell phone number of Yuma Ray.

As the tribal attorney, Yuma Ray had been engaged in a long-standing ongoing battle with the federal government for Native American rights ever since he'd graduated from college. He was currently one of the lawyers working on a lawsuit concerning billions of dollars belonging to the tribes that had been held in trust by the BIA, but were now missing. This was in addition to a lawsuit seeking reparations for Navajo miners who had become ill from exposure to radiation while working in government owned uranium mines.

A busy and important man, Yuma was seen as a tribal protector, heroically battling the federal government on behalf of the Navajos. He had a declarative voice, an authoritative mien, and control over a considerable number of people both in and out of the tribe.

"Did you meet with her?" he asked when he answered the phone.

"Yes."

"So who is in the picture besides John Wayne?" He sounded less worried than she would have liked.

"Lulu and her mother. And Emerson's brother. He looked to be about six. My mother—"

"Did Jilly recognize her?" he interrupted.

"No, I don't think so," she replied. "She didn't say."

"Who else?"

"Keegan said her grandfather was in it. She pointed him out. Said he was the BIA doctor back then. The picture looks like it was taken just before—" She cut off the rest of the sentence, unable to go on.

Yuma was silent a moment. "Well, if that's all she has, that won't tell her anything. I don't think any harm was done."

"Can't you stop her?" Sandra's voice pitched up to a whine.

"There's no law against showing a picture and asking a few questions."

"Yuma, she's a reporter," Sandra said, exasperated at having to remind him. "She's going to keep asking questions."

"That doesn't mean she's going to get any answers."

"I hope not."

"Don't worry."

Long pause.

"But what if—"

"Then I'll take care of it," he said calmly, and rang off without a goodbye.

Sandra pressed both hands to her mouth and waited for her heart to slow down. She didn't know what he meant by that, but trusted him to do the right thing.

In the Tahoe, Jilly's silence freighted the air in a way that told Keegan something was unsettled in her friend's mind. With both hands gripping the wheel, her face frozen and staring straight ahead, Jilly drove slowly over the dirt driveway leading to the rodeo practice grounds. "She's lying."

Keegan's head whipped around, a surprised breath caught in her throat. "Who?"

"My mother."

"About what?"

"About not knowing anyone in that picture."

"How do you know?"

"I just know."

CHAPTER SEVEN

Jilly didn't say any more about it, and silence filled the Tahoe. Keegan didn't press for an explanation, not wanting to pry into what might be a private family matter that had no bearing on the information she was seeking. Yet the puzzling comment stayed with her, and she couldn't forget the expression on Jilly's face when she said it. A mixture of sadness and genuine disappointment.

Rodeo fans in pickups and trucks were quickly filling up the weedy field designated for parking. Jilly pulled in at the back of the dimly lit dirt lot. Keegan got out and together they dodged the incoming vehicles as they made their way to the bleachers. They found seats next to a boisterous group of teenagers Jilly knew from the high school.

Country music poured from speakers mounted above a makeshift grandstand under a banner that said *BULL BASH— DON'T LET IT THROW YOU.* The bulls, massive animals with widespread horns, bunched up in a pen closed off with a chained gate. A few of them were lined up nose to tail in a gangway leading to the mounting chute.

Young male riders wearing western hats and colorful fringed chaps over their boot-cut Wranglers were dragging ropes, gloves, helmets, padded vests, and wire face protectors out of canvas duffel bags all the while sneaking uneasy peeks at the immense bulls.

Pretty teenage girls with cell phones in hand or clipped to the waist of their low-cut jeans huddled together making eyes at the slim-hipped riders, occasionally dissolving into giggles. Four older girls perched on the top rail of the fence wearing jeans, black spaghetti-strap tank tops, and western boots were openly giving the riders a considered once over. Shiny black hair shimmering down their backs, heads all turned in the same direction, they reminded Keegan of sleek watchful blackbirds lined up on a telephone wire.

Jilly waved and called good luck to members of the high school bull riding team. "This is a practice event," she explained, leaning in close so Keegan could hear over the raucous noise of the crowd and the music blaring from the loudspeakers. "Mostly for young riders who are just starting out, but also for riders already on the amateur or semipro circuit who need a little practice before a competition. Some of the older guys do it for fun."

Keegan wasn't sure she'd call being tossed around on the back of a fifteen-hundred pound bull then thrown to the ground with the possibility of being trampled fun for an older guy. She had to admit they were all in great shape, and she was taken by the *machismo* of it all.

After the National Anthem, two rodeo clowns in baggy pants and frizzy yarn wigs back-flipped and somersaulted into the bullring. They greeted the crowd and told corny jokes until the announcer's voice from the loudspeaker declared it was time to begin.

"Welcome to our weekly bull ride practice. Thanks for comin' out to support our young riders. Now! Let's get 'er done!"

The crowd roared.

Keegan had seen rodeos on ESPN, and had actually attended an event where she sat in an upper row in a huge arena that afforded a postage stamp-sized view of the action. Here, she was three feet away from the bullring, close enough to have dirt kicked up in her face, close enough to reach out and touch the bulls in the gangway.

The first rider burst out of the bucking chute on the back of a wildly thrashing bull named Hell Fire. One of his gloved hands gripped a braided rope handle while his free arm cut and flailed the air as he desperately tried to keep his balance on the bucking and twisting animal. The cheering, foot-stomping crowd nearly drowned out the clanging of the cowbells hanging from a bucking strap around the bull's flanks.

"Hangin' on hard as he can, but not enough!" exclaimed the announcer over the loudspeaker as the rider flew off the bull and landed hard on his shoulder. The rodeo clowns immediately rushed over to distract the bull with their antics, giving the rider time to scramble up and dash out of the ring like his boots were on fire. A gate at the far end of the ring slid open, and the bull, who also seemed anxious to be away, left the ring at a brisk trot.

"That was a heck of ride right there," said the enthusiastic Navajo announcer, clipping off the ends of his words. "Hell Fire is a real fast spinner, and if ya don't ride in the perfect spot on his back, he's gonna throw you right off! Now this next half-nasty bull with powerful haunches is called Honey Babe, but don't let the name fool ya. He likes to get things goin' by lookin' one way and twistin' the other . . ."

Despite the clamor and excitement, Keegan couldn't stop her mind from drifting away from the announcer's patter to Jilly's surprising statement that her mother had lied about not knowing anyone else in the photo. Keegan could accept the fact that some Navajos might not want to look at it. The thought that someone would lie one way or the other about knowing anyone in it had never occurred to her. She took her time absorbing this, turning it over in her mind.

Her bullshit meter worked pretty well most of the time, but nothing about Sandra Wolf's story had sounded any alarms. No guarded shifting of her eyes, no flinty edge to her voice, no nervous fingers on the table. No discordant note to the sadness in Sandra's voice when she spoke about the kidnapped child.

Keegan had been swept right into the story, her heart squeezing painfully when she thought about the mother of that little girl returning home to find her baby had been taken. She knew how that young mother felt. The only difference was that the Navajo mother was able to hold out hope of having her child returned. No such promise had been made to Keegan.

Almost certainly it was Lincoln Cole who had treated the ailing adults Sandra spoke of. That meant medical records existed somewhere with names and addresses. She should have asked the nurse practioner who treated her scorpion sting.

Her mind filled with questions.

Could she find those records, and would those names lead her to other names? Where was the little girl's mother now? Who else besides Sandra might have lied about knowing anyone? Where was the missionary school the little girl was taken to? Why wasn't she returned, and what was her name? Where was she now? She'd be an adult, maybe with children of her own. Maybe grandchildren.

Keegan's brain clicked and made another connection. Jilly's grandmother. Sandra's mother. Thinking back on Earlene Cly's reaction to the photo, calling attention to John Wayne might have been her way of distracting attention away from something else. Or *someone* else.

Suddenly, Keegan's vow not to pry into what might be a family matter shattered. When the time was right, she was going to ask Jilly about it. Her thoughts spun away when Jilly touched her arm.

"There's Dante," Jilly said, making Keegan's heart do a little flipover.

She looked where Jilly indicated, but didn't see him. "Where?"

"There. In the ring. He's one of the rodeo clowns, only they call them bullfighters. He's the one in the barrel."

Keegan saw an agitated bull head butt the fat padded barrel hanging from wide straps over the clown's shoulder. The barrel tipped over with the clown still inside, and the bull tossed his horns, giving it another shove, rolling it a few yards.

The other clown yelled and waved his arms. The bull turned and snorted. After a feint charge at the new target, the animal wheeled and calmly exited the ring through the sliding gate. Dante, in clown face makeup, popped his head out of the barrel and did a playful little jig to the uproarious applause of the spectators. But when he walked off, Keegan noticed he limped.

Eight more cowboys took a turn before the final ride was announced.

"Pile Driver is our last bull, a high leapin', belly rollin', real fast spinner. Let's see if our rider has the talent to stay on."

He didn't. At the first thrust of powerful haunches, the cowboy slid off the back of the bull and landed on his bottom.

The riders packed up their gear and the fans dispersed, crowding at the gate that led to the parking lot. A familiar face in the crowd caught Keegan's eye, then disappeared behind a moving sea of western hats and shouldered duffel bags. Then she saw it again. Vicki, the waitress from Goulding's, the one who had taken her order but never brought her breakfast.

Keegan nudged Jilly. "Do you know who that girl is?"

At that moment, Vicki's laughing face turned and caught Keegan looking at her. Instantly Vicki's smile disappeared, and she turned away. A half second later, she was swallowed up by the moving crowd, but not before Jilly caught a glimpse.

"That's Emerson Bedonnie's granddaughter. He's a member of the Navajo Tribal Council. Her name is Vicki. Why?"

"No reason. I just—"

Her words were abruptly cut off as someone plowed into her

from behind, forcing the breath from her lungs and knocking her off her feet. Unable to keep her balance, she went down on her knees as her purse was forcibly yanked from her shoulder. A husky Navajo, her purse in his hands, shouldered his way through the exiting throng, knocking people aside.

"Stop! Stop him!" Jilly cried, then bent to assist Keegan. "Are you all right?" she asked, her eyes full of worry.

"There he goes!" someone yelled.

"He's in the parking lot!" someone else cried.

Keegan got to her feet with Jilly's help just in time to see Dante Covelli break from the crowd in pursuit of the thief, who was darting in and out of a line of 4 × 4 rigs exiting the parking lot. Several other men took off, joining Dante in the chase.

Two security guards came running as Keegan collected herself and checked for injuries. There was a hole in her jeans, and her knee was bleeding.

"What happened?" a security guard asked.

"Someone stole my purse."

"Pushed her down and grabbed it right off her shoulder," said Jilly.

Witnesses immediately came forward, and one of the security guards began taking statements and names. Onlookers milled around waiting to see what would happen next.

While Keegan was giving her information, Dante limped over carrying her purse.

"Did you catch him?" Jilly asked.

"No." He handed Keegan her bag. "The guy jumped into a pickup that was waiting for him," he told security, "and they took off. I found the purse on the ground where he tossed it." He rubbed his hip and winced.

"Anything missing?" the security guard asked Keegan.

She looked through her bag. Her wallet was still there, and she flipped through it.

"He took the cash out of my wallet, but left my credit cards. Thankfully. I had a photograph in here. It's gone."

Jilly's mouth fell open. "Where are the copies?"

"In the car."

The security guard finished writing his report, then gave Keegan his card.

"I'll file this with Tribal Police," he told her. "If you want a copy, you can get it from them."

Keegan thanked him, then turned to Dante.

"Thank you for helping, too. And for finding my purse."

He acknowledged her with a hitch of his chin. "Are you hurt?"

She looked down at herself. "Just a skinned knee and a hole in my new jeans. What about you? Are you all right? You're limping."

He shook his head. "Bruised a little. That bull horned my hip through the barrel. It's nothing."

"Do you need a ride back to your camp?" Jilly asked.

He shook his head again. "Nah. I can drive. I'm not going to the dig site anyway. I'm going to Bluff. I need a few days to catch up on some things at home before I take the exchange students to Cortez on the field trip."

Dante had wiped off the clown makeup and changed into regular clothes, jeans and boots. His voice was a rich baritone that Keegan knew could switch instantly and unaccountably from polite to icy. Right now the expression on his face was calm, but if she looked closely, she could see tension in his eyes. He caught her looking at him, and their eyes ignited for a miniscule instant before he turned to leave.

"Let me know if you need anything," Jilly called after him.

"I will," he said over his shoulder, giving a little half wave behind his back.

Keegan watched him walk away thinking his personality might need some work, but he was a damn handsome man.

CHAPTER EIGHT

The radar in Keegan's limbic brain was picking up something indefinable, and she needed to spade up the turf of the past to find out what it was. Secrets were buried in that old picture, and if she hoped to find people in whom memory might still reside, she needed to stay in Navajoland.

The land held an emotional charge for her and not just because of the missing child. It was a given that she'd do everything in her power to help find out what happened to that little girl despite the fifty-odd years that had passed. Even if all she could do was take the story to a wider audience by writing about the circumstances of her disappearance, there was always a chance someone would surface with information. The child's mother, if she was still alive, deserved that much.

But it was personal, too. It was almost as if by finding out what happened to that mother's child, she came a bit closer to finding out what happened to Daisy.

She didn't expect the police to ever catch the man who shouldered her down and grabbed her purse. They had little to go on. She hadn't seen anything more from her position on the ground than the torso of a boulder of a man dressed in black jeans and a blue shirt pushing through the crowd with the strap of her shoulder bag wrapped around his fist. Shock and the suddenness of the event had blanked the minds of others in the crowd who might have provided a better description. They all agreed on one thing, however. He was Navajo. Whatever the secrets were, they were important enough for him to steal the photo that contained them.

The mechanic had called to tell her he'd located the parts for her 4Runner. Unfortunately, it would be three weeks before he could start the work.

She sighed but didn't argue. Instead she concentrated on what she needed to do and the tools she needed to do it with. Most important was a phone that worked on the reservation. Internet access was critical, too, and she needed transportation. She had Earlene's truck, which, it turned out, ran well enough if she didn't go far; it was surprisingly dependable for its age and condition. That would do until she had her own wheels back.

First, she went to the lodge front desk, where she arranged for a lease of one of the outlying bungalows up the hill from the main lodge building. It was clean and spacious, with two bedrooms, two bathrooms, a small kitchen with modern appliances, and a front porch for viewing the beautiful uplifted red rock pass. Best of all, it provided wireless access. Next best was the treadmill and Bowflex TreadClimber in the second bedroom. She moved in her belongings, plugged her laptop in to charge, and made a shopping list, then chuggered off in Earlene's old pickup to buy groceries.

She snagged a grocery cart from the parking lot and headed for the supermarket entrance. A bench near the door was occupied by an old Navajo man with a long beaky nose in a face as lined as a roadmap. He was wearing black pants and shirt, none too clean, and a black felt reservation hat. A half-smoked cigarette hung from his lips. Tiny bits of leaves and twigs were matted in his long black hair as if he'd slept outside the night before.

He was so still, she thought it was a wax figure sitting there until she got closer and saw smoke rising from the cigarette.

Unmoving, the elder stared straight into the distance, looking cosmically disappointed, let down by everything he'd ever seen or done, with barely enough strength for the bad memories. As Keegan approached, his eyes shifted in her direction, but his gaze remained blank. She wondered if he was blind or mentally impaired, or if alcohol had spoiled his life.

She pushed her cart through the automatic doors, and right away spotted Vicki Bedonnie at the cash register checking out a long line of customers. Keegan headed for the produce section, stocked up on groceries, staples for the kitchen, and meals for the next few days, then waited in Vicki's checkout line.

"Hello," Keegan said when it was her turn.

Vicki lifted the bored, put-upon eyes of a fed-up employee. Her face showed no sign of recognition, her expression neither friendly nor hostile.

Keegan spoke first. "Weren't you my waitress at Goulding's the other morning?"

"No," Vicki answered, and began methodically scanning grocery items, weighing and punching in codes for the produce.

"Remember I showed you a picture and asked if you knew anyone?"

Vicki didn't reply. One by one, she dragged grocery items over the scanner and rang up coffee and creamer and cereal and Lean Cuisine frozen dinners without saying a word.

"Did you enjoy the bull riding last night?" Keegan asked after a moment, compelled to make a connection with this girl.

"I don't know what you mean," Vicki replied, then hurriedly packed groceries into plastic bags, concentrating very hard on what she was doing.

"Your total is ninety-three forty-two. Cash, debit, or credit? We don't take checks." Vicki still had not made eye contact.

Keegan took a hundred-dollar bill out of her wallet, but held it just out of reach and waited, forcing Vicki to look up at her, which she did quickly, then away. Keegan was stunned to see a barely perceptible flash of what looked like fear pass behind Vicki's eyes.

Keegan handed over the money, took her change, then pushed her grocery cart through the parking lot, mentally adding Vicki Bedonnie's name to her list of Navajos with secrets.

Through narrowed eyes from under the brim of his hat, Will Bedonnie watched the white woman leave the grocery store. He had stretched out on the bench and put his hat over his face, pretending to be asleep. He'd done that because he wanted to discourage her from talking to him when she came out.

He wouldn't have minded talking to her. She looked nice and she was pretty, but Vicki had told him in no uncertain terms that he must not speak to the white woman with the light blue eyes. If she spoke to him first, he should walk away.

He hadn't seen her walking toward the supermarket entrance until she was almost to the door. He tried not to look at her when she got close, but couldn't stop his eyes from sliding over to hers. They were such a pretty color. Like lake water with the sun shining in its depths.

Vicki said the *biligaana* was a witch and to stay away from her. But she didn't look like a witch, and he thought about that a long time. He thought about it so long, he must have really fallen asleep, because the next thing he knew, Vicki's hand was on his arm shaking him awake.

"Uncle Will. Wake up, Uncle Will."

He slid his eyelids open and moved his hat. Her face was over his. Behind her head, the sky had lost its blue.

"I'm off work now," Vicki said. "You have to go home."

"Okay," he said. With great effort because of the pain in his stiff, achy joints, he dropped his feet to the ground and slowly sat up.

Vicki was holding car keys and a grocery bag. "Did you walk?"

He nodded.

"Come on," she said. "It's almost dark. I'll drive you home. You can't sleep in the desert. You have to go to your trailer."

He stood up. She took his arm and gently helped him into her creaky Corolla. He sat quietly as she turned right out of the parking lot toward a neighborhood of single- and doublewides. In a few minutes, the old car moaned over some bumps, then stopped next to an aging trailer.

Inside, Vicki unpacked the grocery bag, placed canned goods and a carton of cigarettes on a shelf, and put some frozen meals in the freezer in the top compartment of the refrigerator.

"These go in the microwave," she reminded him.

He smiled. "I know."

Vicki looked around the small trailer. "Promise me you won't sleep out in the desert anymore?"

"Okay," he said.

"You need to get cleaned up," she said. "I'll come by tomorrow and pick up your laundry."

"Okay." He smiled at his great-niece again. "Thank you."

She seemed reluctant to go. "Did you talk to her?"

"No. You said not to. But I wanted to," he said. "If she talks to me, why can't I talk to her?"

"Because Grandfather said you can't." She kissed his cheek and left.

Will listened to the car's engine fade away. He wasn't crazy, even though some people thought he was. It was just that sometimes he forgot things and made mistakes. He got confused and didn't understand everything, but otherwise got along just fine. He could use the microwave, put soup in a pot on a burner, change the sheets on his bed, and drive his old pickup when he felt like it.

His brother, Emerson, had offered to buy him one of those

fancy new pickups with four doors that six people could fit in, but he said no. What would he do with that? He didn't know six people well enough to take them anywhere.

After Keegan put her groceries away, she drove Earlene's pickup to Kayenta, where she signed up for a cell phone service that covered Monument Valley and the Four Corners. She bought legal pads, pens, and a digital voice recorder from the drug store, then stopped at the post office to get a post office box.

When she returned to her bungalow, she called Jilly. School was still in session, so she left a voice mail with her new cell phone number and let Jilly know which bungalow she'd moved into. Then she called Diana to update her, and after that her mother and grandmother.

As always, Keegan's conversation with her mother was superficial and very careful. Ellen Cole Flowers lived on her own family money, which was considerable—and a good thing, since Keegan's father had walked out leaving her nothing. She took good care of herself physically, dressed well, and spent time with other impressively well-kept women friends, all of whom had been thrown over for younger models. The atmosphere in her mother's house was just as cold and forbidding as it was when her father left. Keegan suspected it was a carryover from her mother's own fractious childhood home.

In contrast, her grandmother's voice over the phone was gentle and loving, if a bit delicate as she talked about the morning at her book club with her friends, mostly widows like herself, then about the latest mystery she was reading.

"I'll bring back some new mysteries by local authors," Keegan promised then added, "Love you, Gram."

"Love you, too, Keegan. Hurry home."

Next, Keegan called her cousin Richard. "Are you sure none of his Bureau of Indian Affairs records are there?" she asked.

"I didn't find anything like that," he said. "I'm sure I hauled everything out of their basement. It was mostly personal stuff. Old bank statements, letters from the power company from that time they built their guesthouse, some worthless stock certificates from a drug company, golf tournament ID badges, insurance policies that Grandmother didn't even know existed. Some nice Navajo rugs. I still have a lot to go through, but I already threw a bunch of stuff away, even though Grandmother was reluctant to let anything go. You know how she is."

Keegan did. To her grandmother, every single item she'd ever owned was far too valuable to give up.

"How is she? I just spoke to her. She didn't sound well."

"I don't think she is. She misses Grandfather. Hard to believe, huh? After the way they fought? Besides being lonely, she complains about being tired."

Keegan thought a minute. "I didn't mention it when I spoke to her, but I wonder if she'd know where those BIA files would be?"

"Jeez, Keegan, that was fifty years ago. I don't know that she lived out there with him very long. She never talked about it much."

"No. I don't think she liked it."

"Not civilized enough for her."

"You're probably right."

"Any luck finding anyone in the picture?"

"No." She filled him in on the past few days.

"Well, I'll let you know if I come across anything having to do with the Indian Health Service clinic or the BIA."

Keegan gave him her new phone number and they hung up.

She opened her laptop and stared at it, wondering where to begin her search. She was organized by nature, able to sort, categorize, and compartmentalize pertinent information efficiently, an immensely valuable talent in an investigative writer.

Her Rolodex was full of helpful resources, people and places she could go to for facts and particulars on nearly any topic, but none of them were even remotely connected to the information she sought now.

Her fingers flew over the keyboard, pulling up websites she thought would be helpful. She was disappointed to find that the BIA website had been taken down because of a decades-old still pending lawsuit, but she found a phone number for a regional BIA office in Gallup. She dialed it, and was referred to the American Indian Records repository in Kansas. She called them, and they referred her to Phoenix Indian Health Service, who then referred her to the Navajo Nation Indian Health Service, who further referred her to the Navajo Nation Vital Records. And so it went.

After several more rounds of referrals and dead ends, being transferred, and hanging on hold playing computer solitaire, she finally reached an archivist at the National Archives Field Office in Laguna Nigel, California.

"Justin Bickham here," the archivist said when he came on the line.

She was relieved to hear a smile in his voice. Encouraged, she told him what information she was seeking and why.

"I have an old picture," she concluded. "I'd like to know the names of the people in it."

"No problem," he said. "I might be able to help with that, too."

"Really?" Keegan's spirits picked up.

"But it might take a while. Information about the Navajos and activities on the reservation is contained in the records of several federal agencies," he informed her in a good natured voice. "The BIA is responsible for formulating federal policy relating to the tribe, but implementing those policies fell to local entities."

"Local? Like who?"

"Well, historically, the Indian Agents. Though they didn't keep records with us historians in mind. They were mainly concerned with accounting for every penny they spent and convincing their bosses they were doing a good job, so the bulk of their files consist of accounting records and correspondence with the BIA headquarters in Washington, D.C. When they did record information about individual Navajos, it generally related to the payment of money, or the allotment of land."

"What about school records? Wouldn't there be files and enrollment records?"

"Oh, yes. Each school kept a census, or was supposed to. But you'd need to know the student's name or the name of the school. Unfortunately, there's no central location for school files. And," he went on, "it was during those years that the BIA turned over education of the Indians to the states. So the records are quite scattered. It depends on the school."

Keegan's hopes dipped.

"How about medical records? Or my grandfather's employment records? Those must exist somewhere."

"They do," he said. "Those will be easier to track down. For the most part, they'd be housed right here."

"Would I be able to have access to those? Do I need to come to California and search myself?"

"Not if I want to keep my job. That's what they pay me for." He gave a friendly chuckle. "Seriously, you can come in and look through original documents if you want to, but it's quicker if I do it. I'd love to work on this for you."

"Thanks," she said, relieved. "I'm temporarily without transportation, so I'd be grateful if you could do the search."

"Just give me whatever information you have. You're on your own as far as finding someone who attended an Indian school, though. Without more information, I can't give you much help there."

She thanked him, promised to put a copy of the photo in the mail, and gave him her cell phone number. "Call me as soon as you have anything at all."

"I will," he promised.

She stayed at the computer a while longer, searching for information on government run Indian schools. Most of them no longer existed, having closed decades ago. Some were still around, but for the most part they were now private boarding schools or had transformed themselves into institutions of higher education.

After thinking about it, Keegan decided to begin her search locally. It seemed to make sense that the little girl had been taken to a school nearby. She'd start there, anyway. She had so little to go on, it would be a piecemeal undertaking.

Night fell, and she pushed back from her laptop. Yawning, she stretched her arms over her head, then turned out the light and walked to the front windows to draw the curtains. The instant before they closed, something caught her eye. She tweaked the edge and peeked out.

A set of headlights approached, moving slowly as the vehicle passed. She'd noticed it going by earlier, because of the way the brake lights came on when it reached the bungalow, then off as it picked up speed and moved on.

She peered through the blinds and waited. Sure enough, it came back in the opposite direction, only this time it stopped at the end of the driveway and idled there. It was a high-riding SUV, one of many driving along reservation roads at any given time with nothing in particular to distinguish it except it was new and shiny, with the tell-tale bulky profile of a pricey model.

Keegan didn't recognize it, and it was too dark to see who was driving. She didn't like the prickly sensation its presence generated up her spine. After it finally drove away, she double-checked the locks on the doors, made sure all the windows were closed and secured, then went to bed and lay awake a long time before finally dropping off.

CHAPTER NINE

Archivist Justin Bickham, surrounded by bulging file folders and overflowing Hollinger record storage boxes, studied the copy of the photograph Keegan Thomas had sent. Considering what he'd just learned about it, he couldn't stop a smile from spreading.

It was plain old, blind, dumb luck that her search request had been routed to him from the intake desk, and he silently thanked the powers that be—wherever and whatever they were—for what happened after that. He hadn't expected to find a windfall in this little-used reading room in the attic of the National Archives.

But there it was.

Right in front of him.

His heart picked up a beat, and his furtive glance over his shoulder was purely instinctive. Because he was careful by nature, though some would say indecisive and weak-willed, he took three pulse-slowing breaths so he could review the events of the previous days, looking for any landmines that may have escaped his notice.

Earlier in the week, he'd spent fruitless hours methodically reading thousands of paper and microfilm pages in archival data bases searching for the records Keegan Thomas had requested. He had entered Lincoln Cole's name in the search engine and when that turned up nothing, added the geographic area.

He had managed to gather some records naming the missionary and Indian schools operating in the 1950s, some scanty accounting records from oil and gas payments, incomplete and unrelated records of payments to individual Indians, a few years' worth of payroll records from the uranium mines, but nothing directly related to Lincoln Cole or his BIA clinic. Not a single medical file or report. Not a mention of his name.

With over ten billion documents in the archives, and no overall computerized organization system for most of them, there were endless places for Justin to search. The records Keegan asked for could be stored in as many as twenty-five different areas, and most were not cross-referenced. Justin was nearly ready to give up and tell Keegan no records existed in the National Archives about her grandfather's time in Monument Valley when, luckily, Henry Parker returned from sick leave.

Henry, an eighty-seven-year-old senior archivist blessed with a photographic memory and an assiduous recall of events was the archives go-to guy. All the researchers knew that when a search produced unsatisfactory results, they could count on Henry to suggest the not-so-obvious places that pertinent records might reside. Henry was the gatekeeper, and talking to him was a definite time saver.

Justin stood in the open doorway of Henry's office, studying the old man, watching him work.

"Hey, Henry, when are you going to start using a computer?" Justin quipped.

"Not today," Henry answered without looking up from his ancient Royal typewriter, his fingers moving slowly, one deliberate keystroke after another. Not once had he ever Googled anything.

Justin got a kick out of joking with the old man, and Henry always went along with the banter, so Justin asked the usual follow up question. "When are you going to retire?"

To which Henry gave his usual answer. "Not today."

The old man had stopped typing and looked up, smiling. His furrowed face, full of weather beaten grooves, showed eyes that still shined with youth and excellent teeth. Justin wondered if they were dentures.

"What can I do for you?" the old archivist asked.

Justin explained the focus of his records search for Keegan Thomas. Henry listened with his head tilted, eyes closed in thought. After a moment, he rattled off a series of numbers: record group, entry, stack, row, compartment, and shelf. Although slight and stooping and years past the normal retirement age, the old archivist had no trouble remembering the long sequences of numbers that unlocked the secrets of the archives.

"Ha!" Henry said, opening his eyes and grinning toothily. "Thought you'd stump me, didn't you?"

Justin shook his head. "I'm way ahead of you, Henry. Already looked there."

Justin had set a thick bundle of papers on the corner of Henry's desk and ran down a brief summary of what he'd found.

"Correspondence from the commissioner of Indian affairs. Miscellaneous BIA reports. Indian trust fund documents. Some budget and accounting records showing money paid to individual Indians, but nothing relating to Lincoln Cole."

He laid down the photo Keegan had sent him. "That's her grandfather there," Justin pointed out. "John Wayne and John Ford are in the back row. But I haven't been able to identify any of these other people. That's mostly what she was interested in. She wants to know who they are. Wants to find them, if they're still alive."

Henry picked up the photo, held it to the light, and adjusted his bifocals. "I've seen this somewhere before." He studied it a moment, then a light went on behind his eyes.

"Ah, yes," he'd said at last. "The original was in a shipment of records sent over from the BIA, maybe . . ." he paused, "eight or ten years ago. They haven't been put in the stacks yet. We had a little red-haired intern working on them, but after she went back to college, I had them hauled upstairs."

Justin frowned. He knew what the term *upstairs* meant. Due to a reduction in staff, *upstairs* was where low priority files and documents languished when no one had time to process them. They not only hadn't been shelved, they hadn't even been cataloged.

Records didn't always arrive at the archives in the best condition. Justin had envisioned cardboard boxes bulging from the weight of their contents, sagging from water damage, chewed by mice, stored haphazardly in the dingy attic room. He'd sighed and resigned himself to another time wasting search.

But the time hadn't been wasted at all.

Now, with dust motes drifting in the sun's rays that streamed in through dirty windows, Justin grinned again and laid Keegan's photo next to the original he'd found.

They were identical, except on the original everyone was identified by name, and it was one of the names that set his pulse to racing. He'd seen that same name recurring over and over on a set of ledgers. It had seemed insignificant at the time, but now that name had shown up again on a BIA policy report right alongside Lincoln Cole's name, and on a decades old file from Senator O'Toole's office.

Justin finished reading and sat back in his chair as though someone had shoved him. He couldn't have been more stunned if someone had hit him in the chest.

Well, well, well, Dr. Cole. Just what were you up to out there in the desert?

Justin puzzled over it a long time, until pieces of disconnected information began to fall into place. After a short while, he stood, and began sorting records into two piles, one for Keegan and one for himself. He loaded them into boxes, which he put on a rolling records cart, and headed for the copy machine wondering how he could personally benefit from this astonishing information. Who would be willing to pay money for what he had just discovered?

As he listened to the steady thrum and thump of the old copy machine, an idea came to him not quite fully formed. He'd have to work out the details, make some phone calls, ask questions, get more information.

This was something he definitely would prefer to carry out alone. Justin thought hard about it, but didn't see any way he could pull it off without help. Someone had to do the dirty work. He'd need at least one more person, maybe two, and this worried him. There were plenty of secrets in the government both inside and outside Washington, D.C., but a secret wasn't a secret if more than one person knew it.

He paused, realizing that wasn't quite true. He looked at the papers moving through the copy machine. This had been kept secret for fifty years, and several people had known about it.

Back in the attic room, he packed up the materials he was mailing to Keegan, selecting only the most benign and superficial, nothing that could tip her off. The others, he put aside for his use later.

His cell phone rang, and he glanced at the caller ID. It was his wife, and he cringed. It would be bad news. She never called with good news.

"Hi, Angela."

"You didn't make the car payment again this month," she said without preamble, her voice trembling. "The bank just called."

"Ohhh," he said, as if remembering something important. "I forgot."

"No, you didn't," she shot back. "You went to the casino

again, didn't you?"

"Don't worry, honey. It's not good for the baby." It was a baby he looked forward to. He wanted very much to be a father, but a baby needed a lot of things. Expensive things, and eventually they'd need a bigger house. The pregnancy couldn't have come at a worse time.

"I'll be able to make it up next month."

"How?" she pressed.

He looked at the papers spread across his work table. He didn't want to tell her what he planned to do. Not yet. Not until he had a chance to speak to his old friend, Booker.

When he didn't answer, Angela's breathy sigh came through the phone, quavery and defeated. "Never mind," she said at the end of it. "I'll call my father for a loan."

Again, her tone implied.

"No, baby, don't. You don't need to. We're coming into some money real soon. I promise. I've got an idea."

The plaintive sigh came again.

"What kind of scheme are you cooking up now?" Her words, sounding like they were spoken through clenched teeth, made it clear just how frustrated she was. "Justin, I swear to God, if you get in trouble again, my father will . . ."

At the mention of her father, Justin flicked a switch in his mind and tuned her out. Her voice continued through the earpiece, a strident hum of garbled vocalizations, her undecipherable tirade merely background noise to the thoughts churning in his mind.

His head was filled with what he had to do to put his plan in motion. Phone calls to make. Travel arrangements. He looked at the unorganized boxes and files surrounding him. Who knew how much more research he faced?

The grease of Washington's wheels was simple and as old as dirt: bribes, blackmail, and booze. There was sex, of course, though less so now in light of all the recent scandals, and Justin stayed away from that anyway. Too messy. Money worked better and was easier to hide. The highly beneficial mutual back scratching engendered by an exchange of money couldn't be captured as a digital image on the cell phone of a passerby, and later broadcast all over the world via cable news and YouTube.

He'd always operated on the fine edge of restraint, never quite crossing the line, so had stayed out of jail and mostly kept his jobs. This time, if all went as planned, he and Angela would be in a place where extradition was not an option by the time anybody found out what he'd done.

Angela's diatribe showed no sign of weakening, and Justin's attention snapped back to her. Her unrelieved anger, now fueled by the hormone surges of pregnancy, had not yet run its course.

"My father got you that job," she was saying, yelling, "but he can't help you keep it if you screw up again."

"Look, honey. I gotta go. I've got a lot of work to do. I'll see you tonight. Don't bother cooking, we'll eat out."

"No, we won't!" Her voice pitched up to an ever higher range. "We don't have money to—"

"I love you," he said and hung up.

His thoughts were rapid fire, but making connections. He opened his cell phone again and dialed a number. It was answered quickly.

"Hey, Booker. It's Justin."

"Hey. What's up at the national trash heap?"

"Not much."

Justin and Booker had buddied up in college and now, years later, maintained the kind of long distance friendship that didn't require constant reinforcement. Booker was a Senate aide in Washington, D.C., but the miles didn't prohibit a once a year San Diego beach vacation or golf outing with their wives. Other than that, their work kept them close to their homes.

Small talk dispensed with, Justin worked the conversation over to what he'd really called about.

"How's the job with the senator? You still in charge of money that can't be traced?"

"Hold on a sec."

Justin could hear the sound of footsteps and a door closing softly.

"Yeah," Booker said when he came back on the line. "It's called job security. Why? What's up?"

"Does the name Earlene Cly ring a bell?"

"No. Should it?"

"She's been getting checks from your office for over fifty years."

"That's not unusual. The slush fund comes with the job. It existed before Mike O'Toole took office, and it will exist after he's gone."

"Do you know what the money is for?"

"Not really. Facilitation payments, probably. You know, hush money. That's usually what it's for. I just authorize the payments and make sure there's money to cover it."

"Yeah, but hush money for what? Would you know?"

"I can probably find out. Let me take a look at the database. Why do you need to know?"

"Ah," said Justin sounding annoyed. "I'm working on a special assignment. It's confidential. Probably a dead end, but I have to ask."

Justin heard the clicking of computer keys, then a stretch of silence, then more clicking. Justin pictured Booker sitting forward in his chair, peering at his monitor.

"Well, it looks like she was added as a temporary employee, but never removed," Booker said.

"Does it say why?"

"No, but I can check and get back to you. Hey, how's Angela? When's that baby due?"

Justin talked about the baby, they complained about their jobs, made a friendly bet about an upcoming basketball game, and Justin gradually steered the conversation around to reminiscing about old friends.

"By the way," he said, keeping his voice casual. "Do you know where Charlie Manygoats hangs out these days? Has he gone back to the rez or what?"

CHAPTER TEN

Keegan read aloud.

"The aim of the boarding school system established by the government was to assimilate Indian children into the dominant white society by forbidding their language, clothing, hairstyles, and culture. Harsh measures were often used in the schools to accomplish their goal."

She removed her reading glasses and looked up from the pages she'd printed off the Internet during a week of online research.

Jilly sat across the dinner table in Keegan's kitchen. A wistful look had stolen into her expression during their conversation about Keegan's research on missionary schools.

"A lot of problems on the reservation now stem from those experiences," Jilly said sadly. "Many of those who returned to the reservation had a very hard time adjusting. They took what they'd learned in school and repeated it here. And I'm not only talking about what they learned in textbooks."

"What do you mean?"

"Domestic violence," said Jilly. "Alcoholism, abandonment of children, poor parenting skills. Cruelty and abuse are not the Navajo way of child-rearing, but some of the girls who returned to the reservation didn't know how to treat their children when they became mothers. They treated their kids the way they were treated at the schools. They thought it was the white way."

"Did any of your family members have to endure that?"

"Some did, but most escaped it. Monument Valley is so remote, it was easy to be overlooked out here then. Like now in a lot of ways. And," she added, "that's also why you're going to have a hard time finding that little girl."

Keegan stood up with her plate, and motioned to Jilly's. "Would you like more? I'm having seconds."

"Sure." Jilly passed her plate to Keegan, then continued. "*Shimasani* said she still remembers her mother hiding her when the missionaries and Indian Agents came around. It wasn't that the elders didn't think education was important. They did. They just didn't want their children going to those government boarding schools. Stories of abuse and unhappiness had made it back to the reservation by then. Everyone was frightened."

Keegan returned to the table, set Jilly's dish in front of her.

Jilly nodded her thanks. "One of my great aunts told me how the school administrators shaved her hair, burned her clothes and all her possessions, including the small bag she carried her charms in. She didn't even know how old she really was. When she got to the school, the teachers looked at her, guessed how old she was, assigned her a birth date, and gave her an age."

Keegan's heart swelled, and she was suddenly overwhelmed with the need to apologize. "I'm so sorry."

Jilly looked at her with a half smile. She'd braided her hair today, the plait laying over her shoulder looking like shimmering strands of liquid coal, its end secured with a circle of silver and turquoise. Lean and trim in stature, she appeared almost delicate when compared to the typically lush bodies of most Navajo women. "Sorry for what?" Jilly asked.

"For the way the Navajos have been treated," Keegan said.

Jilly laughed out loud at that, but kindly.

"Oh, I see," she replied. "You're afflicted with that dread disease. *White guilt.*" She shuddered in mock horror when she said it.

Keegan shrugged, and picked up her fork. "Maybe," she conceded.

"I see that a lot," said Jilly. "Most of the whites and *wannabes* living here now suffer from it."

Keegan sighed deeply. "I don't know," she said, looking directly at Jilly. "I can't help but feel I have to make up for it somehow. Maybe finding the little girl in the picture and reuniting the family would be my small way of doing that."

Jilly was thoughtful a long time. "I don't know how you'll ever find her. It happened a lot. Kids literally snatched up, loaded on wagons and taken away, just like my mother said."

"But don't you think it's odd that the rest of the children weren't taken as well?"

Jilly shrugged and nodded at the same time. "I guess."

"Why would they only take one and not the others?" Keegan pressed.

"Maybe because she was the youngest," Jilly offered.

Keegan picked up a sheet of paper from her stack of research. "According to this, they didn't just take the little ones. They took older kids, too."

Jilly didn't reply.

They finished eating through a silence that lasted a couple of minutes. Keegan stood and cleared the table, rinsing the dishes before putting them in the dishwasher.

Conversation seemed to have suddenly dried up, and Keegan wondered not for the first time how Sandra Wolf could remember so much about that little girl without remembering her name. It was on the tip of her tongue to say so, but she hesitated, not wanting to risk offending Jilly by making insinuations about her mother. Instead she talked about something else.

"Something else is bothering me," Keegan said, resting her hip on the edge of the counter and wiping her hands on a kitchen towel.

"What?"

"The night we went to the rodeo. The only thing taken from my purse besides the cash was that picture. I think he only took the cash to cover up. It's the picture he was really after."

To Keegan, that act alone infused the picture with significant importance and hidden meaning. But apparently not to Jilly, whose reply was offhand and breezy.

"Good thing we stopped to make copies on the way to the rodeo."

"Good thing Dante was there," Keegan replied. Then, at Jilly's quick glance added, "I mean, because he brought my purse back with all my credit cards. Otherwise we wouldn't have known what the thief was really after."

Jilly's expression went inward, threads of thought unraveling behind her eyes. A shadow crossed her face for a moment, then a frown. "Yeah," she said vaguely, then quickly changed the subject. "Have you heard anything about your car?"

"Not yet. Is your grandmother worried about her truck?"

"Oh, no. Believe me, she's happy being at her hogan. I call her every other day to check on her. Or she calls me. I insisted she get a cell phone to use out there. She fought me over it for the longest time. Now she has it, you couldn't pry it away from her."

"Well, tell her I appreciate the use of her truck. I hope to have mine back soon. I'd like to visit some of the government run Indian schools. Since your mother said the missionaries arrived by horse and wagon that day, I'm thinking they were probably from a school around here somewhere."

"But you don't even know her name," Jilly said.

"I know. I just want to go and ask some questions. See what I can find out," Keegan replied. She lifted her shoulders in a shrug. "You never know what might turn up."

"That's true," Jilly said, nodding agreement. "I'll check around, too, see if anyone at the high school knows anything."

They sat at the table a while longer, chatting amiably. Jilly talked about school and how the Russian students were faring. Keegan related her conversation with Justin Bickham at the National Archives. She tried to work the conversation around to what she'd wanted to talk about since their dinner with Sandra Wolf, but which up to now they'd avoided by mutual and unspoken accord.

Gathering her courage, Keegan brought it up during a lull in the conversation.

"Jilly, can I ask you something?"

"Sure."

"The other night you said your mother lied about not knowing anyone in that picture. What made you say that? What did she lie about?"

The light in Jilly's eyes dimmed a bit, but other than that her expression didn't offer a clue to what she was thinking or feeling inside.

"Oh, it was nothing," Jilly replied, sweeping the question away with her hand. "I was mistaken about something." She looked at her watch. "It's getting late. I have to go. I've got papers to grade."

She stood and took her car keys from her purse. "Thanks for dinner. I'll call you if I find out anything about the schools." Her smile was genuine, but Keegan saw something worrisome behind it.

After Jilly left, Keegan spent twenty minutes on the Bowflex, then an hour on the treadmill mulling over inconsistencies that laid heavy on her mind. Workout finished, she sat outside on her front porch awaiting the sunset, turning questions over one by one, like playing cards in a mental game of solitaire.

What was the meaning of Earlene's reaction to the photo?

After her initial show of interest, she shut right down. Keegan had felt like a door had been slammed in her face. Dante's response had been far from subtle. His jaw literally dropped.

And the man who snatched her purse and took the photo. How did he fit in?

Then there was Vicki.

Keegan could understand that Vicki might not recognize her after only seeing her once or twice. Waiting tables, Vicki saw hundreds of people. Yet, there was something very strange about her, too. Keegan could swear she'd seen real alarm in the girl's eyes at the rodeo, and then again at the grocery store.

Fear bumps suddenly crept along Keegan's forearms. And who was it driving slowly past the bungalow late at night?

The sun slipped below the mesas, and the western horizon erupted in brilliant orange and deep pink, spreading across the low hanging clouds like flames in the sky. She enjoyed the show until all that was left of it was a reef of dusty rose along the farthest rim. After that, night fell quickly.

She went inside, turned on the shower, and slipped off her shoes, then stopped to listen to . . . what? She turned off the shower and heard the sound again. A light knock at her front door.

She flicked on the porch light and looked out the side window. A rumpled pudge of a man was standing there, older, wearing cowboy boots, and a business suit over a rodeo shirt, his hair in a ponytail.

When he saw her peeking through the window, he stepped away from the door, crinkled his face in a grandfatherly smile, and politely removed his cowboy hat.

She opened the interior door, but left the screen door locked.

"Hello," the man said. "My name is Yuma Ray. I'm the tribal attorney for the Navajo Nation. We haven't met, but I wanted to stop by and have a word with you, if I may."

"Certainly. About what?"

"Oh, it's a small matter. I'm sure we can straighten everything out. I would like to talk to you about it, though. May I come in?"

Keegan never opened her door to strangers, let alone allow them inside, but he appeared harmless. Short and stocky, with some extra pounds around the middle, he had the melting jaw line of middle age and a nose that took up a bit too much of his face.

She opened the door. "Sure. Come in," she said.

He handed her a business card as he crossed the threshold. While she read it, he glanced around the room, his fingers dancing on the brim of the hat he held at waist level.

"Would you like to sit down?" She gestured to a chair. "Can I get you something? Water? Coffee?"

"Oh, no. Thank you kindly. This will just take a minute."

"What can I do for you, Mr. Ray?"

"First of all, I want to welcome you to the reservation. Are you on vacation or is this a business trip?"

She sensed something behind his polite question, a motive behind his inquisitiveness. She answered carefully.

"Well, actually both."

She spoke briefly about her grandfather's history on the reservation, but something, a small voice in the back of her mind that she'd learned to listen to, stopped her from mentioning her interest in the kidnapped child.

"I'm writing a story about it for a magazine."

"Ah," he said, nodding. His eyes flitted around the room and landed on her laptop and the papers stacked beside it.

"Have I done something illegal?" she asked when the silence went on long enough to become uncomfortable.

"Oh, no, nothing illegal. But it's come to my attention that you've been asking questions, and showing an old picture around. Is that true?"

She admitted it was, but added, "I'm sorry if I've broken any laws."

"Oh, you haven't," he said, quickly, smiling again. "No laws have been broken, I assure you. But it's upsetting to some of our people. I just thought I'd mention it to you."

"I didn't realize I'd offended anyone." That wasn't true, of course. She knew she'd upset at least some of the Natives she'd spoken to.

"Some of us Navajos are stuck in the old ways," he went on pleasantly. "The older ones especially regard me as sort of a protector of the tribe. They come to me when they have a problem or they're upset about something. You know, we have certain customs and traditions, myths and stories that perhaps seem silly to white people. For instance, there's an old Navajo saying that people who keep trying to unearth Navajo secrets may find they are digging their own grave." He paused significantly. "Silly, isn't it?"

His smile held until it looked like it had been pasted on with Elmer's glue. He was only half joking.

"No," she replied. "Not silly at all. In fact, I enjoy the Navajo stories. I've learned quite a few since I've been here."

Yuma Ray tipped his head at her laptop open on the table. "Well, I see you're in the middle of something, so I won't take any more of your time." He walked to the door and turned.

"Please enjoy your time in Monument Valley. You can't beat the views, can you? Visit the Navajo Tribal Park. Have one of the guides take you on a Jeep tour. You'll find it interesting." He put his hand on the door handle, then stopped again.

"Oh, yes," he said, turning. "One more thing. While you're out enjoying the sights, there's another old Navajo saying you might want to keep in mind."

"What is that?" she asked.

"Don't walk on steep mountains alone. Evil spirits will make you fall." He stared at her, his eyes very black, peering out from a nest of wrinkles. "I guess that can be interpreted in any number of ways," he added with a low chuckle that lacked any real humor. Something flickered through his eyes, something she couldn't read.

As he put his hat back on, the light from the end table lamp glinted off the ornate silver and turquoise watchband encircling his wrist. He opened the door and walked down the path. After the drama of the sunset, the sky was very dark, but Keegan could see the vehicle he'd arrived in. A shiny, black Hummer. A rich man's car.

CHAPTER ELEVEN

Jilly called two days later, but not with information about schools.

"What does your grandmother want to talk to me about?" Keegan asked, surprised.

"I'm not sure," Jilly answered. "All she said was that she'd made a promise a long time ago, but was going to break it now. I think it was about your photo."

"Is that what she said?"

"In a roundabout way. She hinted."

Keegan understood. It hadn't taken her long to discover that some of the Navajos had a tendency to talk all around a subject, considering it impolite to address it directly.

"Anyway, she wanted me to bring you out to her hogan. Only I can't leave school. Dante is due back with the Russian students, and I need to be here when they arrive. I have to give them the final assignments they need to complete before the semester is over. Can you go alone?"

A nudge of trepidation poked Keegan's middle as she remembered getting lost near Oljato. The nudge turned into a pinch of embarrassment at the subsequent memory of walking into Dante's camp in her bra with her shirt wrapped around her head.

"Sure," she said, "if you give me directions. When does she want me to come?"

"This morning if you can make it. Stop by the school, and

I'll leave an envelope with instructions and a map in the office."

Keegan ended the call, finished dressing, ran a hand through her hair, fingering it into place, put both phones in her purse and headed out. She'd found her off-reservation phone occasionally picked up a signal as she drove along the highway just past Eagle Rock near Viewpoint, so she carried it along with the reservation phone.

She cranked Earlene's truck to life, then rattled it to the gas station. She filled the tank, and went inside to pay and buy a bottle of water.

It was the kind of gas station that also sold pizza, subs, milk, and bread along with paperback books, DVDs, and sunglasses. A bird-thin man with an intense look, his hair tied back with a string of yarn, sat at a table eating pizza and smoking a cigarette. It was the same man she'd seen on the bench outside the grocery store, only now he was reading the newspaper, so he obviously wasn't blind as she'd first thought. He paid no attention to her at first, but he raised his eyes to meet hers as she went out the door.

With Jilly's detailed instructions lying open on the passenger seat, the old pickup rolled south on 163, then west on 160, trailing a thin haze of blue smoke behind it. At the turnoff just past Black Mesa, marked only by two weathered fence posts and an oil drum painted white, Keegan jolted down the steep incline of the ditch bank and rumbled over a cattle guard.

Two dusty, bumpy miles later, the mesa that had been a distant purple tabletop now loomed close, its jagged walls reaching into the sky. She checked Jilly's hand drawn map, then turned off the packed earth of unimproved roads onto an even vaguer track that wound around the wind-strafed arid buttes of Indian Country. Navajo Mountain was a bluish haze in the background.

The faint sweet smell of sage drifted on the breeze, and Keegan rolled down the window to let it fill the cab of the truck. She found herself in a broad flat arroyo, a green line of tamarisk and cottonwood up ahead. That meant water was nearby. She must be getting close to Earlene's place.

The hammering roar of an engine and the bump and slam of a vehicle pounding over gullies came to her from far away. Sounds, like distances, were deceiving in the wilderness, and she couldn't tell from which direction it was coming, but it was getting closer. Abruptly, the pitch changed, and with a horrific grind of gears, a huge SUV covered with muddy earth bounced over the rim of the arroyo, catching air. It landed with a terrific thump and headed directly toward her, throwing up rocks and sand.

Propelled by reflex, Keegan slammed her foot on the brake pedal and yanked the steering wheel to the right just in time to avoid a head-on collision, but not quick enough to escape a metal-on-metal scrape and a shower of sparks.

Earlene's old pickup plowed through a scrawny growth of creosote bush as the speeding vehicle bounced past over the rough terrain, roared down the wash, and disappeared around a sandstone escarpment.

"Idiot!" she yelled. "You moron!"

Heart pounding, Keegan's hands stayed locked on the steering wheel even after the pickup stopped its gravelly skid along the desert floor. It all happened so fast she hadn't caught a glimpse of the other driver, and now the only thing in her rearview mirror was a fast receding cloud of dust. When she tried to recreate in her mind what had just happened, all she could remember was a big black grille guard attached to the front of an airborne vehicle looming up in front of her, a shadowy hulking figure on the driver's side.

The pickup's engine had stalled out, and she took the key from the ignition, opened the door, and got out on shaky legs to check the extent of the damage. Paint was scraped to bare metal from front to back on the driver's side, and the front fender was dented. Earlene would not be happy about that. She hoped the old woman had insurance. If not Keegan would pay for the repairs herself.

Earlene's carpet scraps and all the plastic flowers had been thrown off the dashboard and tossed around the cab of the truck. With shaking hands, Keegan gathered them up and put it all back as close to the original arrangement as possible. She took a deep breath as she turned the key, then let it out slowly, relieved when the old engine turned over. Moving slowly, carefully, remembering how she'd stranded herself when she bottomed out near Oljato, Keegan maneuvered out of the sand and back to the rutted track.

Still fuming about the recklessness of the big SUV's driver, Keegan, hyperalert now, drove through a stand of cottonwoods and down into a bosque of wetlands nourished by mountain runoff, then pulled out of the wash and up an incline. Ahead, sheltered by a thick stand of trees was a hogan, a horse corral, sheep pens, a stack of hay bales protected by a vast sheet of plastic, and a round galvanized metal water tank. A faint trail of smoke rose from the top of the hogan.

She let the pickup roll forward a few yards, then stopped. She got out of the truck, but stood watching the door, waiting for Earlene to invite her in, as was the custom. An unnatural silence permeated the air.

Keegan counted the passing seconds. Next, she counted the fence posts, then the trees, then the number of stacked hay bales. Four wide. Three high. Twelve total.

Still, Earlene did not appear.

Counting her steps, Keegan approached the hogan.

The heavy door was made of wood and hung from metal hinges. She stood outside trying to remember which way to enter, right or left. According to tradition, the door of a hogan always faced east. That meant the kitchen area was north, to her right. That was it. Men entered to the left, women to the right. Still she didn't move.

I'll count to ten and then go in, she told herself. Irritably she shoved the thought away. *That is silly. Just go in.*

One, two, three, four.

She reached for the door and pushed it with her fingertips. It swung open on squeaky hinges just enough for her to see the interior was filled with smoky shadows from the coals in the center fire pit.

Five, six, seven.

She was prickling with a sense of uneasiness.

Eight, nine. A rumble of thunder rolled overhead, and she glanced up at the clouds creeping down the mesa.

"Oh, for God's sake," she muttered. "Go in."

Ten.

Holding a breath, she stepped inside.

It took a moment for the scene to penetrate her consciousness, but even then it didn't make sense. There was a bed to her left, but the sheets and blankets had been tossed on the floor, the mattress upended against the wall and slashed open. An apartment sized refrigerator powered by a generator lay on its side, its door flung open, foodstuffs spilled out, liquids soaking into the dirt floor. An old sofa was tipped over, the upholstery and cushions cut open, shredded foam stuffing bulging out. All the drawers in two small chests had been emptied onto the dirt floor. Earlene's loom, strung with the remains of a half finished rug, was smashed to pieces, no longer usable.

A cold thought shoved itself into Keegan's brain, and she hurried to the bedclothes piled on the floor, pulling them aside, dreading what she'd find underneath. The painful tightness in her chest loosened when she saw Earlene wasn't beneath them.

What happened here? Who had done this and why? What kind of thinking would lead someone to do this to an old woman's home? Into what circumstances would such an action fit? Had the driver of the speeding truck done this? She wished she'd caught a glimpse of him. She couldn't even identify the make, model, or color of that speeding rig.

She went outside and looked around. A pink desert with lavender blue mountains and mesas scalloped the horizon.

"Earlene!" she called. "Earlene!" There was no reply, only her own voice echoing back.

A well worn path led away from the hogan and she followed it down a craggy slope into a place where humps of blown sand supported a growth of Mormon tea. An eddy of wind whistled through the piñons. It stirred her hair. Faint footprints in loose sand led her farther into the desert beyond clumps of rabbitbrush and snakeweed to a place where erosion had formed a sand-floored cul-de-sac in the side of a mesa.

She entered the clearing, and half a dozen ravens squawked into startled flight, startling her and making her jump. The wind rose again and fell. Everything around her stilled and quieted. A lizard emerged from a crevice in the cliff. It turned its cold unblinking eyes on her, then scurried away. She watched it go, and that's when she saw the smear of blood on a rock.

Something cold slithered through her, and a gasp jammed in her throat. She stepped backward, then gave herself a moment to absorb the scene. Leading away from the cul-de-sac, the ground was disturbed with a mixture of footprints—sharp-edged hoof prints of sheep, paw prints of a dog, and the prints of more than one human.

Using her hands to give her leverage, she climbed a steep sandstone slope and looked down on a shallow basin where a small flock of sheep grazed, watched over by a lone shepherd dog. The dog eyed her warily, its tail moving side to side in a slow, cautious sweep. Earlene was nowhere in sight.

Returning to flat ground, Keegan took a closer look at the blood smear. It appeared to be fresh, but whether animal or human, she had no idea.

Head down, eyes to the ground, she scanned the rocks and dirt and desert growth, paying attention to details she would have ignored before. A broken stem, a turned-over rock, a loose skitter of stones, any minor disturbance of the surroundings.

She saw something tucked into a pile of rocks near a growth of Mormon tea, and instantly her consciousness zoomed in on the blood drops surrounding it, trailing off over the boulders. Gingerly she withdrew a small, blue velvet drawstring bag from a sheltered place against the cliff. It was Earlene's bag. Keegan remembered seeing it on the window ledge in Jilly's kitchen.

Quickly, she slipped it in her pocket. Fear growing, she scrambled over the boulders and followed a trail of bloody drops until nightmare and reality became indistinguishable. Filled with a terrible pity, she choked back a strangled cry.

Earlene Cly lay face down in red dirt made redder by the blood pooled around her head. But even an unpracticed eye could tell it wasn't the ugly gash in her head that killed her. It was the ugly pitchfork embedded in her back.

The sob Keegan was holding exploded from her chest, tearing her throat on its way out. She viewed the scene for no longer than a panic-stricken microsecond before racing back to her car to get her phone.

Many hours later, while getting ready for bed, Keegan remembered Earlene's blue velvet bag. She took it out of her pocket, opened the top, and emptied the contents into her palm. Tiny carved amulets in the shape of animals. A frog, a ram, a beaver. Earlene's two elaborate silver and turquoise rings. She stared

113

sadly at the old woman's treasures. Hot tears burned behind her eyes.

When she slipped the jewelry and amulets back into the *jish* bag, she felt something in the lining. Fingering it through the velvet, she turned the bag inside out. A seam had been cut and re-sewn. Using a fingernail to break the loose threads, she inserted her thumb and forefinger into the opening and pulled out a folded piece of notepaper wrapped around an obsidian carving of a snake. With trembling fingers, she unfolded the paper and read the words.

Lulu Etsitty.

Keegan sat a minute, staring at it, then rewrapped the note around the snake and put it back in the bag with the others. First thing in the morning, she'd return it to the family.

CHAPTER TWELVE

Jilly and Sandra wanted to have the funeral right away, but it was several days before the medical examiner would release Earlene's body. When he finally did, only the immediate family went to the cemetery. Keegan was invited to join friends and family at Jilly's house afterward.

Nearly a hundred people attended, far too many to fit inside Jilly's little house. Instead, everyone gathered in the front yard, where buffet tables had been set up end to end. There was plenty of food. Nearly everyone arrived with something. Home-baked bread and rolls, crocks of beans, potato salad, and savory casseroles, as well as pots of steaming soups and stews.

The promise of rain had faded when west winds blew the thunderheads into New Mexico. Left behind were intermittent gusts that whipped the skirts around the legs of the old Navajo women as they set out serving spoons, napkins, paper plates, and plastic knives and forks. Men, some of them wearing the familiar round-crowned, black felt reservation hats, brims pulled low, milled around in clusters talking quietly, their faces drawn. The younger men, with the help of some teenage boys, set up folding chairs on the hard packed earth. There weren't enough chairs to go around, so guests took advantage of porch railings, steps, tree stumps, or flat boulders. Conversations in Navajo were held in subdued voices.

Keegan hadn't had a chance to speak to Jilly or Sandra other than for a briefest moment to offer condolences and comfort.

Sandra had merely looked at her in pained silence, her lips in a tight, hard line. Jilly had opened her mouth to say something, but the words got caught in her throat. Neither woman released the tears so obviously being held back. Now, mother and daughter sat next to each other holding hands, the breeze moving loose strands of hair against their faces. Surrounding them, protectively it seemed, were family members and close friends, speaking softly, crooning and consoling. Even though Keegan didn't understand the language, she couldn't miss the messages of solace.

She didn't see anyone she knew except Jilly and Sandra. After a while, she caught a glimpse of Dante Covelli at the end of the driveway talking to some other men, not Navajo. They were wearing a style of clothing befitting the relaxed dress code on the reservation, as well as the telltale unofficial uniform of local archaeologists. Cargo pants, hiking boots, and wide-brimmed safari hats. Dante didn't notice her, and she was sure he wouldn't acknowledge her if he did.

Despite the natural hospitality of the Navajos, Keegan felt out of place. She'd approached some people she assumed were family members, though the Navajo system of kinship confounded her, and had uttered a few stiff, awkward sentences of comfort. They were met with nods and shaky smiles, but she wasn't sure if her remarks were understood.

Since she was the one who found Earlene's body, most of the relatives tended to avoid her, sneaking peeks out of the corner of their eye from a distance, unintentionally making her feel like the outsider she really was. She felt a mixture of sympathy and guilt.

FBI agents were on the scene, minus suit and tie, but their straight-backed military bearing gave them away. They'd been called in, as they always were for unexplained deaths on the reservation, to work with the Navajo Tribal Police in investigating Earlene's death. They stood at the perimeter of the gathering, two of them, steely-eyed and grim, taking in the scene and everyone in it.

They'd questioned Keegan at length, and she'd told them what she knew, which wasn't much. She hadn't mentioned finding Earlene's amulets. She knew if she had, the tiny carvings would have been confiscated as evidence and maybe never returned to the family. Instead, at her first opportunity, she had surreptitiously slipped the blue velvet bag into Jilly's palm and closed her fingers over it. When the time was right, she would ask Jilly about the hidden note.

The line at the food tables had thinned out, so Keegan walked over and picked up a napkin and a paper plate. She hadn't eaten since breakfast; it seemed impossible that appetite could exist in the face of recent events, but she put some food on her plate anyway. Green salad, sliced chicken breast, some fruit.

When she turned from the table, she nearly bumped into Yuma Ray, who was standing close behind her. She nodded and tried to step around, but he deliberately blocked her way and looked at her with eyes wounded and laced with blame.

"See what happens when you dig around in the past?" he said.

His voice was quiet, but filled with such anguish and accusation her heart squeezed tight in her chest. She couldn't think of anything to say so didn't say anything at all. He stared at her a moment longer, his expression slightly hostile, then walked away, shoulders slumped.

Keegan moved off to sit alone on a pile of stacked firewood covered with a sheet of plastic held down with cement blocks. She stared at the food on her plate, trying to work up an appetite, then set her plate aside untouched, and dropped her forehead to her fingertips. Her vision was suddenly blurred with tears. Maybe Yuma Ray was right. Maybe it was her fault Earlene was murdered.

Boots crunched on dirt and stones, drew near, then stopped next to her. It was Dante.

Gently, he lifted her hand from her lap and pressed it in both of his. She looked up at him, grateful for a human touch. Gone were the sharp lines and flinty expression that usually commanded his face. The churlish glint in his eyes had been replaced by smoky shadows.

"Come on," he said, softly. "Let's get out of here."

The Jeep Grand Cherokee with Dante at the wheel sped north through a vermillion universe created by a sun getting ready to drop below the ridge of a distant mesa.

"Where are we going?" Keegan asked.

"To my house."

"Why?"

"Because I've got frozen pizzas. And wine and beer, and Diet Coke."

When she didn't comment, he went on. "I noticed you didn't touch your plate. Aren't you hungry?"

She gave a half nod, half shrug. She didn't know.

"You'll feel better after you eat. And I want to talk to you."

"About what?"

"I'll tell you when we get there."

After that, neither of them spoke until Dante turned his rig into a dirt driveway and pulled the hand brake.

It wasn't the kind of house Keegan would have pictured for Dante: a big old stone Victorian hunk of junk in need of a paint job, three blocks from the paved highway at the dead end of a dirt street in the tiny village of Bluff. Most of the decorative gingerbread and cornices were intact, a bay window commanded the street front, dormers over the second-story windows were deep and dramatic, and there were both front and side porches.

But all of it needed work. It was a style of house better suited to a new life as a bed and breakfast, after renovation, of course, than the abode of a rugged, dirt-digging, outdoor type like Dante Covelli. When he told her the house was on the National Historic Register, she silently took back her hunk of junk assessment.

Inside, she gazed around a living room furnished with cushy leather furniture, neutral in color and supple to the touch. A big mocha-colored sectional, dressed up with Indian print pillows and a Navajo blanket, invited long afternoon naps in front of a fireplace that actually worked. Dante ducked out the side door to retrieve some logs and got a fire going right away.

The kitchen had been updated with modern stainless appliances, the kind usually found in homes where cooking was a passion. But not in this house, apparently. Dante opened the oven, threw in a couple of frozen pizzas, and set the timer. He took a bottle of wine from the pantry and a can of Coke from the refrigerator, and held them up, one in each hand. He quirked his brows in question, asking her preference.

"Wine, please," she told him.

He poured two glasses, handed one to her, and motioned her to the sofa. He lowered himself into the cushions at the other end, and set the wine bottle on the coffee table.

The fire wasn't so much for heat as it was meant to soothe. Keegan welcomed it, letting its glow wash over her, loosening the web of tension that had held her in its grip since finding Earlene's body. She took a sip of wine, rested her head against the back of the sofa, and sighed deep and long.

"Thank you," she said. "For bringing me here." She slanted a look at him.

He smiled, a warm smile that softened his features. She smiled back.

"You looked like you needed a friend," he said.

"I did," she said. "I do," she amended. She took a long breath, let it out slowly. "Thanks for coming to my rescue. I was feeling pretty uncomfortable." She sat upright, took another small sip, and set her glass down.

"Don't feel bad. Most white people are uptight with the Navajo view of death. They don't understand it. They don't understand how the Navajos don't like to look at dead people or touch them or say their name, yet sometimes the family prepares the body of their loved ones for burial."

"They do?" She could imagine no pain like the washing and dressing of a deceased loved one, and wondered if Jilly and Sandra had been the ones to do that for Earlene. Poor Jilly. Poor Sandra. It must have been unbearable.

Dante went on. "They feel if the body's not prepared the right way, the person's spirit will return to haunt the family. Traditionally, anyway."

Keegan thought about that a moment. "Jilly and her mother seem more modern than traditional. Earlene did, too, in some ways."

"Like many of the Natives in Monument Valley, they walk with one foot in each world. Even though Jilly and Earlene treated me as part of the family, I'm not really and never can be. The Navajo kinship and clan system overrides everything. Jobs, friendships, everything. I sometimes feel like an outsider, too, but I don't take it personally. You shouldn't either."

"Mmmm. I suppose not." She stared at the flames.

"It's interesting how much of the Navajo belief system is pragmatic. Even some of the myths and legends. Have you ever heard the Navajo story that explains why people die?"

She shook her head. "No."

"Well, it goes like this. One day the first Navajo people placed an animal hide in the water. They believed that if it didn't sink, no one would ever die, but if the hide sank into the water, then death would always occur on earth. But none of the Navajos kept watch over the hide, and behind their backs, Coyote deliberately threw some rocks on it, making it sink." He paused. "Do you know why he did that?"

"No. Why?"

"Coyote came to the very sensible conclusion that if no one ever died, there would come a time when there wouldn't be enough land on which the people could live."

Keegan had to acknowledge the sageness of the story. "Unfortunately that's not why Earlene died," she added, lowering her eyes.

Dante let a beat of silence go by.

"It must have been pretty awful. Finding her that way." He shook his head as if imagining it.

"It was *horrible*." Memories churned, conjuring up the awfulness of that moment. Keegan forced the images from her mind. She couldn't keep reliving it.

"Earlene didn't deserve to die that way," Dante said. "And I'd be surprised if a Navajo did it. That was a white man's meanness."

Her mind stopped, stuck on that thought. "You think so?"

"Hell, yes." A glimmer of anger flashed briefly then died in his eyes. "Navajos get drunk and kill, or they fight and kill, but they don't murder harmless old women."

"I don't think the FBI is ruling anyone out. I just wish I'd been able to get a look at the driver of that truck." She told him about the vehicle she'd seen speeding away on the trail from Earlene's hogan.

When she finished, Dante held her look, his eyes reflective. "What did the FBI say when you told them that?"

"Nothing. I'm sure it didn't help them much."

"What did the truck look like?"

Keegan described what she remembered. "Does it sound

121

familiar to you?"

"No. But I'll keep an eye open for it."

Dante refilled his glass, then hers, and then the oven timer buzzed. He set the bottle down, and she started to get up to help him in the kitchen.

"Stay here," he said. "Relax. I'll get it."

"Are you sure?"

"I'm sure."

He returned with forks and napkins, and two plates with two slices of pizza on each. The smell of the pizza ignited her appetite, and she ate hungrily. The food had a calming effect, relaxing her even more. A log tumbled off the grate setting off a tiny shower of sparks. Dante got up to close the fireplace screen.

"They blame me for it," she said after a while.

"For what?" Dante asked, wiping the side of his mouth with a napkin. "Who blames you?"

She shrugged, flipped a palm. "All of them."

"The Navajos? They think you killed Earlene? Why do they think that?"

"No, they don't think I killed her, but they think it's my fault she's dead."

He stopped chewing. "Why?"

"You know. The picture. You warned me they wouldn't like me showing it around and asking questions, and you were right. Some of them don't. Especially Yuma Ray." She used a napkin on her greasy fingers. "Do you know him? He said he was the tribal attorney."

"I know who he is. I've never met him, but he's a big shot in the tribe, and sort of a hero to the Navajos. He's helped them recoup from some of the wrongs done to them by the Washington bureaucracy. You know. Broken treaties, missing land trust money. Mining royalties. Things like that."

"Well, he paid me a visit one night. It was late."

Dante's slice of pizza stopped halfway to his mouth. He looked at her with sharp interest. "He did? What did he want?"

"He said he wanted to welcome me to Monument Valley. And then it was just small talk, but I couldn't help feeling an undercurrent of something else, something not being said. You know how some of the Navajo don't always come right out with what they're getting at."

"Yeah," Dante put in, grinning. "They like to sneak up on their point."

"It was all very furtive. It scared me a little."

Dante digested this, his expression thoughtful. "What exactly did he say?"

"Something about people who dig up the past end up digging their own grave. He said it was an old Navajo saying."

Dante stared at her and lowered the piece of pizza he was about to take a bite from. "There's no Navajo saying like that. He was threatening you."

"Well, that's what it sounded like to me at the time. And then today, at Jilly's, he said, 'This is what happens when you dig around in the past.' Something like that. I took him to mean what happened to Earlene."

Dante's expression was perplexed. "You mean he thinks your photograph is somehow connected to Earlene's murder?"

She shrugged. "I guess so."

"How could it be?" Lines creased the corners of his eyes, and his frown deepened.

She shrugged again. "A few nights before he knocked on my door—" She stopped suddenly, remembering. "Oh. I moved out of the motel. I'm in a bungalow up the hill now. Anyway, for a few nights before Yuma Ray came over, I'd seen a car driving by late at night, after dark. Slow. I think it might have been him."

At that, Dante fell silent, focused on private thoughts, and Keegan wondered if she should be more worried about Yuma

Ray's visit. Dante popped the last bite of pizza into his mouth, went to the kitchen, and came back with the rest of the pizza on a platter. He set it on the coffee table and helped himself to more.

Keegan did, too. "How well do you know Jilly's mother?"

Dante shrugged. "I've met her a few times. She rarely comes to Monument Valley. Why?"

Keegan related the conversation she'd had over dinner with Sandra in Window Rock.

"It was the night I went to the bull riding with Jilly. I showed Sandra the picture, and she said she didn't know anyone in it, yet she knew that one of the little kids had been kidnapped. By missionaries."

"Really?" said Dante, his expression interested, but dubious.

"But later Jilly told me she thought her mother was lying."

"Lying about what?"

"I don't know. When I brought it up later, she didn't want to talk about it."

Dante was sitting very still, his eyes busy with thought. "Did you tell the police all this?"

Keegan shook her head. "Well, no. I didn't see it had anything to do with what happened to Earlene. And I don't want to just throw it out there, you know, maybe cause trouble for Sandra and Jilly. They've got enough to deal with."

"It all might mean something. You probably need to tell them," he said.

"That's not the only thing I didn't tell them." She hadn't planned on mentioning Earlene's amulet bag, but suddenly found herself telling him about it.

When she finished, he agreed that giving the amulets to Jilly for the family was probably a good idea, but asked, "What did Earlene want to talk to you about?"

"I don't know exactly. Jilly said she thought it had something to do with my grandfather, or someone else in that picture." Dante held her look, his eyes reflective, his gaze drawn inward to someplace private. "Well, that picture is what I wanted to talk to you about."

Keegan bristled, instantly defensive. She thought he was going to tell her to stop showing it around again, and she started to put a little starch in her voice. "Dante, I'm not here to take advantage of anyone. Honest, I just—"

But he didn't let her finish. "I've been thinking about that guy who grabbed your purse at the rodeo grounds—"

"Thank you again for getting it back," she interjected.

He accepted her thanks with a combination nod and head shake. No problem. "Have the police found out who it was?"

"No."

He looked pensive. "I thought it was strange he left your checkbook and credit cards, and only took cash and the picture."

She nodded in agreement, acknowledging a strangeness her reporter's mind couldn't ignore.

They ate in silence for a time, and then he shoved his plate aside. "I owe you an apology."

"You do?"

He nodded. "About the picture. That night at Jilly's when you talked about it. I didn't believe what you said. That you were looking for people in the picture. I was rude then, and since. And I'm sorry."

She smiled. "What, you thought I was just a nosey *wannabe?*"

It should have been a cue for laughter, but instead he looked grim, and her grin dissolved. "Who did you think I was looking for?"

He gazed at her with a serious expression. "Me."

"Why would I be looking for you?" Was he someone famous? A celebrity she didn't recognize? A movie star on hiatus or hiding from the paparazzi?

125

She studied his handsome face, acknowledging a sneaking attraction that had begun at her first sight of him. Longish blond hair framed his face, setting off brilliant gray-green eyes. A quick and vivid fantasy of being ravished by him right there on that mocha-colored sofa was shattered by Billy Bob Thornton's voice floating up, barely audible, Keegan's cell phone playing its tune in her bag.

She snapped out of her reverie, grabbed her purse, and raked through it looking for her off-rez phone. She found it and flipped it open quickly, catching the call without looking at the caller ID.

"Hello."

"Keegan?" It was Jeffrey.

"Oh," she said, more than a little surprised to hear from him. "Hello, Jeffrey."

"Didn't you get my messages?" His voice was tight with urgency.

"No. My phone doesn't always work here. Why? What's wrong?"

She heard him take a shaky breath before going on. "The FBI called me. You gave them my number as an emergency contact in case there was news about Daisy and they couldn't reach you."

Instantly, her heart thumped. "Have they found her?"

Jeffrey let out another long breath. "Keegan, honey, you need to call them right away. They want you to go to San Diego to identify a body. I'm sorry. It's Daisy."

CHAPTER THIRTEEN

Two years and forty-eight days ago, Keegan Thomas and four-year-old Daisy arrived at the beach under a buttermilk sky. The lumpy clouds, looking like a herd of sheep standing close together in an overhead pasture, meant that thunderstorms would roll in by noon, ruining the photographs she needed for the Southern California travel article she was writing. It was due Wednesday.

They'd been late starting out that day, because Daisy had misplaced her beach sandals, and it took thirty minutes to find them. Then she dawdled at breakfast. In the car, Keegan noticed the gas tank was on empty. It took another twenty minutes to fill up, and by that time her patience was stretched to breaking.

"Come on, Daisy. Hurry."

They started down the creaky cliffside stairway, Keegan carrying beach towels, a blanket, a low-slung beach chair, a small cooler with water and snacks, and a camera case. Daisy, in front of her, took one careful step at a time, her arms clutching a duck-cloth drawstring bag containing beach toys.

"Why are we in a hurry?" she asked, her flip-flops slapping the wooden-slatted steps as she descended.

"Because I want to get pictures of the blowhole before it rains."

"Are we going to see the whales again?"

"No," answered Keegan. "It's not that kind of blowhole. It's a hole in the cliff where seawater shoots out the top of a sea cave so it looks like . . . well, it sort of looks like a whale's blow. Come on, honey. We're losing the light. Can you hold on to the handrail? You'll be able to go a little faster."

"Okay, Mommy."

Sunrises in Southern California occurred over land rather than water, here specifically over downtown San Diego. Less colorful than sunsets, because there is less dust in the atmosphere at that time of day, the sunrises were no less dramatic, the ocean views enhanced by the deflected light. Keegan hoped to catch in her camera lens the sun-washed surface of the ocean and the pink and pale lavender streaks on the horizon behind the droplets of water shooting geyserlike into the air from the blowhole.

The beach was almost empty at that hour, except for the early risers and ocean worshipers draped in blankets or ponchos and wearing big hats. They sat cross-legged along a dune ridge under scraggly trees that leaned in the direction of the prevailing winds.

Keegan and Daisy gave them a wide berth so as not to disturb their morning meditation, staking out a place in the sand several hundred feet away near a natural seawall. The long, low embankment of boulders at the high water mark offered protection from the waves crashing dramatically at the shoreline, but still allowed Daisy to remain safe and in sight as Keegan shot pictures.

Keegan spread the blanket, holding down the corners with rocks. Daisy upended her bag, and unceremoniously dumped out her beach toys. Keegan knelt on the blanket setting up the camera and sorting through her equipment case.

A noisy barking caught Daisy's attention.

"Look. Seals." Daisy was pointing to a narrow spit of land jutting away into the water, where a colony of sea lions rested on the rocks.

Keegan glanced up quickly, then turned her attention back to adjusting the camera settings.

"They're sea lions," she said, "not seals. See the whiskers and the little ear flaps?"

Daisy nodded.

"Don't go down there," Keegan warned. "Stay here by the blanket, okay?"

Daisy, compliant and obedient, nodded, then busied herself digging a hole and scooping sand into her pail.

"I'm going to make a big sand castle. Big enough for a giant," she said, immediately getting on with it.

Keegan checked the camera's battery level, inserted the media card, made sure the lens was clean, then stood.

"Daisy, promise you'll stay here, okay? I'll be right over there on those rocks taking pictures."

Daisy looked where Keegan was pointing and nodded again.

"You'll be able to see me the whole time, okay? If you need me, just call."

"Okay, Mommy."

The weather was changing fast and along with it, the light. Far out over the ocean, a distinct dark line of a weather front moved doggedly toward shore, tumbling rows of mangled waves that grew bigger and more powerful as they neared the beach. Rising winds were beginning to break up the beautiful cottony clouds, stretching and shredding them into gunmetal gray rows. Here and there, bits of pale blue sky showed between.

Keegan scoped out a level place to set up her tripod, attached her camera, then framed the shot through the viewfinder. The digital sensors did the work of measuring distance and light electronically. She leaned into the camera, composed and previewed the shot in the rear mounted liquid crystal monitor, then waited for a wave to create the striking effect she sought.

Patience was called for. Any old wave wouldn't do. Long rolling swells didn't have enough energy to produce the dramatic phenomenon she was hoping for. She needed a breaker, a monstrous thrust of water with enough power to propel itself in, up, and out the top of the sea cave. Wave after wave washed ashore while she waited, concentrating.

Between advancing wave fronts, Keegan's gaze alternated between the sky and her daughter. Daisy was one of those imaginative children who played easily alone, and though she had many little friends from school, she was comfortable in her own skin, content to keep her own company. Keegan smiled at the sight of her, bent at the waist, the seat of her jeans damp from sitting in the wet sand, her serious face set on her task as she earnestly formed arches and battlements and sand pail turrets.

As if feeling her mother's eyes on her, Daisy turned and waved, calling out, but her words were indistinguishable, drowned in the roar of the thunderous surf.

Keegan waved back. "I can't hear you," she shouted, motioning with her hands and shoulders, knowing Daisy couldn't hear her either, indicating to the child that verbal communication was impossible.

Daisy turned and hunkered down again, the architect of a castle for a giant.

Wave action increased, bringing in a school of phosphorescent fish, their scales glinting, briefly lighting up the water. Keegan snapped off a series of shots that were suitable, not what she hoped for, but would do in a pinch. The sky was changing, and she was almost ready to give up when she saw in the distance the makings of a horrendous wave.

Sea smoke, those transitory patches of fog formed when cold air flowed over warm sea water, drifted onshore and danced along the ground. High stratus clouds, moving fast, covered the sky diffusing the solar light, making the sun appear anemic as if she were seeing it through ground glass. Rain would be falling soon, and it was going to be a downpour.

Keegan turned back to the ocean and watched the distant monster wave churn and grow over the depths. When it reached the shallows, its forward motion would be severely impeded, causing its energy to explode with tremendous force, creating a crescendo of motion madness.

Keegan caught a movement out of the corner of her eye. Daisy had stopped digging and was standing, looking off to her right. The sea lions were hauling inland, away from the waves crashing on the shore.

Steam fog became ground fog, ghostly images drifting across the sand and rocks, settling into crags and crevices. Waves pounded the beach, rising fifteen feet into the air, the remaining rays of the sun lighting them from behind with a transparent glow.

Daisy was calling again, her hands cupped around her mouth, but most of her words were carried away by gusting winds.

"Mommy, Mommy, look—" Animated now, the child was standing, pointing excitedly at the sea lions.

"Just a minute, sweetie." Quickly Keegan focused and recomposed the shot, waiting for the mammoth wave to crash and lift in a predetermined spot. Briefly, she shifted her gaze from the LCD monitor to Daisy.

"One more picture," she called to Daisy. "I'll be right there."

Her finger hovered over the shutter release. The massive breaker gathered speed as it approached. Near shore, the wall of water grew so steep, the crest outpaced the body of the wave curling into a pipeline before collapsing in a turbulent mass at the mouth of the sea cave. A microsecond later, a geyser exploded straight up out of the rocks, the top of the gusher percolating to apex before breaking apart into a sparkling coronet of water drops caught by the dying rays of the sun, all of it captured perfectly in her camera.

She got the shot!

Jubilantly she celebrated her sense of timing and good fortune, because within seconds the surroundings utterly changed. A faint mist plumed upward and merged with a low cloud hanging in shreds, followed by a heavy fog bank that rolled in obliterating the sea cave, ending any further picture taking. Keegan unmounted the camera, collapsed the tripod, and headed for the sea wall, now nothing more than a faint outline in the mist.

"Okay, Daisy," she called. "Let's go home before it starts to rain."

Cold foggy air hugged the sea wall and swirled around the castle built for a giant, but Daisy was gone.

CHAPTER FOURTEEN

White lane divider lines spooled out on the highway heading west toward San Diego. Dante was driving. Keegan, wound so tight Dante was afraid she was going to snap, stared straight ahead not speaking. He could feel the tension pulsing off her in waves.

The remoteness of Monument Valley made it difficult to travel any way other than by car, especially if you had to leave in a hurry. The closest major airport was in Salt Lake City, a six-hour drive north, the opposite direction they needed to go. Sky Harbor International Airport in Phoenix was about the same distance away in the right direction, but if they were going to drive that far, it was easier and more convenient to just drive the rest of the way to San Diego than deal with the airport hassle.

Only Keegan couldn't drive there at all.

After the phone call from Jeffrey, she jumped to her feet and grabbed her purse. "My car!" she cried, her eyes wide. "My car is still being repaired."

Dante didn't have to think twice. He stuffed a change of clothes in a duffel bag, drove Keegan to her bungalow so she could pack, and ninety minutes later, as sunlight abandoned the sky, they were on the road heading for California.

Now, a dome of inky blackness pinpricked with a million stars stretched in all directions overhead. Dante pushed his speed as much as he dared, his eyes probing the darkness beyond the headlights, keenly aware of the danger of animals on the road in this open range country. Once they reached the interstate, he could pick up speed and make up some time.

Keegan's hands were in her lap, clasped tight. Her face displayed no panic, just angry defeat. Her rigid posture hardly changed, except now her head was turned slightly off center, eyes moving, watching the roadside utility poles approach then race by in a blur.

She made a small sound.

"What?" he said. "I didn't hear you."

"I didn't say anything," she answered, words clipped, voice taut.

"Oh," he said. "I thought I saw your lips move."

"No," she replied, then compressed her lips and closed her eyes.

There was no other conversation. What was there to say? He had no words of comfort for her. It was pretty common knowledge that strangers abduct children for only one thing, and chances of her daughter being found alive after that weren't good. Statistically no chance at all. She must have known that on some level. Yet she'd been sustained by hope.

He wished she'd fall asleep, release some of the awful tension holding her body so rigid. But when she woke up in San Diego forced to face the reality that her daughter was dead, then what? Did she have friends to stand by her? Where was her family? He wondered if she was in a relationship with someone, if there was someone she loved.

He knew almost nothing about her personal life, and that especially was none of his business. He switched his thoughts back to the questions surrounding Earlene's murder, and his conversation with Keegan, which raised even more questions. About Sandra Wolf's story of a kidnapping, and Jilly's claim that her mother lied about not knowing anyone in the photo.

He'd have to have Keegan show him the picture again so he could take a closer look at it.

And Yuma Ray's strange behavior. He was a man of standing in the tribe, influential, prominent, respected in the hallowed halls of Washington, D.C., as well as on the reservation. Why would he be driving around and knocking on her door late at night?

Dante felt a frisson of unease and followed the thought a little further. Was Keegan in some kind of danger? Was Earlene's murder connected? Secrets abounded on the reservation, but who was harboring a secret worth killing for?

On the ramp to the interstate, he kicked up his speed and merged into the sparse traffic hurtling along the moonlit freeway. After he settled into the speed lane, he slid his eyes sideways, glancing at her profile.

She had reclined her seat a little so she could stretch out her legs. Light and shadow danced over her face. Despite her taut features, she looked like a woman who had been well cared for. Through a door ajar in her bungalow, he'd caught a glimpse of the treadmill that no doubt contributed to her great body. He couldn't help noticing what good shape she was in the day she appeared in his camp with her shirt wrapped around her head.

Her short dark hair lay wispy and glossy in a precisely razored, expensive looking cut. Her hands and nails showed the attentions of a manicurist. Either that, or she spent a lot of time on them herself.

Her skin looked smooth and soft, but now, in her distress, lacked luminosity. Her face was drawn, devoid of makeup that had worn off hours ago. Makeup wouldn't have done much to hide the gray tint washing under her eyes, the lines between her sculpted brows and along the sides of her full mouth. The struggle to control her emotions was taking a heavy toll.

A three-quarter moon hung halfway down the sky as they

crossed the state line and entered California. A shudder reverberated through him, dark memories rumbling to escape.

He dreaded going back and knew it was risky. He might still be recognized. San Diego was where it all happened. Where his world fell apart, his marriage broke up, his career and good name destroyed. The legal expenses broke him, and when the money was gone, his wife left, too.

His face had been on the front of every newspaper, gossip magazine and tabloid on every newsstand and supermarket checkout counter. Demonized and discredited by the media, he'd been dogged by a trail of investigative reporters intent on ferreting out any real or perceived wrongdoing, all the while flaunting First Amendment rights and hiding behind the privilege of protecting their sources.

It hadn't been all that difficult to come up with Dante's signature on an incriminating document. After that, there was no stopping them. He was tried and convicted by the media. They had taken everything from him but his life. That they left for the vultures.

It was just beginning daylight when the highway cut through a flat expanse of desert dotted with sage and thorny scrub brush. Dante cast a look to his left, where the Mexican border was close enough to touch with his elbow. To the north lay the ghost of the eerie Salton Sea, two hundred feet below sea level. As he neared the city, more memories careened back. The betrayal, the rage. The lies, the deception. The threats.

To the men he'd worked with, men with grudge and ambition, whistleblowers were the worst kind of vermin; they were snitches. Dante's bosses, and their bosses, the ones who hadn't gone to jail, had scores to settle, payback prompted by revenge. Dante knew they had the right kind of contacts, other men who, with no more than a nod, were powerful enough to make someone disappear.

But he hadn't waited for them to do it. He did it himself when he went to the Navajo Reservation, a remote and mysterious land within a land, where it was easy to vanish. Where people didn't like answering the questions of strangers. Where it was easy to hide from the outside world.

As the sun brightened over San Diego, Dante wandered the dark corridors of his memory.

They arrived too early. The security guard at the desk in the lobby of the building on Farnham Street where the medical examiner's office was located told Keegan they didn't open to the public until nine. Dante took her across the street to a Starbuck's. She sat outside while he went in to order lattes and scones. At that early hour, there was a long line at the counter.

Keegan was grateful for the opportunity to sit down and collect herself before facing the ordeal that awaited her. She needed the time to calm down and catch her breath. A faint flutter of anxiety that was never too far away brought on a shiver. Someone walking over her grave, her grandmother would say.

She felt groggy, achy and drained. She'd slept only fitfully despite the sleep inducing hiss and hum of tires on pavement.

A burning sob rose in her chest at the thought of what she had to do, what she was about to see.

Oh, please, God, make this go away. Don't let it be Daisy.

She watched the cars passing. When the fifth black car goes by, she thought in desperation, I'll wake up from this horrible nightmare.

One.

Two.

Three.

Dante came out the door, pushing it open with his hip and elbow. He set the coffees and a bag of scones on the table, took sugar packets out of his pocket.

"Here are some extra sugars. Is that enough cream? You said plenty, so I just guessed."

"Yes. That's fine. Thank you." She took the coffee gratefully. Her first sip sent a burst of badly needed energy through her.

Dante, looking tired and jittery, took the scones out of the bag, set them on paper plates, and fussed with the napkins. He pushed a plate across the table toward her, and held out a fork.

"Here," he said.

His skin was sallow, his eyes sagged with a weight that wasn't his to bear, the corners of his mouth turned down by fatigue. But here he was, rescuing her again. What would she have done without him to drive her here? She was indebted to him and told him so.

"No thanks needed," he said, shrugging it off. "I'm glad I was there to help. Have you called your mother to tell her?"

Keegan nodded. "She's in Phoenix. She drove up from Tucson to be with my grandmother in the hospital. I said I'd let them know as soon as . . . as soon as it was over."

She finished her coffee and pushed the cup away. The sun moved higher in the sky, warming her back and neck. Across from her, Dante put on sunglasses and looked at his watch.

"It's after nine," he said. "We should go."

Her stomach clenched. "Yes." Her eyes darted to the street. No black cars.

When they returned to the glass-domed marble lobby, Jeffrey was sitting on a vinyl and chrome sofa with Special Agent Joe Porfino, the FBI investigator working on Daisy's case. Both men rose when Keegan entered. Jeffrey opened his arms and rushed to her, slipping Dante a curious, disapproving look.

She let Jeffrey embrace her briefly, then turned to Agent Porfino. He was tall and long-boned, a scarecrow of a man who looked like he was called upon daily to smother his joy and replace it with the worst the world had to offer. Things like accompanying mothers to view the dead bodies of their children.

With effort, she struggled to control a rush of emotion. Daisy had been missing for two years. After the first few months, the investigation had gone nowhere. In her mind, Agent Porfino had quit on her, and she had to work hard not to let her anger at him become overwhelming.

How could a child disappear into goddamn thin air from a goddamn public beach?

Daisy would never have willingly gone off with anyone. Stranger danger lessons were too deeply ingrained. Daisy must have screamed and called for her, but Keegan had heard no sound on the beach that morning except the crashing of the waves. Guilt expanded inside her chest. She didn't know why the weight of it didn't crush her where she stood.

Agent Porfino held out his hand, and Keegan shook it, then introduced Dante. Porfino said hello and shook Dante's hand, but Jeffrey just glared rudely at Dante while subjecting his hand to a bone-crushing grip, after which they ignored each other in mutual disregard.

They took the elevator to an upper floor, where a receptionist directed them to a family counseling room. It was decorated in various shades of beige and contained comfortable upholstered furniture in warm soft colors. At the far end of the room was a set of windowless double doors.

After a minute of ear ringing silence, the doors opened and a heavyset man came in. He greeted Porfino, then introduced himself to the others as a medical investigator. He had stick straight black hair and a carefully cultivated soul patch under his bottom lip. He was wearing a long white lab coat over jeans. Latex gloves covered his hands. Around his neck was a big, brushed silver cross on a silver chain. He carried a clipboard securing several sheets of paper. He looked at the topmost sheet, then at her.

"Keegan Thomas?"

Keegan stepped forward. Jeffrey gave Dante a poisonous look and stepped forward with her, taking her arm. Keegan politely shouldered him away.

"Are you the mother?" the medical investigator asked.

"Yes."

He swung his eyes from Dante to Jeffrey. "Is this the child's father?"

"No. Daisy's father and I are divorced."

The medical investigator made a notation on his clipboard, asked more questions, and wrote down her answers. When he finished, he looked at her with sympathy in his eyes.

"Mrs. Thomas, I need to let you know, this will not be easy. The body was in the desert long enough for decomposition to begin. Before she was left there, she'd been pretty badly beaten."

Keegan held a breath and counted her heartbeats. Slowly, she released it, steeling herself.

"They found her in Anza Borrego," Porfino added. "A hiker spotted her at the bottom of Font's Point. It looked like she'd been there several weeks."

"Several *weeks?*" Stunned, Keegan's thoughts leaped around, making connections too horrible to grasp. "But she's been gone over *two years!*"

Porfino stared at her, his face unreadable, saying nothing.

"So that means she's been alive all this time? Someone's had her for two *years* . . ." Keegan's voice trailed away, and she fought off the unbearable unthinkable. Her mind tried to take her to places she didn't want to go, tortured her with horrible images of Daisy subjected to the nightmarish desires of a sexual predator.

The medical investigator spoke next. "We've done some DNA testing using hair from the hairbrush you provided when your little girl went missing, but we won't have the results for some time. Agent Porfino said you had asked to be notified immediately if we found her. You've agreed to view the body."

Accepting the inevitable, Keegan nodded, a cascade of dread tumbling through her. Words wouldn't come because of the tears crowding her throat.

"Come with me," he said.

With Porfino, Dante, and Jeffrey trailing behind, the medical investigator led Keegan into a viewing room that was as cold and spare as a hospital operating suite, all shiny metal surfaces and a slick tile floor. In the middle of the room was a stainless steel gurney covered with a sheet. Keegan smothered a gasp at the sight of the tiny shape shrouded beneath it.

Anxiety leaped and turned in her like a flock of frightened birds taking wing. Her heart was racing. She swallowed hard, and had to look away, staring instead at the lights in the ceiling.

The medical investigator pulled the sheet back revealing a translucent plastic bag unzipped at the top exposing the upper torso of a little girl. It took enormous concentration for Keegan to turn her head and look at it. With fierce resolve, she lowered her eyes to the lifeless body. The first sight was a savage blow to her heart.

The skin on the child's body was the color of gray wax, a stark contrast to the purplish red of her face. Mouth gaping, eyes swollen to slits, the face so badly damaged from a beating, and later the effects of sun and desert scavengers, it was unrecognizable.

Keegan swallowed hard. "Was she . . . sexually . . ." She couldn't bring herself to ask the question, not sure she wanted to know.

"Sexually assaulted?" the investigator finished for her. "Yes."

Inside, she crumbled. "May I see her hands?"

The medical investigator reached under the sheet and pulled out the child's arms. He laid them across her middle on top of the plastic. The fingernails were ragged and torn, the cuticles split, no doubt signs of a struggle. Keegan could see the little finger on the left hand was broken. The callous cruelty of this child's fate was unfathomable. Clearly death had not been instantaneous.

Keegan made herself slow her breathing, forcing the air past the knot of nausea in her stomach. She swayed, feeling lightheaded, and was shaking so hard, Dante reached out to steady her. She leaned into him.

She opened her mouth to speak. Words backed up in her throat for a long time, then broke forth like an ice jam had given way.

"That's not Daisy."

CHAPTER FIFTEEN

In the Fountain Café at the Doubletree Hotel in Mission Valley's Hazard Center, a long-haired movie star hopeful, leggy and angular with the look of a saluki, pranced over to the table to take their order. Dante was punchy with exhaustion after driving all night, and Keegan, running on adrenaline, agreed that it was a good idea to spend the night in San Diego before heading back to the reservation. Dante went to the front desk to get rooms. Keegan sat over a cup of coffee trying to sort her emotions.

When Daisy was born, the first thing she and Brady looked at were her hands, afraid the baby had inherited the Thomas family's worst physical trait—unattractive wide, flat fingernails. Brady was, uncharacteristically for a man, self-conscious of his hands, and his mother and sisters were so ashamed of theirs, they were never seen without artificial nails.

"She has beautiful fingernails," Brady had said of the tiny newborn, even before counting the fingers. Keegan, through a post delivery haze, insisted on seeing for herself. He was right. They were pearly pink, oval-shaped and delicate.

The fingernails on the dead child in the San Diego County morgue were broad and flat-planed.

Keegan's emotions floundered in that oceanic space filling the gulf between grief and relief, and for a brief second an irrepressible spark of happiness filled her. Though she would still be forced to live the nightmare of not knowing where Daisy

143

was, she could continue to hold out hope that her daughter was alive.

Keegan opened her phone and punched in the international code for Brady's personal cell phone number. Earlier, she'd left a message at his office, but hadn't heard back. He still wasn't answering, but there was a time zone change she was too tired to calculate. He could be out to dinner, or at one of his countless meetings, or traveling out of signal range, or in bed with someone. She left another message telling him the happy and sad news about Daisy, then called her mother to tell her.

Keegan's mother was still at Hazel Cole's bedside. "Your grandmother is asking for you," she said. "Is there any way you could stop at the hospital in Phoenix on your way through?"

"Is she worse?" A new dread began to form in Keegan's chest, something else to worry about.

"No. She's out of intensive care. Thankfully it was a minor stroke, but the doctor wants her to stay a few more days and rest. She's sleeping now. She's anxious to see you, though."

"Okay. Give her my love and tell her I'll be there tomorrow."

Keegan closed her phone and watched Dante coming across the lobby carrying a newspaper. He had the body of an athlete, long and lean in jeans and boots, his legs swinging forward in an easy, unstudied stride. He put two keycards on the table and sat down just as the server arrived with their lunch. Keegan told him about her conversation with her mother.

"Do you mind stopping at the hospital?" she asked.

"No. Of course not. Not at all."

His smile was weary, but it reached his eyes, so she knew it was genuine. He unfolded the newspaper, extracted the sports page and the business section.

"Do you want some of this paper?" he asked.

She nodded. "Thanks. I'll take whichever sections you aren't reading."

He handed them over, then picked up his fork.

She studied his face while he ate. His skin was bronzed, his thick hair burnished by the sun; he had that whole rugged outdoorsman thing working for him. Tired and hungry, worn out by troubles not his own, yet he'd still been able to work up a smile. That said a lot about him. He was a good man. A man of compassion.

She'd barely begun glancing through the paper when the quality of the air around the table changed, its energy so charged she could feel it shimmering on her skin. She looked up to see Dante staring at the newspaper in the grip of some thought that washed ripples of pain over his features. He was reading fast, his eyes darting over the words. He paled.

"Dante? Is something wrong?"

His brow clouded, and tight lines appeared around his mouth. He didn't answer.

She lowered her fork. "Dante?"

Quickly, he folded the newspaper and laid it to the side.

"No, nothing. It's nothing," he said, his eyes bouncing off hers. He glowered and motioned to the newspaper beside his plate. "I just read something about my old boss. The company I used to work for here in San Diego. Venture Real Estate Development."

She waited for him to go on, to say something that would explain his reaction. When he didn't, she asked, "What about them?"

"They're bidding on that new Navajo resort construction project in Monument Valley. Just surprised me, that's all." He picked up the sports page, and his face slipped into the kind of expression that told her it wasn't a subject for further discussion.

After lunch Dante headed straight to his room to sleep, but Keegan was too full of energy to settle down. She hadn't heard from Justin Bickham at the National Archives. The archives building was less than an hour away, so Dante had handed over the car keys and she drove to Laguna Nigel.

She exited I-5 at Oso Parkway, and parked under a eucalyptus tree in front of a squatty tiered building that reminded her of a Mayan temple with the top tiers lopped off. Inside she approached a studious looking young woman furiously typing away on the computer, and asked to see Justin Bickham.

"Justin is no longer with the National Archives," the woman told her.

Keegan's heart fell. This was a major setback. Now she'd have to tell the whole story and start all over again with someone new. Her disappointment dissolved at the receptionist's next words.

"But you can speak to Henry Parker," she said. "He took over all of Justin's research requests. I'll call him for you."

Henry Parker appeared through a door and greeted Keegan at the counter. He was wearing a suit and tie, an unusual sight in any workplace these days, and the kind of running shoes old people wore to comfort aging feet. He had a shock of thick white hair and a wide mouth just meant for smiling, which he did now, showing a beautiful display of teeth.

She started to repeat everything she'd told Justin, but he stopped her.

"I'm familiar with what you're looking for," he told her. "Justin spoke to me about it before he left." The old man promised to finish the search that Justin had begun and call her in a few days. "What's your phone number, dear?"

She gave him both cell phone numbers, thanked him, and left.

Henry Parker watched Keegan walk across the lobby and out the door. He sighed tiredly. He was swamped with research requests. Even though he promised to call her next week, he didn't really know how soon he'd be able to start looking for the records she needed.

Henry shook his head, thinking about Justin Bickham. His leaving had made a short staff even shorter. Everyone was buried with work. Only Justin hadn't resigned, as he'd let Keegan believe. Justin had been fired, caught trying to sneak documents out of the archives hidden under his belt and in his sock.

Even with the new records tracking system Henry had designed, he had to admit stealing records wasn't impossible. He wondered what else Justin Bickham had managed to slip past security before being caught. Henry was old enough to know that the first time someone was caught doing something wrong did not mean it was the first time they'd done it.

Back in his office, he put Keegan's note aside and sat down at his typewriter. As soon as he had a chance, he would go upstairs to see how much progress Justin had made on his research project for her.

The next day, Dante dropped Keegan off at the Paradise Valley Hospital, while he went off to take care of some personal business and make some phone calls. Keegan found her grandmother propped up by pillows watching television. Apparently, not even a stroke could disrupt her usual routine of afternoon talk and reality shows. The closing credits for *Judge Judy* were rolling when Keegan peeked in from the hallway. The room was neat and clean, everything tightly tucked and folded, with nothing out of place, as squared away as a hospital room should be. A flower arrangement on the deep window sill added color.

Hazel Cole didn't look to be in particular distress, considering she was past her mid-eighties. Her white hair floated around her head, surrounding it like a nimbus. A nasal cannula under her nose was connected to a plastic tube that hissed with supplemental oxygen. In point of fact, Hazel Cole looked more annoyed than sick, but she smiled and her expression softened when Keegan came in.

After a prolonged hug, Keegan took her grandmother's hand, blue-veined and more frail looking than she remembered, and held it gently. It felt like a sack of tiny bird bones. They talked a long time about Daisy and how empty life seemed without her in it, then about the stroke that had sent Hazel to the hospital, and finally about how much her grandmother missed Lincoln Cole.

"Life isn't the same without him," Hazel said, plunging into remembered gloom. "He was the only man I've ever loved. I'm just sorry I didn't show it when he was alive." After a moment of quiet reflection, she gathered her emotions and changed the subject.

"Where are you staying in Monument Valley? I think you told me, but I forgot. I can't seem to hold on to things so well anymore."

"I rented one of the bungalows at Goulding's," Keegan told her. She went on to describe its convenience and coziness, but was interrupted by a question from her grandmother.

"Have you found anyone in that photo?"

"No," she replied. "It was so long ago, Gram, either no one remembers or they don't want to talk about it. And besides, those people may not even be living now."

"But there are children," Hazel insisted. "They'd still be alive."

"Yes, but no one recognizes them after all this time. And they may have moved away from the reservation," she added. "Lots of the kids leave to go to college and get jobs elsewhere. There are any number of reasons they wouldn't still be there. One of the kids in the picture was kidnapped."

"Which one? Which child?"

Keegan studied her grandmother's suddenly animated face. Her upper body was striped with sunlight falling though the blinds. Outside the window, a Gila woodpecker excavated a nest cavity inside the pulpy flesh of an old saguaro.

"The little girl," Keegan answered. "She was taken by missionaries and sent to a boarding school. Only she was never returned. No one ever saw her again."

Hazel's fingers tightened around Keegan's hand. "Are you going to look for her?"

"I don't think so, Gram. I have no idea where they would have taken her. Most of the Indian schools closed years ago."

Turbulent currents of poorly disguised urgency swirled behind her grandmother's eyes, and the pressure of her hand on Keegan's increased even more.

"You have to look for her," Hazel said. "Please don't give up."

"But I don't know where to look. I don't even know her name," Keegan protested.

An expression of extremely personal pain crossed the old woman's features. Her eyes were sad and imploring. "Her name is Lulu Etsitty," she said.

Keegan's mouth fell open and she stared. That was the name she found on the note in Earlene's *jish* bag. "How do you know that?"

Hazel slipped her fingers out of Keegan's, pressed them to the bridge of her nose, then let her hand fall to her side. She laid her head back against the pillow and spoke of an earlier time.

"Your grandfather and I went to the reservation as newly-weds," she said, recalling happier days. "When he was offered the opportunity to run a BIA clinic in Monument Valley, he jumped at the chance to help those so desperately in need of care. At the time, Monument Valley was so isolated, so cut off,

149

the Indians were dying for lack of transportation. The poorer ones especially had no way to get to doctors for badly needed medical care. Your grandfather was the only physician located on that part of the reservation."

A smile crossed her face, swinging wide a door in her memory. "Oh, my, he was handsome. Tall and strong, with a full head of wavy hair. I was so proud to be his wife."

The television droned in the background as the past came scrabbling back to her. She looked as if she were reliving every minute of it.

"At the time, the Gouldings still lived above the trading post. They let us live in one of the guest cabins, an old potato shack, really, and the clinic was set up in a tent. At first the Indians were suspicious. They didn't trust white doctors, thought the BIA sent them to practice and experiment on them. Many of them wouldn't go for necessary surgeries, and refused to let their children be vaccinated or receive other life-saving treatment. But your grandfather was so gentle and kind, he eventually persuaded the mothers to bring their children, and eventually the adults came to him, too."

Her eyes fell closed and when she spoke again, an edge of bitterness crept into her voice.

"At first, it was a romantic adventure. But I came to hate living there. Your grandfather was at the clinic all day and late into the night. I had no place to go and nothing to do except stare out the window at miles and miles of red nothingness. I think I started to go a little crazy with it after a while. I begged your grandfather to leave, but he refused."

She paused and sighed before going on.

"After your mother was born, it was a little better. Your grandfather was still busy, hardly ever away from the clinic, but I wasn't so lonely anymore. I had a baby to care for and I loved doing that. For a while."

Keegan listened intently. Her grandmother had never before talked so openly about her life in Monument Valley.

"You have to understand, Keegan. It was nothing more than a primitive tent-strewn outpost surrounded by a stillness that was no longer peaceful for me. After a while none of it was beautiful. Everything looked fractured and broken. There was dirt and dust everywhere. It was impossible to stay clean. Hygiene was poor. Food was sometimes scarce. No running water. Blistering hot in the summer, snow and freezing rain in the winter. The roads would be closed for days. If they weren't blocked by snow, they were impassable because of the mud."

She shook her head at memories she no longer wished to recall.

"And there was so much sickness! All the children wheezing and coughing all the time, and the adults, too. Always sick." Her eyes glistened with tears.

"Then I had another baby, and I wanted to go back to Phoenix. We argued about it all the time. Your grandfather refused to go. He didn't want to leave the Indians without a doctor. I insisted. We had a terrible fight. I left him and came back to Phoenix with my babies."

"Oh, Gram. I didn't know. That must have been hard."

Her grandmother looked at her a long time.

"But that's not the only reason I left," she replied. Then, "Do you have the picture with you?"

Keegan opened her bag and took it out. Hazel gazed at it, tears gathering. She touched it with her fingertip.

"This is Lulu Etsitty. The woman holding her in the shawl is Teaya. She was this lovely Indian girl, about eighteen, very sweet. Beautiful long black hair, big dark eyes. She adored your grandfather. And, considering how much hell I was giving him, I don't blame him for adoring her in return. Teaya is Lulu's mother. Your grandfather is Lulu's father."

Thunderstruck, Keegan's thoughts tumbled, a rush of emotion coming from nowhere and everywhere at once.

"Teaya is the reason I left," Hazel went on. "I was so angry and hurt. I cried for three days after Lulu was born. Then I came back to Phoenix."

Keegan stared at her grandmother, too flabbergasted to say anything.

"After a couple of years, the BIA sent another doctor and your grandfather came back to us. I never forgave him for being unfaithful and I never let him forget how much he hurt me. He wanted to send money to care for the child, but I wouldn't let him. Threatened to leave him if he did. I demanded he forget that part of his life. To please me and to keep his family together, he did. But I think he died inside."

The tap-tap-tap of the busy woodpecker sounded from outside. A nurse came in, white-soled shoes squeaking on the linoleum floor. She smiled and nodded hello, checked the drip on the IV bag, and left.

"Does my mother know she has a . . . a half sister?" Keegan asked.

"No, not yet. I was hoping you'd be able to find Lulu before I told your mother."

"Does Richard know? Is that why he gave me the picture? Does he know those people?"

"No. Your cousin had no idea how happy I was when he told me you were going to the reservation to find them for a story. No one in the family knows. Except you."

Keegan pulled in a breath and tried to think of something to say. A terrible sadness overcame her. Her grandmother had lived almost an entire lifetime clutching the shards of a fierce and painful past. Now she was nearing the end of her life. She looked into her grandmother's eyes and saw them filled with remorse.

"Will you find Lulu and bring her to me? I owe her an apology and so much more. Please don't let me die with this regret. I was hateful and selfish. I'm asking you to help me find forgiveness for denying her all these years. I don't deserve forgiveness, I admit, but I'm going to ask her for it anyway."

Silently, Keegan did some quick calculations in her mind. Lulu would be in middle-age by now. Even if Keegan could find her, would she want to come to Phoenix to meet Lincoln Cole's wife?

"Bring Teaya, too, if she's still alive."

"Gram, look at the picture again. Do you know anyone else? Please look closely. I'll do whatever I can to find Teaya and Lulu, but I have nothing to go on."

Hazel looked at the photo, her eyes moving slowly studying each face.

"This was your grandfather's nurse." She pointed to a woman standing to his left and slightly behind. "Not really a nurse, but she helped him at the clinic. Gave shots, swabbed throats, administered vaccinations, that kind of thing. She could read and write, so she did the recordkeeping, too.

"Her name was Earlene Cly."

Chapter Sixteen

Back in Monument Valley, good news waited. Not only was Keegan's car ready, the mechanic was willing to deliver it. For this she was grateful. Dante had already gone out of his way for her. She didn't want to impose on him further. Earlene's family was still in mourning, so Keegan was reluctant to ask Jilly to drive her to Farmington to pick it up.

Her stomach knotted around thoughts of Jilly and Earlene, and Sandra, too. Earlene hadn't pointed herself out in that photo nor had she mentioned being Lincoln Cole's assistant. And while Keegan could believe Jilly might not recognize a younger version of her grandmother in an old faded photograph, surely Sandra would know her own mother.

Now that she had something to go on—the names her grandmother had given her—she called Henry Parker to tell him.

"Lulu Etsitty. Teaya Etsitty. Earlene Cly," Keegan told him, spelling the names and speaking slowly so Henry could write them down.

"It might not be so easy finding records on individuals," Henry said. "The lineage for most Navajo families was unrecorded in the old days. Most of it was passed down from one generation to the next. It's not like today," he added. "We like to document and chronicle everything now. I'm recording oral histories for my grandchildren."

The mechanic arrived with her car, and she wrote out a check for the repair including a healthy tip for bringing it to her. Then she drove to the post office to check her mail.

Unlike her grandmother, who saw Monument Valley as an empty and inhospitable land, Keegan found that, after only a few days away, she had missed its stark beauty and quiet inspiration. The desert called out to her soul in the red dawns and orange sunsets that draped the land in a mantle the color of life, and in the golden afternoons that echoed its history. It was impossible to believe the cathedral-like monuments rising so majestically into the air were not emitting a strain of music too finely tuned for outsiders to hear.

But Keegan could hear it, and it was with a rush of warmth that she realized her DNA was here. She wasn't just *in* Monument Valley anymore, she was also *of* it. Because her grandfather had breached a matrimonial boundary, she was connected to this land and its people in a way she couldn't deny, indisputably connected by blood and an act of love.

Regardless of the circumstances, and without diminishing her grandmother's pain, Keegan saw this as a gift rather than something to be ashamed of or angry about. If anything, her desire to find Lulu was stronger than ever.

She was still reeling from her grandmother's stunning revelation about Lulu's parentage, but strangely, her knowledge of Lincoln Cole's indiscretion didn't change the way she felt about him. It had happened so long ago, the chasm created by the distance in time made it easy for Keegan to imagine her grandmother had told a story about people she didn't know. Distant relatives maybe, or neighbors on the next block.

As long as Keegan could remember, her grandfather had been a person in no particular need of words, a man who did not readily call them up, but he'd been a loving grandfather nonetheless. Now, though, Keegan wondered if his reticence wasn't the result of Hazel's admittedly bitter, soul-searing re-

155

criminations.

Keegan's mother rarely talked about her childhood, only hinting at the strained relationship between her parents and, in turn, her strained relationship with them. Once, after too much Christmas wine and in the mood to unburden her heart, Keegan's mother had sullenly referred to the atmosphere in her childhood home as a sort of choked silence interrupted only by the harsh words of her parents when they couldn't avoid speaking to each other.

When Keegan was a child, the behavior of her grandparents seemed little more than odd. As she got older, she became accustomed to it. Now she understood the dynamics. Still, she chose to restore her grandfather to the version she knew and loved, the kindly old man who took her to the park and pushed her on the swing, or let her sit on his lap and put pink pinchy clips in his snowy white hair while he watched the baseball game on television.

She arrived at the post office, a slope-roofed boxy building, a modified mobile home really, at the end of a bumpy, washed out dirt road. A yellow slip in her post office box instructed her to pick up her mail at the counter.

"You got a lot of mail," the Navajo postal clerk commented. She hefted three small boxes, and a half dozen bulking manila envelopes in a cardboard sorting tray onto the wooden countertop, all of it imprinted with a National Archives return address. A crisp, official looking white business-size envelope lay on top.

"You must be doin' research or something," said the clerk. "Are you from the college, or writing a book?"

Keegan shook her head. "No, not a book. But I am writing a magazine article. I'm doing some family research."

Dubious, the pretty Navajo studied Keegan's face. "Searching for Indian ancestors, huh? You don't look Indian."

Keegan laughed. "I'm not," she responded, knowing but not

minding that she'd just been labeled a *wannabe*.

Keegan carried it all out and stashed it on the passenger seat, but unable to wait, she opened the white envelope right away. Inside, was a letter from Justin Bickham, obviously written before he left. He informed her that her grandfather's BIA records had been misplaced in the bureaucratic tangle that was Washington, D.C., but he was sending her some unrelated records she might find helpful. He promised to keep looking. Now that he'd quit his job, she knew she'd never hear from him again. She was depending on old Henry Parker now.

Back at her bungalow, she sliced the boxes open with a kitchen knife, and removed bundles of photocopied documents. Some of the pages were held together with paper clips, some were stapled and folded. Many were loose sheets in seemingly random order.

From the look of the copies, some of the original documents must have been in very poor condition. She could discern torn edges, crease marks, and water damage. It looked like some of the documents were simply deteriorating from age. Whole paragraphs of text were faded, making them difficult to read.

Expectantly, she thumbed through the files, looking for mission school records. All she found were a few incomplete attendance reports signed by school social workers, and a partial list of schools, some of them sponsored by local churches or mission outposts. Most were located in New Mexico, Colorado, and Arizona, but not all. With a red pen, she checked off the schools that had been located nearby. She'd visit those first.

The bulk of the material appeared to be statistical in nature, the kind of pencil pushing busywork that had always been required by the government. Handwritten ledger sheets of accounting records, endless pages of legalese relating to land leases and land sales, more detailed ledger sheets.

Someone had meticulously logged population and census tallies, as well as the names of Indians of more than half white blood holding trust land, each with a notarized affidavit attached. She paid close attention to these and anything with a list of names. There were lots of Clys and Etsittys showing. Large extended families had apparently always been commonplace on the reservation. She couldn't be sure any of them were related to Teaya or Lulu or Earlene.

It wasn't long before her eyes glazed over from reading endless columns of figures and dates, and her mind strayed from the repetitious reports documenting everything from births and deaths to mining activities on Indian land. She sat back, blinked her tired eyes, and rubbed them to ease the strain. Why had Justin sent her all this? Except for the list of schools, most of it had little to do with what she'd asked for.

She flipped through the remaining records until she came to some reports that related directly to Indian Health Service activities. A thick stack of correspondence between the Indian Health Service and Washington, D.C., dealt almost exclusively with congressional hearings held to examine the poor quality of care available to Indians. Reading further, she found the hearings had been prompted by the results of a sanitation survey.

She skimmed through annual and semiannual reports that consisted mainly of more eye-crossing columns of numbers, but took her time over patient lists from hospitals, dentists, and field nurses. For the moment, she skipped over a general health survey of the tribe, coming at last to copies of actual medical files of individual patients, all of them written by visiting nurses from one of the distant hospitals.

It seemed the nurses assigned to Monument Valley traveled to other settlements on the reservation as well, remote outposts like Dennehotso, Rough Rock, and Rock Point. Most of their reports consisted of statistical information such as how many visits were made to which patients each month, how many were for prenatal care and child welfare, mainly newborn care or household hygiene. It confirmed what her grandmother had said. Disease was prevalent. Tuberculosis, pneumonia, whooping cough, dysentery. Skin lesions were common. Carefully documented was how many new patients were seen each week, and how many had been treated previously.

Some of the reports included narrative sections, but the amount of detail varied greatly depending on which nurse wrote it. Some were quite descriptive, mentioning things like the progress made with household cleanliness and hand washing, the kind of dental care given, and the condition of the roads, which seemed to be a popular topic, especially in the winter months. They all included the names of individuals and their specific ailments, noting whether the patient was diagnosed by a nurse, or by a physician who had actually made the trip out to see the patient.

Something spun through her mind too fast to catch, a fleeting thought that gave her a swift kick, then dematerialized before it could register in her brain. She sat a moment, staring out the window at the late afternoon sunlight that flooded the valley, her foot doing the nervous little jiggle it always did when she was trying to figure something out. She caught herself counting the jiggles, then got up, fixed a cup of tea, then settled in again, opening an envelope labeled *Indian Health Service, Phoenix Area Office.*

According to what she read in the memos and reports in those files, government physicians were assigned to various hospitals at Fort Defiance, Window Rock, and Tuba City. No physicians were assigned to Monument Valley or any other outpost on that part of the reservation. It was the field nurses who traveled throughout the reservation, each assigned to various districts and responsible for preventative care and education among the Navajos.

She stopped reading, went back, and read that last part again, turning it over in her mind.

"Hmmm," she said aloud. "That can't be right."

If the BIA hadn't dispatched any physicians to Monument Valley, why had they sent her grandfather there? Or if it wasn't the BIA who had sent him, who was it? She laid the questions out side by side in her mind, thought a moment, then shrugged, deciding the answers were in the misplaced files she hoped Henry Parker would be able to locate.

She gathered up the papers spread across her tabletop, sorted them into neat piles, separating out the list of Indian schools and other school related documents. Those she put in her purse. Tomorrow she'd try to find the schools that had been on this part of the reservation. Jilly had mentioned an old mission in Bluff along the San Juan River. She'd start there.

With luck, and Keegan held only faint hope here, someone over the years had managed to retain student records. Finding the school where the missionaries had taken Lulu was the first step to finding Lulu.

Exasperated, Dante slapped his hand on the hood of his truck and swore through his teeth.

"What the hell!"

He'd left so unexpectedly for San Diego with Keegan, he hadn't secured his dig site the way he normally would have if he'd known in advance he was going to be away for more than a day.

But he hadn't worried about it too much. There were dig sites all over this area of the West, and most people living here had a tenacious respect for archaeologists and their work. Normally, anyone accidentally coming across his camp wouldn't disturb it. The only reason he ever staked a tarp over his dig was to protect it from weather and wildlife, not necessarily from people.

But this destruction was not weather related nor had it been caused by wild animals. The tire treads furrowed through the excavation grid and imprinted on the side and roof of his flattened tent proved that.

He looked around and swore again.

Items he had painstakingly unearthed during the preceding months by slowly removing layers of soil, rubble, and ash from what had been an ancient community built a thousand years ago were scattered about the camp. Potsherds with the familiar gray and black on white design, and other rounded bottom vessels, some wholly intact, had been trampled to dust.

Inside the tent, artifacts he had carefully categorized and sorted into corrugated boxes, or laid out on the worktable for photographing, were now crushed and pulverized. Thankfully he hadn't left his laptop, but he had stored his handwritten field notes and some photographs inside the tent. They'd been ripped to shreds then trampled under someone's boot soles.

Angrily, he strode through dirt that had long since had its moisture sucked out by the baking sun and dry air to the midden pile he'd just begun to explore. In that spot, his trowel had uncovered dozens of tiny bones, the remains of many turkey dinners disposed of into the refuse heap by inhabitants of a long buried ancient village. Broken hand tools made of stone, and wrecked pottery, the mistakes of early artists, had also been tossed into what was essentially a garbage dump, but to researchers represented historical treasure.

Dante gusted out an irritated breath and sighed, doubting any of it could be salvaged. When the dig season ended in the fall, he had planned to backfill the entire site by replacing the soil, a fiercely protective act of preservation. Now, the destruction of the artifacts was so extensive, he had no choice but to rent a backhoe and bury it now.

He walked around, dismally toeing up potsherds from the dirt. Thankfully he hadn't found any human remains, but that didn't mean there weren't any. Under the terms of a federal law, all human remains and funerary objects excavated at archaeological sites or exposed in construction were to be returned to descendents for reburial.

Dante had considered that an appropriate and practical solution to a problem that had vexed Native Americans and archaeologists for years. It was also at the heart of his problems with Venture Real Estate Development.

He didn't have to wonder who had done this. He was pretty sure the media hadn't tracked him down, though it had crossed his mind that Keegan may have leaked his whereabouts to her media friends. He gave her the benefit of the doubt by dismissing that notion, and besides, the media wasn't interested in destroying his dig site. They had wanted to destroy him.

No, he had a pretty good idea who had done it and how Peter Venture had tracked him down. Dante's name along with everyone else being considered for work on the resort construction was listed in the bid packet, information that was readily available.

And Peter wouldn't hesitate to inform Emerson Bedonnie and the rest of the tribal leadership about Dante's questionable past.

The sun blazed over the rim of a broad mesa to the west, illuminating the message scrawled on the collapsed tent canvas. Dante gazed at it.

WE FOUND YOU, it said.

Just as Dante always feared they would.

Chapter Seventeen

Will Bedonnie stepped outside his trailer and looked up at a sky washed with color by the arrival of the sun. The celestial palette, the colors all swirled together, reminded him of the kaleidoscope Vicki brought him last year from a carnival in Shiprock.

He stood a moment looking into the east, then opened his *jish* bag and took out a pinch of corn pollen. He said a prayer welcoming the sun in a singsong, off-key, smoke roughened voice, then blessed the dawning day with a sprinkle of pollen into the air.

After another mumbled prayer, he made his way around back to a metal storage shed, walking on aging, sleep-stiffened legs. From inside the shed, he took out a coil of flexible wire, a ball of twine, a hand trowel, and a small hand rake. Then, reaching behind some old tires where it was hidden, he extracted a plastic Basha's grocery bag.

He glanced around, making sure he was alone, then opened the bag to check its contents. A stuffed teddy bear. A pink satin heart-shaped pillow. Plastic flowers woven into a garland. A thin silver chain with a tiny heart. His own heart pinched with emotion when he looked at it.

He sighed, closed the bag, and shut the door. He had to hurry. He didn't want to be gone long in case Vicki decided to come over to check on him. She came every few days, usually when his food got low. It was getting low now.

He shuffled to his pickup, which was nearly half as old as he was, the stiffness in his knees taking longer than usual to dissipate today. Lowering the tailgate, he put the wire and the string and the hand tools in the back, then climbed behind the steering wheel clutching the grocery bag.

The engine coughed and groaned when he turned the key, then caught and choked to a start. When the noisy rumble settled into an unsteady growl, he shifted into gear.

Vicki would be angry with him if she knew what he was doing. So would his brother Emerson. He had promised them he wouldn't go there anymore.

Will smiled to himself and chuckled out loud. Everyone thought he was a foolish old man, senile and forgetful, and maybe he was. But there were days, like today, when his memory of things that had occurred decades ago was as clear to him as if they had happened yesterday.

Gravel crunched under the tires as he rolled slowly out of his yard and down the dirt road until, with a bone-jarring bounce over the lip, he was on the paved highway. He scanned the distant horizon looking for the familiar outline of Meridian Butte, his destination. Before long, its massive bulk appeared in the long view, reaching into the rose and purple sky. He turned off into the red desert, gritty dust pelting the jolting vehicle, and speaking in Navajo, said a prayer of protection as he headed toward the special place in the rocks.

Keegan was on the road early under a glowing red-orange morning sky, heading for one of the local mission schools.

Nothing on the reservation was within walking distance. With few exceptions, any errand involved a twenty-mile drive. Traffic on the highway was light, and Keegan guessed that most of the traveling in Monument Valley was done over an unmarked network of unimproved back roads.

Just outside Mexican Hat, something in the gulley at the Valley of the Gods turnoff caught her eye. A highway fatality marker, a big one, down the incline several yards off the road. Curious, she pulled onto the shoulder and walked over to take a look. Her heart bumped when she laid eyes on it.

She remembered this horrible accident. It had been in all the papers. A busload of skiers returning to Phoenix from Telluride had skidded on a patch of ice and slid off the road, rolling over and over in this empty expanse of desert. The top of the bus had been sheared away, bodies thrown about into the darkness. It was January. There was snow. The dead and the injured had lain in the bitter cold and black nastiness for hours. The crash site was so remote, nobody's cell phone worked. It was two hours before a passerby appeared. His cell phone couldn't pick up a signal either, and he had to drive to the next town to summon help.

An inscription on the cross above the names of the survivors read *Utah Bus Crash—By The Grace of God.* A separate marker heralded the passing of those who didn't make it. *May You Ever Be Enjoying a Powder Day,* it said beneath a bronze engraving of a skier on the downhill.

Keegan let her gaze wander, the hair on her arms lifting ominously. The ground was still disturbed, roughed up. Deep ruts where the bus's tires dug into the earth had hardened in the mud. Crash debris was visible fifty yards or more into the desert. Broken pieces of the bus, of the luggage, of the ski equipment. Shattered glass glittered in the sun.

Keegan shuddered. The bad energy of the place jumped along her nerves making her jittery. Some of the souls are not at rest, she thought. They're still here. She hurried away and got back in her car, wondering how the Indians felt about this very visible reminder of the violent deaths of so many innocents.

In Bluff, she turned right at Twin Rocks, still thinking about the bus accident. She would have missed the mission entirely if it hadn't been for the sheep blocking the road. While she waited for the flock to cross, she noticed a small brass marker telling her the mission was a National Historic site.

The sheep took their own good time crossing despite some impatient horn honking from a driver in an oncoming vehicle with out-of-state plates who had been forced to stop. Over the fluffy backs of the sheep, Keegan could see him scowling through his windshield and waving his arms.

Two young Navajo girls and an energetic black and white shepherd dog worked hard to keep the strays from wandering off. Before long, the sound of bleating sheep and tinkling bells faded away into the desert. Keegan waited for the other car to go by, then turned left over the metal grate bridge onto the mission property.

It was a hodgepodge collection of buildings, some of stone, some of logs, some of adobe, all of indeterminate age that meandered over the grounds into an escarpment of sandstone. One of the larger structures, which looked like some sort of community center or all-purpose room, stood out, by its A-frame construction and bank of picture windows, as possibly having been built in the seventies. Nothing looked any newer than that. She drove slowly over mostly bare ground, past a clay brick building with a cross over the door.

She didn't see any people, but there were a few vehicles, so she knew someone was around somewhere. A sound carried on the breeze, and in the distance she saw a man on the roof of a barn, hammering.

Keegan parked under a cottonwood tree and walked around the grounds trying doors, which were all locked. Cupping her hands around her face to block the light, she looked in the windows of a classroom with a kitchenette on the far wall, but saw no one. The door of the administration building was locked, too, and she stood on the porch looking around for someone to speak to.

Farther back, behind a thicket of wavy leaf scrub oak and tucked into a rise of land, was a short, squat stone hut built into the earth. Its wooden door hung wide open. Parked nearby was a four-wheel-drive SUV with a black grille guard on its front end, and scrapes along the driver's side.

A scene rose up in her mind complete with sound and color, everything clear and vibrant except the make and model of a similar mud covered vehicle as it raced away from Earlene's hogan. She took a moment to study it, trying but failing to come up with a detailed vision of the truck she'd seen that day.

She approached the hut, rapped her knuckles on the doorframe, waited a moment, then peered into the dim interior. It was a windowless dirt-floor dugout with barely enough room to stand erect inside, but someone was living there.

An unmade bed, a thin mattress atop a cot, its sheets and blankets thrown back had the look of having been recently vacated by someone. An open box of Triscuits and a bag of chocolate chip cookies were propped next to an overflowing ash tray on an upturned cardboard box beside the bed. A gaping canvas duffle bag on the floor contained men's clothing. She could guess the size of the owner by the quantity of denim in the jeans. Next to the duffel bag, two very large size hiking boots worn down at the heels were turned toe to toe at an angle.

On a makeshift wooden table along the wall, a portable single-burner propane cookstove with a saucepan on the heating element rested on a platform of stacked cinderblocks.

Warily, she looked back at the bed, the covers thrown back, the indentation on the mattress so recently occupied she could almost feel the body heat emanating from the sheets. The hair on her forearms rose.

"Can I help you?"

Keegan jumped and yelped as if she'd been goosed, and spun around at the sound of a voice behind her. It belonged to a woman, about sixty, wearing a plaid flannel shirt and baggy jeans. Her silver hair hung in a long braid.

Keegan's heart was banging like a drum and her instinct was to immediately apologize for intruding, but she was too busy trying to catch her breath. The woman apologized instead.

"Sorry to startle you," she said. "Are you a friend of Charlie's?" Her kind gray eyes twinkled.

"Oh, no, I'm not. I was looking for . . . I'm doing research on . . ." Keegan stumbled over her words, jumbling her thoughts. She gave her head a shake, introduced herself, and started over.

"I understand there used to be a school here. I was hoping to speak to someone who could give me some information about it for an article I'm writing."

The woman smiled. "Indeed there was a school here. A clinic, too. Lots of babies were born here back in the day."

Wondering how far back that day went, Keegan explained what she was looking for and why. "I know it was a long time ago, but would you possibly have records of any of the students who went to school here?"

"We do," the woman replied. "When I came here as the administrative assistant back in the 1990s, the first thing I did was clean out the storage rooms. They were filled with boxes and boxes of records, some of them more than fifty years old. Many more than I could manage on my own. I was fortunate enough to get a federal grant and have VISTA volunteers come in during the summer to input the information into the computer system before I sent the records to the National Archives."

A bubble of hope rose in Keegan's chest.

"My name's Lillian Greyhaven," the woman said. "Who did

you say you were writing an article for?"

Keegan told her, leaving out some details and skipping the part about the kidnapping, as well as her personal connection to Lulu.

"Well, if you'll come with me to my office, I'll take a look on the computer and see if we can find who you're looking for."

Lillian led the way to a low roofed stone building, chatting all the way about the worship and pastoral care that, despite minimal funding, took place at the mission. She stopped outside a door, reached under a rock, and removed a key ring.

"We're on the National Register of Historic Places," she said proudly.

"Yes," Keegan replied. "I saw the sign out front."

Keys on a ring clinked together as Lillian looked for the right one. She found it, turned it in the lock, and the door swung open.

"Here we are," she said as if she were welcoming a guest into a cozy bed and breakfast room.

Because of the age and slightly rundown condition of the building, the sleek new looking computer stood out in stark relief against the old furniture hunkered there. Lillian positioned herself in front of the monitor, clicked a few keys, and asked, "What's the name you're looking for?"

"Lulu Etsitty. I think that's spelled e-t-s-i-t-t-y."

"It could be," said Lillian. "There are several spellings and variations of some of the Navajo names. But let's start with that."

Lillian's fingers flew over the keyboard, and a list appeared in a grid on the monitor. Keegan peered over Lillian's shoulder, reading the names as they scrolled up the screen.

"Hmmm," Lillian said. "I don't see that name." She clicked a few more keys and pulled up another screen. "No, not there either. I guess she wasn't here."

"Are you sure?" Keegan asked, disappointed.

Lillian nodded, tried a few more databases, then shook her head. "No. I don't find that name."

"What about Teaya Etsitty?" Keegan asked and spelled the first name. "That's Lulu's mother."

"Oh, I know Teaya," Lillian said, taking her hands off the keyboard and turning to Keegan. "Haven't seen her in a long time. Last I heard she worked at the Oljato Senior Center. That was a while ago, though. I didn't know she had a daughter named Lulu," she added thoughtfully.

Keegan's spirits lifted at this bit of news, but fell again when Lillian said she didn't recognize the name Lincoln Cole or Earlene Cly. Keegan looked at her watch. She could probably make it back to Oljato before noon. That would still leave time to visit the school in Kayenta.

She thanked Lillian for her trouble. Lillian walked with her to the shady spot where she'd parked.

"We have services every Sunday at nine and eleven," Lillian said, motioning to the little chapel. "We'd love to see you. Reverend Hornbuckle is marvelous. He was educated in Scotland."

"Thank you. I'll try."

"Well, good luck," Lillian said, shading her eyes from the sun. "Let me know if you find her, okay? I'm here all the time. I live here."

Keegan pressed the remote on her keychain, sounding the *tweet-tweet* that unlocked her car. "Do you live in the dugout?"

"Oh, no, Charlie Manygoats stays there. He lived here at the mission until he went away to college." Lillian went on, indulging in a little harmless gossip, the currency of every realm, even the church. "His parents abandoned him when he was a baby, and we took him in. He comes back every now and then, and stays with us. We still have some dorm rooms, but he prefers the dugout."

At Keegan's quizzical expression, Lillian was quick to offer an explanation. "I'm afraid Charlie hasn't yet found his path in life, despite an excellent university education. But with God's blessing, he'll find his way. We don't worry about him."

Lillian stood waving until Keegan could no longer see her in the rearview mirror.

Keegan pushed her speed up to eighty, more than legal but expedient, until she realized the old pickup turning onto the highway up ahead wasn't going nearly that fast. She applied gentle pressure to her brakes, slowing until she hit 25 mph, apparently the top speed of the vehicle limping along in front of her. She rounded a wide curve trailing the pickup, not daring to pass until she was again on the straightaway.

When she saw the road ahead was clear, she swerved into the passing lane and accelerated. It only took a couple of seconds for the 4Runner to gain on the pickup, and she glanced over at the driver framed in the side window as she went by. She recognized him as the old man she'd seen at the grocery store and at the gas station. His gaze engaged with hers and followed as she passed.

That was strange, she thought. It was almost as if he were trying to tell her something.

Charlie Manygoats, wearing only boxer shorts and holding his iPod in his hand, slowly emerged from behind a brushy hump of red sandstone boulders partway up the rocky slope where he'd dashed when he saw Keegan get out of her car. He almost didn't hear it pull in, because he had his ear buds in and the volume turned up. It was only because he caught a faint movement in the distance, a lizard darting away into the underbrush, that he saw her headed his way.

With no time to dress, he bolted out his open door, head low, darting behind the crowded scrub shrubbery, and clambered up the fractured bluff behind the dugout with the agility suggested by his surname. From that vantage point, he watched her approach, take a good look at his truck as she went by, then stand in the doorway of the dugout. He worried she would get nosy and go inside, start poking around in his things. Luckily, the church lady stopped her, and took her to the office. Now she was gone, but he waited for a while just to be sure she didn't come right back.

He'd been on the lookout for her. Ordinarily it wasn't hard to find a *bilagaana* on the reservation—all he had to do was ask around some—but he didn't want to be too obvious and call attention to himself. He wondered if she'd told the church lady where she was staying.

He already knew what she looked like, had a good mental picture of her face through the windshield when he'd nearly rammed her as he raced away from the old lady's hogan. That day, she'd been driving a battered pickup. Today she showed up in a new SUV. He was too far away to read the license number, and there were dozens of silver 4Runners on the reservation, but at least now he knew what to look for.

Charlie climbed down from the rocks and slipped back into the dugout, put his earbuds in, and turned on his iPod. He plopped down on the mattress, closed his eyes, and fell back into his music, the half-smile of a new idea curving his lips.

CHAPTER EIGHTEEN

Keegan spent three days on the road visiting the sites of Indian boarding schools within driving distance of Monument Valley. Farmington, Shiprock, Ignacio, Kayenta.

There were, or used to be, other schools located farther away in places like northern Utah and Colorado and Arizona. In 1984, the Intermountain Indian School in Brigham City, Utah, closed after tribal tensions pushed to the breaking point led to a student riot. The Phoenix Indian School operated for almost one hundred years before being turned into a museum and historic site. Both schools were in existence when Lulu was taken, but Keegan's instincts told her Lulu had not been taken that far away.

It was after dark when she returned. A Jeep, its profile lit by the flicker of her headlights through the trees, was parked in front of her bungalow. It was Dante's car. She pulled to a stop next to it, but didn't see anyone, and cautiously stepped out. Suddenly, Dante's head popped up.

The overhead light came on when he opened the door and he stepped out, a tired smile on his face, his eyes half-lidded, his hair ruffled from sleep. Seeing him sent a little spiral of pleasure inside her. He was in jeans and boots again, looking too damn tempting.

"Hi," he said. "Where've you been?" It was a casual question asked in the offhand manner of intimates and good friends.

"I've been to the Indian schools looking for Lulu Etsitty."

173

Keegan reached back into the 4Runner, pulled out her purse, and slipped the strap over her shoulder.

"Any luck?" he asked.

She dragged her overnight bag from the back seat. "No, not much." They regarded each other for a long moment. "Would you like to come in?" she asked. "I'll tell you about it."

The eagerness with which he accepted her invitation told her something was amiss. He had a lonely look in his eye, the look of someone who needed a friend.

"Here, let me help you with that," he said, reaching for her overnight bag while she looked for the door key in her purse.

"Thanks," she said. Their gazes met and held a moment, sending a pleasant little pulse of warmth to her chest as she unlocked the door.

"I saw Jilly yesterday," he told her once they were inside. "She said she left a message on your cell phone."

Keegan turned on the lamp, the light warming the room with its glow.

"I didn't get it. I must have been in a cellular dead spot. I need to talk to her, though. I haven't seen her since we got back from San Diego."

"You haven't told her what your grandmother said about the picture? About Earlene? And Lulu?"

"No, not yet," Keegan said. "But I'm glad she called. I was afraid she was mad at me for leaving so abruptly last week."

"She isn't," Dante assured her. "I told her I took you away, and then we had to go to San Diego. I hope you don't mind, but I told her why. She said she's sorry about your little girl, and wants you to call her as soon as you can. Summer school doesn't start for a couple of weeks, so she'll have more free time during the break."

"I will. Did she say if there was anything new on Earlene's murder? Does the FBI have any leads?" She wondered if she'd ever be able to think about Earlene without a twist in her stomach.

"Not so far."

Keegan relieved him of her overnight bag, took it into her bedroom, and set it on the bed. She eased out of her jeans and slipped on a pair of sweatpants.

"I left you a message, too." His voice carried in to her from the other room.

She stepped back through the doorway tying the drawstrings, eyebrows raised in question. "You did?"

He executed a one-shoulder shrug and said, "I wanted to talk to you."

"Oh. Is something wrong?"

He didn't have to answer for her to know something was bothering him. The frown on his face said it all, but he dodged her question.

"Have you got anything to eat?" he asked.

"Dante, how long have you been waiting outside?"

"A few hours. I was here last night, too. When you didn't come home, I got a little worried."

She smiled. "Sit down. Let me fix you something." She opened the refrigerator, then the freezer. "I've got chili and frozen pizza."

He managed a small smile in return. "Since we had pizza last time, how about chili?"

"Chili it is."

She moved her laptop and files from the kitchen table to the bedroom. It had only been a few weeks, and already she was outgrowing the bungalow.

Dante watched while she heated the chili, set out placemats and napkins, bowls and spoons. "Which schools did you visit?" he asked. "What did you find out?"

"I went to all the schools on the eastern side of the reservation and over into New Mexico, but I didn't learn a lot. For the most part, student records weren't kept on site. They've either been destroyed or damaged, or sent to federal facilities. Only no one knew exactly which federal facilities they were sent to, so it's going to take a lot more searching."

She emptied a box of cornbread mix into a bowl, added water and an egg, stirred, poured the batter into a baking pan, and put it in the oven. She set the timer and sat down at the table with Dante.

"The mission in Bluff had all their school records on computer, but we couldn't find Lulu's name. I did find out Lulu's mother works at the Oljato Senior Center."

"How'd you find that out?"

"The woman who works in the office at the mission told me. I drove out to Oljato, but Teaya wasn't there. She's with the Navajo Adopt-an-Elder program. She visits outlying hogans to check on the grandmothers who choose to stay in their homes. She makes sure they're eating properly. Taking their meds. That kind of thing."

Dante gave her a questioning look. "What did you plan to say to her if you found her?"

She shrugged, folded and refolded a napkin, and then fiddled with the corner of it, thinking.

"I don't know. It was an impulse." She looked up. "I guess I just wanted to get a look at the woman who gave birth to my grandfather's child. After all, Lulu is my blood relative. And I wanted to let Teaya know I was looking for her daughter. She's a mother who's been in pain for fifty years. Can you imagine it?" She shrugged again. "I thought it might help her to know someone cared. No matter what I say it will be a shock to her."

When Keegan finished telling him about her trip, Dante fell into silence, lost in thoughts of his own. She went to the stereo, looked through a pile of CDs, put in a James Blunt and a Billy

Bob Thornton. Billy Bob came on first, singing about California in his gravel-and-stone voice.

The stove timer went off, and Keegan served up steaming bowls of chili and hot cornbread with butter. Dante ate hungrily, reminding her of all the late suppers she'd had with Brady. For all her ex-husband's faults, he liked her cooking and never failed to tell her so.

There was little conversation while they ate. After Dante finished a second bowl, he thanked her and politely offered to help clean up.

She waved him away. "That's all right," she said, declining. "I can do it. It'll only take a minute." She eyed him sideways. "Go sit down and relax. Would you like a beer?"

He said he would, and she told him to help himself. He grabbed a beer from the fridge, and flopped back against the couch cushions, popped the top, and took a big swallow.

Finished in the kitchen, Keegan wiped her hands on a kitchen towel, pumped a dollop of lemon oil hand lotion into her palm, and joined him there, sitting sideways so she could face him.

"What's wrong, Dante? Did something happen while I was away?"

"Yeah," he said. He leaned forward to set his empty beer can on the coffee table.

"Something bad?" She worked the lotion into her hands, waiting for him to go on.

He sighed and ran a hand through his hair. "Yeah. Bad." He told her about the destruction at his dig site.

She was flabbergasted. "Who would do a thing like that?"

"I have a pretty good idea."

"You do? Who?"

He released a sad chuckle. "I'm afraid my past has come back to haunt me."

She took her time considering what he said. "Does it have

177

something to do with what you read in the paper in San Diego? At lunch, remember? About where you used to work."

"Yeah," he said. "It does."

"Does it have something to do with you thinking I'd come here looking for you? We never did get to finish that conversation." The one interrupted by the phone call from Jeffrey. She'd been wondering about it ever since.

"That, too," he said, nodding.

"So what happened?"

He jutted his jaw and sighed again, quiet for a long time.

"I'm sorry," she said, picking up on his silence. "I'm being nosy, as usual. You don't have to tell me if you don't want to talk about it."

"But I do want to. I want to tell you because I don't want you to believe things you might read about me in the paper. Or hear from someone else, or on the news. I want you to know the truth about what I did and didn't do."

She waited patiently for him to go on, prompting him with a look of encouragement. He stared at her, frowning slightly, as if debating with himself whether or not to trust her. The moment dragged on, and when it got too weighty, she tried to lighten it to let him know it was safe to confide in her.

"Hmmm," she said, compressing her lips and narrowing her eyes in mock consideration. "Let me guess. Are you a terrorist?"

"No."

"A foreign spy?"

"No!"

"An ax murderer or sex offender?"

"God, no!"

They laughed then, he nervously, and the tension dissipated.

"Dante, I'm your friend. What could you possibly have done that was too horrible to tell me?"

"I made a stupid mistake," he said, relenting. "I trusted

178

someone who betrayed me, when I knew better than to expect anything from anyone."

"We've all done that," she replied. She studied his eyes, saw the weight of his memories hidden there. The temptation to throw her arms around him was overwhelming. Instead, she reached over and laid her hand on his arm.

"What happened?"

"Remember in San Diego I told you about Venture Real Estate Development? Where I used to work?"

She nodded.

"They're bidding on the new casino resort project with the tribe."

"Yes. You told me."

"Eight years ago, I was their compliance archaeologist. It was my job to survey building sites to make sure archaeological information would not be inadvertently destroyed during construction. I reported directly to Peter Venture. Peter and I had been friends for years. Our wives, too. We were a pretty tight foursome."

His wife? He's married?

"Peter took over the company after his father died, and was working hard to expand the business from strip malls and gas stations to high-end shopping centers, and medical clinics and hospitals.

"He won the bid to build a children's hospital south of San Diego near the Mexican border. The medical facility would be on the U.S. side, but it would serve the people and children of the many small villages in Mexico along that part of the border. An agreement had been made to allow access back and forth between the countries for medical care. Peter had persuaded the United States to provide shuttle bus transportation for poor families in Mexico."

"What a wonderfully philanthropic thing to do," Keegan said, impressed.

"Peter contributed to many worthy causes, especially anything to do with children. So, yeah, he was well liked, and had a lot of credibility in the community. He was a handsome guy, very charming, very intelligent.

"I led the compliance team. It was a huge project in a part of the desert not easily accessible, but Peter was going to build roads, too. There was a lot of work involved, but the project looked like a go. Except for one thing."

"What was that?"

"During the survey, we turned up artifacts and evidence of human remains."

Keegan straightened. "You did? Whose?"

"I don't know. They were old. Ancient, in fact. The artifacts looked to be about a thousand years old, so we figured the bones were, too. The site wasn't on Mission Indian land, but it was adjacent to it, so the chances were good there was a cultural relationship."

"What did you do?"

"Well, when you find cultural remains, everything stops. Or it's supposed to. By law, developers are required to work with local Indian tribes to determine the ancestry and identity of the remains, so the tribes can take their ancestors and sacred objects home. The items I found on the site would have significantly delayed construction. Maybe even canceled the entire building project.

"But Peter had been overextended. He was in a money bind. He needed to move forward with the construction, and insisted I exclude certain findings from my cultural resource survey reports so the project wouldn't have to be delayed. Or scrapped. I refused. We argued, and he fired me. The company went ahead with construction anyway, and in the process they destroyed the burial site. I reported them, and Peter and his partners were subpoenaed."

"Oh," Keegan said, drawing out the word. "That must have been a hard decision to make."

"It was, and maybe not the best one considering what happened after."

"Why?"

"The story made the news big time because of Peter's high profile, and because of the inherent emotional impact of the story. You know, Indian burial sites *and* hospitals for poor kids.

"Peter denied everything. Claimed he had no idea anything of a historical nature had been found. Pointed his finger at me, claimed I was the one who initiated a cover up. He and the partners swore to it. Eventually, documentation turned up showing I had approved the survey findings."

"Did someone forge your signature?" Keegan asked from the kitchen where she'd gone to get him another beer. She brought it back, handed it to him, and he thanked her.

"Either that, or I might have signed it inadvertently," he admitted.

She sat down and opened a Diet Coke for herself.

"I suspected my new assistant was involved," he went on, "or at least knew a hell of a lot more than he let on. He was a smart-as-a-whip young guy out of New Mexico. Peter must have offered him something. Money, or a promotion. Anyway, either he forged my signature, or he slipped the falsified report into a stack of papers awaiting my signature, and I just signed it without reading it thoroughly."

He lifted his shoulders in a hey-what-can-I-say shrug. "I trusted the guy, so I did that sometimes. Anyway, I was charged and arrested, but my lawyer got me released in a few days. In the end, the charges were dropped. Not enough evidence."

"So it ended there?" Keegan asked.

"Only as far as the courts were concerned. Not the media," Dante answered. A shade of bitterness slipped into his voice. "They tried and convicted me in the press, demonizing me to the point where I was guilty either way. If I *had* signed falsified documents and allowed construction to proceed, I was guilty of destroying cultural remains, and lying about it. If I *hadn't* approved the surveys because of the find, which would have stopped construction, then I was guilty of depriving poor children of needed medical care."

Keegan recalled his frosty reaction the night they met, after he learned she was a reporter. This explained it, she realized. He didn't harbor any love for reporters. She could see why and looked at him with sympathy.

"It was too good for them to let go," he went on. "The reporters couldn't prove anything, but they didn't need to. People are always eager to believe the worst. It sold newspapers. But it also drew attention away from the real culprits, wealthy, important men with ties to political decision makers across both borders."

Some of the light snuffed out of his eyes, and his shoulders sagged.

"After they took everything else from me, my wife took the kids and went back home to Minnesota . . ."

So he's not married, she thought with a tiny pinch of delight.

". . . Peter didn't go to jail, he wasn't even charged with anything. But he still had a score to settle. To him and others in the industry, I was worse than a snitch. I was a traitor. I came to Monument Valley to lay low. I figured it would be the last place the press, or anyone else, would look for me. I hoped I could blend in with all the other shovel bums in the Four Corners."

His tight smile couldn't hide his worry, and she felt the spark of attraction she'd been carrying flare up into a tiny flame.

Without thinking, she leaned forward and kissed him lightly on the lips.

That's not quite true. She'd been thinking about it for some time.

It was a soft kiss that lingered, but didn't ask for more. When it was over, he looked at her, a wisp of a smile on his lips, clearly not sure what to make of it.

"What was that for?" he asked.

"You needed it," she said, smiling.

"I did," he replied. "Thanks."

She hoped he wouldn't read more into the kiss than she meant. Friendship. Comfort. A warm touch to let him know she understood his pain and even felt it a little. She wasn't the kind to sleep around or seduce men she hardly knew. She didn't want him to think she was.

His forearm was resting along the back of the sofa. She laid her hand on it, feeling its warmth seep into her palm. "Do you think these men want to harm you? Physically, I mean."

"Yes." He said it matter-of-factly, without fear or the faintest note of trepidation. "They want revenge."

"What are you going to do now?" she asked after a few moments.

"Nothing until I meet with Emerson Bedonnie and have a chance to explain. He's the tribal council member making the hiring decisions. I applied for the compliance position on the casino project. Since Venture Real Estate Development is one of the bidders on the construction, Emerson will be talking to Peter Venture, if he hasn't already. I'm sure Peter will be only too happy to give Emerson all the dirt about what happened in San Diego."

"Maybe Emerson will believe you."

"Maybe he won't," Dante interjected. "People almost never survive that kind of public investigation. I couldn't prove anything then, and I can't now."

There was a short lull.

"What about the damage to your site? Can any of it be salvaged?" Keegan asked.

"I backfilled it. It's better to preserve it that way than leave everything exposed. I've got some new projects in mind."

"What are they?"

"Solstice markers. Those celestial calendars used by ancient cultures to mark off the seasons. I've always been interested in them, and there have been some recent discoveries near here. I want to study existing ones, and look for new ones. Maybe write some research papers."

"Oh, that is interesting," said Keegan. "I saw a PBS special on solstice markers once. It's amazing how accurate they are. I'd love to see one."

"I'll take you," Dante said. "I know the location of one that can record meridian passage of the sun to within a few minutes." Some of the sadness left his expression with the talk of a new project.

"Okay."

He yawned, taking a big gulp of air, then sat there looking at her but not speaking for a long time, his expression taut with unasked questions and unspoken words.

"What?" she said finally, catching on that he had more to say. "Don't tell me you have more surprises in your past."

"No," he replied, smiling. "It's not my past I was thinking about. It's yours."

"My past?" She laughed lightly. "I don't have one. At least not that you don't already know about."

"What about Jeffrey? The FBI called him looking for you. Where does he fit into your life?"

Keegan's eyelashes fluttered to her cheeks, and she chuckled softly, surprised that he remembered.

"I'm sorry," Dante said quickly. "That was too personal a question, huh?"

"No, not at all," she answered. "I just didn't expect it."

He waited for her to go on.

"Jeffrey was . . ." she stopped, searching for the right words. "An escape," she said at last.

"Was? Or is?" Dante asked.

"Was. I needed someone to help me not feel so numb after Daisy was taken."

"Did it work?" he asked.

"For a while," she said. "We broke up just before I came here."

"Why?"

Keegan heaved a sigh, remembering. "We were on vacation in Cabo San Lucas and had a fight. He complained because my work took up so much of my time. I wasn't available enough for him. And it's true. I am very involved in my work. He didn't understand." She shrugged. "And some of my habits bothered him."

"Like what?"

She hesitated, not sure she should tell a slightly embarrassing story about herself. "Well, I have this annoying habit of counting things." She looked at him. "Some people get headaches when they're upset. I count things." She waited for a reaction from him. When none came, she prompted, "Crazy, huh?"

Dante shook his head. "I don't think so."

"Billy Bob Thornton does the same thing. I guess I kind of identify with him. He wrote a song about counting things. I can relate."

"And for that, this Jeffrey dumped you?"

"Well, I'm not exactly sure if he dumped me or I dumped him. He was having an affair."

Dante gazed at her a long while, his green eyes shimmering,

gentle and kind. "What an idiot your Jeffrey is," he said, reaching out and gently stroking her cheek with the back of his fingers.

"After that, we didn't really have anything more to say to each other, so he left and I stayed on. He'd already paid for the room for the week, so I figured what the hell."

Dante let out a robust laugh at that. "He must have thought there was some chance of getting back together when he met you at the medical examiner's office in San Diego."

She held his gaze. "Yeah, he did, but there's no chance in hell," she replied. "He knows that now."

Dante yawned hugely, and then silence fell between them. The stereo had recycled back to the first CD, and Keegan got up to turn it off.

"If you plan to visit more schools looking for Lulu maybe I could go along," he offered, his voice sleepy. "Help with the driving. Or whatever."

She turned and looked at him. "Sure," she said. "I'd like that."

"What other schools do you plan to visit?" His words were garbled from speaking around another yawn.

"There are only a few more," she said. "Let me get my list. Maybe you know where they are."

She went into the bedroom where she'd stashed the files. She looked through the folders, pulled out the one labeled *Government Schools,* and returned to the living room.

"Next week I planned to go to . . ." She stopped.

Dante, head flopped back, eyes closed, his lips slightly parted, had dozed off. She stood a minute watching him. The tension she'd seen in his face earlier was gone, and in the silence she could hear his breath moving past his lips.

There was something about a man sleeping on her couch that had always given her a little kick. There was something intimate and comfortable about it. She felt it now and considered lying down and snuggling up against him. Instead, she covered him with the sofa throw, turned off the lights, and went to bed.

Chapter Nineteen

Henry Parker stood with hands on hips, legs spread wide, feet braced. He scowled, then exhaled in disgust at the mess left behind in the upstairs room of the National Archives where Justin Bickham had been last working. No one had been in this room since Justin was fired, and Henry was only here now because Keegan Thomas had called with a question.

Why, she had wanted to know, had the BIA sent Lincoln Cole to Monument Valley if it had not been their policy to send physicians there?

Good question and one that had tweaked his own curiosity.

Henry's eyes traveled over the disarray: boxes emptied with no clue to what they had contained, records spilled out of folders, documents spread across the table and elsewhere around the room in no apparent order. Briefly, in the interest of time, *his* time, Henry considered scooping up all the papers and files and photos and dumping everything back in the boxes. But Henry prided himself on being punctilious in obligation so couldn't bring himself do such a thing.

And there was another reason.

Recently a report on a cable news channel, intending to call the National Archives to task, alleged blatant incompetence in the security and management of records. This assertion set off all kinds of alarms, especially after a highly publicized attempted theft of government records by a former presidential aide who had been caught sneaking out with smoking-gun documents during a previous administration. This energized some activist groups who raised holy hell about it, inciting some members of Congress to call for an investigation.

Fortunately, the outcry was halted after it was found that much of the missing material was simply misplaced, not lost or stolen as originally believed. Most of the records were either misfiled on nearby shelves or marked with the wrong call numbers.

Only the records in this room weren't shelved or marked with call numbers at all. Justin was supposed to have been sorting and coding these materials for retrieval, but clearly that task had not even begun.

As Henry scanned the room, he began to discern a sort of pattern to some of the disorder. The work table itself, like an island in the midst of a turbulent ocean, seemed to be a repository of orderly chaos. Various documents were stacked and sorted by date and record group. Upon closer inspection, Henry saw they were medical field reports, and accounting records relating to the Navajo Indian Reservation.

Clearly, Justin had been in the midst of doing *something*. Henry didn't know what, but he suspected Justin had planned to return to this room to finish up. Or cover his tracks. He hadn't counted on being fired and having his electronic ID deactivated from the system.

Feeling the press of long hours and too much work, Henry sat down and began to read.

Hours later, he removed his glasses, closed his eyes and rubbed his face. Threads of thought began unraveling, and he let his mind drift. He got up, walked to the window, and stood looking out. The lowering sky was gray with clouds bleaching the color from the buildings and gardens outside.

He hadn't found the answer to Keegan's question. Instead, many more questions had taken form and were now swirling in his brain. After a few moments, he left the room, locked it, and went back to his office.

Squeezing past a stack of boxes, he sat at his cluttered desk and stared at a large map on his wall. It was the AAA guide to Indian Country, a roadmap covering the Four Corners states of Utah, Arizona, Colorado, and New Mexico showing the Navajo Reservation borders.

Making a decision, he opened a drawer, took out a much used Rolodex—no BlackBerries or electronic phone directories for him—and thumbed the cards until he found the phone number he was looking for. Adjusting his spectacles, he read the number, imprinted it on his mind, then reached for the phone and dialed.

It was answered quickly and crisply.

"Senator O'Toole's office."

"Is he still there?" Henry asked, unable to keep a dash of impatience from slipping into his voice.

"Who's calling please?"

"Henry Parker from the National Archives."

"The senator has asked not to be disturbed, Mr. Parker. He's studying a bill at the moment."

"Put him on, Clarissa. It's important."

"One moment, please."

The senator was supported by a very large staff of highly efficient aides and political intellectuals who ran his office and did much of the work that needed to be done for the country. O'Toole oversaw most of it, always studied the bills that crossed his desk, and never missed a vote, but didn't have as much historical recall of details as he once did.

What Henry was calling about couldn't be discussed with any of O'Toole's aides. This was something the senator needed to handle himself.

★ ★ ★ ★ ★

Eavesdropping at the adjoining door between their offices, Booker heard the senator hang up the phone. He scooted back to his desk, and was in front of his computer with his hands on the keyboard a moment before the door opened and O'Toole came through.

"You're still here, Booker?" the senator said with a weary smile.

"Yes, Senator. Just finishing up some reports before I go home."

Senator O'Toole handed him a slip of paper. "Would you mind taking care of this for me tomorrow? The National Archives is trying to verify some information."

Booker read the note.

"Of course, sir."

"I think I'll head home."

"Are you feeling all right, Senator?"

"Just tired is all. Good night."

"Have a good evening, Senator."

Soon after O'Toole was gone, Clarissa left. By the time the rest of the staffers departed, night had fallen and thunder was rumbling.

Booker opened his cell phone and called Justin.

"What are you up to, Bickham?" Booker barked when Justin answered.

"Wha—What do you mean?" Justin stammered.

"O'Toole just got a call from Henry Parker at the archives. He wants to know about those payments to Earlene Cly."

"Oh, shit." Justin's voice sounded worried.

"I gave you that information in confidence. I could lose my job the same way they fired your ass."

"I didn't say anything to Henry. I swear."

Booker went on, making sure his point was crystal clear. "I

191

don't know what you're involved in, but whatever it is, don't drag me into it."

"Don't worry. I won't."

"I mean it, Justin. We've been friends for a long time, but this isn't the old days. I'm done with scamming. That was college kid stuff. I'm playing with the big boys now. Don't screw it up for me."

Not waiting for Justin to reply, Booker snapped his phone shut and tossed it on his desk.

"Shit!" he said, and sat back angrily.

CHAPTER TWENTY

Keegan roused at the first ring of the phone on the bedside table. Through sleep-bleary eyes, she peered at the clock radio's glowing red numerals. Three twenty-seven. She picked up the phone, read the caller ID, and felt a sudden drop in the pit of her stomach. It was a San Diego area code.

"Hello."

"Keegan Thomas?"

"Yes."

"This is Special Agent Porfino."

At the sound of his voice, she came fully awake. "Do you have news about Daisy?" She sat up and turned on the light.

"Yes. How soon can you be in San Diego?"

"Have you found her? Do you have her?"

The pause was ever so slight, but it was there. "No, but we know where she is."

Keegan's heart began beating like she'd just spent an hour on the Bowflex. "Where?"

"We'll fill you in when you get here. We're still gathering information. By the time you arrive, we should know more."

"Is she alive?" Keegan couldn't help asking, dread beginning to form.

"If the information we have is correct, then yes. She's alive."

After she hung up, a dizzying rush of adrenaline made her light-headed. Questions spun through her mind and she held on to the bedpost until her thoughts slowed. She dressed quickly, tossed deodorant, a toothbrush, and a change of underwear in her purse. Within twenty minutes she was speeding down the highway.

She waited till the sun was up to call Dante from the road. She hadn't seen him since the night he'd fallen asleep at her place. She had wakened the next morning to the delicious aroma of toast and coffee. He'd found the fixings, helped himself, and started breakfast without being told. Her kind of man.

For the past week, he'd been on a field trip to Canyon de Chelly with the Russian exchange students, but they'd talked on the phone every day. He was expected back tonight.

His voice mail picked up, and she left a message telling him where she was going and why. "They said she's alive. That's all that matters." She was breathless with anticipation, allowing herself to feel a welling of joy. "I'll call you later when I know more."

She arrived at police headquarters in the middle of an extended rush hour, the delay making her irritable. The parking garage was nearly full, the elevator wasn't working, and she had to hike down from the uppermost level. By the time she pushed through the double glass doors of the main lobby and cleared the security checkpoint, her nerves were stretched to breaking.

At the front desk, a bottle-blonde police officer with a wrist brace on her arm took Keegan's name and made a phone call. Porfino appeared and escorted her down halls and through doors. Keegan peppered him with questions, none of which he answered. He ushered her into a conference room where some men were already seated at a conference table.

Porfino introduced them as members of the Joint SDPD FBI Missing Children's Task Force. Keegan didn't catch any names. She was only interested in what they had to say about Daisy. Using the courteous manners they'd all learned in FBI 101, they offered her coffee, water, iced tea, and a seat. She declined everything except the seat. It felt like they were preparing her for bad news. The atmosphere in the room was strained.

"Where is Daisy? You said she was all right."

"That's what we've been told," said a man who'd been introduced as chief of the task force.

She felt a stirring of anger. "What do you mean 'that's what you've been told'? Don't you know?"

Porfino opened a file folder and removed a set of color prints, slid one over to her. "Is this your daughter?"

The pictures had been taken at a playground. Keegan was held captive by the image of Daisy running through the grass chasing a puppy. She was six now and had grown a lot. Her hair was long, tied in a ponytail at the top of her head, hanging down between her shoulder blades. The playground equipment in the background looked colorful and new. Keegan could see other children playing on the swings, climbing the fun house ladders, stepping along the catwalks.

"Yes, this is Daisy." She looked up at Porfino, but his gaze bounced away. He looked nervous.

He took the photo back, slid another one in front of her. Daisy emerging from a yellow plastic tube slide, ponytail flying, mouth open in childish glee. Keegan heard Daisy's laugh like a tinkling bell in her mind, an infectious giggle that had never failed to provoke the same response in her, sparking a prolonged mother-daughter gigglefest.

Glumly, Keegan nodded.

He handed her two more pictures. In these, Daisy was seated at a table in an outdoor café, sitting primly on an elaborate wrought iron chair. Her head was turned slightly away from the camera, and she was talking to an adult. Keegan couldn't see who she was talking to because the image was partially blocked by pedestrians passing by on the sidewalk.

Keegan looked up at Porfino. "This is her, too. Where were

195

these taken? Who is she with?"

Porfino exhaled audibly and exchanged a grim look with the others around the table.

"She's with your husband," he said.

It was such a ridiculous statement, Keegan would have laughed if she wasn't so confused.

"Your ex-husband," Porfino clarified. "And no, there's no mistake."

"Daisy is with her father, Brady Thomas," the head of the task force said from across the table.

A cold hard lump formed in her chest. "Brady has her?"

"Yes."

"He took her?" she answered dumbly, her mind rejecting the reality of what they were telling her.

"It appears so. That's what our investigation turned up."

Keegan shook her head from side to side, dismissing this with a wave of her hand. "No. No, that's not possible. I spoke to him after she went missing. He—" Her voice was stolen by a clutch of disbelief trying but failing to take over her thinking.

"It's him," Porfino said. "There's no doubt. Authorities in Spain have confirmed his identity. And Daisy's."

Keegan's mind skittered from one irrelevant thought to another, frantically avoiding the truth of it. The quicksand of the past sucked at her feet. A picture popped into her mind, a moment that separated itself from all others, one detail rising up in bold relief: Daisy at the beach, shrouded by thickening fog, looking to her right and pointing, smiling. *Mommy, look.*

Keegan had thought she was looking at the sea lions on the move, but she was really looking at her father. That's why Daisy didn't scream or struggle. That's why she went willingly.

A tremor went through her, and tears pricked the corners of her eyes. "Where did he take her?"

"They've been spotted in London and Spain. These pictures

were taken in Madrid."

"Well, go and get her!" Frustration swirled inside her building to outrage.

"I'm afraid we can't do that."

"Then tell *me* where they are," she shouted, her eyes drilling into his. "Where *exactly?* I'll go and get her myself." Her voice was hoarse, raw with anger.

Porfino held her look, his eyes reflective, as though he were weighing his words.

"You can't. They aren't there anymore. They left. Task force members in Madrid were closing in on them, but they slipped away. By the time investigators arrived, they were gone." He swallowed, and his eyes filled with sadness. "Now we don't know where they are."

A powerful rush of emotions swept through her. She wanted to scream. Her stomach spasmed from the fury that had her in its grip. Her heartbeats pounded in her ears, and she counted them off. *One. Two. Three.*

Forcefully, she willed herself to *stop it! Stop counting! Calm down!* But she was caught in a waking nightmare, her mind refusing to obey the commands of her will.

"Let me assure you, we're doing everything we can to find them," Porfino was saying. "We've had some more leads . . ."

But Keegan wasn't listening. She struggled against a sense of loss so huge and irreparable her mind balked at taking its measure. Why would Brady take her? *God in Heaven, why would he do that?*

A life-size image of Brady came to her. A complicated man with an on-switch for charm that manifested mostly in his role as a father. He loved Daisy, was attentive to her, changed diapers and fed her. Took her places with him even when she was a baby. To Home Depot. To the mall. To well-baby checkups at the pediatrician's office.

But his discontent with the constrictions of marriage, his dissatisfaction and quiet hostility toward Keegan, had inflicted a daily ration of pain until finally their marriage was torn apart, shattered by enmity, the very air they shared becoming as abrasive as grit. By the time she'd filed for divorce, there were no more ways for Brady to inflict pain on her except by taking Daisy away.

"His work," Keegan said, interrupting Porfino. "His office. Has anyone gone there? Questioned his employees? Talked to his secretary? I think her name is Madeline. Somebody must know where he is."

Porfino shook his head. "There is no such office. The address he gave you belongs to a mail forwarding outfit. The phone number is an answering service. His cell phone was GPS-tracked to a trash barrel in Verona, Italy."

Vivid sensations and memories flickered, and Keegan forced her mind to retrace a series of events. Brady moved out. The divorce was final. Saying he wanted a completely new start, Brady had accepted a high paying position in Italy as U.S.-European liaison for some sort of international manufacturing and trade agency.

The day Daisy disappeared, Keegan had called him in Rome to tell him. His secretary answered. Mr. Thomas wasn't in. She left a message, and Brady called back ten minutes later on his cell. Tearfully, Keegan told him the devastating news. He seemed inconsolable, beside himself with wretched misery.

He'd arrived at Phoenix Sky Harbor on a flight from Italy two days later, or so he'd told her. But from what Porfino was telling her now, Brady had lied. He must have already been in the States, following her around, waiting for his chance. In La Jolla, he took advantage of the fog and her inattention. When he flew back to Italy, Daisy was with him.

Grimly, Keegan pulled herself back to the present, to this

room full of men who were supposed to be helping her.

She felt like her mind was falling in on itself. Guilt-fueled anger swelled inside her, squeezing her heart. She was losing control of the rage that resided just below her surface, always ready to emerge, the same rage she fought to suppress every single day of her life since Daisy disappeared.

"Mrs. Thomas?" One of the investigators rose from the table and took a step toward her, holding out his hand. "Can I get you something? Do you need a doctor?"

"Better call her a doctor," another voice said.

Keegan shot out of her chair. "I don't need a doctor," she said as she headed for the door. "I NEED MY DAUGHTER!"

She could barely muster enough strength on wobbly legs to get back to her car. Insane with fury, her vision blurred from the tears spilling from her eyes. She didn't have the energy to drive back to the reservation. She'd used up all her energy looking for someone else's child when she should have been looking for her own.

In the rapid fall of night just past Phoenix, she exited I-17 at Carefree Highway and headed home, to her *real* home, the home she'd lived in with Daisy.

The house was dark and cold, just like she felt. She looked around the rooms trying to absorb the memories of the happy days she'd spent there with Daisy. She went upstairs into Daisy's bedroom, yanked open the closet, and pulled a box off the top shelf, emptying its contents on the yellow bedspread. Pictures and greeting cards spilled out. *Congratulations on the Birth of Your Child. Happy First Birthday. Happy First Mother's Day.*

Tears flooded her eyes and ran down her face. She picked up a handful of pictures and looked at them one at a time. A picture of herself six-months pregnant, her tummy round and plump. Daisy as a newborn asleep on her shoulder. Daisy's first outing. First step. First trip to the park.

Would she ever hold Daisy again? Would she ever see her little angel face so full of innocence? She longed to stroke her daughter's silky cheek, touch her feathery hair. Hear the music of her laughter.

Keegan's eyes felt like they were filled with acid, burning deep into the sockets. She pressed her trembling fists against them and fought for control. She went downstairs and tried to eat, but couldn't taste anything. Instead, she took a bottle of bourbon from the pantry, poured some in a glass, and planned righteous revenge.

She held her anger tightly and fed it with thoughts of reprisal. Her entire body ached to strangle that bastard Brady. She wanted to put her hands around his throat, dig her nails into the flesh of his neck and kill him, and not an iota of remorse would tweak her conscience.

A door swung wide in her imagination and through it she pictured him gaping and gasping for air as she punched him in the face again and again, trying to pound her fist through his face. She would try her absolute best to break his goddamn nose with her knuckles. She could almost hear the pleasurable crack and snap of the bones of his cheeks and around his eyes.

How many bones were there in a face? She wanted to break each and every one of them, counting out loud as she went. She put the bottle to her lips and swallowed.

I'll kill you, Brady Thomas. I swear I'll kill you dead.

CHAPTER TWENTY-ONE

Something was wrong. It didn't feel right.

Dante hadn't heard from Keegan in two days. She hadn't called him back as promised, and she hadn't answered either of her phones or returned his messages.

Something must have happened in San Diego. She left on Wednesday. This was Saturday. Her car wasn't parked outside the bungalow, and when Dante looked in the windows, he saw her things were still there, but she wasn't. Jilly hadn't heard from her, either.

So now Dante was going to find her. He was a little worried, afraid that she'd had bad news about Daisy, and if that was the case, he wanted to be with her. Also, he missed her.

He booted up his laptop, clicked on MapQuest, and called up a map of Cave Creek, Arizona. That's where she said she lived, and she'd mentioned the name of the street, but he couldn't remember it. It was Saddle something. Saddle Mountain, Saddle Ridge, something like that. He zoomed in and enlarged the map for a closer view so he could read the street names, but still didn't find it.

He closed out MapQuest, pulled up a people finding website, and typed in her name. Her address on Saddle Canyon Ranch Road popped up right away.

He unfolded a southwestern states map and studied it a minute, letting his eyes trace out the shortest route from Monument Valley to Cave Creek. It was the same general direction they'd traveled to get to San Diego, except he'd have to turn off the interstate just before he got to Phoenix.

It was an easy drive with little traffic and minimal road construction. He found Cave Creek with no trouble. The town wasn't very big, mostly desert with a main drag through its center lined with art galleries, restaurants, and shops that catered to tourists. He stopped at one of the shops to pick up a local map, and the storekeeper showed him where Saddle Canyon Ranch was.

Following instructions, he turned left at the stop sign, and after a mile turned east into the desert. Saddle Canyon Ranch Road was a bumpy, dusty road with no more than a handful of stucco-textured, tile-roofed Southwestern-style houses with plenty of acreage in between. A couple of the houses were partially hidden behind rambling adobe walls set far back from the road, which ended at the bottom of a rugged-looking mountain dotted with saguaros.

He drove slowly, looking for Keegan's address. Not all the houses showed street numbers, but he could rule a few out right away. It was the weekend, and some of the neighbors were outside working in their yards, cleaning garages, loading ATVs onto trailers, or washing cars. They gave him a curious glance as he went by, a stranger in a strange car on a street where everyone probably knew everyone else.

He ruled out another house, because the family name was painted on a large rock at the foot of the driveway. Only two remained, but he couldn't see the house numbers. One, a latte-colored territorial adobe with a flat roof had a kiva-style courtyard in front. Across the road, fronted by a bosque of twisted mesquite, a stylized pueblo followed the contours of the mountain, its color blending in with the desert sand.

Letting the Jeep idle, he studied the two houses, hoping he wasn't arousing the suspicions of the neighbors. Both houses had extensive landscaping in front, and redwood play sets in the back yard. The territorial had three day's worth of newspapers in the driveway. Dante guessed Keegan wouldn't have neglected to stop her paper delivery. And even if she had, there would be more than three papers laying there.

He shifted into drive and pulled up close to the tawny pueblo. The only sounds were the low rumble of the Jeep's engine, and stones crunching under the tires as he braked to a stop in the turnaround area outside the garage. Dante got out and walked a tumbled stone pathway to the front door's covered portico. A slab of stone with letters that spelled out *THOMAS* leaned against one of the concrete planters. He'd guessed right. This was Keegan's house.

He rang the bell and waited, then rang again. He rang a third time, then clapped the wrought iron knocker on the solid alderwood door. Nothing. He tried the latch expecting the door to be locked, and it was. Stepping out of the entryway, he studied the windows. They were all shut, closed off with interior shutters. No sounds came from inside. A fist of unease turned in his gut.

He walked around to the back, still not sure if Keegan was inside. Not wanting the neighbors to mistake him for a prowler, he strolled casually, examining the roofline as if looking for cracks in the stucco, hoping he looked like someone who had business there. He wondered if her car was in the garage, but there were no windows. He tried the utility door on the side of the garage. Locked. So were the French doors off the back patio.

His gaze traveled over the pool enclosure, the wrought iron furniture, the barrel cactus and mesquites in the back yard, looking for a likely place Keegan might hide a house key. Desert willow branches stirred in the breeze. A cactus wren twittered in an ocotillo. Beyond that, the landscaping was left to nature, with big views and no neighboring houses in sight.

He picked up a rock, then rapped his knuckles on the French doors once more to alert Keegan, in case she was inside and hadn't heard his knock at the front door. When that brought no response, he used the rock to shatter the glass pane next to the latch. Still no one came running, so he reached in, turned the lock, and stepped into the kitchen.

Dirty dishes filled the sink, cabinet doors hung open. Crumbs and spills covered the smooth surface of the granite countertop. Something was hardened in a saucepan on the stovetop, and an empty liquor bottle topped off an overflowing trash can. Wafting through the kitchen was the unmistakable odor of an unrefrigerated carton of milk left out on the counter. Holding his breath and turning his head to the side, he emptied it down the drain.

The rest of the house was meticulously maintained. Its interior multileveled architecture was all high ceilings, rounded corners, arched doorways, and rough textures. The walls were a crazy quilt of Navajo rugs and paintings depicting tales of mythic battles won, enemies tricked, spirits honored, and stories told.

Dante climbed a rounded, curving stairway cut into the wall, and found himself at the end of a hallway painted deep red and lined with Native American artifacts. Several doors opened off it, and he tried them one at a time. A guest room done up in an Old West cowboy theme. A bathroom. A little girl's room with yellow ruffles at the windows, and a puffy spread on the bed with five green throw pillows that spelled out *DAISY* propped against the headboard. A box was upended on the bed, pictures and greeting cards scattered about.

Next to Daisy's bedroom was a small room with a desk, a computer, and a phone. The red message light on the phone blinked furiously. The computer screen glowed, and he stepped in to take a look at it. The browser showed a people-search website with the name "Brady Thomas" in the search field.

He found Keegan in the master bedroom, sprawled fully dressed on top of an unmade bed, her mouth open in a perfect O as she slept. Crumpled tissues were everywhere, on the bed, on the floor. The television was on low, casting moving shadows around the darkened room, while the voice of an entertainment news host dished the latest dirt on a celebrity. A half-empty bottle of bourbon was on the dresser next to the bed.

"Keegan?" he called softly. She didn't stir, and he said her name again, a little louder. "Keegan? Are you all right?"

He went in, turned off the TV, and gazed down at her. She didn't look all right, but he was relieved to see she was breathing. A wash of smeared mascara tinted the delicate skin under her eyes. Makeup stains smudged the pillow, and her face was puffy from sleep and crying and booze. She needed a shower.

"Keegan, wake up." He put his hand on her shoulder and shook gently.

She groaned and rolled away from his touch.

"Come on. Wake up."

She groaned again and feebly batted his hand away.

Dante sat on the edge of the bed, slipped his arm under her shoulders, and lifted her to a sitting position. She opened her eyes, then grimaced, and pressed her fingers to her forehead. "Ohhh," she moaned.

"What happened in San Diego?" he asked.

She mumbled something, but he didn't catch it.

"What?"

"Brady's got her," Keegan said, sounding like her mouth was stuffed with cotton.

"Who?"

Slowly and ever so gently, she massaged her temples with her fingertips. "Brady," she said, without looking at him. "My ex-husband. He took Daisy."

205

"Where did he take her?" Dante asked after a stunned moment.

"They don't know." She sounded helpless and defeated.

"Okay," he said, lifting her chin so he could hear what she was saying. "Tell me everything. Go slow."

Her long-lashed blue eyes met his, and there was such torment in their depths it broke something inside him. Haltingly, in a voice barely above a whisper, her shaky words jamming up in her throat, she repeated what the joint task force told her their investigation had turned up. When she finished, tears began to leak out of her eyes. He handed her a tissue from the box on the bed. He couldn't take away her pain, but he could share it.

"I'm so sorry, Keegan."

She responded by letting him hold her, her head falling naturally to his shoulder.

"What are you going to do now?" he asked after a minute.

Her shoulders hiked in a shrug. "I dunno, but I'm not going back." She moved away from him to put her head back on the pillow.

"Oh, no, you don't," Dante said, refusing to let her lay down. "That isn't helping."

"It's helping me," she said.

"Well, it won't get Daisy back," he replied, handing her another tissue. "Or Lulu, either."

For a moment the silence hung. His arm was still around her, and she leaned against him, her shoulders sagging. He could feel them move as she breathed in and out.

Finally she spoke, her voice low and raw. "Losing Daisy was like an amputation, like having a limb sawed off."

"Teaya probably felt that way, too," Dante replied. "She's probably felt that way for the past fifty years."

Keegan sniffed wetly and stared at the floor. She held a balled-up tissue to her nose and mouth.

"At least you know Daisy is alive, and thank God for that. Teaya doesn't know anything about her baby. Lulu could be alive, too."

Keegan cleared her throat, but didn't say anything. Her breathing had calmed, her breath coming slow and even. Dante glanced down at her. She seemed to be listening, so he went on, speaking softly.

"Agencies all over the world are looking for Daisy, and you've got to believe they're best equipped to do the job. But Teaya has no one. Except you. You were the only one looking for her little girl. If you don't go back, Lulu will never be found. And," he added, "you promised your grandmother you'd do it."

At that, Keegan started crying again, silently, tears squeezing out between her lashes and rolling down her cheeks.

"Stop," he whispered, wrapping her in both arms, cupping his hand around her head and holding her face pressed to his chest. Pressed so close, her heart seemed to beat against his. He rocked her gently for a moment and let her cry. He was surprised she had any tears left. Eventually they subsided, and she pulled in a deep shuddering breath.

"Come on," he said, giving her shoulders a little squeeze. "Get in the shower, and I'll fix us something to eat."

She nodded, and he stood up, bringing her along with him. He walked with her into the adjoining bathroom, turned the shower on full blast, and adjusted the temperature. She stood there, dejected.

"Do you need some help?"

"No. I can manage." Her fingers trembled as she began unbuttoning her jeans.

"Do you need some aspirin?"

"Yes, please." Her voice teetered on the last word.

He found a bottle in the medicine chest, took out two, then filled a paper cup with water and handed it to her along with the tablets. She swallowed them, then pulled her jeans down over her hips.

Ignoring his primal instincts, he reluctantly averted his eyes, and strode back into the bedroom. As much as he wanted to kiss those lips and stroke that silken skin, he wasn't one of those insensitive horndogs who took advantage of women weakened by an emotional meltdown, or otherwise whacked out.

He waited a moment for the heat that flared up in his middle to fade, letting his eyes linger on the shower curtain. Then, sighing, he stripped the bed and went to the linen closet for clean sheets.

While she showered, he remade the bed and wondered what kind of asshole her ex-husband was to run off with their only child, while at the same time imagining what it would be like to step into the shower with her.

He put the wadded up tissues into a plastic trash bag he found under the bathroom sink, scooped the dirty laundry under his arm, and picked up the half empty bottle of bourbon from the dresser.

On his way to the kitchen, he stopped in the laundry room, dumped clothes and detergent in the washer, and turned it on. Her purse was spilled on the living room floor, its contents scattered over the Saltillo tile. He picked it up, and put everything back inside except her cell phones. Those he put on the charger on the kitchen counter. He opened the French doors to air out the house, swept up the broken glass, loaded the dishwasher and turned it on, wiped the counters, the stovetop, and the floor.

He opened a can of chicken noodle soup from the pantry, and heated it on the stove. The shower had stopped running, and he listened for the sound of her footsteps on the stairs. Minutes passed, he wasn't sure how many, but when she didn't come down, he poured the steaming soup in a cup and took it upstairs. She was back in bed sound asleep.

He gazed at her beautiful face that was, if not peaceful, at least more tranquil than it had been a little while ago. Unwilling to wake her from what he hoped would be a restorative sleep, he went back downstairs, where he ate the soup in front of the family room television, and eventually fell asleep during the opening credits of *Saturday Night Live*.

"Oh, my God!"

Keegan woke with a jolt in the velvet gray of the hour before dawn, and two thoughts came to her in quick succession hitting her in the face like icy waves.

Daisy is alive!

Dante is here!

In the lucidity of a post booze binge and many hours of needed sleep, reality and gratitude took hold.

Daisy was alive. *Somewhere.* Somewhere in this world, her daughter was alive and breathing and cared for. Brady would never hurt her, but he could, and most certainly would, make sure Keegan never saw her again.

What had Brady told Daisy? He'd probably said her mother was dead. The thought twisted painfully inside her. "The bastard." She ground out the words between her teeth, and wondered if Daisy was thinking of her. The only thing greater than the pain of missing Daisy would be the pain of Daisy forgetting her.

Her love for Daisy was so deep, so fierce, it sometimes scared her. Anger began to billow again, but she instantly pulled it back, letting it vaporize. It was important she keep her focus on the things she could control instead of lashing out blindly. Runaway emotions distorted perceptions. It was control she needed now. Calculated, unbending control. She processed this thought with no small amount of resolve, then took a deep breath to compose herself.

She had to try to seek some comfort in the knowledge that Daisy was with her father instead of a child predator, but the ugly truth was, Keegan didn't know how she could spend the rest of her life without her daughter and not go insane.

Her marriage to Brady had begun in a whirlwind of bliss and promise. She had once loved him more than anything in the world, but the infertility treatments, a multiyear cycle of false hopes and cruel disappointments, were tough on their relationship. The time before she got pregnant with Daisy, she had made it to the fourth month when she miscarried, blood soaking her dress during a trip to Babies "R" Us.

After that, she didn't know how to talk to him. He didn't know how to love her. Together their lovemaking had not been charged with any hint of emotional resonance. It was babymaking. Looking back on it, she was sure that's when he began straying. The only good thing to come out of the marriage was Daisy.

The sheets under her hands were smooth and crisp, and she skimmed a glance around the room. She didn't remember changing the bed or cleaning the room. Dante must have done it. She was wearing an oversized University of Arizona T-shirt and drawstring pajama bottoms. Did Dante do that, too?

But, no. The fog of amnesia brought on by extreme inebriation was drifting away. She remembered taking a shower, the hot water pelting her, doing its best to clarify and define her anger into something useful.

She put a hand over her eyes. Her mouth was dry as dust, a headache pounding her temples.

What had she been thinking to drink that way? She didn't even like whiskey. The two bottles of expensive limited edition bourbon had been a Christmas gift from her cousin Richard. Richard, an irredeemable geek in his youth, was now a man of wealth and impeccable taste and style who put a lot of thought into the impression his pricey gifts would make. The fact that she wasn't much of a drinker had been beside the point. She reminded herself to call him and the rest of the family with the news about Daisy.

The barely discernable sound of a television drifted up from downstairs.

Tossing the covers, she swung her legs over the side of the bed and got up, walking barefoot down the stairs. Dante was asleep, sprawled in an overstuffed chair, his head tilted to one side, resting as best it could on his shoulder. A Jerry Springer rerun was on the television at low volume. Images flashed across the screen, a raging, chair-throwing fistfight staged for the cameras and cheered on by ill-mannered audience members.

An onslaught of intense alcohol dehydration propelled her to the kitchen sink for a glass of water. The light under the microwave cast the room in amber and shadow, and she could see it was immaculate. Dante must have done that, too. The refrigerator began to hum, and the ice maker chattered. Dante's car keys were on the kitchen counter next to his sunglasses. His boots were on the floor by the French doors. One of the panes where glass should have been was covered with cardboard and tape.

She drank two full glasses of ice water, then stood next to the chair watching Dante sleep. Her heart began beating a little too fast, and she gave conscious resistance to the thoughts that accompanied it. Heat rose to her skin.

Movement on the Jerry Springer stage caught her eye. A woman in a beehive hairdo wearing an orange tank top that showed her substantial middle stood up looking eager to join the ongoing fray. *If I can count to seven before she throws a punch,* thought Keegan, *I won't wake Dante.*

One.

211

Two.

Three.

Four.

Beehive woman took a leap, landed on her boyfriend's back, and began pounding on his head.

Keegan picked up the remote and clicked it off.

"Dante?"

Slowly, he opened his eyes, his emerald gaze smoky with slumber, his lashes dark as night. She felt an involuntary little jolt.

"You're sleeping in your clothes."

"Huh?" he said, coming awake. He squinted up at her, getting his bearings, then looked down at himself. "Oh. Yeah."

"You can take them off."

He blinked. "What?"

"Come upstairs with me, and you can take them off."

It took a moment for her words to sink in. When they did, he gave her a long, long look full of question.

She dipped her head and stared at him leaving no doubt of her meaning. She smiled and held out her hand. With a rich chuckle, he took it, then followed her up the stairs.

In the bedroom, she fell back on the bed carrying him with her. His gray-green eyes were no longer sleepy. They were dancing. A tremor went through her, delicious and surprising. He put his arms around her, and she let herself be gathered close. He kissed her lips lightly, and she relished the taste of his mouth. It was a warm, sweet kiss that told of something much more wonderful to come.

The next morning, she felt his hand drifting lightly up her thigh. He pulled her in and folded his arms around her. "What do you want to do?" he asked.

"I want to make love again," she answered.

"Okay," he said. "I meant after."

"Call the glass company to fix the window you broke."

He nuzzled her hair, his breath warming her ear. "Okay. Then what?"

"Go back to Monument Valley and find Lulu."

He reached for her hand and entwined each of his fingers between each of hers.

"Okay," he said a third time, and with promise in his voice added, "We'll find Lulu. And we'll get Daisy back, too."

He spoke in the kind of voice that told her everything was under control, everything was going to be all right, and made her believe it, too. She pulled his hand to her lips and kissed his fingertips.

CHAPTER TWENTY-TWO

Jilly, having recently returned from a Native American Educators Conference in Denver, looked up from unpacking her bags and listened to Keegan with her mouth open, too astonished to question or interrupt.

"I knew it would be a shock," Keegan said apologetically, "but I thought you needed to know what my grandmother told me."

Jilly brought her hand up to cover her mouth, then raised it to cover her eyes. She bowed her head, and dropped to the edge of the bed. She uttered soft words in Navajo, her voice barely audible. Keegan wasn't sure if she was praying or swearing.

"I knew my mother was lying about something," Jilly said, slowly shaking her head. "I just didn't know what."

She sat that way a long moment. When she looked up, her expression was one of absolute bewilderment.

"Why wouldn't my mother say *shimasani* was in that picture?" She gazed, trancelike, at a spot over Keegan's shoulder, in the grip of thoughts that washed ripples of disappointment over her features. "Why didn't my grandmother point herself out or say she knew your grandfather?"

Keegan shrugged helplessly. She'd been asking herself those same questions, and more. "I don't know."

Jilly put her head in her hands again briefly, then raised it and stared at the ceiling as if praying for deliverance.

"God. What else didn't they tell me? We Navajo are even

secretive with each other." She sighed. "I still haven't gone through the clothes and things my grandmother kept here. Now I'm afraid what else I'll find." Jilly tried to laugh, but the sound strangled in her throat.

Following tradition, the family had already burned Earlene's hogan. They'd given her sheep to the neighbor who had tended them in her absence and after she died. Her loom had been destroyed by her attacker, but Jilly had taken possession of Earlene's handspun yarns and whatever finished and unfinished weavings she'd been able to salvage. Keegan could see them stashed in boxes, taking up a lot of floor space in the bedroom across the hall where Earlene had slept when she stayed there.

Jilly's eyes suddenly widened and focused on Keegan as a new thought came to her. "But you must have been shocked to find out your grandfather is Lulu's father." Then the fuller implication of that hit her, and she took a quick, sharp breath. "That means you're related to Lulu."

"Yes."

Jilly let a silent minute go by. Keegan could see questions swirling behind her eyes. "Does Teaya know?" Jilly asked. "About you, I mean."

"No, not yet, but I want to tell her. My grandmother wants her to come to Phoenix so they can talk. I found out Teaya does outreach volunteer work for the senior center in Oljato, but I haven't been able to get in touch with her."

Jilly flared her eyes and choked out a sound that was half laugh, half snort. "It will be such a blow to her."

Keegan agreed, and had been wondering about the best way to break that particular bit of news. She hoped Jilly would help.

"Do you know Teaya?" Keegan asked.

"A little. *Shimasani* knew her. She's a weaver. I've seen her the times I went with *shimasani* to weavers' gatherings, and at festivals. She sometimes has a jewelry booth near the visitor's center in the summer."

"She'd be, what," Keegan calculated in her head. "Sixty-eight years old now? She's nearly an elder herself."

"Yes, she is." Jilly went back to unpacking her suitcase, folding clothes and putting them on hangers, her expression pensive.

"Would you go with me to talk to her?" Keegan asked. "Teaya might feel more comfortable if you were present. So would I," she admitted.

Jilly agreed immediately. "When do you want to do it?"

"Tomorrow? We could drive out to the senior center, and if she's not there, maybe they'll tell you where her eldercare assignment is."

Jilly slid her closet door shut with more a little more force than necessary, then turned and looked directly at Keegan. "The sooner the better," she replied decisively. "Then I'm going to Albuquerque to talk to my mother."

The Oljato Senior Center was a square concrete block building on the right as they entered the tiny town. Inside, a middle-aged Navajo woman was working at a computer when Keegan and Jilly entered. A noisy air conditioner rattled nearby.

"Teaya is at Minnie Shebala's house over in Montezuma Creek for a few days," the director said. "She'll probably be happy for some company. Take the third turnoff after the elementary school," she said. "Follow it a couple of miles. You can't miss it."

Keegan had no idea where that was, but Jilly seemed to know. After turning off the rutty road, she drove across open desert and down a bumpy wash, then veered onto an even ruttier road that obscured the windshield with dust. A tumbleweed rolled out of the flats and bounced off the hood of the Tahoe before continuing its windswept journey.

Jilly came to a small cement block house. She steered onto

the hard packed dirt in front, staying back a polite distance, and waited until a woman came out.

"That's her," Jilly said, getting out of the car. *"Ya'at'eeh,"* she greeted Teaya, who stood on the porch with her arm raised, shading her eyes from the sun, watching them approach. Recognition dawned on Teaya's face as they drew near.

"Ya'at'eeh, Jilly Cly," she said. "I haven't seen you since the craft fair last fall. Have you driven all this way to visit me?"

Teaya was small and slight, with kind eyes and a smile that lifted clouds. Keegan could tell she must have been ravishing as a young woman, because she was so attractive now. Though the contours of her face and body had softened, Keegan would never have guessed this vigorous and youthful appearing woman with lively black eyes was in her late sixties.

"Yes," Jilly answered, then gestured to Keegan. "This is my friend, Keegan Thomas. She's writing an article for a magazine and has a picture she'd like you to look at. Would you mind talking to her?"

"Not at all. Come inside." Teaya smiled and held the door open, stepping aside so they could enter. She walked quickly to a bedroom and closed the door. "This is Minnie's nap time," she said lowering her voice an octave. "She always drops off when I read to her."

The neat as a pin little house had only a front room, a kitchen, and one tiny bedroom. The kitchen and living area flowed together, separated by a round table and four straight backed chairs. The space devoted to the living room held a recliner chair, a television set with rabbit ears, and a saggy sofa.

Teaya invited them to sit at the table while she fussed at the kitchen counter. She set out a plate of blue cornmeal muffins, and poured iced tea from a pitcher.

"Now," she said pleasantly, sitting down. "What do you have to show me?" She took the picture Keegan was holding out to her. After one look at it, a smile immediately appeared.

"Oh, that's me," she exclaimed. "And that's Doctor Cole next to me." She looked at Keegan, her eyes lively with interest. "Where did you get this?"

"Doctor Cole is my grandfather," Keegan said. "He's passed on now. This was in his belongings." Keegan caught her words up short, unsure how to handle the subject of death with the Navajos now that she'd learned how uneasy it made them.

Teaya beamed. "You're Dr. Cole's granddaughter?" She studied Keegan's face, taking an inventory of her features as if searching for a resemblance. Then her expression turned serious. "Your grandfather was a great man. A wonderful doctor." There was heartfelt admiration in her tone.

"Thank you," Keegan said, warming with familial pride. She fastened her eyes on this pretty woman, the mother of her grandfather's child, and waited for Teaya to make the further connection, but she didn't. Instead Teaya regarded Keegan mildly a moment, then turned her gaze back to the picture, moving her eyes over the images.

"And this," she said, speaking to Jilly, "is your grandmother standing next to me. Your grandfather is in front here, sitting on the log with the blanket over his knees. He wasn't well."

Jilly's mouth dropped open in surprise. "My grandfather is in there, too?" She moved closer to gape at the photo she'd already looked at a dozen times. "*Shimasani*'s husband?"

"Oh, yes," Teaya replied, smiling in remembrance. "Your grandfather loved it when John Wayne came to visit. He liked listening to stories of Hollywood."

Jilly let out her breath in a burst and leaned back in her chair, looking fretful, looking as if one more surprise would cause her to fly to pieces.

Teaya was still studying the photo. "Oh, and next to your grandmother is Mrs. Bedonnie, and that's her little boy Will.

You know Will Bedonnie, don't you?" Her forehead crinkled, and the corners of her mouth tightened into a sad little grimace. "He's Emerson's brother. He's not quite right in the head, you know."

"Yes," Jilly answered. "I know."

Slowly Teaya's expression melted into perplexity. She pursed her lips and frowned. "But I wonder who this is," she said. "Whose little girl I'm holding?"

Keegan and Jilly exchanged a quick glance.

"That's your daughter," Keegan said gently.

Teaya met her eyes without blinking, a small puzzled frown forming between her brows. "I don't have a daughter," she said. "I don't have any children."

A silence heavy as a blanket fell on the room. In a dim corner of Keegan's mind, where primitive fears lived, something stirred. The hair on her arms rose and fell.

Jilly cocked her eyebrows and leaned forward. "That's Lulu," she said. "Your little girl."

"But I don't have a little girl," Teaya insisted. "I wasn't able to have children."

Keegan and Jilly darted a pointed look at each other, their stunned gazes clashing in midair before sliding back to the old woman's face.

Teaya looked at them, bemused, her head tilted a little to the side. Her eyes squeezed imperceptibly as her thoughts seemed to travel inward to a long distant past. A swell of tenderness washed over her face, here and gone in an instant, then she returned to the present.

"Whatever made you think I had a child?" she asked uncertainly, looking first at Keegan and then at Jilly.

Keegan drew a shaky breath, then reached out and took Teaya's hand.

"I'm mistaken," Keegan said with compassion. "I'm very

sorry, but I made a mistake." The words sounded forced, but she couldn't help it.

A sound came from behind the closed bedroom door, the creak of a mattress, someone getting out of bed.

"Oh," said Teaya with a smile. She handed the photo back. "That's Minnie. It's time for her lunch."

Keegan and Jilly hurriedly stood. "We'll be going then," Keegan said. "Thank you for your time."

"Oh, it was no bother," Teaya said brightly, all trace of her previous confusion gone. "I enjoyed visiting with you." She walked Keegan and Jilly to the door and waved as they drove away.

In the car, Keegan swung a confounded look at Jilly, who was staring straight ahead, her face stony. She was pushing the Tahoe too fast for the bumpy ground, her hands clenching the wheel as the SUV bounced and bottomed out.

Keegan's thoughts raced, questions trailing through her mind in an endless loop. "How could she not remember her own child?" she asked out loud.

Jilly twisted her lips, her velvety dark eyes thoughtful, but she said nothing.

"Teaya doesn't appear to have dementia."

"Someone's lying," Jilly replied angrily. "I can't tell the truth from the lies anymore."

Keegan was confused, too. Her mind shuffled possibilities like a deck of cards. Who was capable of varnishing the truth?

Sandra and Earlene both were. They'd lied about knowing anyone in the photo. Did Sandra also lie about the little girl's kidnapping? And if so, why?

And who was that little girl? Was her name really Lulu? Was Lincoln Cole really her father? Hazel Cole was certainly capable of embellishing a story, but Keegan didn't think her grandmother would lie about something like that. Yet, Teaya denied it was her child.

Keegan resisted the temptation to make accusations against Jilly's mother or grandmother, though it was becoming clear the secrets in that family were more than harmless little privacies, the kind anyone could be forgiven for keeping to themselves. They were beginning to look like secrets that affected others in deeply personal or harmful ways.

Jilly chittered the tires in the gravel getting back on the pavement. She stared straight ahead, her features frozen, though Keegan was certain she was feeling a mixture of hurt and anger at the deceptions of her closest loved ones.

Keegan made a helpless gesture, briefly touching Jilly's arm. "Don't be too hard on your mother," Keegan said. "She probably has a very good reason for saying what she did."

"Or maybe," Jilly replied bitterly, "my grandmother was murdered because of it."

The same thought had spun through Keegan's mind, but she didn't say so, and they rode the rest of the way in silence.

CHAPTER TWENTY-THREE

The engine muscled the Jeep up an incline. Ahead, red cliffs loomed large on the rough trail. The ground leveled off at the top, and Dante steered along a rocky corridor of tumbleweed and dense clutches of sage. This was a place where there were no roads, just wheel paths leading to collapsing log shacks, skeletons of trailers, and hogans abandoned long ago.

Keegan was relating what happened at Minnie Shebala's house, bringing him up to date on the new development, Teaya's denial of a child. Dante listened intently just as mystified as she was.

"And Jilly thinks her mother knows something about Earlene's murder?" asked Dante, dubious. "That hardly seems likely."

"She doesn't think Sandra knows anything specific about the murder. She just thinks her mother knows more than she's telling. And what she knows might somehow be connected to Earlene's death."

"Hmmm." Dante nodded, his interest sharpened.

"She's in Albuquerque now," Keegan went on, "talking to her mother about our visit with Teaya. I'll be interested to know what Sandra has to say about Teaya denying she has a daughter named Lulu." She paused. "Of course, there's always the chance Jilly might not want to tell me. I hope she does, but she might feel it's family business, and too personal to share."

Dante slid her a sideways look. "Since when has that stopped you from asking questions?" he asked with a slow smile.

Keegan acknowledged his good-natured gibe with a mock punch on his arm. "Well, it's my family's business, too," she went on undeterred. "Lulu shares my bloodline." Keegan's thoughts spun out, the inconsistencies continuing to nag at her, frustrating her. "My grandfather. Earlene. Teaya. Whatever it is Sandra isn't telling. It's all connected somehow."

"Have you told your grandmother what Teaya said?"

"No. I'm going to wait a while. I need to find out more before I shock her with that." Keegan shook her head. "I don't understand why she would tell a story like that about my grandfather if it wasn't true." The tangle of dark connections was impossible to navigate, and her exasperation grew. "And I'm still waiting to hear from Henry Parker at the National Archives about why my grandfather went to Monument Valley if the BIA didn't send him."

"When are you going to the Indian school in Santa Fe?" Dante asked.

"Next week," she said. "I called and spoke to their historian. They have paper records they'll let me see. Student enrollment registers, some pictures. All the students had their picture taken when they arrived."

Dante reached out and covered her hand with his. He squeezed her fingers gently and smiled. "Do you want me to go with you?"

She gazed at his handsome face. "If you want to."

"I want to," he said, his smile lingering.

The trail dipped and followed a curve. A dry bluff rose up, sparsely dotted with dark green sage. Its jagged crest was outlined against the jeweled blue sky.

"Thanks for coming to celebrate the solstice with me," Dante said, interlacing his fingers with hers, resting their entwined hands on his knee. "Have you ever seen a solstice marker?"

"Only in pictures, and on television," she replied. "Never at solstice. I've always wanted to. My friend Diana said she always feels a burst of energy near summer solstice."

"Lots of people do," Dante said. "I have to admit I do, too. Most people merely think of solstice, if they think of it at all, as the longest day of the year. You know, the beginning of summer. In astronomical terms, it's when the sun is directly overhead on the Tropic of Cancer.

"But for ancient cultures, solstice was a practical seasonal milestone. They used sun migration symbols to track the path of the sun through the sky and mark important dates. Agrarian societies depended on sun calendars to tell them when it was time to plant. For many others, solstice also held spiritual significance. Like the Navajo Enemy Way ceremony. That's only held during the summer months."

They rounded the last bend. On the horizon, fractured and upturned landforms whipped into shape by wind and rain and earthquakes rose dramatically above the earth. Late morning sun fired up the buttes and mesas, painting them with a blaze of color. Dante slowed the Jeep to a crawl, slithered it through a field of sandstone boulders, then stopped in a clearing that offered a breathtaking view of Monument Valley.

"We get out here and walk the rest of the way. It's rocky, but a fairly easy hike."

Keegan stepped out and looked around. "Someone's been here. I see tire tracks."

Dante glanced at the marks on the ground and shrugged. "Probably photographers. They come up to shoot the sunrise. Like on Mokie Dugway," he said, referring to the stunning overlook on Cedar Mesa known for its views.

Dante shouldered his backpack, handed Keegan hers, and plopped a canvas outback hat on his head. "Did you bring a hat?" he asked. His words, spoken with a smile, were gently reproachful, reminding her how he'd chided her for going without that day she got stuck on Oljato Mesa.

"Yes," Keegan replied. She took a soft-brimmed hat from her backpack and put it on.

"Okay, let's go," he said. "It's not far."

Dante led the way along a gently rising path that curved around a sheer rock face stained with black, streaky canyon varnish. It was narrow at first, and they proceeded up single file for a short distance. When they made the last turn, the pathway broadened into a wide horseshoe-shaped upland backed by a sheer cliff face. The outside flanks dropped off sharply, but a rocky slope terraced down the center of the horseshoe at a forty-five degree angle. The sun, flaming over a distant ridge, turned it orange.

"We can sit here."

Keegan slipped off her backpack and sat on a flat boulder facing a slightly concave wall of rock. On a narrow ledge that followed the curvature, two stone slabs stood on edge, slightly off vertical and fanned out at a gentle angle. They were close together, but not touching. It looked like the slabs had once fit together to form a solid block. The place where the block had once joined the cliff face was marked by variegated layers of strata charting the geological eons.

Dante lowered himself beside her. He took off his hat and wiped his forehead with his bandana, then put it back on and adjusted the brim.

"With the sun coming from behind us, those slabs cast shadows on the cliff face except near midday, when the sun shines between them. Then they'll form patterns of light that illuminate the petroglyphs on the rock. You can barely see them now, but when the sun brightens they'll stand out in relief."

"I can see them," Keegan said. Figures of snakes, birds, animals, and human forms were pecked and carved into the rock wall. A large spiraling concentric circle, partially shadowed, was located behind the two slabs, but visible between them.

"I've seen a rock art wall like this at Sand Island in Bluff," Keegan said. "Down by the river. Some of the carvings look like religious symbols." She remembered a feeling of being transported back in time a thousand years as she tried to decipher their meaning, imagined hearing ancient voices raised in prayer.

"There's another interesting rock art wall with eight-hundred-year-old handprints at Newspaper Rock near Monticello," Dante said. "I'll take you there sometime. I'm guessing these are that old, too."

Sunlight was beginning to touch the cliff face. The two stone slabs bent the sun's rays in a way that made parallel shafts of light shine on the spiral.

"Which of those carvings are the solstice markers?" Keegan asked.

"The spiral, but all the symbols work together with light and shadow to mark the sun's passage. The sun illuminates them each day near noon in a pattern that changes throughout the year. The big spiral in the center marks the solstices and equinoxes. See? It has thirteen turns, suggesting that each turn represents a twenty-eight day lunar cycle. And see those peck marks?"

Keegan looked where Dante was pointing. Clusters of deep grooves were scratched into the stone beside the spiral.

"Yes, I see them."

"There are twenty-four of them," Dante explained. "The length of time the sun shines between each one indicates a day, sunrise to sunrise."

"How did they figure that out?"

"That's one of the mysteries of these ancient cultures. Sometimes they built their pueblos so the sun would enter from one side and shine on key features inside like doorways or niches or certain corners at the solstices and equinoxes. There's a kiva in Chaco Canyon where the sun shines through a window on the northeastern side of the structure into a niche on an interior wall at the exact moment of solstice."

Keegan felt like she was sitting in an outdoor temple. A sacred place where people came to meditate and pray.

"See that wedge of sunlight to your left?" Dante asked. He was speaking in a near-whisper as if he, too, were showing respect to a sacred place.

"Yes."

"As the sun moves across the sky, that beam of light will move across the markings on the cliff face. Eight days ago, it was there, just touching that symbol of a human carrying a bow. At solstice it will be in the center of the spiral. In three days it will be there on that petroglyph that looks like an animal. I want you to see what happens at solstice." He looked at his watch. "It's just past eleven-thirty."

Keegan felt a vague excitement ripple over the surface of her skin. Within minutes the first beam of light began to move above the top edge of the slabs.

"It's starting," said Dante. "Watch where the sun is shining right there. It's going to start moving down through the spiral." A narrow shaft of sunlight touched the outer spiral and slowly, second by second, moved toward the center.

"Now that big shadow there will start to move at the same time. As the sun climbs, the light will follow the irregular rock edges of that butte, and cast the shadowed silhouette of a human face."

Keegan watched in fascination as the distinct profile of a face touched the center of the spiraling concentric circles at the same time a shaft of light traveled downward through its center and drifted across the eye symbol. The sun had reached its northernmost point.

It was solstice.

All at once Keegan felt energized. A spontaneous wave of peace and power surfed through her. Something pivotal was happening. She had the feeling of going through an open door, of leaving something behind, walking into something new. The word *forgiveness* came to her, but she didn't know if it was whispered in her ear or written across her mind.

Forgiveness of who, she wondered. She'd already forgiven her grandfather, and would easily forgive her grandmother no matter what. Even her cold and distant mother could be forgiven for actions she was incapable of anticipating or controlling. Who was it she needed to forgive next? Earlene? Jilly? Teaya? Sandra?

The sun passed its vortex, and she stood and walked to the overlook at the edge of the rocky stepdown, overcome by a strange kinetic dynamism. Her eyes roamed over the treeless red terrain falling away in front of her. It came to her in a flash, as clearly as if someone spoke to her, that it was Brady she was supposed to forgive. The thought pinched painfully, and her mind rebelled in guilty anger. Forgiving Brady for taking Daisy was something she could never do. Ever.

Dante came to stand beside her. She turned to him, and her heart bumped at the almost mystical expression in his eyes. He'd obviously been moved in some similar fashion by the sun's rite of passage.

"Oh, Dante, thank you for bringing me here. I loved it. I want to do this every year."

They put their arms around each other and stood that way, not speaking. She took in the warmth of his body, felt the strength and security of his arms around her. She went up on tiptoe and touched her lips to the corner of his mouth. She laid her head on his chest, letting her eyes rest on the awesome wildness and the distant monuments that rose to towering heights in the distance.

The thin dry desert air carried a faint aroma of cedar and sage. A long-tailed raptor circled overhead, eyeing something on the ground. She watched its effortless flight as it glided on rising shafts of air, then followed it as it dipped and skimmed the rocky crags below.

Keegan lifted her head and stared. "What's that?"

"What? Where?"

She stepped out of Dante's embrace, but held her gaze on a flash of light, a ray of sun glinting off something in the rocks below. "Did you bring binoculars?"

"Yes."

"Let me have them." She made a *gimme* motion with her hand, not moving her eyes, afraid she'd lose track of it if she looked away.

Dante took the binoculars out of his backpack and handed them to her.

Keegan steadied her elbows at her waist, and focused on a jumble of rocks near the bottom of the slope. "It looks like a . . ." She stared, trying to make it out. A light breeze ruffled her bangs and the hair on the back of her head, and caused the glint to flicker.

"It looks like a pinwheel."

"A what?" Dante squinted where she was pointing.

"You know. Those metallic thingies we used to get at the fair and on Fourth of July? They were shiny and turned around when the wind blew. We called them spinners."

"Let me see," he said.

She handed the binoculars back, and he scanned the lower rocks. "Yeah," he said after a few seconds. "You're right." Then, "Hey, where are you going?"

But Keegan was already making her way down to take a closer look.

"Be careful in those rocks," he called, stowing the binoculars and starting down after her.

It was steep, but manageable if she maneuvered a diagonal path back and forth across the fall line. Clambering over boulders, and keeping her distance from prickly pear and cholla, she lost sight of the pinwheel behind an outcropping halfway down. She saw it again when she reached the bottom, where she halted, stunned to see a roadside cross where there was no road.

Dante caught up to her and stopped, equally stunned.

It wasn't a casual memorial. It was deliberately assembled and showed the effects of being cared for, despite its obvious prolonged exposure to the elements. Three pinwheels, all of them spinning in the breeze, were attached with wire to an unpainted wooden cross that leaned against a large boulder and was held in place with a small pile of stones. Draped over the crossbar was a silver garland, the kind used on Christmas trees. Hanging from the garland was a heart-shaped turquoise pendant on a thin leather cord, and a turquoise bead necklace. Bunched up at the base of the cross as if huddling together for companionship was a collection of stuffed animals. A teddy bear. A puppy. A bunny.

The cross's vertical piece was topped by bouquets of bleached out silk flowers deteriorating from the sun. Pink roses, yellow daisies, sprigs of greenery held in place with wire. Bordering the entire memorial was a circle of flat stones, the ground inside its perimeter freshly swept with a broom.

"Oh, Dante, look," Keegan said on a sob, the shock of discovery hitting her full force. She went down on her knees and gently touched her fingertips to the faded letters that spelled out the name of the deceased. "It's Lulu."

CHAPTER TWENTY-FOUR

The National Archives and Records Administration was a labyrinthine facility with over five hundred miles of mobile shelving, and Henry Parker was familiar with every inch of it. The number of records stored in the facility easily outnumbered the employees by a million to one. It could take as long as thirty minutes of walking the corridors to retrieve a single document. This, the walking, had become more difficult for Henry with the passing years, but he had the tenacity of a pit bull when it came to tracking documents and solving historical puzzles.

Most people had no idea how to conduct their records research or even where to begin. Henry's archival memory, his grasp of world history, and his ability to locate pertinent documents made him a one-man memory bank. He had been written up in magazines because of it, and was acclaimed by researchers worldwide for his knowledge of primary sources and his uncanny recall of events.

It was that superhuman memory that was urging him on today, propelling him to a section of the National Archives not open to the public. The classified stacks. Even the archive technicians, who usually assisted with searching and retrieving records, weren't cleared for entrance into that inner sanctum. But Henry, by virtue of being not only a senior archivist but a senior archivist with the most seniority, had a security clearance allowing him unlimited access everywhere.

The thick cushioned soles of his shoes made almost no sound

on the polished marble floor as he approached the main reading room. It was the beginning of the day. The sun shining through a bank of framed windows three stories high created a grid pattern of shadows that fell across the floor, over the study tables, and up the opposite walls. Early arriving archivists and researchers rolling wheeled carts piled high with archival storage boxes were claiming the preferred reading tables adjacent to the wall of windows. Soon the tables on the mezzanine would be full, as well.

The archives permitted outside researchers to freely comb through original records, a practice Henry abhorred with all his heart. He felt it defeated the mandate of records preservation. There were strict rules about handling records here, and archive room monitors made sure everyone followed them to the letter. Even so, and despite the security cameras, collections still got misplaced or messed up. And Henry hadn't yet figured out how Justin had defeated the other more stringent security measures in use at the archives.

As Henry entered the reading room, he nodded to the archive junior staff and volunteers stationed behind the information counter. He'd been a volunteer many decades ago when he started at the archives, and remembered spending summers answering all manner of questions that ranged from *Where can I find a list of Nazi concentration camp survivors?* to *Where is the restroom?*

The staff greeted him when he came in, their eyes lively and smiles bright with the eager expectation and high hopes of the young.

"Good morning, Henry."

"Having a good day, Henry?"

"You're looking sharp this morning, Henry."

That they spoke his name in reverential tones indicated the level of respect with which they regarded Henry for his knowledge and ability as well as his age.

For his part, Henry truly liked the young staff members and enjoyed spending time with them. They always remembered to invite him to birthday and engagement celebrations after work, or drinks on Friday, invitations he'd recently begun to politely decline.

He returned their pleasant greetings with a smile of his own today, even though he was in a hurry and his mood was prickly.

"Good morning to you. Yes, it is a wonderful day! You look pretty, Peaches."

Usually he stopped to chat, but today he kept walking, the trajectory to his destination unflagging. There was no time. He was on a mission.

Henry crossed the reading room and exited through a door on the far end. He continued along corridors of locked doors until he reached a room marked *NO ENTRY—RESTRICTED AREA*. He stopped, punched in his nine-digit security code, and placed his palm on the handprint scanner. When he heard the beeps, he hauled open the heavy door and went in. He let the door close behind him, checking to make sure it was secure, then proceeded to the classified stacks where he hoped to solve an archival puzzle.

When federal agencies sent records to the National Archives, Henry was often the first to take a look. While reading the documents abandoned in the attic room after Justin was fired, Henry had recalled that other similar documents had arrived in the same shipment ten years before. Financial statements, census data, oil, gas, and mining reports, and other records documenting activities on the Navajo Indian Reservation during the 1950s.

Only those records had been separated from the rest at the time and sent here, over Henry's objections, to be shielded behind a national security classification.

It was often a tug of war between historians and the federal agencies over whether to classify or declassify documents. Henry usually argued against it if the information didn't jeopardize national security, often enlisting the guidance of the Information Security Oversight Office.

The ISOO reviewed requests for declassification of federal records, and worked closely with the archives about what records can and should be declassified and open to the public. Often, the archives would approve the declassification of records, but the federal agency that sent them would not. This forced the archives to restrict the information, because classified materials couldn't be released without the agreement of the agency that provided them originally. Getting that agreement was often easier said than done, and in this case, the sending agency had refused to budge.

Sometimes, the refusal to declassify was based on simply not having enough staff to process the thousands of pages that needed to be reviewed line by line before being released. But usually it was political, and Henry had a feeling that was the case with the records he was looking for now.

He glanced around the room, his eyes trailing over shelves that were crowded with material overflowing into carts, and out of the stacks onto the floor. Some of it hadn't been touched since the day it arrived.

Archival holdings were arranged by record group, the basic unit of archival control. After that, they were organized by key word, number, and name of the original agency or bureau that created them. By law, documents had to be kept in the order in which they were received. Consequently, if items were misfiled fifty years ago by the creating agency, they must remain that way at the archives.

This practice, as Henry was aware, provided a much maligned but often used method of hiding smoking-gun documents and other incriminating materials. No wonder the Tribes were suing for an accounting of their missing trust fund money, he thought.

Henry trod the corridors between the stacks, his thoughts filtering back, recreating the day the records arrived from the BIA. Suddenly he stopped walking, his mind racing backward in time. *Wait a minute.* Were they from the BIA or from Senator O'Toole's office?

Like a movie playing in Henry's mind, images appeared. Scenes, people. His son Jake had started his new job at the Department of Justice. It had been his granddaughter's birthday. Melanie was turning six. A birthday dinner was planned that evening: pizza, cake, candles, and gifts. Henry was going to leave work early, but his director had asked him to look through the shipment before he left for the day. All this went through Henry's mind in a calm and orderly manner, leading him to a section containing seldom requested materials.

And then he saw them. Three archival storage boxes, stacked on the same cart where he'd deposited them ten years prior.

Henry cleared some space on a table, extracted documents from the first box, and sat down to review the material. Quickly, he checked the contents of the box against the index sheet. As expected, there were agency reports and financial records relating to the uranium mines located on the reservation. These he browsed, but found nothing relating to Lincoln Cole or Earlene Cly. He set them aside.

It was the same with the second box. Carbon copies of letters with handwritten corrections in pen from a time before computers, internal memos and reports from the Indian Health Service, annual budget requests, and health reports.

But it was the third box labeled *Pipeline Surveys* that made Henry sit back in surprise. He stared at the contents, letting a guilty memory wash over him.

In a hurry to get to Melanie's birthday party, he'd only given the shipment a cursory inventory at the time, looking at the first and last documents in the box and generalizing about the middle, a common archival practice he did not as a rule engage in or endorse. Even so, he'd argued for declassification at the time, seeing no reason to restrict the information. Oil and gas correspondence, expense reports, and pipeline output records did not threaten national security.

But the sending agency had been adamant, and Henry's director, a man close to retirement, a man of terminal indecision and weakness of spine, did not support Henry's argument. These boxes had been separated out from the others and sent here to the classified stacks where they had remained untouched. Until now.

Henry's heart picked up its beat as he carefully removed the contents of the third box, and flipped through journals filled with cramped but legible pen and ink script. *Lincoln Cole's diaries written in his own hand laying out the details of Project 32.*

CHAPTER TWENTY-FIVE

There was no body under the mound of stones holding the cross in place. No bones either. Eventually crime task force officials released the site to the tribe, which called in a team of cultural preservation specialists. They confirmed it wasn't a grave, it was someone's personal memory marker, a contemporary one, and let it go at that. Their determination didn't answer the question at the forefront of Keegan's mind. Who put it there, and why?

The problem was, Keegan had no one to ask. The tribe wanted to keep the whole operation quiet. They did not publicize the discovery because they didn't want shovel-wielding bulldozer-driving outsiders flooding in, tramping around and digging up the site, doing their own search.

Because Monument Valley was so far removed from population centers, it was fairly easy to keep secrets from filtering out, but within Monument Valley absolutely nothing was secret. Everyone was talking about the mysterious roadside cross in the desert. Keegan and Dante talked of nothing else for days, speculating and offering up explanations, each one more implausible than the next.

She was in her kitchen emptying the dishwasher, thoughts of the discovery still heavy on her mind. Dante had just settled in to watch a rerun of *Ice Road Truckers*. She didn't know which was louder: the crash of the platter as she dropped it to the floor, or her scream as her gaze met a pair of eyes staring in through the glass panel in her back door. Dante bolted to his feet and came running.

An old man, a Navajo with a deeply creased nut-brown face, was standing outside. He backed up a step when he saw Dante, but didn't run away. Instead, looking doubtful, he waved a big hand motioning Dante to come out.

The two men had a brief conversation outside, then Dante came in with the old man. "This is Will Bedonnie," Dante said. "He wants to know if he can talk to you."

Keegan recognized him as the man she'd noticed at the grocery store, in the gas station, on the highway. He stood uncertainly in the doorway, watching her. He studied her face, his eyes slightly defiant but mostly curious.

"Would you like to sit down?" She gestured to a chair, but he hesitated, looking as if he was afraid she might yank back either the invitation or the chair if he accepted it. With obvious reluctance, he came in, taking slow steps. He sat down at the kitchen table, perching awkwardly on the edge of his seat.

"What did you want to talk to me about?" Keegan asked.

"About Lulu's special place," he answered, surrounding each word with great significance.

Keegan and Dante exchanged a quick look.

"Okay, Will," she said softly. "What did you want to tell me about it?"

Will paused heavily. "It's not there anymore." His tone was petulant and offended.

Keegan knew he was talking about the cross. "No, it isn't," Keegan said. "The police had to take it away." Patiently she waited for him to go on.

Will lowered guilty eyes and shifted his weight, looking as if he was debating his next words, or maybe his wisdom in coming. "Now I can't take care of it anymore."

"Are you the one who put it there?" asked Dante. "The cross

and the flowers and stuffed animals?"

Will nodded. "But now they're gone." The look on his face seemed to demand some sort of an explanation.

"Why did you put it there?" Keegan asked.

Will lowered his eyes.

"Lulu's name was on the cross. Is she buried there some-where?"

The old man shook his head. "No, I don't think so."

"Well, did something happen to her there?" Keegan pressed, trying to put pieces of the puzzle together.

Will hesitated a long time, thinking about this, fidgeting. Agitated, he began pumping his leg up and down, the heel of his boot tap-tap-tapping on the floor. "I don't know," he said finally.

Keegan decided to move on and not press for an answer. Not yet. She asked another question.

"How long have you been taking care of her special place?"

"A long time." Will's dour expression suddenly softened, and his eyes showed a twinkle. "She liked the little toys. The bear and the puppy."

"What else do you remember about Lulu?" Keegan prodded gently.

He bobbed his head in delight. "She was pretty." Memories held a smile in place. "Her face was round and she laughed. Yeah, all the time. She was happy. Until . . ."

In the pause that followed, Dante asked, "What happened to her, Will?"

But the old man's smile was already sliding away. His face pinched tight, and he shook his head, looking bewildered, as if he were trying to recall something that happened a long time ago. "I don't exactly remember," he said. Then suddenly he was animated again, speaking with urgency. "But I have to take care of it. I have to give Lulu her bunny and her beads and her . . ."

Sounds from outside stopped him. Tires on gravel. A car door slamming. Vicki Bedonnie hurried to the door. Keegan let her in.

"I've come to pick up my Uncle Will," she said, a little out of breath. She walked over to him and gently took his arm. "Come on, Uncle Will."

"No." He waved her away, a gesture that was like a slap.

Undaunted, Vicki took his arm again and spoke in a low voice close to his ear. "Come on," she said to him. "Grandfather said you can't—"

But Will held back, pulling his arm out of her grasp, refusing to get out of the chair. "But she's not a witch like you said," he protested, causing Vicki to flick an embarrassed glance at Keegan.

"Never mind about that," Vicki said, taking his claw-like hand in both of hers. "We have to go."

"But she's not a witch," he insisted. "Look. She has blue eyes, just like Lulu."

A resounding silence erupted in the room. Keegan felt the percussion on her eardrums.

Vicki looked at her uncle with a stern expression. "What did you tell them?" she asked, anxiety pitching her voice. She spun around and glared at Keegan, waving her arm as if to clear the air of Will's words. "Don't believe anything he tells you."

"But he said he put that marker at Horseshoe Point. He said he knew Lulu. He remembered her. What happened to her, Vicki?" Dante's voice was commanding.

Vicki shook her head from side to side furiously. "Nothing. He gets mixed up," she insisted. "Sometimes he doesn't know what he's saying."

Will interrupted. "Yes, I do! I remember Lulu." He cut himself off as an image seemed to rise up in his memory then without warning take flight. His gaze darted around the room as if tracking its errant route. Confusion melted his expression, and a solitary tear ran down his cheek.

"Don't cry, Uncle Will. C'mon, we have to go." Vicki took his arm, forcefully this time, but he still refused. Memories chased each other in his eyes, and tears began to flow, flooding the wrinkles on his cheeks.

"Lulu was gone," he said sadly. "I wanted to go find her, but Emerson wouldn't let me."

Vicki gave up trying to dislodge him from his chair. Instead she leaned over and put her arms around his shoulders. "Shhh. Shhh," she soothed. "Don't cry, Uncle Will. It's okay," she said over and over, patting his back, trying to comfort him.

Her own tears glistened, and she wept silently with him. After a while she cleared her throat, sniffed wetly, and looked up at Keegan. Sadness ran down her face like a slow rain.

"Can I use your phone?" she asked, her voice wracked. "I have to call my grandpa."

CHAPTER TWENTY-SIX

The next day Sandra flew in from Albuquerque. Emerson Bedonnie and Yuma Ray coming in from Window Rock drove the extra miles to pick her up at the airport in Farmington. It was out of their way, but Keegan was sure they wanted time alone for a private conversation. The three of them arrived at Jilly's house and walked in with the unwilling fervor of soldiers having been sent off to war.

Will wasn't there. The others agreed it was best. Talking about Lulu upset him. Keegan wondered if Teaya should be included. Both Jilly and Dante argued against it.

Sandra was a bundle of nerves, all jittery hands and trembling lips. She barely managed a nod of greeting.

"It happened pretty much the way I told you," she said with an apologetic look at Jilly, who stared back silently. "Except missionaries didn't take Lulu."

Emerson and Yuma eyed each other gloomily, then stared at the floor seeming relieved that Sandra was willing to start.

She took a deep breath and wiped an unsteady hand across her eyes.

"I was at Aunt Mary's like I said," she began. "Teaya was living there with Lulu. Aunt Mary and Teaya must have eaten something bad because they both got sick. We didn't know what was wrong at the time, we just knew they were really sick. Emerson's mother came over to help." Sandra looked over at Emerson expectantly. *Your turn,* her expression said.

Reluctantly, he picked up the story. Lines of strain were evident beside his eyes and mouth.

"Yes, that's true. She took me and my brother Will along, but right after we got there, my mother sent me over to Yuma Ray's house. I ran all the way."

Yuma Ray, looking like he'd rather be anywhere but there, cleared his throat. "We lived on the other side of the mesa," he said. "Just my dad and me. My mother died when I was born. My father had a horse and wagon. Emerson's mother wanted him to take Mary and Teaya to the doctor. He said he would, but I remember he didn't want to go alone. He wanted Emerson's mother along to take care of the sick women. He didn't want to be alone with them if they died in his wagon."

"There was an argument," Emerson said, adding some detail. "My mother didn't want to leave the children alone, but she was also afraid we'd get the sickness if we got in the wagon and went along. Finally it was decided that since I was the oldest, I'd stay and watch the young ones until they came back."

"How old were you?" Keegan asked.

"I was nine," said Emerson. "I knew what to do. Sometimes I watched Will when my mother had to leave the trailer for short periods of time. Anyway, my mother and Yuma's father managed to get Mary and Teaya in the back of the wagon. They told us kids to stay there and not go out of sight of the hogan. My mother was very strict."

"Very *bossy*," Yuma said, jumping in. "She threatened us. Told us Spider Woman would boil us and eat us and put our bones on Spider Rock if we disobeyed her."

Keegan remembered Jilly telling a Spider Woman story the night she went to dinner and met Earlene. She looked over at Jilly, who was staring out the window. Sandra's face was drawn in a tight mask, her gaze riveted on her trembling hands. Yuma's eyes were boring a hole in the floor. No one seemed able to make eye contact.

"Anyway, like all children, we didn't always do what we were told," Emerson went on, speaking in a subdued tone of regret. "At first, we didn't think about how sick the adults were. You know how self-absorbed kids are. It wasn't often we were left unsupervised for long periods of time, and this was a real treat. A chance to run and play and make noise without being told to quiet down.

"When they weren't back by nightfall, I started to get worried. Lulu was crying for Teaya, and Sandra was getting irritable, wanting to go home. I got to thinking that maybe all the adults would get the sickness and not come back at all." Emerson looked over at Yuma. "I think it was Yuma who first mentioned performing a healing ceremony."

Yuma nodded, his face sorrowful. "I knew it was forbidden. I knew that only medicine men were allowed to do it. But the longer we were alone, the more scared I became. I think I had just turned six."

Emerson sighed as floodgates opened to more memories. "The next morning we ran out to Horseshoe Point. We had no idea how to perform a ceremony. Didn't have the sacred objects necessary. Didn't know the words to the chants and songs. And by then Lulu had stopped crying, and Sandra, too, so we gave up on the idea. The girls were playing in the rocks with a doll. Will and Yuma were having a stick race, seeing who could kick a stick the farthest. But I was still worried. I just sat on a rock thinking about what I'd do if my mother never came back, how I'd take care of the others if I had to. After a while, Will asked me where Lulu was."

Emerson's voice crumbled. He tried to go on, but failed. Across the room, Sandra pressed her fist against her mouth, but tears came anyway. Jilly went to sit beside her mother and hold her hand. Dante sat forward expectantly. Anxiety tightened in

Keegan's chest as she waited for someone to say something. Finally, Yuma spoke up. "She'd been playing with Sandra. Will and I were so involved in our own game, we weren't paying attention to what the girls were doing."

He swallowed a couple of times, and tears glazed his eyes. Keegan watched him struggle with his emotions, thinking what a very different image this was of the man who had intimidated her with nighttime visits and veiled threats. The silence dragged on too long.

"What happened to Lulu?" Keegan pressed, her voice insistent. "Please. I have to know. Lulu was my grandfather's child."

Sandra had already learned this from Jilly, so she didn't react with surprise. Apparently she hadn't mentioned it to Emerson and Yuma on the ride over, because they looked at each other, then back at Keegan, with their jaws dropped in shocked disbelief.

Keegan told them what her grandmother had revealed about Lulu's paternity.

"We never knew who Lulu's father was," said Emerson. "Everyone wondered. I heard my mother talking about it with her friends. They said Teaya got sick because she had a white man's child."

"What happened to Lulu?" Keegan repeated. "Please tell me."

Emerson's shoulders rose and fell in a sigh. "She wandered off," he said helplessly. "One minute she was there. The next minute she wasn't. We looked everywhere. We yelled and called her name, but she didn't answer. Will found her doll at the edge of the drop-off."

The sound of Sandra's renewed weeping stabbed Keegan in the heart. Yuma buried his face in his hands. Emerson struggled pitifully, but failed to keep his composure. His face crinkled and he wiped away a tear.

"Will was hysterical," Emerson said when he could speak again. "He begged me to go down and find her, but it was impossible. It was a sheer drop to the bottom of the canyon at that point. There wasn't anything I could do."

The words carried the weight of finality, but there was still a lot left unsaid. Keegan needed to hear it all. She looked from Emerson to Yuma, and forced the issue.

"You two were the oldest. You didn't tell your parents when they came back?"

Yuma lowered his eyes. Emerson answered.

"We were terrified. We were afraid if we told them, they'd have Spider Woman come and take us like my mother said. We didn't want to be eaten or woven into Spider Woman's rug." He gazed at Keegan, his expression daring her to ridicule such beliefs.

"That probably sounds foolish to you," Emerson said, defensively. "But that's how deeply our beliefs were embedded back then. We were kids. It was fifty years ago, but stories like that are still the fabric of our culture. Every generation is told about Spider Woman. Kids today may say they don't believe it, but it's still there, buried deep inside."

Keegan didn't think it was foolish at all. She could well imagine four frightened children, left alone, bewildered, torn by grief, and paralyzed by fear.

"I can understand," she assured him. "It must have been a horrible experience."

"And we certainly weren't going to tell her we went out there intending to perform a healing ceremony," said Yuma. He rolled his eyes as if imagining a punishment too awful to contemplate.

Emerson agreed. "So we made a promise to never tell what really happened. We concocted the story about missionaries.

When Yuma's father brought the women back, that's what we told them."

"What did they say? Did they believe you?"

Emerson frowned, reliving the moment in his mind. "My mother was furious, but thankfully at the missionaries, not at us. Teaya was completely heartbroken. I remember she couldn't stop crying. She wanted to go find Lulu, but . . ." Emerson shrugged. "They had no way to go look for her. They didn't have transportation. They didn't know who the missionaries were or where the schools were." He sighed. "Aunt Mary tried to console her by saying she'd have Lulu back some day. That the missionaries almost always brought the children back eventually."

Guilty glances collided and ricocheted off the walls.

"But, later," Keegan said. "Why didn't you tell the truth later?"

Yuma half raised his hand in a gesture of futility and let it drop to his lap.

"Later, when we were teens . . ." He shrugged. "It had happened so long ago. I guess part of the reason we didn't tell was because we were afraid we'd be blamed for it. By then, so many of the high school kids were getting in trouble, drinking, stealing cars. Drugs were beginning to come to the reservation from the cities. We were afraid no one would believe it had been an accident."

"But when you grew up," Keegan insisted. "Why not then?"

"We were still afraid. By then we had jobs and families and careers," explained Emerson. "Sandra got a scholarship and went on to college, earned a PhD. She was a college professor, a respected historian, married to a famous heart surgeon. Yuma was moving up in the tribe. He was highly respected, too, and gaining influence. I owned several businesses. I was a youth leader. I mentored teenagers from the high school. By then, we all had a lot more to lose. It would have ruined us."

Emerson lowered his eyes. "Except for Will. He never got over it. He reacted by slowly losing his mind. He just gradually shrunk into himself." Emerson glanced around at the others. "But for the rest of us, so much time had gone by it was easy to pretend it never happened at all."

"Until you came here showing that picture around," said Yuma. "We were worried someone would recognize Lulu and start asking questions. Stir things up. Some of the people in the picture are still alive."

Sandra's head bobbed weakly in agreement. "I was afraid Teaya would see it and the story would come out then."

"But Teaya did see it," Keegan told her. "She recognized almost everyone in it except Lulu. She denied being Lulu's mother."

Again, eyebrows hiked up in surprise.

"She didn't remember Lulu?" Yuma asked.

Emerson was incredulous. "How could she not know her own child?"

Sandra shook her head forlornly. "It's a blessing she was able to erase the heartbreak from her mind." She wiped her eyes with a tissue. "I've lived with the memory every day of my life."

Dante spoke up with a question. "Why did Will place the memorial in that particular spot? It wasn't in the canyon or anywhere near the dropoff where she fell."

"He can't get down to the bottom," explained Emerson simply. "It's too treacherous for him to even try."

"But searchers went down there," said Keegan. "They didn't find anything."

"That's not surprising," said Dante. "During the rainy season, flash floods race through that canyon. And scavengers . . ." He stopped, sparing the others painful mental images.

"When did Will erect the memory marker?" asked Keegan.

"A long time ago," Emerson replied. "I think he was in his early teens. I didn't know anything about it until many years later."

"How did you find out?"

"When I moved from Monument Valley to Window Rock, I couldn't watch over Will anymore. My granddaughter Vicki still lived here, so I asked her to keep an eye on him. Will could live on his own, take care of his basic day-to-day needs, but I gave Vicki money each month to make sure he had food and gas money. Things like that. I added a little extra for her."

"Did Vicki know about Lulu?" Keegan asked. "About what happened at Horseshoe Point?"

"No. Not at first, but she found out. One day when Will went out to refresh the marker, she followed him. When she asked me about it later, I told her everything. I wanted her to know why it was so important to keep an eye on him. Make sure he wasn't talking to people about it. It turned out he had a copy of the same picture you were showing around. Vicki found it in his trailer one day when she was cleaning. Whoever the photographer was must have made several copies. You know, like souvenir photos sold to tourists back then. Somehow Will got hold of one, recognized Lulu, and kept it."

"Did you ever see the memory marker? Any of you?"

Three heads went back and forth indicating no.

"I never went back there," Emerson said. "They say spirits of babies who die in infancy hang around earth and wait for another chance at life. Lulu wasn't an infant, she was three, but still . . ."

"I didn't go, either," said Yuma.

Sandra lowered her eyes and slowly shook her head.

"Does anyone else besides Vicki know about this?" Keegan looked from face to face, waiting for an answer.

"My mother knew," Sandra admitted.

Emerson thrust himself erect. "Earlene knew? You told her?"

"I had to," Sandra said, defending herself. She looked him straight in the eye daring him to argue with her. "I couldn't stand it anymore. The guilt was eating me alive. Just before I went away to college, I told her." Sandra sat back, crossing her arms at her waist, her intensity diminishing just as quickly as it had flared up. "She promised not to tell."

Keegan and Dante exchanged a look, asking a silent question. Up to now, everything had been one huge puzzle with no discernible pattern. Suddenly pieces of the puzzle were starting to slide into place, but they fit imperfectly. Keegan had thought Earlene's guilty knowledge of the relationship between Lincoln Cole and Teaya Etsitty explained why she had lied about the photo. Now it seemed she might have lied to cover up her knowledge of Lulu's death. What did she want to talk to Keegan about that day? Lulu's paternity? Or how Lulu died? Or was it both?

"Someone stole Keegan's purse at the rodeo," Dante said, changing the subject, "but the only things missing were the picture and a little cash. Whoever took it left her checkbooks and her credit cards. Did any of you have anything to do with that?" He looked at them one at a time.

Sandra's fidget started up again. "No," she said with a quick shake of her head.

Emerson and Yuma shifted uncomfortably in their seats, doing a good job of not looking at each other or at Dante.

"No," they said at the same time.

Dante looked doubtful, but let it drop.

Yuma cleared his throat. "I've already made arrangements to bring this matter before the Tribal Council," he said, breaking into everyone's thoughts. "The events occurred on tribal land. Earlene's death is in the hands of the police and the FBI, but this other . . ." He paused. "Lulu and what happened to her, that's a Navajo matter and should be taken care of in a Navajo way according to tradition." He looked dismally at Keegan and Dante. "I trust you won't have any objection to that?"

"No," said Dante.

"Of course not," said Keegan.

Later, driving home in the Jeep, Dante asked her if she was going to press charges about the purse snatching.

"No," she answered. "They didn't mean to do me any harm, and they've all suffered enough, don't you think? Having that terrible experience as children. Held captive by a horrible secret all their lives."

"Yeah," Dante agreed, "but it's not a secret worth killing for."

She looked at him. "What?"

"I don't think it's tied to Earlene's murder, do you?"

She sat back, her mind going over what had just transpired. "No," she said very slowly, thinking out loud. "No, I don't. There's something else."

She stared at the ribbon of road unfurling in the headlights and counted the tire thumps on the pavement seams.

CHAPTER TWENTY-SEVEN

When Henry finished reading Lincoln Cole's journals and the other Project 32 files, he knew he had to bump it up the chain of command. He immediately asked the new NARA director, Douglas Corbett, to take a look at the records and requested his assistance in getting the files declassified so they could be released to the public. His request was thunderously ignored. Henry then made an appointment to meet with Corbett to discuss it face to face.

He was cooling his heels in the director's sun-filled waiting room, listening to soft music drifting in through overhead speakers, reading old *Smithsonian* magazines. He'd already been kept waiting an hour and a half, a practice he knew established hierarchy. But Henry wasn't about to give up. That Project 32 had been kept under wraps for the past fifty years was unthinkable.

He stared at Corbett's closed door, turned his gaze to his watch, then compared the time to the digital clock on the receptionist's desk. The receptionist smiled bleakly at him, then shrugged in apology.

"I'm sorry, Henry. He's still tied up. Would you like to reschedule?"

Henry resolutely shook his head, shifted his weight in the chair, and folded his arms over his chest. "No thanks," he answered.

While he waited, he thought about Justin and speculated

about what exactly that young man had found in those unprocessed files. Wondered if Justin had comprehended the entire scope and goal of Project 32, and if so, what he intended to do with the information. The document Justin had been caught with stuffed down his underwear was benign on its own, but Henry had no way of knowing what else he'd managed to sneak out prior to being fired.

If Henry had known some of Lincoln Cole's Project 32 files were stashed there, he never would have sent Justin up without looking at them himself.

An equally important question was, why had only a portion of those records been designated classified while the rest hadn't?

There was only one explanation for that, Henry knew. Human error. Somebody slipped up.

Douglas Corbett's door opened, and the director peered out with an aggressive beaky look, no doubt disappointed that Henry was still there.

"Come on in, Henry," he said with a resigned sigh. "I've only got a few minutes." He turned to the receptionist. "When I'm done here, I'll be leaving for the day."

"Yes, Mr. Corbett," the receptionist replied.

Corbett motioned Henry into a visitor's chair in front of his desk, then installed himself into a creaky leather chair on the other side. "Sorry to keep you waiting, Henry. What can I do for you?"

As if you didn't know, thought Henry, but he said, "I wondered if you've had a chance to review those Project 32 records sent over from O'Toole's office and the BIA."

Corbett stared across the desk, his face pinched, looking as if he needed an antacid. His arms rested on the desk, one brown-spotted hand on top of the other.

"I have," he said, then shook his head impatiently. "Look Henry. We can't release those records. Not now. You know that.

That BIA lawsuit has a settlement offer on the table. Do you know what it would mean if details of Project 32 were released?"

"Yes," Henry replied matter-of-factly. "Congress would hold hearings, and it would *all* come out then. The secret drug testing. The fact that money from the Indian Health Care fund was spent on it."

"The tribes would reject the settlement offer," Corbett said tepidly, speaking the obvious.

"As they should," Henry said.

"The government has been tied up in court on this case for over twenty-five years," Corbett went on. "The tribes could tie it up for twenty-five more."

"That's right. They could sue for misappropriation of Indian Health Care funds. For harm done to the families. For harm done to the tribe—"

Corbett interrupted. "Look Henry, don't go getting all politically correct on me here. Okay? Your job is not to question the legitimacy of federal programs, even failed ones. Your job is to archive the material that comes in here, assign coding numbers, and see that it gets put in the proper place."

"I'm not questioning the legitimacy of Project 32," Henry replied earnestly, leaning forward. "I'm questioning the ethical underpinnings of it."

"You aren't the arbiter of the government's ethics," Corbett shot back, "and neither am I. The sending agency won't agree to declassify Project 32, and that's that. I don't want to hear any more about it. Just do your job, Henry. Just do your damn job."

Henry pondered this through a thoughtful silence.

"And if you're thinking about going to ISOO," Corbett added, "don't bother. I've already spoken to them. They won't get involved in a fight over this one. The blowback would be incalculable."

Blowback. The CIA term for unintended negative consequences resulting from clandestine operations. Douglas was an old CIA man. Apparently you could take the man out of the CIA, but you could never take the CIA out of the man.

It was Henry's idealism, a holdover from a pre–World War II youth, that led him to make a monumental decision. He sighed as the weight of it pressed down on him.

"Thanks for your time, Douglas." Henry stood and reached across the desk to shake the director's hand. "No hard feelings."

Corbett stood up, extended his hand, but didn't come out from behind his desk. "Let it go, Henry. Please. For everyone's sake, let it go. No good can come from digging up those old bones."

Henry had no intention of letting it go. As he looked into Corbett's worried eyes, he wondered not for the first time who in the BIA was powerful enough or had connections powerful enough to cover up something as malevolent as Project 32. He considered the possibility that the BIA might not have ordered it. Maybe there was a BIA within the BIA, a sort of rogue government agency. A renegade operation within the department. Henry examined these possibilities as he made the long trek back to his office.

His steps were slower today than they were last week, and would be slower in the coming weeks. He knew this, but couldn't quite believe it, so he had stashed it in some unvisited corner of his mind. He hadn't told anyone what was coming, hadn't repeated the words his doctor had said, not even to his son Jake.

Henry was living with Jake and Carol now, in their big house on the ocean in what the real estate people liked to call a mother-in-law apartment. Jake, worried about his father's wellbeing in the declining years, had insisted. Henry knew he was perfectly capable of living on his own, but he had agreed to the new arrangement mostly because Jake's wife, Carol, was like the daughter Henry never had. She spoiled and catered to him like he was her own father. It was a loving household full of life and activity and constant goings-on. The older grandchildren were grown and out on their own, but Melanie still lived at home and she filled their house with noise and commotion and love.

Henry was going to have to tell them. He didn't have long. Not days, not weeks, but maybe a couple of months. He chose not to think of that either. He intended to put whatever time he had left to good use. Lincoln Cole's Project 32 would not die with Henry Parker.

He wasn't going to do anything as sophomoric as trying to sneak smoking-gun records out of the facility. After all these years, he didn't want his noteworthy career with the archives tarnished with a wrongdoing. Instead he was going to put his photographic memory to work. There wasn't a security system in the world that could detect his memories.

The brilliance of the morning sun splashed the walls of Henry's bedroom with a lemony yellow glow. The house was quiet. Melanie had spent the night with a girlfriend and hadn't yet returned home. Carol was out for an early morning beach run. Henry was putting underwear and shoes in a small travel bag. Jake, wearing pajama bottoms and carrying a cup of coffee, came to stand in the doorway looking perplexed.

"Hey, Dad. What are you doing?"

"I have to go away for a little while."

"Where?"

"Monument Valley."

"What for?"

"There's something I have to do." Henry walked into the bathroom, came out with toothbrush and toothpaste, put both in a shaving kit, and zipped it shut.

"Can't it wait? If you postpone it until next week, I'll go with you."

"No, son. It can't wait."

Jake ruminated on this while Henry folded a shirt and then a pair of pajamas and placed them in his bag.

"When will you be back?" Jake asked.

"A couple of days."

Henry knew his son objected to him traveling alone so far from home, but Jake had learned long ago it did no good to argue with his old man. The disapproval on Jake's face gave way to resignation.

"Just promise me you'll call and keep in touch. Okay, Dad?"

"I will," Henry promised.

Henry smiled at his handsome son, thinking again how much he was going to miss Jake and Carol and Melanie when his time came. Rationally, he knew he'd be dead and wouldn't be capable of feeling any emotion, but while still living he found it impossible to conjure up such a state of nonexistence. He preferred to think of death as a long lonely road trip from which he'd never return.

Fortunately his demise wasn't imminent. There was still time to talk to Keegan Thomas and give her the documents he'd imprinted on his brain, then typed from memory when he arrived home each night. Melanie had showed him how to use the computer to type pages and print them out. He was sorry now he hadn't learned that bit of magic long ago.

"Did you remember to pack your cell phone charger?" Jake asked.

Henry picked it up from the bedspread. "Got it right here."

Jake sighed then hugged his father, holding on longer than usual. "Okay, Dad. See you in a few days. Be careful," he said, then left.

Henry's black Mercedes was old, but he'd bonded with it

and saw no reason to replace it even though he could easily afford to. He was as used to it as if it were an old friend. His fingers fit snugly around the leather wrapped steering wheel. The knobs and levers on the dash were familiar and within easy reach. He could adjust the air conditioning and change the radio station without ever taking his eyes off the road. The indentation made by his body on the driver's seat cradled his old rump comfortably, which was especially important on a long car trip.

He popped the trunk and put his travel bag inside, then slid the boxes of Project 32 documents onto the back seat. He got behind the wheel, fastened his seatbelt, checked his stash of road snacks, then turned the key. Exiting the exclusive gated oceanfront community, he gave a two fingered wave to the security guards in the gatehouse, then drove past the beaches he once lolled upon, back when there was less humidity and far fewer people.

On the freeway heading east, he picked up his speed and set cruise control at seventy. If all went as planned, and if he could avoid most of the highway construction, he'd arrive in Monument Valley before dark. He'd already called Keegan Thomas, and she was expecting him. Though she was gracious and inviting, he could tell by her voice that she wondered why he was personally delivering her grandfather's records instead of just shipping them to her.

But he wasn't going to risk that, wasn't going to take a chance they might be lost or damaged in shipping. And he certainly couldn't tell her over the phone what he'd discovered.

He wasn't sure how she would take it. It would probably be a shock, so he'd do his best to break it to her gently. What she did with the information afterward was up to her, though he'd certainly encourage her to make it public. The Navajo culture didn't allow many reasons for hatred, even when deserved.

Henry wouldn't be surprised if Project 32 proved to be one of the exceptions.

Chapter Twenty-Eight

"Christ, man. Why'd you do that?"

Justin practically did a spit-take when Charlie told him he'd taken a job in maintenance at Goulding's when he found out Keegan Thomas was staying there. They were drinking beer in a bar in Utah on the bank of the San Juan River just over the boundary line of the Navajo Nation. Alcohol was prohibited on the rez.

"She might see you!" Justin rasped in a hoarse whisper.

"So what if she does?" replied Charlie. "She doesn't know who I am." He picked up his beer, leaving a wet ring on the bar, and took a long swig.

"Jeez, Charlie. You're gonna blow the whole damn thing."

Charlie's beer bottle came down sounding a sharp *clack* on the bar's polished surface. "Give me some credit, would ya?" he said, his voice low. "I already jimmied the locks on her doors."

This shut Justin up. He clamped his mouth shut, annoyed that he hadn't thought of that.

"Besides, I need the money," Charlie complained. "You still haven't paid me for that other thing."

"You'll be paid, don't worry. When we're finished, money won't be a problem for either of us. My contacts have deep pockets."

Charlie gave a skeptical grunt. "Oh, yeah? Who are these contacts you're talking about? The feds?" He said the last two words as if he were dislodging something nasty off his bottom lip.

"Yeah."

Charlie gave a little snort of contempt and looked at Justin's reflection in the back-bar mirror. "You trust those pricks?"

"Yeah," Justin said again. "They've got a lot to lose. They don't want Project 32 to get out, and they're willing to pay big money to see it doesn't."

Charlie was silent a long time, mulling this over. His face was wide, with dark careful eyes set in a flat stare. Long hair down his back twisted in a loose braid tied off with a string. He grunted. "If you say so."

Suddenly Justin wasn't convinced he could trust Charlie after all. Liabilities were beginning to surface. The emotional absence he'd seen in Charlie, and what Justin had been counting on to help him carry out the necessary dirty work, was turning into a lack of focus. Charlie's deficiency of conscience was beginning to look like instability instead of remorselessness.

But it was too late now, and Justin felt a disconcerting twitch in his butt. He needed Charlie for this. He couldn't do it alone.

"Don't back out on me now, Charlie. You'll have the money. In cash. Just as soon as we—"

He cut off his words when a juiced-up bunch that didn't look old enough to drink came in and filled the stools along the bar next to them. The bartender checked their identification, then served them. Their noisy presence put an end to Justin's conversation with Charlie. He looked around for an empty booth, but there weren't any. He motioned Charlie to keep quiet.

Justin was tired and wired, the surface of his skin crackling with nervous energy. He gazed at Charlie, watching the Indian use his thumbnail to work the label loose from his beer bottle. Thick, dark-skinned fingers picked at it until it peeled off in

261

tiny pieces. Charlie's face was blank as a cinder block. Justin couldn't begin to guess what he was thinking, and that worried him. A twist of doubt swirling in Justin's brain became a maelstrom.

Charlie had a gut hanging off the front of him. His jeans looked like they had suffered a long and difficult existence. He'd turned into a somber, brooding stranger. Quite different from the jovial jock Justin knew at the University of Arizona, where Charlie was a political science major and inept at just about everything else except football and partying.

In those days, Justin, Booker, and Charlie shared an apartment off campus, testosterone filled digs that very quickly came to be known as party central. Between the three of them, some sort of booze-and-sex-fueled activity went on practically every night. And one of the three, if not *all* three, always seemed to have a minor scam going, a way to put a little extra tax-free money in their pockets.

Back then, Charlie had a warm and ready grin, the shoulders of a quarterback, and hard, muscular arms from his daily weight lifting workouts in the gym. He was known as the Big Indian. Even the girls called him that. *Especially* the girls.

But something happened to Charlie in his senior year. He lost interest in everything, even football. His grades plummeted. At the time he confided to Justin and Booker that it was because the more he learned about American history and its political system, the less he wanted to do with the federal government. He scraped by through graduation, but said goodbye to his dream of following in the footsteps of Ben Nighthorse Campbell, a United States senator from Colorado who was at the time the only American Indian in Congress. Instead, Charlie dropped out of sight, only surfacing now and then during the intervening years via emails and phone calls to ask for a loan.

As for Booker, he went off to Washington as an intern in the

Senate Office Building. He became a lower level aide, then a legislative assistant, then an upper level staff member in Senator Mike O'Toole's office. Booker held strong positions on international issues and aspired to be a cabinet member in a Republican president's administration some day.

Justin, dogged by bad luck and trouble, hadn't fared so well. He'd tried his hand at any number of unsuccessful businesses. A wine bar that failed in the first year. A contracting business that went under after he was caught employing illegals. Just as he was beginning to see some success selling real estate, the housing bubble burst, and before he knew it he was watching daytime TV in his pajamas. When he'd had enough of that, Angela's father called in some favors and got him the job with the National Archives.

Nothing in Justin's academic background was remotely related to archival records management, but he had other attributes attractive to the National Archives and Records Administration. He was smart, given to orderly thinking, possessed an ability to collect and evaluate data, analyze the information, and draw conclusions from it, so they provided him with on-the-job training. He took to it right away. It was a position that allowed him to work without supervision while providing him with the "job for life" security of government work.

That is, until he got caught stealing files, but by then it didn't matter. He had what he needed.

When Justin found the Project 32 prototype and reformulation data analysis records, he knew right away the possibilities to profit from the knowledge were manyfold. There were people both in and out of the government who would pay substantial sums to have those final validated formulary results turned over to them. Certainly the military would want them. He suspected they were already working on similar projects.

Then there were the private military companies, like Black Opal, and other security contractors in the Middle East. He'd heard those groups were highly funded, sometimes by unscrupulous sources, but what the hell. Money was money. Black Opal didn't care where their money came from, and Justin didn't care where his came from, either.

He'd briefly considered offering the information to foreign governments or one of the America hating terrorists groups. There were plenty of Jihad Johnnies who would gleefully pay for it first and figure out some nefarious use for it later. But selling the information to a foreign entity would be difficult. He didn't have the international contacts that could make such a thing happen. And it would be dangerous. Chances were good he would lose his head—literally!—when the transaction was completed.

Justin eventually came to the conclusion that the only alternative to selling the information would be to sell it back. That would be far easier to do. He knew people who, without asking too many questions, could put him in touch with other people who had the ability to set up a meeting with a decision maker at the BIA. Someone who could say yay or nay to Justin's proposal, a proposal he was sure they couldn't refuse.

Justin couldn't have been any more surprised when they made an offer of their own, one that instantly wiped out all his bargaining chips. Not only did they agree to pay him to turn over the records of the program's purpose and study results, but they upped the ante considerably. Their counteroffer was contingent on Justin's guarantee that anyone who already knew about Project 32 would be eliminated. That's the word they used. *Eliminated.*

This was an unexpected development, one that shook him to his very core. They were asking the unthinkable with the promise of life-changing money. Getaway money. New-identity-disappearing-from-the-face-of-the-earth money. He and Angela and the baby could live in unimagined luxury in a foreign country or on a South Sea island. Hell, maybe they could even buy the island.

He asked for some time to think about it. They gave him twenty-four hours, then virtually sealed the deal with a veiled threat by asking when the baby was due and whether they planned to live long enough to have more children.

Justin was stunned. His analytical mind had failed him, and he knew he'd made a horrible mistake. He'd been so wrapped up in his own hubris, he'd neglected to consider that powerful men would have options, too.

They'd made him an offer *he* couldn't refuse, and he accepted it the next morning.

He was in way deeper than he ever imagined.

A booth in the corner cleared. Justin elbowed Charlie and nodded to it, then held up two fingers to the bartender ordering up another round. They carried their half-empty bottles over and sat facing each other over the table, nudged up against the wall for privacy.

Justin leaned in, keeping his voice low. "What about the old nurse? What's the buzz on the reservation? Does the FBI have any leads?"

Charlie shook his head. "They turned it over to the tribal cops. They think some dudes from Farmington needed drug money. She had all those rugs she wove there. Some of them were worth seven or eight thousand dollars."

Justin hoped that line of investigation would keep them occupied for some time, and he breathed a little easier.

At least the old woman was out of the way now. According to what he'd uncovered, she had kept the Project 32 test records and administered at least some of the injections. Justin was pretty sure she hadn't told anyone. If she had, he was sure it would have come out by now. And if she hadn't told anyone about her involvement in Project 32, she probably hadn't told anyone about the hush money she was receiving, which meant she was stashing it someplace.

"You sure you didn't find any bank statements in her hogan?"

Charlie speared an indignant gaze on Justin, his expression livid. "How many times you gonna ask me that? I told you. No."

"Okay, okay," Justin said, backing down. "I'm just asking. Calm down. I'm nervous is all."

Charlie huffed, rolled his eyes, and tipped his bottle.

It had crossed Justin's mind that he might be able to redirect Earlene's payoff money to a post office box in his name. If no one knew she was receiving it, no one would miss it. All he'd need to do is put in a change of address form at the post office. He'd hoped Booker would do it on his computer, but no chance of that. Booker had flat out refused.

Justin discreetly scanned the room. "We're gonna have to do it tonight."

"Why?"

"Henry Parker, the old dude I worked with at archives, is on his way here. He's coming to see Keegan Thomas."

"How do you know?"

"I called his house and spoke to his son. Told him I used to work with Henry, and heard he'd been sick, and wondered how he was doing. His son was glad to hear from me, but said he was worried about his father. Henry had packed a bag and left for Monument Valley in a hurry."

Charlie said nothing.

"There's only one reason he'd come here," Justin explained impatiently when Charlie didn't react. "To tell Keegan about her grandfather and Project 32. Once he does that, she'll blow the whistle for sure. It's got to be tonight."

Charlie sat there, stone-faced and silent.

"Charlie, did you hear what I said?"

The Indian shifted his gaze, his ebony eyes hard as stones. "I don't like to be rushed," he said.

Justin's butt twitched again.

Chapter Twenty-Nine

Keegan was reeling, stunned, like she'd walked into a plate glass door. She stared open-mouthed at Henry Parker, who was sitting on the sofa in a stiff tea party posture.

"That can't possibly be true," Keegan said in disbelief. Yet it must be true. This man had driven over nine hours to personally tell her that her grandfather had conducted secret medical experiments on the Navajos. And he had documents to prove it! She mentally tried to grasp something—*anything*—that would ground her in some reality she could understand.

The room filled up with silence. She looked at the string of questions unraveling in her head. She wanted to ask them all at once.

"Are you sure?" she offered weakly.

Henry nodded, his expression rueful. He looked as if the burden of what he knew, what he must tell her, was almost too much for him to bear.

"I'm afraid so. Your grandfather was originally sent to Monument Valley by the BIA to run an Indian Health Service medical clinic. That part is true. But also to conduct medical experiments."

The revelation made Keegan's head swim. Her shoulders slumped, her energy visibly draining away.

Henry's eyes widened. "Oh, dear. I'm afraid I've done a poor job of breaking this news to you. Can I get you something? A glass of water? Do you need to call someone to be with you?"

She wanted to call Dante, but he was in Colorado working a rodeo. He wouldn't return until after midnight. Jilly was in Albuquerque with her mother. Keegan wasn't sure when she'd be coming back. Slowly she shook her head.

"No. Thank you. I'm all right. I just—" She released an audible breath and shook her head in confusion. "I don't understand. How could that possibly be?"

"Let me start at the beginning," he said. "It might be easier for you to comprehend if I set it in an historical and cultural context."

She doubted that would help, but nodded anyway, indicating she was listening.

"Your grandfather was recruited while he was still in medical school to work on a CIA program called Project 32. It was an offshoot of an old CIA mind control program that was active after World War II. The fighting overseas had ended, but sophisticated espionage techniques being developed by foreign countries were rapidly becoming a threat to our national security."

Keegan blinked and stared. "My grandfather was in the CIA?"

"No, not really, not in the way you're thinking. He wasn't an undercover operative or anything like that, but he did participate in some clandestine mind control programs as a physician. By the time he became involved, most of the laboratory research had been completed. He was recruited for the field work."

"I see," Keegan said, but she didn't. She was quiet as Henry went on.

"In the earliest mind control studies, which were secret, of course, CIA researchers found that short term memories last just a few seconds. That's why phone numbers are usually no longer than ten digits, though they used to be seven. Street addresses are also limited to seven numbers. That's about what the human brain can hold on to over the short run, and if

C. C. Harrison

they're forgotten, it's of little consequence.

"But long term memories are the primary drivers of human behavior, so that's what the researchers focused on. Most events in a person's daily life are trivial and routine, and quickly forgotten, but when an event provokes an emotional response—like terror or sadness or anger—the body is flooded with stress hormones.

"These hormones wash over the part of the brain that processes those strong emotions and send a signal to the brain that what's happening *at that moment* is worth remembering. Adrenaline burns those stressful memories into the brain. It's all part of the instinctive fight-or-flight response. The researchers discovered that by introducing a drug that blocks the action of those stress hormones, the system can be prevented from working. In other words, those strong emotions can be weakened to neutrality. Even eliminated."

"What does this have to do with the Navajos? Or my grandfather?"

"I'm coming to that," Henry said and paused a beat before going on. "At first," he raised a finger for emphasis, "they tested the drug on lab rats and found that they were able to remove a specific memory from the brains of rats while leaving the rest of the animals' memories intact. Further tests showed that by modifying the drug, they could erase certain memories deep in the brain. Have you seen the movie *The Manchurian Candidate*?"

Keegan's mind began tumbling over itself anticipating and at the same time dreading his words. A hollow sick feeling opened in her stomach. "Yes. It came out a few years ago."

"That one was actually a remake of an old sixties movie. Shelly Winters was in the original. So was Lawrence Harvey. Anyway, it was about a man who was brainwashed into becoming an unwilling assassin for the CIA. The movie and the book it was based on were fiction, but not far removed from reality.

270

The CIA really did conduct mind control experiments with the aim of creating Manchurian Candidate type operatives for use as agents or couriers in foreign countries."

"*That's* what my grandfather was doing? Making Manchurian Candidate assassins out of the Indians?" She said it as if it was the most ridiculous thing she'd ever heard which it was.

Henry waved her question away like so much smoke in the air. "No, no, no. Nothing like that. As you're probably aware—most everyone is these days—the Indians were horribly ill-treated in this country's early history. Treaties were broken, their land was taken from them. They were forcibly removed from their homes. By the end of the World War II, the government wanted them to forget about that. The BIA asked the CIA researchers for help.

"They wanted a drug that could create amnesia barriers and erase memories. The goal of Project 32 was to eliminate the memories of the Navajos and defuse the tribal anger. Make them less likely to seek retribution for the government mistreatment and injustices of the past. They wanted to render the Indians more compliant in the government's attempts at integrating them into the white culture and away from their primitive ways."

"Make it easier for the government to control them, you mean," Keegan said.

"Well, yes," Henry replied. "Plus, the Navajos had a very strong oral history tradition. Project 32 was the government's way of preventing the anger and memories of those old injustices from being passed down through the generations."

The implication of this struck Keegan like a knife to her heart. "The government's version of the final solution?" she asked bitterly. "They wanted to erase the Navajo culture?"

"Not entirely. Just certain memories. Just the memories that would make them reluctant to blend into mainstream white culture."

"And prohibit them from seeking reprisal later," she put in.

Henry nodded. "But don't misunderstand. I'm not talking about the entire U.S. government. It wouldn't be fair to cast aspersions on our entire political system. This was a small rogue group of people who acted on their own."

"And my grandfather . . . he knew about this? He knew what he was doing?"

"I'm afraid he did," Henry said. "Lincoln Cole was a willing participant."

Keegan was forced to let go of the tiny smidgen of hope she'd been clinging to that Lincoln Cole was as unwitting as his victims.

For a minute or more, neither of them spoke.

"But how?" she asked. "How could something like that happen? How could he get away with it? I don't understand how the Indians let him do it."

"Your grandfather was very popular with the Navajos because he seemed to understand them and respect their ways. He allowed the Navajos to live according to their culture."

Keegan closed her eyes and slowly shook her head. "So in addition to everything else, he was a hypocrite, too." Her one-note laugh lacked any hint of amusement.

"They came to trust him," Henry said, "and eventually let him administer penicillin and other necessary medications that made them feel better or cured them. They let him inoculate their children against life threatening diseases. From there it wasn't much of a leap to injecting the memory erasing drugs."

"How long did this go on? These," she waved the back of her hand in the air as if she were swatting away a mosquito, "these experiments?"

"The BIA ordered them discontinued after a few years.

Researchers eventually realized that emotional memories, however painful, serve a purpose. They help us learn to adapt in order to survive. Early humans needed to know that certain animals were dangerous. Cave men needed to understand that saber-toothed tigers were to be avoided or killed. Children today need to learn that fire burns, and that if they play in the street they can get run over by a car. In order to survive, mankind had to learn to avoid harmful things by remembering the bad experiences.

"By then, some of the newer people coming into the BIA heard rumors about Project 32 and strongly objected. And some of the doctors on other reservations began to balk, too. They were uncomfortable experimenting on unwitting subjects, but more than that, they saw what was being done as a gross human rights violation. It violated their Hippocratic Oath. It was unethical."

"It was illegal," Keegan put in. "It was against the damn law."

"It was," Henry agreed, his voice sincere. "But your grandfather didn't want to call it off. He knew what he was doing was probably illegal, but he didn't feel it was unethical. He thought he was doing the Indians a favor by erasing those painful memories. Felt he was giving them some peace of mind, especially the old ones living out their final days."

"So he kept giving them the drugs on his own after the project was cancelled?"

"Yes." Henry nodded toward the document boxes he'd brought in and set on the coffee table. "It's all there in his personal journals. His purpose was not to tinker with the memories that represented personal identities, the *self* that represents a person's authentic being, so he didn't think the Navajos were being harmed in any way. He believed it wasn't such a bad thing to eradicate painful memories. He firmly believed he was helping them by ending their suffering. But he did stop eventually. The drugs didn't always work the way they were supposed to."

"What happened?"

"Sometimes they wore off. And there were side effects. Sometimes they short-circuited other areas of the brain. The children began having learning difficulties at the government schools. The unintended consequences were mental retardation and erratic behavior. Anger and violence. Problems worse than the perceived problems the drugs were supposed to prevent or alleviate."

Keegan's stomach knotted painfully around that knowledge. She took a deep breath and sat back in her chair, trying to rein in her thoughts. After a moment, she got up, removed the top of one of the document boxes and stared at its contents.

A part of her didn't quite believe this man. Yet he was a dedicated archivist, a keeper of memories, and had used his own memory possibly at great risk to himself to bring her the truth. A truth she had asked for, she reminded herself.

But still, it was insane. Like something from a movie or one of those political thrillers that were all the rage. She wanted to laugh at the absurdity of it. Lincoln Cole was her grandfather. How did he turn into an isolated renegade doctor performing medical experiments on unsuspecting victims? Earlene Cly had been a kindly old Navajo woman, not a mad scientist's assistant. It was all so sinister. Every line of logic was falling apart.

Frustrated, she asked, "Whose idea was this to begin with? If it wasn't governmental policy, how did it start? Who came up with it?"

Henry pressed his mouth into a tight line and heaved a great sigh.

"I wasn't sure about that for the longest time," he answered. "Couldn't pin it down right away. When the program began to wind down, everyone scrambled to cover their tracks and hide any trace of their involvement. But the CIA was used to cloaking their activities. It was their job, after all, to be clandestine, and everyone knew it. Nobody ever questioned them or what they did back then, so they didn't bother covering their tracks in the same way. And if anyone were to question them, they were experts at plausible denials, disinformation, and cover-up."

"Do you have any specifics? Any names?"

"From what I could tell, the original proposal came from a newly elected senator who discussed the idea of creating amnesia barriers with a friend of his in the CIA. The friend knew the CIA had been experimenting with something similar. Apparently the CIA approached the BIA, and the bureau thought it would be a good solution. Not the whole bureau, of course. Project 32 was run from inside a tiny division, just a few people were involved."

"Who was the senator?"

"Macavity O'Toole. He's dead now, but his son Mike O'Toole was elected to his Senate seat. The other man is Douglas Corbett. My boss at the archives."

"Does Corbett know you're telling me this?" Keegan asked.

"Not yet, but he will. At least I hope he will. I'm hoping you will agree to make this information public."

Keegan thought about that. That would be her task. To tell everyone, including her family, that Lincoln Cole was an active participant in such grossly unethical medical experimentation. Her mother would be shocked. Her grandmother might not ever get over it. And her cousin Richard Cole. He was such a proud man. How would it affect his standing, his career?

"What kind of trouble will you get into if I do make it public?" she asked Henry.

"Nothing that will make a difference in my life," Henry replied. "I won't be going back to the archives. I've retired myself."

Keegan gazed thoughtfully at the documents in the box open in front of her. She ran her finger over the top edges of the file folders reading the labels. *Internal Memos. Financial Audits. Drug Delivery System. Human Drug Testing Results. Lab Results. Human Behavior and Verbal Signals. Cultural Adaptation. Brain Stimulations Study. Stimulus Response Results. Ideological Conversion Study.*

"How could this be kept secret for so long? It's been fifty years. I didn't think anything could be kept secret in the government for that long."

"You'd be surprised," Henry replied, his tone verging on caustic. "Back then they didn't have Internet or email or Black-Berries or twenty-four hour cable channels. News didn't spread the way it does now.

"But the main reason it was able to be covered up is the same reason it was able to go on at all. Details of the program were kept secret even from other personnel of the BIA. That led to loss of central control and eventually independence from supervision by the regular chain of command within the agency. Project 32 wasn't subject to any regular review of activities by senior officials. As I said, not many people knew about it to begin with, and most of those who did have passed on.

"And no one person knew everything," he added. "Even the drug formula. No one researcher knew all the components."

"But you found all kinds of paper records," Keegan pointed out. "It doesn't seem like anybody was reluctant to write things down. Wasn't this information available under the Freedom of Information Act?"

"Not really. Not most of it anyway. Most of the records were classified, and those that were available under the FOIA were unreadable. Several generations of photocopying made the documents difficult to decipher. Others were heavily redacted. Whole pages were blacked out.

"The program was so secret that, to put it simply, one hand

didn't know what the other was doing. Either information wasn't shared, or it was shared too much. There was a lot of duplication of effort. Someone made a file copy of a document, not knowing that three or four other people had done the same thing. And, the records weren't stored in any one place. On the whole, it was pretty sloppy recordkeeping."

A new wave of apprehension came over her, and she wondered if her grandmother knew the nature of Lincoln Cole's work on the reservation. Then something else jolted in her mind. *Teaya.*

Was Teaya given the memory erasing drug? Is that why she didn't remember Lulu? Did Lincoln Cole give it to her to alleviate the painful memories of the child she thought was kidnapped?

"Did you find names of the people who received the drug?" she asked.

Henry nodded toward the record boxes. "I made out a list. It's in there."

She wondered if Will Bedonnie's name was on the list, then had another sudden thought.

"My grandmother lived in Monument Valley with my grandfather for a while. She told me Earlene Cly was his nurse," Keegan said. "Did Earlene know what he was doing?"

"Not at first. Dr. Cole had somehow determined the beta blocker that was the active ingredient in the drug. That's what enabled him to continue giving it. His records show that after the BIA ended the program, he shared everything with Earlene Cly. He explained his purpose, how he was trying to help the Navajos, and apparently she agreed with him. Or at least, she didn't object. According to his journal, her response was that she saw so much pain and suffering of her people, it was a relief to be free of it."

Keegan digested this, thought about Jilly and Sandra and

how they would take these new developments.

Henry went on. "Eventually the government found out Dr. Cole hadn't stopped administering the drug, and ordered him home. The BIA wanted your grandfather and Earlene to sign a secrecy agreement, but before he left Monument Valley he negotiated compensation for Earlene."

"What kind of compensation?"

"Lifetime monthly payments. Out of O'Toole's office."

"Ah," she said. "Hush money."

"That's what it amounted to," Henry agreed. "But what the BIA didn't know was that your grandfather had given Earlene the formula for the drug, too. Told her to hold on to it. He told her it could make her family a lot of money some day. All she had to do was keep quiet until science had advanced enough to make the drug safe."

"Well, it looks like she did a good job of that. Unfortunately it probably got her killed."

"What do you mean?"

"Earlene was murdered."

Henry's eyes widened slightly. "Do they know who did it?"

"No," she said. "But her hogan was ransacked, so whoever did it was looking for something."

Henry didn't reply right away, but she noticed he had paled.

"There's a connection isn't there?" she asked. "What are you thinking?"

"Justin Bickham, the archivist you originally worked with, was fired. He didn't just leave like I told you. He'd been caught trying to sneak some records out of the archives. The document he was caught with was harmless, and it wasn't classified, so they decided to quietly end his employment rather than go through the time and expense of prosecution and potential litigation.

"But we don't know what he took before he got caught. We're

thinking he made copies instead of taking originals. He'd been researching what you'd asked for, so my guess is he came across records relating to Project 32 and saw an opportunity for himself."

"What would he do with the information?"

"I don't know, but it can't be anything good. Blackmail maybe. Perhaps he was going to sell the information. In the wrong hands, memory extraction drugs can be used in any number of dangerous ways. Imagine if terrorists got hold of one."

The thought chilled her blood. "Was he capable of that? Had he done anything like that before?"

"I don't know. He was a preferential hiring in the first place. That means he came to us through a referral from someone higher up. Those applicants are hired as a favor. Sometimes they aren't vetted very thoroughly."

A curtain of weariness fell over Henry's eyes. His face was drawn and ashen.

"You must be exhausted," she said. "You've had a long day, a long drive."

"Yes, I am tired," he said, and looked out the window into the darkness. "I guess time got away from me. I should leave." He stood.

"Where are you staying?" she asked.

"I don't have a room yet. I came straight here. I wanted to talk to you right away."

"Look, it's late. I have an extra bedroom. Why don't you stay here? You can get a good night's sleep and leave tomorrow if you have to."

"Thank you," he said politely, "but I've taken enough of your time already. I couldn't impose further."

"Don't be silly," she said. "It's no bother at all. And besides, I have more questions. I can ask them over breakfast."

"All right. If you insist," he said, gratefully accepting her invitation.

"I do insist," she said, smiling at the old man, glad to be able to help him out. "Thank you for doing this. For coming here to tell me."

She showed him to his room and turned down the bed. "Sleep well, Henry," she said. "Good night."

After Henry retired, Keegan sat up awash in thought. Keyed up, nerves jangled, she skimmed through the Project 32 files, pulling them out at random to glance at the contents. They were damning indeed. She took out some of the folders she especially wanted to ask Henry about and laid them on the coffee table, setting the box aside. Then she turned out the light, went to bed, and eventually slipped into a light and troubled slumber.

CHAPTER THIRTY

The white Ford Explorer was tucked so far back under the low hanging branches of a musty desert willow, in the shadow of a soaring mesa across the road from Keegan's bungalow, it was imperceptible to a casual glance. Charlie was behind the wheel, staring as if mesmerized into the rearview mirror. Justin, growing more uneasy with each passing minute, slouched in the passenger seat worrying about the Indian, halfway regretting his decision to include him in the plan.

Charlie was juiced up on some kind of drug. He was spaced out and jittery, his movements jerky, his leg bouncing, his pupils wide and intense, boring a tunnel into the dark void reflected in the mirror. Suddenly, his knee stopped bobbing up and down, and he froze.

"What's that?" he rasped.

"What?" Justin jumped and jerked his eyes to the right, trying to catch a reflection in the door mirror on his side. "What's what?"

"A light. Back there. Something moved."

Justin ducked and hunched, then turned to peer nervously over his shoulder. "What? I don't see anything."

In a moment, Charlie grunted, and his knee began bouncing again. He continued staring, his eyes glued to the mirror.

Justin faced front and hunkered down low, resting the back of his head on the seat. "Come on, Charlie," he implored. "Get a grip. How many of those pills did you take?"

The Indian's jaw tightened, but he said nothing.

"I know you took something."

Still the Indian was silent.

Justin narrowed his eyes and rolled his head in Charlie's direction. "Look, Charlie, don't screw this up! Don't—"

Charlie's head spun so fast, Justin instinctively drew back.

"Shut up," Charlie snapped. He looked like a rattlesnake just before striking.

"Take it easy," Justin replied, his tone conciliatory. A light sweat broke out on his forehead.

Charlie turned back to the mirror and said nothing.

Justin slid a sidelong look at the Indian. Oh, man, he thought grimly. The guy's a loose cannon.

The bungalow glowed with interior light, but one by one the lights went out plunging it into total darkness.

"What, the old man's spending the night with her?" Charlie said giving a little snort and emitting a lewd chuckle. "I thought you said he was in his eighties."

Justin ignored Charlie. He was running his plan through his mind.

"That's okay," Charlie said to himself, grinning lecherously. "I don't mind sloppy seconds."

Justin flung a fisted backhand sharply into Charlie's bicep. "Hey," he warned. "Cut it out. That's not what this is about. Stick to the plan."

Charlie elbow-checked Justin's fist away. "Don't worry. I'll stick to the plan. But that doesn't mean I can't stick it to her before we're done."

A hollow, sinking feeling plummeted to the pit of Justin's stomach. *Oh, man,* he thought again. *Oh, shit!*

Charlie fell back into his sulk, and Justin looked at his watch. "Are you sure she can't lock the doors?" he asked.

Charlie nodded. "I jammed the deadbolt. The thumb turn

won't work. She can push the button in the lockset, but I jim-mied the mechanism. From the inside she'll think it's locked, but we'll be able to turn it from the outside and get in."

"Okay," Justin said, satisfied. Breaking windows and smash-ing down doors was not part of his plan. Such obvious signs of a break-in would instantly alert passersby and casual visitors, who would immediately call the police. He and Charlie needed to get in, get out, take care of business, and then leave Monu-ment Valley before anyone raised an alarm, hopefully many days later.

He took a deep breath and let it out quickly. "Okay," he said. "Let's go."

Without a word, Charlie turned the key and let the SUV roll into Keegan's driveway. The two men exited the vehicle and stepped quietly up the porch steps. Justin gave the screen door a hard yank, snapping the flimsy latch. Soundlessly he opened the interior door and stepped across the threshold, only to trip on a cardboard box and fall to his knees.

The shuddering bang startled Keegan awake and she sat up. She heard voices coming from the living room, swearing. Then a light came on showing through the crack under the door. She threw back the covers just as her bedroom door flung open. The figure of a man lit from behind filled the doorway. She opened her mouth to scream, but before she could make a sound, he was on her, his hand jammed over her face.

"Stay quiet," he rasped. "Don't fight me. You don't have a chance. I can break you in two."

Logic and the size of his bulk told her what he said was true, but intuitively she fought back, kicking out with her legs, prying at his hand on her face. He was pressing her mouth so hard, her teeth were cutting the tender skin inside her lips. He dragged her into the living room and slammed her onto the sofa. Terrified, she cried out. He smacked the side of her face, instantly cutting off her scream, then looked down at her, his eyes dark and expressionless.

She'd seen him around the lodge carrying tools, driving a service vehicle. He worked for Goulding's.

"Who are you?" she asked. She was trembling, fear making the muscles of her arms and legs shake uncontrollably.

Another man stepped forward. She knew him, too. She gasped. "Justin! What are you doing here?"

Just then the door to the guest room opened, and Henry Parker came out holding a gun in front of him, steadying it with both hands. He glared at Justin.

"I always knew you were a no good son-of-a-bitch," Henry said. He looked skinny and frail, his cotton pajamas hanging in folds on his bony frame, but his eyes were blazing.

"Hey, Henry," Justin said with a surprised little laugh. "I didn't know you had a gun."

"Of course, I do," Henry replied. "A man would be a fool to come out West without a gun."

Just that quick, Charlie launched himself from across the room in two long strides. In a single motion, he swatted Henry's hands aside and snatched away the gun. He clamped his big hand on the old man's shoulder, and squeezed his thumb and fingers painfully into the tender muscle. Grimacing, Henry tried valiantly to resist, but he was no match for the Indian. With a cry of pain, he sagged to the floor like a bag of bones.

"Stop it!" Keegan screamed. "Don't hurt him!"

She jumped up to go to him, but Justin stopped her. "Leave him be," he said, taking a gun from his jacket pocket and pointing it at her.

Frozen in fear, she stared at the barrel pointed directly at her face. "He's hurt. Let me help him. Please," she begged. Henry was on the floor, grimacing in pain.

"I said leave him be," Justin barked, and swung his arm smashing the gun into her cheek. Her hands flew to her face, and she let out a squeal. Breathless, she asked, "What do you want?"

"Shut up," he said.

Charlie was standing over Henry, his legs spread wide, checking to see if the old man's gun was loaded. Satisfied that it was, he bent down, picked Henry up by his arm, and shoved him into a chair.

"Are those the Project 32 records?" Justin asked Keegan, tipping his head toward the boxes by the door.

Keegan nodded.

"Put them in the car," Justin instructed over his shoulder.

"You can't take those," Henry croaked bravely.

Charlie spun around. "You gonna stop me, old man?" he said, then calmly raised the gun and shot Henry in the chest. Henry slumped over the arm of the chair. A red splotch appeared on his pajama top. Bubbles of red foam burbled out from his lips.

"No!" Keegan screamed, horrified. "Look what you've done! You killed him!"

"Shut her up," Charlie yelled, frantic and agitated. "Shut her the fuck up!"

She heard a pop and saw a flash an instant before her shoulder exploded in pain. She fell forward and dropped to her knees. Trying to drag in a breath, she clutched the arm of the sofa and struggled to pull herself up.

Charlie elbowed Justin aside and sent a sharp kick into her ribs. In agony, she crumpled to the floor, pulling her knees to her chest, pain radiating through her body. She lay there, listening to her heartbeat reverberate in her ears, its beat gradually slowing and growing faint. From somewhere far away, a phone was ringing. Then everything went black and quiet.

Justin grabbed his phone from his jacket and looked at it.

"Don't answer," Charlie snapped.

"It's Angela," Justin said, helplessly, then, "Hello."

"Justin! Where are you? My water broke!"

"But you're not due for another month!"

"Don't you think I know that?" she screamed. "Get your ass home!"

"I'll—I'll be home as soon as I can get there," he sputtered. "Are you having pains?"

"Yes, of course I am," she said in a wail.

"Call your mother. No! Call *my* mother. Call my sister."

"Please come home, Justin. Hurry!" she yelled, her voice screechy with panic.

"Hang in there, baby. I'm on my way. I'll meet you at the hospital!" he said, even though he knew, but she didn't, that he was hours away. He shoved the phone back in his pocket and took a shaky breath.

"Come on, hurry up," he said to Charlie. "You carry those two out. I'll get the boxes."

"What about their cars? We have to get their cars out of here, too."

"Never mind about the cars now!" Justin yelled. "We'll come back for them later. Let's get out of here and finish this. Hurry. Angela's in labor. I've got to get home."

Keegan heard them talking. Voices coming from far away. She lay very still, slowing her breath so she could hear what they were saying. The words were angry.

She was in the flat, hard back of an SUV, not hers. She heard footsteps then the sound of streaming water. Someone was urinating against the back tire. Footsteps receded, then the argument began again. Justin wanted to leave. Charlie wanted her. They'd had the same argument at the house.

"No, leave her alone. There's no time," Justin said bitterly. Frustration had ratcheted his voice up to panic.

"Come on, Charlie. Help me dump them over the edge. I've got to get back."

The argument continued. More angry shouts, then a grunt. Sounds of a scuffle. They were fighting.

A gunshot!

Someone came running. The driver's door flew open and Charlie jumped in, breathing hard. Tires spun in the dirt throwing clumps and stones against the fenders. Suddenly the SUV lurched forward.

Keegan was in the cargo hold jammed in next to the Project 32 boxes. Henry's lifeless form was crumpled against the tailgate. She tried to sit up, but pain ripped through her shoulder and she fell back, light-headed and breathless. The inside of the vehicle smelled of dirt and smoke and beer. Empty bottles rolled around and clanked together. One of them kept bumping against her hand. She closed her fingers around it stilling its motion.

She struggled through searing pain to pull herself up to her elbow and look out the window. Rock, sage, and cactus were ghostly images in the moonlight. Charlie steered over terrain devoid of roads, dodging the worst of the erosion gullies and furrows cleaving the desert floor. He was driving with determination. His hands on the wheel were sure and steady. He knows where he's going, she thought.

Don't let a kidnapper take you in a car.

The warning cut through the fog in her brain. That's what they always tell you. If you get in a car with them, they'll kill you after they rape you. Instinctively, she tightened her grip on the neck of the empty beer bottle in her hand.

She had to get herself out of this. No one was coming to save her. A primitive survival instinct surfaced in her befuddled brain giving her clear choices. Go along with the inevitable or fight back. Wait until Charlie reached his deadly destination, or do something now and take him by surprise. She might die trying to escape, but she was going to die anyway. There was no way he'd let her live. Not after what she'd witnessed.

He killed Henry. Then he shot her. She'd heard a gunshot when he was arguing with Justin. Was Justin dead, too?

Charlie's shoulders were hunched over the steering wheel, his eyes focused on the vast open space ahead. Staying low, Keegan braced and pulled back her arm sending pain from her shoulders to her ribs. With all her weight behind the blow, she smashed the empty bottle on the back of Charlie's head.

Caught off guard, he howled, twisting around swinging a powerhouse backhand. The vehicle swerved wildly.

"You bitch!" he bellowed.

Suddenly, the ground in front of the SUV fell away, dropping the front end into emptiness before crashing against a vertical wall of sandstone. Glass exploded. The SUV's rear end flew up in the air then dropped with a bone shattering bang, jarring loose a thunderous hail of rock and stones. A terrifying shriek of metal scraping against rock cut the air as the rig made a slow, grinding descent before coming to a stop, wedged between the vertical sandstone walls of a narrow slot canyon.

The deafening roar of an engine wildly out of control echoed against the rocky walls before dying to a whine and choking to a stop. After that, there was only silence, except for the broken rocks avalanching down to the void below.

Momentum had slammed Keegan hard against the back of the front seats. Glass was everywhere. She could tell by the pull of gravity on her body that the SUV was tilted at a sharp angle, nose down, rear end pointing to the sky. The liftgate had been wrenched away and Henry's body was gone. Through the opening, she saw moonlight and stars. The top section of the canyon's walls sloped upward toward solid ground.

There was no sound from Charlie. She peered through a cloud of dust into the cockpit. He was spread-eagled over the steering wheel, covered with glass and blood. His head and shoulders filled the space where once had been the windshield.

Gritting her teeth against the blistering pain, she climbed out of the cargo hold and onto a rocky ledge. She looked at the Explorer, which was now a crumpled mass of metal suspended precariously over a gaping black chasm. Above her, loose talus covered the sloping sides leading upward to the safety of level ground.

Painfully, on her hands and knees, she dragged herself up the incline toward the surface and away from the unstable wreckage. Near the top of the slope, a river of dirt dislodged and deluged downward in a mini landslide that carried her along with it.

Panic-stricken, she dug her toes for purchase, desperately grasping for something to stop her miserable downward slide, bare hands burning and scraping on razor sharp pebbles and coarse dirt. She slowed when her foot caught on a half-buried rock, twisting her knee and sending a hot poker of pain up her leg. Awash in hurt and tears, she slithered to a halt just above the twisted wreckage that emitted another high-pitched squeal and grind as it slipped six more inches down the cemented canyon walls.

Below was a yawning black presence, felt rather than seen.

Move, her mind commanded. *Keep going. Move your arms and legs. Get to the top.* Calling on her last reserve of strength, she made her way with agonizing slowness to the rim, struggled over the edge, and collapsed exhausted in the sand.

There was pain, so much pain. It was impossible to ignore, and she eagerly gave in to the dark part of her brain that promised to bring it to an end. Her final thought was of Daisy.

I'm sorry, baby. I tried to find you. I did the best I could.

Chapter Thirty-One

Someone was breathing close to her face, long, grating, rattling intakes of air. She heard a moan, a low mournful cry. Someone needed help.

Wrapped in a haze of pain and confusion, Keegan turned her head toward the sounds and felt the prickly sting of rocks and cactus needles on her cheek as it scraped over the gritty ground. That's when she realized the tortured breathing was her own. The moans were coming from her.

Oh, my God, what happened to me? Where am I?

She waited for the cacophony in her head to quiet down so she could think. In bits and pieces, it came back to her accompanied by a sense of futility. No one knew where she was.

She was drowning in pain. Her head throbbed like someone was hitting it with a mallet over and over again. When she tried to take a deep breath, pain stabbed through her chest and side. Her knees and the palms of her hands were sore, the flesh scraped and torn during her desperate attempt to reach safety.

It was daylight. She could feel the sun bearing down on her, burning the raw skin of her face and arms. She tried to push herself into a sitting position, using the palms of her injured hands to lift her body, pressing the lacerated flesh into the sharp decomposed granite and sandstone. But the pain was too much and she dropped back.

It hurt like hell to breathe. A new surge of pain overtook her, and she hollered out with the sheer effort of keeping it at bay.

When at last it ebbed away, she gently rolled her body onto its right side. She gasped, feeling again the powerful punch of the bullet as it slammed into her. Charlie's boot had broken her ribs.

Pushing with her good arm, she heaved herself up, struggling to keep her head from spinning. Moaning loudly, she mustered the energy to ease herself into a sitting position. She touched her throbbing shoulder. It was a bloody mess, and her hand came away wet and sticky.

She was still in the clothes she'd put on for bed, T-shirt and pajama bottoms, now dirty and torn. One-handed, she rolled up the bottoms of her pant legs and examined the cuts and bruises on her shins and thighs. Her left knee looked swollen. Gingerly she touched it and saw the skin turn white where she prodded it with her finger. Even if it was only sprained, she'd have that pain to deal with, too. And she'd be immobilized. It would be impossible to hike out even if she knew where she was.

Directly to her left was a cavernous gorge, a fissure whose sides narrowed as it deepened. The crevasse looked like it was created when the surface of the earth abruptly split apart. Canyons like this cracked the desert floor in hundreds of places, and were nearly invisible to the eye until almost on top of them. Distracted by the blow from the beer bottle, Charlie had driven right into it.

Her gaze drifted over the edge of the gorge, and she quickly squeezed her eyes shut to stop the vertigo. When she opened them again, she could see the mangled Ford Explorer wedged between the canyon walls, suspended two hundred feet above the sculpted knobs and pointy rock turrets below.

A wide-winged buzzard circled overhead, then swooped down to alight on the tangled roof rack. The wreckage shifted slightly sending up a grating squeal, and the buzzard took flight. Keegan edged away from the drop-off.

Soon her breathing slowed, and she was able to calm herself a little. She looked around to assess her environment, studying the battlement of eroded sandstone across the wide flat stretch of sand. At its base was a shallow cave.

She had no idea where she was, and guessed her chances of being found accidentally were probably nil. She scanned the horizon beyond the vast expanse of dusty, ochre-colored earth burning under the sun. To the east, she could see the starkly dramatic folds of uplifted rock and sandstone eroded into a layered chevron pattern the locals called Indian Blanket. That told her she was still in Monument Valley, or near it.

Her watch was gone, ripped off in her climb to the top. She guessed it was noon. The sun's intensity would increase many times in the hours before it went down. The heat would leave with the light. After dark, it would be cold. Such was the dichotomy of the desert. Stranded travelers died from the heat or died from the cold all in the same spot.

But I'm not going to die.

She closed her eyes and fought off the despair that rushed in to overwhelm her. When she steadied herself, she focused on the cave in the base of the cliff. Gritting her teeth and straining with the effort, she hobbled across the sandy flat and peered inside.

It was a concave curve of sandstone protected on three sides as well as overhead with only a few eerily shadowed corners inside. Clearly, she wasn't its first inhabitant. A scattered pile of ashes from an old campfire confirmed the presence of a previous resident. Next to it was a ragged nylon sleeping bag, its fabric disintegrated with age. She picked up a twig and poked at it, then lifted it to see what was underneath. Nothing living, only an old *Newsweek* magazine. The date on the cover was 1972.

A low shelf along one interior wall was wide enough to sit on, wide enough in places to recline. She painfully, gratefully, limped over to it and lowered herself onto it. Her ribs and shoulder hurt a lot less sitting down. She lifted her leg with her hands and propped it on the flat surface to rest her knee and relieve the strain. Wincing, she picked at the sharp tiny stones embedded in her palms and bare feet.

She had a clear view through the cave's wide opening. Outside, the long vista stretched into a wilderness that showed no sign of human life. Few shadows, no movement, no sounds save a few birds overhead. Far away, she caught the reflection of a miniature rain-filled seep, a watering place for the countless desert animals that would appear after dark.

She stared fixedly at the distant landforms, concentrating on each profile, calculating their distance. Before long, the bright sun hurt her eyes, and energy draining heat dropped her eyelids. She squinted and cupped her hands around her eyes to cut off some of the persistent glare.

A hawk spiraled in the sky, then circled and dove to make dinner of some tiny desert animal skittering to the safety of a rock pile. She wondered if there was something out there with its heart set on having her for dinner, and a new sliver of fear danced along her spine. She'd have to figure out what to do about food for herself.

Minutes and hours dragged by. She dozed off and on in the heavy heat, waiting for the pain to diminish, for healing to occur.

As the sun neared the horizon, cool air rolled in, bringing a measure of relief from the heat. She opened her eyes to see a furry tarantula meander across the sand and disappear into a hole in the wall. The desert seemed to be coming alive now. More birds flitted about. More insects were trying to dodge them. Blazing shades of red, orange, and purple flowed into scarlet and crimson, turning the sky into a brilliant kaleidoscope of liquid light. The sunset's afterglow outlined the rough shapes on the horizon.

Night fell quickly and with it, the temperature. With nothing to impede its trajectory, light from the moon provided her with just enough brightness to see nighttime desert creatures, released from the strict bondage of daytime temperatures, darting about seeking water and food.

A frantic who-eats-who battle was occurring in her midst. Insects eat pollen. Rodents eat insects. Reptiles eat rodents. Owls eat reptiles. The never-ending cycle that assures perpetuation of life in the desert.

Soon she was shivering from the cold. Though she'd elevated her aching knee, the pain wouldn't let up. She reached for the ratty sleeping bag. Holding it between thumb and forefinger, she draped it gingerly over her knee, hoping for pain relieving warmth. She huddled back into her cradle of rock and closed her eyes.

Her stomach rolled. She hadn't eaten. She'd tasted a few leaves from some of the wild plants, but didn't remember which ones were poisonous and which ones were edible. She wished she'd paid more attention to all those desert survival articles she'd read over the years.

Tomorrow, she told herself. Tomorrow she'd figure something out. Right now she was too tired and weak. And hopeless.

Dante, are you thinking about me? Are you wondering where I am? Are you looking for me?

If he is, please let him find me, she prayed silently, even though she knew there was no way in hell he could.

Closing her eyes, she drew in a shuddering breath and began counting . . . nothing.

One. Two. Three.

The sight and sound of the numbers scrolling through her

mind were a silent deflection of thoughts too painful to bear.

Four. Five. Six.

Numbers were something she knew. Something definite she could hold on to. They were familiar. They occurred with regularity, and never deviated from their inflexible order.

Seven. Eight. Nine.

Numbers did not lie. They did not change their value or appearance. She could count on them as well as count them.

Ten. Eleven. Twelve. Thirteen. Fourteen. Fifteen. Sixteen. Seventeen. Eighteen. Nineteen. Twenty.

It was a small sound like a twig snapping, or a tiny bone breaking. When she first opened her eyes, she thought she'd dreamed it, but in the shadows outside her cave, there was movement. An animal of some kind was stirring, something big. Whatever it was caught her scent and stopped, interrupted in the midst of its nocturnal hunt. It moved again and she crouched back, gripped by fear.

A mountain lion was standing next to a gnarled juniper not far from the entrance to the cave, its small head lifted, its nose sniffing the air. When it looked in her direction, it growled and flicked its black-tipped tail.

She knew mountain lions were strongly territorial and unpredictable. They were known to attack humans who invaded their turf. Their habit was to stalk their prey, positioning themselves for an ambush, but this one had been caught off guard by Keegan's unexpected presence. It wasn't very big, and she guessed it was a young one. An older more experienced mountain lion would not have been caught unawares.

It continued its low threatening growls, asserting its territorial dominance, becoming more and more nervous, unsure what to do. Keegan, equally unsure, sat up, moving slowly, unwilling to let the cat pounce on her while she was lying down.

The cat caught the movement and snarled, curious now, but didn't move any closer. In the pale moonlight, she saw its gaping maw and long pointed teeth. Its ears lay flat against its skull, and it snarled again, then began to pace, huge padded paws plodding soundlessly in the sand. The cat was making tentative movements toward the entrance to the cave, lashing out with its big paw.

Keegan froze with fear and anger. A vision of Daisy's sweet face appeared in her mind along with the sound of the child's joyous laughter. If she was dead, she'd never see her daughter again. As long as she was alive, there was always a chance she'd have her precious Daisy back.

She looked around for something to use as a weapon. The cat picked up its pacing, back and forth, moving closer to the entrance with each sweep. Bracing her hands flat against the wall, and never taking her eyes off the animal, she pulled herself to a standing position. The pain in her ribs assaulted her like hot knives.

The cat was within ten feet of the entrance now, not charging, but snarling ferociously, moving slowly, swatting the air with its paw.

"NO!" Keegan shouted.

The sudden sound cleaved the dark silence. Surprised, the cat halted its advance.

Encouraged by this, Keegan yelled again. "NO!"

Groaning from the pain stabbing at her injured shoulder, she raised her arms over her head to make herself appear bigger than she was.

"NO! GO AWAY! GO!" she bellowed. In tortuous agony, she waved her arms back and forth in the air.

Flustered, the cat took a wavering step backward, and halted, forepaw lifted, still staring into the cave.

"NO! You may not come closer! NO! You may not hurt me!

NO! NO! NO!"

Keegan continued to shriek, and to her amazement the cat backed up on its haunches, then turned and loped away, looking just once over its shoulder.

Instantly her anger turned into angry determination.

Dammit, she was *not* going to be killed by a mountain lion. She was *not* going to die of thirst. She was *not* going to starve to death, and tomorrow she was *not* going to be overcome by the burning sun and relentless heat.

Tomorrow she would find food.

Tomorrow she would find a way out of there.

She hunkered back into her rocky reserve, bent her good leg and wrapped her arms around it, pulling it close to capture as much body heat as possible. Thunder growled in the distance like a drum roll. A coyote howled and was answered by a high wavering cry that ended in a frenetic, high-pitched yapping. The sound stirred a tingling fear of primitive danger that raised the hair on her arms.

I will not die.

The sun was just tipping the ridge of Indian Blanket, not yet high enough in the sky to warm the land or the air when Keegan woke the next morning, cold to the bone and hungry. Night fog scudded away like ghosts, fading into nothing. She fought back the hopeless tears that were threatening to spill over, refusing to give in to them.

Slowly, she moved one part of her body at a time, stretching, flexing, testing for pain, taking stock. She had slept little, daring to doze only sporadically, keeping vigil for fear the big cat would return.

She pulled herself up, putting all her weight on her uninjured leg. She moved around, first balancing on one foot and bracing against the rocks, then gingerly putting her other leg down to test how much weight her injured knee could take. Not much, and she sucked air through her teeth. Moving around warmed her a little, but her shoulder throbbed relentlessly and was sticky with pus. It was beginning to give off a putrid smell from the infection.

If she could build a fire, the smoke would be seen for miles and someone might come to get her, but she had no matches. Her eyes scanned the ground looking for flint rocks and something to burn. The sky was getting lighter by the minute, and she hobbled around collecting green leaves and small sticks with which to make a smoky fire. She moved slowly, taking deep breaths and focusing on her task.

Within an hour, she was drowning in furious sunlight, panting from the heat, and still no fire. She stood helplessly, trying to figure out what to do. A fire had sounded good in theory, but even if she got it started and kept it going until tomorrow, she had no food or water to sustain herself. She was beginning to feel the effects of dehydration.

Suddenly a horrendous shriek erupted from the canyon, and she startled, heart racing. Something, an earth tremor, had jolted the wrecked Explorer, jarring it loose, allowing its weight to be pulled by gravity in an ear-piercing, screeching plunge into the depths.

Dust, stones, and pieces of the canyon wall dislodged, cascading wildly, bouncing and tumbling. The wreckage descended, shuddering and screeching, until moments later, it landed with a thunderous crash at the bottom. Waves of sound boomed and reverberated up from the depths, rolling out across the desert.

A giant plume of dust geysered hundreds of feet into the air, carrying with it a flurry of white. Propelled upward by gusty ground winds at the bottom of the canyon, thousands of sheets of paper fluttered and flapped in a billowing paper blizzard that spread for miles. Ears ringing and coughing from the dust, Keegan watched devastated and fascinated at the same time as the Project 32 files disappeared into the sky.

The stillness was ever more so in the aftermath of the thundering crash. She thought she heard a buzzing, but after a moment decided she must be hallucinating.

Then it came again, faint but unmistakable.

Expectantly, her gaze swept the distance, probing the expanse, seeking the source of the mechanical rumble. Nothing moved. She had to choke back a sob when the resonance faded and disappeared until the only sound in her ear was the rush and gurgle of bodily fluids pulsing through her veins and organs.

Then she heard it again, and tilted her head trying to catch its direction.

Above.

She looked up.

Behind, not in front.

She turned around. It was still faint and far away, but definitely coming closer.

She strained to see, but the glare hurt her eyes and she ducked her head. Then the sound stopped again, and for a moment, her heart almost did, too. She stared until her sun-weary eyes began playing tricks on her. In the wavering heat, her vision blurred.

She closed her eyes again to relieve them. She was weak and sick with hunger, beginning to question her logic and doubt the visual and aural messages coming to her brain. Then the buzzing grew louder and blended into the sound of hollow thudding.

A helicopter!

The chopper came over the top of the mesa, circled, then hovered low enough for her to read the writing on the side. *DESERT SEARCH AND RESCUE.* She could see the yellow helmet of the pilot through the clear plastic canopy. He was waving and smiling as he maneuvered into position.

The door opened, and Dante, beautiful Dante, wonderful Dante, was standing there, buckled into a harness. He sat down on the deck and dangled his legs over the side. He wasn't smiling. He looked ravished with worry, and was saying something. She couldn't hear over the noise of the rotor, but she could read his lips.

"I love you," he mouthed, then shoved off and was lowered to the ground. Members of the rescue team followed with first aid kits, water, blankets, and a stretcher basket.

Keegan stood there shaking and crying in gratitude as Dante gingerly wrapped her in his arms and held her close.

"Thank God you're alive." His voice was choked with tears. She felt them mingle with hers on the side of her face.

"How did you know where I was?" she croaked.

"I didn't," was his muffled reply. "I came back early from the rodeo and saw Henry's car next to yours in the driveway, but neither of you were there. Then I saw blood on the chair inside and called the police." Tenderly, he kissed her parched lips.

A yellow-shirted crew member approached with a first aid kit. Together, he and Dante gently lowered her into the stretcher basket. Somebody strapped her in, somebody else poked her arm with a needle, and within seconds her pain began to seep away. Her limbs felt weightless, floating, and her eyelids grew heavy.

Dante's face was over hers. It was the most wonderful sight in the world. "Search and rescue got the helicopters in the air at dawn," he told her. "We've been searching since yesterday. We'd never have found you if we hadn't seen that plume of dust and all those papers flying around. Whose car is that down there?"

"It's Charlie's. He's a friend of Justin's." Her words tumbled out, muffled and fuzzy.

"Justin the archivist?"

"Yes. Charlie's down there. He's dead. So is Henry. He's an archivist, too. He came to tell me about my grandfather. Charlie shot him at my house," she said, tears flooded out of her eyes. She was babbling, talking in circles, frantic to tell Dante everything that had happened, afraid she might forget, or die, and no one would know the truth. "I think Charlie shot Justin, too. Somewhere in the desert, I don't know where because I passed out, but Henry brought the files and then—"

"Shhh, shhh. Don't talk," Dante whispered. "Later you can tell the police all about it." Using the pad of his thumb, he gently wiped away her tears. "Rest now."

She closed her eyes, letting herself fall and fall in slow motion until a gentle swoop lifted her into the air to safety.

CHAPTER THIRTY-TWO

Six months later

Keegan gazed into the darkness through the window of a guest bedroom in her cousin's mansion northeast of Phoenix. Richard hated it when she called it a mansion. He liked to pretend he was solidly mainstream, but what else would you call a house with seven bedrooms and eight bathrooms? Sometimes his eagerness to make his new money look like old money was at odds with his desire to make an impression. It was a mansion on a street of mansions in a community of mansions.

Sighing, she turned from the window, and sat at an antique writing desk lit by a tiny lamp. She blinked a couple of times, holding back tears. It had been a sorrowful day.

That afternoon Hazel Cole had been laid to rest, having died with uncommon dignity and a spirit so brave it soared. Friends had gathered at Richard's house to pay their final respects, following a simple graveside service where Hazel was buried beside her beloved Lincoln.

Keegan would miss her terribly.

During Hazel Cole's long life she'd had to suffer much bad news. Losing her mother when still a girl, two brothers in a war, a stillborn child early in her marriage, her beloved husband, Lincoln. And finally Lulu, the child from the past she'd never known, her husband's child by another woman. She'd forgiven his wandering eyes, his wanderlust ways, his need for love and approval outside the marriage, but not until he was gone. Then, she wanted nothing more than to join him in eternity. Lulu had been Hazel's last tenuous connection to him, a connection that was abruptly severed when Keegan told her Lulu was dead.

Each death and hardship had scarred her and surely broken her heart. Thankfully, she'd died without the added burden of knowing about the harm done by her husband.

All sound had faded from Richard's house. Everyone was gone now; respects paid, condolences whispered, hugs bestowed. The kitchen and pantry were full of food, the living room filled with the cards and flowers sent by friends, neighbors, and Richard's many business acquaintances. The house was dark and quiet, empty except for Keegan in this comfortably appointed upstairs guest room, and Richard alone in the master suite. His wife left him months ago taking the children. His divorce would soon be final.

Dante was on his way to Monument Valley to prepare for an early morning meeting with Emerson Bedonnie. Dante was on Emerson's short list for the compliance archaeologist position on the resort construction project. He hoped Emerson was going to offer him the job tomorrow, or at least let him explain about the Venture Development scandal.

Keegan had originally planned to leave when he did, following in her own car. After spending so much time in Monument Valley, she found it difficult to be in the city even for a short time. Crowds and congestion were in sharp contrast to the solitude she'd found in the wide open desert. She was anxious to get back to Monument Valley, but Richard had asked her to stay over till morning to discuss some of the provisions of Hazel's will. His request had surprised her. Like very wealthy men everywhere, he was used to running things, liked having his own way without consulting with or deferring to anyone. More from curiosity and a desire to be obliging than anything else, she agreed to stay the night and leave the next day.

Her thoughts wandered back to Dante, and she pictured him behind the wheel of his Jeep, driving through the night. A warm feeling spread behind her heart every time she thought of him.

He'd walked into her life and littered it with tenderness and comfort and kisses and desire, green gazes and touches that instantly sent fire through her body. He made love to her with a selfless abandon that was both thrilling and fulfilling, and she couldn't stop herself from loving him.

A sudden urge to hear his voice compelled her to call him, but he didn't answer and she got his voice mail instead.

"Just me," she whispered a message. "Just miss you. Just love you. See you tomorrow."

She hung up, and her mind flooded with loneliness. Idly, she counted the pens in a heavy silver cup on the desktop. There were an even dozen, all expensive fine point writing instruments. Richard didn't shop at Wal-Mart for anything.

It was getting blustery outside. Barefoot, she walked across the plush carpeting to the sliding glass doors and looked out. The wind swept down from the mountain, agitating the coyotes in the wash across the road. One of the metal garden art fixtures in the front yard had toppled over. Thunder built and faded in the distance. An Arizona monsoon, one of those late summer storms that brought much needed moisture to the dry desert, was forecast to begin sometime during the night. This looked like the start of it. She hoped Dante made it back before any of the roads washed out.

Predictably, the government was taking its time releasing the Project 32 records. Someone pretty big was still sitting on it, someone with connections powerful enough to force a cover-up. After her rescue from the desert, federal authorities rushed in and took over the investigation, quickly putting a lid on it. The case became heavily cloaked in secrecy. A total news blackout infuriated reporters and editors. In return, they released their pent-up frustration in anger-fueled columns and reproachful blogs. The media was having a field day speculating and second guessing, filling up air time and newspapers with rumor and conjecture.

Eventually, Congress announced a probe, and finally, a formal investigation. A legislative committee was formed to look into unspecified allegations against various departments of the federal government including the BIA, allegations that hinted at misconduct, bribery, misappropriation of funds, and mishandling of records. The details remained shrouded.

It was for that reason Keegan had begun writing a book exposing Project 32 and the grossly unethical medical experimentation done for no other reason than political expediency.

Hazel Cole hadn't been told about the book, of course, but Richard strongly objected to it, begging her to abandon it. He didn't want Lincoln Cole's reputation ruined or the family name sullied, but Keegan stood firm, determined that the government's egregious policies be brought to light. Besides that, she felt an obligation to the Navajo people. They were her family now, too.

A gust of wind whipped mesquite branches into a frenzy. They scraped along the deck railings and slapped at the yard lights making them flicker. A sudden flash of distant lightening illuminated a strange car parked on the driveway next to her 4Runner. A tell-tale rectangle of light from a downstairs window lay across the tumbled stone courtyard below. Richard had a guest.

She gazed at it a moment, wondering who was visiting so late at night. Guiltless curiosity drove her to slip quietly from her room and down the stairs toward the low rumble of conversation coming from Richard's study. Fragments of sentences drifted to her, isolated words seemingly unconnected to each other. The agitated quality of the voices urged her to tiptoe into the shadows where she eavesdropped with unabashed nosiness.

The door to the study was ajar, lamplight illuminating the scene inside. Richard was sitting forward in an upholstered chair, talking excitedly to someone opposite him. There wasn't enough of the other person showing to see who it was. Only sharply creased trousers legs, expensive looking shoes, and two hands angrily cutting the air in response to something Richard said.

She held in a breath, and strained to hear.

". . . PHARMACO will never get approval for MemRelease if that happens," the visitor asserted, speaking in a tone not to be reckoned with.

It was a voice she'd heard before and she went into her memory trying to call it up. It wouldn't come to her. The voices floated on the silence of the house.

"I know," Richard replied in response to the stranger's impatient remarks. "This couldn't have come at a worse time."

"Does she have a publisher for her book yet?"

"She said she did. It's supposed to come out next year. But she hasn't finished writing it. She's working on it in Monument Valley."

They were talking about *her!*

"Well, she can't finish it, you know that, don't you? I can have MemRelease approved by the end of the year, but if it comes out that a version of the drug was unsuccessfully, *and illegally,*" the other man emphasized, "tested on the Indians, approval will be withdrawn in a heartbeat. You want to come to Washington as labor secretary? Well, the only way that's going to happen is if I'm president. The money from our agreement with PHARMACO will go a long way toward financing a presidential campaign. I haven't worked all these years to give that up now. Or go broke," he added. "You either, I assume."

"No," Richard answered. "I staked everything I have on MemRelease. If the deal doesn't go through, it will bankrupt me."

"And PHARMACO, too," the other man reminded him. "They've spent millions and taken years bringing MemRelease to market. You've got to stop her, Richard. Now."

"I've tried. She's determined to write that book."

"Well, what are you going to do about it?"

Keegan held her breath in the ringing silence.

"I don't know," Richard said finally.

"You said she was here now?" the other man asked.

"Yes. She's going back tomorrow."

"Then there's no time like the present. She has to be stopped. Permanently."

"I'll take care of it."

"Do you catch my drift, Richard? I said *permanently.*"

The shock of what she heard froze her in place, but just for a moment. Heart racing, she backed away, and tiptoed up the stairs to the guest room. Once inside, she closed the door and pressed her back firmly against it as if Richard and his visitor might come batter it down. Panic unfurled in her stomach and gripped her there.

She had to get out of the house and tell someone what she'd heard. With her mind stampeding toward panic, she grabbed her phone and speed dialed Dante again.

C'mon, answer. Answer.

But he didn't. She tossed the phone in her purse, and slipped the strap over her shoulder. Frantically, she gathered her things and stuffed them into her suitcase. She turned out the light and opened the door a crack, peeking out. The muffled voices were still coming from Richard's study. She shoved her shoes in her purse, picked up her bag, and made her way down the stairs to the front door.

Quickly, she stepped outside, silencing the click of the latch. The interior light in the 4Runner came on when she opened the door, and she froze, and glanced at the window in the study, but no one looked out. She tossed in her suitcase into the back seat, scrambled behind the wheel, and silently closed the door. It was too dark to see, and blindly, frantically, she dug in her purse for her phone and her car keys.

She speed dialed Dante again, and thankfully he answered this time, his voice rough and muffled from sleep.

"Hello."

"Dante, it's me. I'm getting out of here. Richard is involved in some sort of kickback scheme with a drug company to release Project 32's memory erasing drug." Her hand was shaking so hard she couldn't get the key in the ignition. "He wants to stop me from writing my book. I think he wants to kill me—"

"Keegan, you are such a goddamn snoop. You always were, even as a kid . . ."

The voice was coming through the phone but also from outside her window. The car door flew open. Richard stood there with Dante's phone to his ear, a gun in his hand, and a bullying sneer on his face. Fear flared inside her like a lighted match.

"Get out," he said. "You're not going anywhere."

"Richard, what are you doing?" She was nearly paralyzed with panic and tried to force a nervous laugh, like *hey-Richard-quit-your-kidding*, but it broke in half and lodged in her throat. Moving quickly, she reached for the door handle in a frantic attempt to pull it closed, but Richard was quicker and yanked it out of her hands.

She made a move toward the passenger door, but Richard chucked Dante's phone to the ground, reached into the car, grabbed the front of her shirt in his fist and dragged her out.

The back of her hand and the top of her head hit the doorframe sending her phone flying and her purse spilling from her lap. A lightning bolt of pain crashed inside her skull. Dazed, her knees buckled and she nearly collapsed onto the cobblestones, but he yanked her up before she hit the ground.

"Get back inside," he said, giving her a shove toward the house.

She could feel the hand holding the gun shaking as he shoved it into the small of her back and propelled her into the house and down the hall to his study, where she collapsed in a chair. She squeezed her eyes shut and put her hands to her throbbing head. A bump, tender to the touch, was already forming where her head hit the door frame.

"Well, who have we here?" a voice said.

Keegan opened her eyelids to a squint, then closed them against what felt like a blast of high-intensity light stabbing her retinas. She clasped a hand over her eyes, then slowly lowered it, adjusting to the light. She focused her gaze on the man who had spoken.

The familiar voice she'd heard belonged to an equally familiar face, one she'd seen on the news dozens of times. Senator Mike O'Toole, influential member of the Senate Special Committee on Aging, Health Care, and Medicine, and head of the congressional committee investigating Project 32. Richard stood next to him, the gun still in his hand.

"Meet Senator O'Toole," Richard said, giving her a sharp look full of anger and superiority. "This is Keegan Thomas," he said, addressing the senator, motioning with the gun. "Good thing her boyfriend forgot his cell phone or they'd be on their way to the U.S. attorney's office right now."

"Richard, why are you doing this?" she asked.

He didn't answer, but his eyes were hard on her.

Senator O'Toole calmly re-crossed one leg over the other and looked at her like he was expressing disappointment in a recalcitrant child. There was a long pause, followed by a shrug and a heavy sigh.

"We might as well explain it to her," he said. "She won't be telling anyone."

He paused again, letting her think about that. The throbbing in her head was persistent, nearly drowning out the sound of his voice in her ears. She fixated on the senator, studying his face. No emotion touched his eyes. Richard stood quiet behind the senator's chair, his features settled into stone, cold determination.

"Put the gun down, Richard. We're going to have a talk. We're civilized people, aren't we?" said the senator in the too slow, too patient voice of someone trying not to get riled at blatant stupidity.

Richard lowered his hand, holding the gun at his side.

Satisfied, O'Toole began. "With my help, a drug company called PHARMACO is on the verge of bringing a miracle drug to market. It will relieve the distress of millions of people around the world by making it possible to dampen or erase their painful memories forever."

Keegan swung her eyes from the senator to Richard and back again. "You mean the drug from Project 32."

"Yes," he said, confirming it with a slow nod.

Her gaze jumped to Richard. "I thought you didn't find any of those records in grandfather's files."

"I found them later. Unfortunately, I'd already given you the picture."

O'Toole ignored the exchange and went on.

"The drug is called MemRelease," he said, his voice commanding attention. "Just imagine, Keegan, the wonders of a drug like this. How merciful it will be if victims of violent crimes, or children who have been abused, can be spared the trauma of those terrible memories. If soldiers returning from the Middle East wouldn't have to live with flashbacks of the horrors they've witnessed in war. MemRelease will make this possible."

An ocean of anxiety flooded her mind as she listened.

"It will be used in emergency rooms for both patients and medical staff. For plane crash survivors. For traffic accident victims. People won't be forced to spend a lifetime having their stressful events recreated in their minds, forever in agony. Do you know what happens after a plane crash?"

She shot him an icy look.

"It involves collecting human remains. Body parts." He frowned distastefully and tipped his shoulders up in a shrug. "Someone has to clean it up. When the World Trade Center was struck by terrorists, many of the brave men and women who rushed inside to help committed suicide later. They were absolutely haunted by the memories they carried with them of what they saw, what they heard. What they smelled. You see, Keegan, people want to be rid of those memories."

Her anger bubbled up. "But you can't manipulate people's thoughts that way," she protested. "It's not right."

O'Toole looked at her sadly, as if she'd somehow, stupidly, missed an obvious point.

"Not right for whom?" he replied, his voice testy. "Not right for people suffering depression and post-traumatic stress disorder? Not right for victims of automobile accidents or heinous assaults? Or torture?"

"It's repression," she insisted. "Medicine has a less harmful way of helping those people that doesn't involve mind control. Freedom of thought is a fundamental right. People have a right to control their own minds and mental processes. You have no right to take that away from them."

The senator flipped her statement back to her with a backhand through the air, disregarding it. "Everything in life isn't one way or the other. Nothing is all *right* or all *wrong*. Most things fall on a continuum in between. Life isn't black and white." He threw up his hands in capitulation. "Some things are gray. You have to accept that." His gaze was level.

"It's a violation of First Amendment rights," she insisted. "Freedom of thought is at the core of our freedoms guaranteed by the Constitution. Freedom of thought is central to First Amendment protections. You're a senator, sworn to uphold the Constitution. You have no right to mess with a person's brain chemistry that way. There are very harmful side effects. Read my grandfather's records, it's all there. He documented a multitude of mental disabilities as a result of that drug."

O'Toole met her eyes with a look of utter indifference. "I've read them. His experiments, by the way, were extremely helpful in the development of MemRelease. Lincoln Cole worked closely with my father on Project 32 when it first began."

Keegan wanted to cry, she wanted to scream. "As human beings, we have a social obligation to remember past events for the communal good. Like the holocaust. Like the government's mistreatment of the Indians. You're not God," she said again.

O'Toole and Richard exchanged a look she couldn't read.

She tried to think of something to say. Something that might dissuade her cousin from this detestable plan. Something poignant that might reach him and make him change his mind, but she couldn't think of anything.

"You'll never get away with it," she blurted.

"Why not?" the senator said. "Once MemRelease is approved, it will be legal."

"Just because it's legal doesn't make it right. What you're doing isn't legal. Taking kickbacks is against the law."

His reply was curt and sullen. "Only if someone finds out about it." Then, letting his impatience show, he said, "Look. Would it be easier for you to think of MemRelease as a morning after pill for remorse or pain or guilt? A pill that makes the horrible less horrible for innocent people? What does it matter if Richard and I make a little money from what's essentially a humanitarian endeavor?"

He paused, and his expression softened. "Look. How about if we cut you in on it? We could do that, couldn't we, Richard?"

Richard nodded, his gaze cold and remote.

"All you have to do," said O'Toole, "is agree to abandon your book, and you could be a very rich woman."

She glared at them. "Never. And now you've given me a final chapter. Your part in this illegal scheme with PHARMACO." She looked at her cousin. "And Richard's, too."

O'Toole's jaw set with visible anger. "I would think you would be less concerned with ethics and more concerned with your future. Your *life*. You seem to forget who you're dealing with here. Whether you agree or not, I can make one phone call and arrange to have a large sum of money deposited into an account in your name, so if there is a probe, you'll be implicated. Even if you're dead."

"I'll take my chances," Keegan said, still full of argument. "As I said before, you won't get away with this."

"Yes, we will, and I'll tell you why," the senator countered icily. "Richard tells me all your resource material, all your grandfather's records, all the documents that old archivist gave you were lost in the desert when you had your unfortunate accident. Without them it will be impossible to verify your story. Old Henry Parker is dead. He can't back you up. Douglas Corbett won't declassify those records in the archives. There's no one left to confirm or validate your assertions."

When she still didn't answer, the senator's face turned to stone. "Your only other option is to die where you sit."

Richard raised the gun, and fear sucked the breath from her lungs.

"No, wait!" she pleaded.

Suddenly there was a shout. All eyes turned to the doorway as Dante burst into the room.

"Hold it!" he yelled, charging at Richard and knocking him back against the desk. They both fell to the floor, and Dante's hand closed around Richard's wrist, wrenching his arm to the side. Richard fought back, but Dante managed to climb on top of him, his knees straddling Richard's chest.

Sirens blared outside, coming closer, then dying in the courtyard. Footsteps thundered over the cobblestones, into the house and up the hallway. O'Toole blanched, terror etched on his face.

Richard continued struggling with Dante, trying to get away. Suddenly his gun swung around toward Keegan. She threw herself to the floor as a shot went off into the ceiling. Another shattered the wide-screen TV.

Dante wrested the gun away from Richard just as the police burst in the door, weapons drawn. He got up and stepped back. Richard was on the floor, holding his arm, moaning. "You broke it! You broke my arm!"

"Stay where you are, O'Toole," an officer shouted. The senator, wearing the look of a man standing in front of a firing squad, didn't resist when two officers snapped on handcuffs and pushed him into a chair.

Dante put Richard's gun on the table and went to Keegan, sweeping her up in an embrace.

"Thank God you came back," she said, throwing her arms around his neck.

He squeezed her tight, then stepped back, his hands on her shoulders, and looked at her with a mildly exasperated expression. "Keegan, do you think you could stay out of trouble for just a little while?"

"I promise to try," she replied, pulling him back into a hug.

Richard, one arm handcuffed to a chair, was being treated by an EMT. O'Toole had asked to make a phone call and, still in handcuffs, was ranting to whoever was on the other end. Two policemen stood next to him, one on either side.

An officer approached Dante and introduced himself. Dante handed him his cell phone. "It's all on there," he said. "I recorded most of what they said and managed to get a little video, too."

The policeman took their names and wrote down their information. "Thanks," he said and walked away.

Dante looked at her face and gently smoothed back her hair. "You've got a bump on your forehead. Do you want the EMTs to look at it?"

"No, I'm fine. I just want to get out of here," she said, then locked her arms loosely around his waist. She put her head on his shoulder, enjoying the feel of him, grateful for his presence. "What made you come back?"

"I was halfway to Flagstaff and wanted to call you before I lost the cell signal. That's when I realized I'd forgotten my phone. I didn't want to be without it in case Emerson Bedonnie called, so I came back for it. When I saw your car door hanging open and your purse dumped out on the ground, I knew you were in trouble. Don't worry. I heard everything that was said, and recorded it on my cell phone. Someone had conveniently left it out in the courtyard."

"That was Richard," she told him. "I'd been trying to call you. He heard your phone ringing in the house and answered it. He caught me just as I was leaving and forced me back inside."

Dante motioned to the sergeant in charge. "Is it all right if we leave?" he asked.

"We need your signed statements first," the sergeant said.

"Sure," Dante replied. Then he took Keegan's hand and laced his fingers through hers. He was looking at her with desire.

"Come on," he said. "Let's get this over with and go back to the rez where we belong. We have some things to talk about."

"Like what?" she asked.

"Like what we're going to do and where we go from here."

A rush of emotion came from nowhere and everywhere at once. She kissed him and tasted all the delicious possibilities of their life together. "I love you, Shovel Bum."

He laughed, and circled her in his arms. "I love you, Nosey Pants."

EPILOGUE

"Keegan, what a nice surprise!"

"Hi, Mom," Keegan said, stepping into the cool marble foyer.

Ellen Cole Flowers reached out to embrace her daughter, a rare but warm display of affection. "What brings you to Tucson?"

"I came down to talk to you," Keegan answered.

"Well, come on in. I'm just making iced tea. Do you want some?"

"I'd love some."

"Let's sit in the family room," Ellen said, leading the way. "Now that the worst of the summer heat is gone, I can open the doors and windows and enjoy the breeze."

Keegan sat down, and Ellen went for the tea.

"Have you finished your book?" Ellen asked, calling in from the kitchen.

"Yes," Keegan answered. "It will be out next spring."

She heard her mother chuckle softly. "All hell will break loose then, I'm sure." Ellen came into the family room with glasses and a pitcher on a tray. "The heads of some very important people will roll when that book hits the shelves. Some big names."

"I hope so," replied Keegan, accepting a glass. "That was my intention."

She took a cooling sip, then put her glass on a side table, noticing a photograph, the photograph that had started it all. Her mother had begun displaying it along with all the other

318

family pictures. Keegan picked it up and peered at Lulu, studying her face. The Thomas family resemblance was vivid, the vis-
age of her grandfather in Lulu evident in the lightness of the
eyes, the thinness of the nose. She was surprised she hadn't
seen that the first time she looked at it.

"How is Teaya?" Keegan's mother asked.

"Fine," Keegan answered. "The same. Are you sure you don't
want to meet her?" Keegan set the picture back on the table,
sliding it into place.

Ellen Cole frowned and tilted her head from side to side.
Maybe, the gesture meant. *Not sure.* "I did at first, but . . . no. If
Teaya ever remembers Lulu, then, yes, I'd like to talk to her."

Mother and daughter sat through a comfortable stretch of
silence.

"I'm sorry, Mom."

Her mother looked at her, a mixture of surprise and sadness
infused in her expression. "For what, honey?"

"For everything. For Richard and for what he was trying to
do. For what Grandfather did do. For Gram and Gramps, and
for the way their anger spoiled your youth."

Her mother was beginning to show her age, Keegan noticed.
Beginning to resemble Hazel Cole. "Did you know about
Grandpa and Teaya? And Lulu?"

Ellen shook her head. "No. But now that I do, it certainly
explains a lot that went on in the house when I was growing
up."

Keegan's heart ballooned with sympathy. "Oh, Mom, I'm so
sorry," she said again.

Ellen reached out and put her hand over Keegan's, patting it
gently. "Don't be, sweetheart. I gave up wishing for a better
childhood a long time ago. They did the best they could. And so
did I. With you."

"I love you, Mom."

"I love you, too, Keegan. I hope you always knew that, even though I didn't say it much in the past."

"I did. I do."

Ellen's eyes perked up. "But this is not what you came to talk to me about, is it?"

Keegan looked at her hands. She pressed her lips together and blinked. "No."

Ellen sipped her tea and waited patiently. "You never were very good at hiding your emotions, Keegan. I know something's happened. Is it Daisy?"

"No." There was a pause followed by a heavy sigh. "I called off the wedding," she said. "Postponed it, I mean."

Ellen's eyes widened, but she didn't otherwise react.

Calm and collected as always, thought Keegan, wishing she'd inherited that particular character trait instead of some of the less attractive ones.

"Why?" Ellen asked, probing gently. "Have you stopped loving Dante?"

"Oh, no," Keegan said quickly. "I still love him, and he loves me. It's just . . ." She shrugged. "It's me. Not him. There was a time I thought he completed me. I only felt whole when I was with him, as if somehow he made up the parts of me that were missing."

"But that's changed now?"

"Yes," Keegan replied. "Because he isn't my missing part. Daisy is. And because of that I can't be wholly available to him. Just like I couldn't be available to Jeffrey. Until I have Daisy back, I can't give myself completely to anyone. Certainly not a husband. It wouldn't be fair. Dante rescued me, but it's time I started rescuing myself."

Keegan was surprised to see understanding in her mother's eyes.

"Then you've made the right decision," Ellen said.

"I think so," Keegan answered, even though she was full of unresolved conflicts, not completely certain of anything. She'd always been good at picking up the pieces, but not so good at putting them back together. "I hope so, anyway."

Ellen's thoughts focused inward for a while. "What about Dante? How did he take it?"

Keegan broke a pained smile, remembering his less than understanding reaction. "Not very well, I'm afraid. He was angry at first, then sad and disappointed. But his job with the tribe will keep him in Monument Valley for at least the next couple of years. We'll still see each other when we can." That was the plan, anyway. "But I have to do something else. Something important."

"What?"

"I'm going to look for Daisy myself."

"Keegan, dear, the authorities are searching for her using every available resource they have at their disposal."

"Mom, the police and the FBI can only do so much. They're looking for lots of kids. They're not concentrating on just Daisy. They know she's with her father, and probably not in danger. I don't think she's a high priority to them. Take a look at their website. Hundreds of children have gone missing. Daisy isn't their only one. But she is *my* only one. And I'm going to find her."

"How? What are you going to do different?"

"I've made a decision to use the money Grandmother left me to start an organization dedicated to helping mothers search for their missing children. The ones the police haven't found or have given up on. Diana, my editor at *Offbeat Arizona*, wants to work with me. We'll only search for one or two kids at a time, so we can focus intense effort on each one." She noticed her mother's quizzical expression. "I don't know how we're going to do that yet. I just know it's something I have to do."

Ellen's eyes softened, her expression wistful.

"I admire you, you know that? You're so full of love." She paused, gazing mildly at Keegan, going backward in time. "I guess you get that from your dad." A melancholy smile curved her lips, a smile without any hint of ill will.

Keegan smiled back. "If I don't do it, I'll feel like I've failed Daisy. Let her down."

"Have you heard anything new about Daisy?" Ellen asked after a pause.

"Nothing I haven't already told you. There's a federal arrest warrant out for Brady, but so far he's been staying under the radar."

"And how is Jilly? Do you talk to her much? How is she holding up?"

"It's going to take her and the rest of her family a long, long time to get over everything that's happened. Oh," Keegan said, remembering. "Did I tell you she found out where all that money was? That hush money paid to Earlene from O'Toole's office?"

"No. Where?"

"In a bank in Farmington. Every month for the last fifty years, fifty dollars has been wire transferred into an account in her grandmother's name. Earlene never touched a penny of it, just let it accumulate. Jilly found some bank statements hidden under the rug in the room where Earlene slept when she stayed at Jilly's house."

"It must amount to quite a sum. What is she going to do with it?"

"She hasn't decided yet. Maybe give some to the senior center. Maybe give some to Teaya. She thought that seemed appropriate."

Ellen did, too. They chatted a while longer, then Keegan said good-bye.

"Come back soon," Ellen said at the door. "Oh, by the way. I forgot to tell you something. I'm thinking of moving into your grandmother's house in Scottsdale."

Keegan hugged her mother. "I hope you do, Mom. I'd love it if you lived closer to me instead of two hours away." They parted, Ellen waving from the door.

Just after Keegan pulled onto the interstate, her phone rang but stopped before she could answer it. She looked at the caller ID. It was a Monument Valley area code.

Jilly stood in the center of Earlene's bedroom, her arms hanging limply at her sides. Her sense of loss was beyond words, and she closed her eyes as the pain cut through her. Sandra had wanted to come along and help sort Earlene's things, but Jilly insisted on doing it by herself. She wanted to be alone.

Outside a low gray ceiling of clouds hung over the desert from horizon to horizon, silent and still. She looked around at the nearly empty room. Her grandmother's essence still hovered, almost as if the old woman were still there. The closet was empty except for a box on the top shelf. She looked at it dolefully. She'd get to it in due time. Right now she was still hurting.

Emotionally exhausted, Jilly sat on the bed picturing Earlene. Her hands were what Jilly had loved the most about her grandmother. Ready hands that had soothed and stroked. Hands that shined with silver and turquoise as she wove intricate patterns on her loom. Hands that were often covered in flour, performing feats of magic with a ball of dough, transforming it into delicious triangles of fry bread.

Jilly exhaled a tired breath. She was worn out, utterly incapable of easing her grief. I should be grateful I had *shimasani* as long as I did, she thought mournfully.

Wiping away a tear, she got a small half ladder from the shed out back, and carried it to the closet. She braced the legs, climbed the steps, and removed the last box from the shelf. It was the size of a shoebox, but heavier than it looked. She set it on top of the bedspread, then sat on the edge of the bed.

When she removed the top, she was barely able to control her surprise. The box was filled with letters still in their envelopes, which were slit open at the top. All of them were addressed to Earlene at a post office box in Kayenta, stamped with a Cortez, Colorado, postmark.

Who in the world did Earlene know in Cortez, seventy miles away?

When her eyes fell on the name above the return address, her heart dipped into her stomach and she took a quick sharp breath. She was so shocked she couldn't even conjure up any questions in her mind.

Stomach churning, she took out the letters and began to read. When she finished, she sat a while, staring into space, putting the pieces together. A half formed thought hovered just beyond her reach. After a long while, she shook her head slowly, picked up her phone, and dialed Keegan's number, but changed her mind and hung up after two rings.

It was best, she decided, to leave the dead—*and the living*—in peace.

ABOUT THE AUTHOR

Author **C. C. Harrison** has won national recognition with her suspense novels. THE CHARMSTONE was voted 2008 Golden Quill's Best Romantic Suspense and Best First Book, and was a Colorado Award of Excellence finalist. Tony Hillerman called it "a valuable book." Her award-winning mystery RUNNING FROM STRANGERS was a 2009 National Readers Choice finalist. SAGE CANE'S HOUSE OF GRACE AND FAVOR (written as Christy Hubbard) was honored at Aspen Institute's Summer Words Literary Festival as a 2010 Colorado Book Award finalist.

When she's not writing, reading, or working out at the gym, she can be found in the mountains of Colorado or some far-flung corner of the Southwest. Visit her website at www.cc harrison-author.com.